OTHER WISE

a novel by

Mary Lou Bagley

Copyright © 2018 *Other Wise* by Mary Lou Bagley

Published by Piscataqua Press
an imprint of RiverRun Bookstore
32 Daniel Street
Portsmouth NH 03801

ISBN: 978-1-718065-20-8

For **Bob**, my constant, my center, my heart

Melanie, my blessing, my gift

Jeremy, my joy and delight

I wish to thank

My editor, Elizabeth Barrett.

My publisher, Tom Holbrook.

Mentors,
Martha Barron Barrett
& Sue Wheeler.

The Molasses Ponders
with whom I've shared
space, time, and stories.

Titia Bozuwa for her friendship,
inspiration, and the Twin Farms experience.

Rebecca Rule for her wisdom,
advice, and good humor.

Kimberly Cloutier Green for
companioning me as poet,
friend, and seeker.

The South Berwick Library (and every library)
for being a light, a third place, an open doorway.

The Maine Writers & Publishers Alliance
for conferences, workshops, and community.

My family, friends, and readers
for their faith and support.

Prologue

Humming, she bends over the rounded clumps of herbs in the back garden. She gathers lavender and rosemary and mint, releasing fragrance into the morning air with each snip.

Suddenly, she raises her head. Letting the last sprig of mint slip from her fingers, she straightens, listening. Nearby in the grass, two golden heaps rise up onto all fours and stand erect, pointing off toward the trees along the horizon.

Sheets dance and snap on the clothesline in the rising wind. A trio of crows lifts off into raucous flight, leaving fine branches of the giant oak shivering. And beneath it all—the snap, the caw, the shiver—a soft rumbling. Out of the woods and down the far hill it travels, spreading across the fields, coursing beneath the stream, and moving ever upward until the ground on which she stands trembles.

A portrait of stillness, she remains, blue eyes searching. Strands of chestnut hair streaked with silver escape the clip at the base of her neck and whip around her face.

The wind drops to a whisper as the buzzing beneath her feet softens into the familiar subtle tug of the earth.

She nods, sighs, and bends back to her work.

Sophia and Grace settle into the grass once more, their golden coats shining in the morning sun.

Chapter 1

Emily settles on the porch swing and closes her eyes. Bits of conversation float in and out as she half rests, half listens. This reunion with her mother's people in Maine—this respite from her disintegrating life in Boston—has been sweet. The only sour note, her mother's absence.

"Saw Margaret in town today," Uncle Otis says. "Told me to get that right rear tire fixed 'fore I end up in the creek."

"You gonna fix it?" Uncle Merton asks.

"Damn right!"

Long silence.

"There's a right puzzler for you," Mert says.

"Yup. Never seen anyone like her."

Emily leans in. For a long while there is only the occasional click of a captured chess piece on the glass-topped table and the clearing of a throat.

"Always at least three jigsaws going," Mert continues. "Once, when I was out there upgrading her electrical service, she finished one of the big ones only to find a piece missin'. I woulda' exploded, been me. But not her. Just said, 'Well, what do you know. I been looking for the one with the yellow tip and it was among the missing all along.' And she just moved on to the card table in the corner where she had a big round one going."

Otis chuckles.

"When she saw me gawpin' she says, 'Here I have to find the piece with the umpteenth gradation of gray.'" He pauses. "Some people say she's a couple pieces shy of a jigsaw puzzle herself."

"Others say worse. Jacob Pill swears she's got the evil eye. Typical Jacob. Everything he doesn't understand must be about the devil." On this last word, Otis mimics the exaggerated style of a tent-revival preacher. More quietly he adds, "She just sees things differently from the rest of us."

"Not only sees things differently. Sees different things than the rest of us." Mert laughs.

Long pause. Emily looks over as Mert relights his pipe and watches the puffs of smoke lift off and dissolve.

"Sometimes she works from the inside out," he says. "Darnedest thing. Most people start by finding all the edge pieces and framing it so's they can work inward. But not Margaret."

"And I'd go buggy, jumping from puzzle to puzzle like she does."

"Yeah. One easy one at a time is more than enough for me. Five hundred pieces, tops."

Intrigued by this exchange, Emily slides to the other end of the swing, closer to the uncles. "I visited a puzzle shop up in Vassalboro once," she says. "It had antique wooden ones of all shapes and sizes, some quite valuable. I spent two hours in there. Where does this woman live? I'd love to—"

"Margaret's kind of private, Emily," Otis says, cutting her off. "Has her reasons. Had some troubles years ago. Learned to keep what they call a 'low profile' since. You're better off staying put and filling up on potato salad and barbequed shrimp. And pie. Better grab some of Lily May's pie before it's gone. You get skinnier every time I see you. Don't people eat down there in Boston?"

"Lives up off Old Fields Road about four miles into the woods," Mert says as if Otis hadn't spoken. "Interesting place, hers. Family land since way back. Fields and woods that go on for miles. She rents out a fertile chunk to a couple of local potters, real artists."

"She's an artist herself. Watercolors and squiggly little Japanese poems. Right up your alley, Miss Museum Assistant. I could take you up there before you leave. Maybe she'd invite us in for a look."

"Maybe not," says Otis.

"Emily's just a kid, Otis. Margaret surely wouldn't mind a curious kid, especially since she's one of ours. And she might offer something besides a look-see at her puzzles and poems to a hollow-eyed girl who's working too hard and not getting enough sleep."

"Thanks for the offer," Emily says, "but I'm leaving early in the morning tomorrow. Maybe next time I'm up? And, I'm not a kid. I'm twenty-nine now!"

Both uncles laugh.

৵৽

An hour later, Emily eases her car up the dirt road, bouncing through shallow potholes and skirting axle-deep craters. She can't get the image of puzzles and her uncle's words—*sees different things than the rest of us*—out of her mind.

A thick mix of hardwoods and evergreens crowds the roadway on both sides as shafts of sunlight slant down through the lush canopy. The play of shadow and light, the varying shades of greens and browns, the contrast of sharp branches and soft moss-covered stumps, has her imagining fairy huts and magical carryings-on. Finally, she rounds a bend, and the road opens out on the right side into a rolling expanse of meadow grass and wildflowers that sweeps uphill. She stops the car and looks up to where a scattering of herb gardens and dense flower beds yields to a stand of lilac trees in front of a gray cottage. A huge oak rises behind the house, dwarfing a cluster of birch trees in the side yard. Beyond the ridge on which the house sits, the land slopes up to woods all around.

Getting out of the car, Emily hears the distant tinkling of wind chimes. Two golden retrievers race down the hill, barking wildly. Emily draws back toward the car, but they stop short of her and dance about, yelping and wagging their tails. A woman tops the knoll from the back of the house. Her hair, chestnut streaked with silver, whips around her head in the wind. She whistles, and the dogs bolt toward her.

The woman watches her all the way up the drive. When Emily reaches her, they stand eye level in silence. Emily is the one to break the gaze, looking instead at a burst of bright coneflowers and hollyhocks and then clearing her throat more loudly than she intends.

"Hi. I'm Emily Donne. I'm here visiting family. I'm staying at my aunt's—Lily May Tyler—until tomorrow morning. I think you know Uncle Otis? And Uncle Mert? Well, anyway, I came upon this beautiful meadow and I'd like to pick some wildflowers. If that's all right?"

Deep blue eyes continue to stare at her as the woman makes no move of welcome, utters no sound. Emily takes in the fine wrinkles around her eyes and mouth, the deep cleft in her chin, and the roundness of her sun-pinked cheeks. Her attention rests briefly on a faint scar, a pale crescent running from forehead to temple above the left eyebrow. She is slightly taller than Emily's five-foot-two, with a slender build. Wearing jeans and a barn-red tank top beneath an unbuttoned denim shirt, she radiates ease and natural grace.

"Actually," Emily says, "I heard my uncles talking about a Margaret who has quite a puzzle collection. If that's you, they say you're quite the 'puzzler.'" She laughs, again too loud, her discomfort edging into giddiness. Her blood thrums in her ears. A metallic taste blooms in her mouth.

Drawn to come here, she now feels awkward and rude and foolish. Her impulse is to turn and run back to her car, but the woman has a magnetism that keeps her planted.

"Yes. I'm Margaret. And, yes, I know your uncles." The older woman has decided to put her out of her misery. "Interesting pair, those two. And they call *me* a character!" She pauses. "I know your aunt but not as well as I'd like to." She looks away, smiling as if remembering something pleasant. "Good people, your family. Good people."

"I call Aunt Lily May my saving grace. And my uncles, life's comic relief." Another laugh, this one releasing the tightness from her chest.

"Help yourself to a gathering basket by the door and pick your aunt a bouquet. Then perhaps you'll join me for a cup of tea before you go. Maybe talk puzzles."

"I'd like that."

"Just come around to the back door when you're done. This is Sophia and Grace. They'll keep you company if you don't mind dogs?"

Emily kneels, and the girls vie for pats and slather her with wet kisses. When she rises, Margaret is gone.

৵৶

Emily leaves the wildflowers in a pail of water by the door and knocks lightly.

"Come on in."

Emily steps inside a kitchen warm with fragrance. Potted herbs line the window sills. Garlic braids and dried flowers hang from the beams overhead. To her left, a basket filled with birch bark and mosses sits on a harvest table against the wall. On the huge range that anchors the right side of the room, a pot of tomato sauce simmers over a blue flame. Clumps of parsley and basil lay ready for chopping nearby.

At the far end of the room, a turquoise cabinet with copper fittings draws Emily's eye. It is filled with bright dishware painted in a distinctly southwestern style. On an upper shelf, a pair of cloth dolls, yarn hair interwoven with sweetgrass, slumps shoulder-to-shoulder, feet dangling.

Margaret indicates one of the mismatched chairs at the oak table in the center of the room. "Have a seat."

"Aunt Lily May will love the flowers." Emily sits as Margaret puts down fresh bowls of water for the dogs who have followed her in.

"That's not why you came up here though, is it? For wildflowers." Arresting blue eyes look deeply into hers. "You came here on purpose, but not for flowers."

Emily looks away. "To be honest, I don't really know why I came. My uncles talked about you and your puzzles, and I couldn't stop thinking about what they said. I did want to pick flowers when I saw the field, but it was the hope of meeting you that brought me here."

"You're not the first." Margaret pours two cups of tea from a squat china pot and sets one down in front of Emily. "You might want to taste it before adding anything. Most find it quite sweet as is."

They sip in silence.

"People have come to me for years. But not for my puzzles or flowers."

Emily says nothing.

"I suspect you have some puzzles of your own to work out, and I may be of some help there. That may be why you've come."

Emily looks at her over her teacup, her brows drawn together, questioning.

"I see things," Margaret says simply. "Know things. Things that have happened or are going to happen." She pauses and lets her words settle around them as the clock ticks and the kettle simmers on the stove.

"I don't see them all the time. They come to me unbidden, and I have to wear a sort of mask and not flinch sometimes. But the people who come looking watch me closely. Some too big in their nonchalance. Way too big. They say they want me to tell them what I see, but they don't. Not really. They want me to tell them what they *want* me to see." Margaret looks off, teacup poised before her lips. She shakes her head and sighs.

"Once in, some sights don't let go of me for a long time after. Sometimes never. I keep those to myself. No point in telling hurtful things that can't be changed."

With an edge of bitterness, she adds, "Some fear these eyes of mine, yet they're drawn to them like mosquitoes to a crackling bug light. Hoping against hope I'll say what they want to hear." She sips her tea. "And, frankly, so do I."

Emily doesn't speak for fear Margaret won't keep talking.

Margaret looks into her eyes again. "You have your own kind of sight, something beyond those green eyes of yours." She pauses and cocks her head, then continues. "It's more about *feeling* than *seeing*. Yes..." She nods slowly. "I think you intuit more than most. You listen with more than your ears. Though you're pretty adept at using those too, aren't you?"

"Do you see anything now?" The words are out before she can

stop them.

"Yes." Margaret pauses. "That's the simple answer."

Emily inhales. She's sure her heartbeat is audible.

"I see words around your head in bold typeface. And a scene. Midday, judging from the lack of shadows in full sun. You're little. Standing under a tree crying. A very old woman..." She pauses. "...also an Emily, bends over you.

"You dig a hole, starting it with your heel but then kneeling and digging with your hands until your fingernails are black. You drop something into the hole and pack the dirt back in around it. Your little face is streaked with black mud trails. You know you will be spanked but you don't care. In fact, you want to feel the sting of your mother's hand. Contact, at least. Lightning flashes in the now dark sky. The other Emily tries to comfort you. She wants you to know something, to remember something..."

Emily is leaning forward now.

"Another scene." Margaret sits back. "Another woman and a circle of little girls seated around a small fire. The woman, flushed and animated, gestures as she talks. Then she drops to a squat and points to one of the children—"

Margaret stops suddenly. "Fading. ...Gone now."

Emily shakes her head. "No."

"I'm sorry. I—"

"Oh!" Emily sits back. "I just remembered." She scowls, then tentatively goes on. "I dreamed of my grandmother last night. I was named after her. But there was no tree or fire in the dream."

"Symbolic, perhaps. Except maybe the circle." Margaret's brow is wrinkled, rippling the pale scar, as she looks into the middle distance. "Just set it aside for now. I think your grandmother has something to say to you."

"What? What does she have to say?" Emily is suddenly terrified that Margaret can't, or won't, tell her any more.

"What do you remember most about your grandmother?" Margaret asks, looking now into Emily's eyes.

"Not much. I was so little and..." Emily cries out in frustration.

"Just breathe and relax. Allow yourself to be with whatever comes, no matter how vague."

Margaret's breathing slows, and her voice soothes as Emily follows her lead into a hazy state of relaxation.

"Wait." Tears come, and Emily sits up straight in her chair. "She used to tell me stories. Or I should say, she would *start* telling a story and then stop and say, 'Make it yours,' and I'd have to finish it." She sucks in her breath. "She called me Emily-Memily, Teller of Tales. I'd forgotten all about that!"

"Sit with this while it's fresh in your mind. Later, you can write it all down on that laptop of yours."

"Thank you."

"I can't take credit. I'm just a catalyst somehow. Or a lightning rod, some would say." Margaret rises and moves to a small round table in the corner.

Emily strains to remember more.

"There you are," Margaret exclaims.

Emily turns in surprise.

"Sorry. Been looking for this piece with a bit of sky and here it sits. Just when I'd let go of trying."

Emily joins her. A round puzzle, two feet in diameter is half completed, worked from the center out in streaks like spokes of a wagon wheel. A pastoral scene. Autumn foliage under a clear blue sky. Pond, red barn, cows, mountains in the background. Large gaps of missing sections reveal the white tablecloth beneath. Emily picks up a piece and snugs it into place on the barn door, then pulls her hand back. "Oh! I'm sorry. I should have asked."

"Just draws you right in, doesn't it? You see the piece, zero in on the spot, and you can't help yourself. You have to fill in the blank."

Emily looks around the room, realizing she's been seeing through the tunnel vision of self-absorption since entering Margaret's home. Puzzles everywhere. A smaller round one on a low table is nearly finished—a complex riot of primary colors in a kaleidoscopic pattern. It shifts and changes as she moves past it, dizzying in its impact. A large rectangular one—an iconic view of the earth from space—sits on a card table. A single piece is missing. The piece, a mix of green and blue and white, sits off to the left. Emily notes she has no urge to put this piece in place. She looks at Margaret.

"I'm putting off the moment," Margaret says. "It's not about savoring so much as internalizing an understanding of timing."

Emily moves on to the scattered pieces on the coffee table in the sitting room. A new beginning, no form yet. She looks around. No box, no map of this terrain. Just colors and shapes. Two thousand pieces at least.

"People bring them to me in brown paper bags or old shoe boxes," Margaret explains. "'Think you'll like this one,' they'll say. Or, from my humorous friends, 'I'll give you a hint: it's not a famous work of art.' Some bring them as a challenge. *Figure this one out without a picture!* they'll think, but not say. And we'll both pretend they came bearing gifts."

Margaret settles into a worn wingback chair and indicates the nearby end of the couch. Emily sits.

Both are quiet for a while. Bird chatter draws Emily's gaze out the window.

"How long have you been puzzling?" she asks.

Margaret's sudden laughter startles her. "All my life! No one has ever known what to make of me. 'Puzzling,' indeed."

"But—"

"Sorry. I know you meant, how long have I been *doing* puzzles. But, you must admit, the way you put it begged for an answer of another kind."

Margaret continues to chuckle as if Emily has disappeared for a moment. Finally, her distant gaze refocuses. "My family was a right tribe of 'puzzlers' in every sense of that word. But my mother was the one who always had a jigsaw puzzle laid out in here." Her voice drifts to a near whisper. "Way back in time before it all came apart."

She suddenly straightens as her attention returns to the room and Emily. "It may have skipped a generation, but you come from a long line of storytellers—on both sides. Your mother has kept her stories pretty much to herself, though, hasn't she? You well understand the expression 'deafening silence,' don't you, child?"

The quiet question stirs a mixture of sadness and surprise in Emily.

"How did you..."

"She loves you both gently and fiercely, Em."

Emily hears her mother's voice in that single syllable, *Em*. She feels the simultaneous airy softness and pulsing intensity that is her mother. She shivers and folds her arms across her chest.

Margaret continues. "She is steeped in mystery. She shields herself against my prying, against all prying."

Margaret is silent for a moment. "It was not my intention to go there. It happens more often than I like to admit, though. This slipping into other people's 'personal space,' as they say. But in this case, it felt necessary somehow."

Emily sighs. "I wish she would let me into that space. She's *my* 'puzzler.'"

"I have a feeling you'll get to know her story one day. The scribe taking it all down. Mind you, I said I have a feeling. That doesn't mean I've seen it. It might be like anyone else's *wrong* feeling."

But Emily has a feeling that this feeling is right. And she doesn't like the idea much.

"I do see an armadillo."

"What?"

"From the Spanish, *little armored one*. I suspect solving the mystery that is your mother is crucial to letting your own guard down. To letting others into *your* space. In your wake, I see a string of rebuffed young men—one not long ago—and friends who could never quite get inside." She pauses. "Worth exploring in writing, perhaps?"

"Sounds ...scary."

"How long are you staying with Otis and Lily May? Maybe you could share some of your stories before you go."

"Oh, I stopped telling stories when I was little," she says quickly.

"Then what's in all those notebooks in the box in the closet? And that file in your computer?" Margaret smiles.

"Oh, those." Emily grins in spite of herself. "Instead of reading before bed, I write. It quiets my mind so I can sleep. But they're like doodlings. I'd be embarrassed to show them to anyone."

"Suit yourself." A pause. "What do you do for work?"

The turn surprises Emily. "I work at a museum. For now, anyway."

"Oh?"

"There are grumblings that the board is slashing the budget and cutting positions."

"What's missing in your work life?"

"Nothing!" Emily responds sharply. "I like my job. Why would you ask that? It's what I trained for. I love being around art. I've been working my butt off to prove my worth to them, and some of what I do is tedious, but that's true of any work."

"I'm wondering why your grandmother is so intent on reminding you of your storytelling self. Perhaps she sees from her wider perspective a coming shift—"

Emily shakes her head, interrupting Margaret. "That's too unsettling."

"Perhaps," Margaret goes on, "she's come to prepare you for something wonderful. Not turning away from art but toward a fuller expression of who you are. Of course, I could be wrong." Margaret's smile says anything but.

Emily looks out the uncurtained window, past the clusters of potted plants on the outer sill. The shadows in the backyard have deepened. How could it have gotten so late so fast?

𝕒𝕖

She feels her way down the dirt driveway, images of the day tumbling through her mind. In her car, she sits with her hand on the key but does not turn it. Darkness filters in and around as crickets sing and fireflies flicker in the fields and woods beyond. Lost, but not lost, Emily remains in silent absorption.

Slowly, shadows of doubt creep in to dispel the sense of excitement tingling within her. She shivers herself awake and turns the key.

Inside the house, Margaret turns her head toward the window at the sound of the car's engine, then fits the piece of earth, water, and sky into place.

Chapter 2

Emily sits on a ladder-back chair in the front bedroom of Otis and Lily May's house. The jagged strands of the caned seat prick at her bare legs, but she is deep into journaling, too intent to let them pull her focus. The glowing screen of her laptop is the only light in the room.

There's a tap at the door, and Aunt Lily May steps in. Emily hits *save* and stifles an exasperated sigh at the interruption. Dear Lily May is her *great*-aunt actually, her grandmother's oldest sister. Eighty something. Although stooped and deeply wrinkled, she exudes a fiery ageless spirit.

"Out for my bedtime constitutional and saw your 'light.'" Lily May laughs quietly. "Thought I might get you to join me under the stars since you're leaving in the morning. We haven't had much chance to talk this trip."

Emily wants to beg off. Already, the sense of flow is evaporating. She wants to reconnect with the current that has been moving her along so smoothly, making her fingers dance across the keyboard and her mind hum. But she closes the lid and follows her aunt down the stairs and out into the front yard.

The two women turn toward the back garden and the path to the pond. A low mist sits in the shallow dips along the way. "Fog in the hollow, good day to follow," they say in unison and laugh.

They walk without words to where the path abruptly divides. Lily May stops as her flashlight beam catches the glint of silver on the ground. "The fork in the road." She laughs aloud, and Emily remembers the oft-told story of how that salad fork came to be planted here in this patch of wooly thyme.

"Uncle Otis and his penchant for literalism," she says. "I spent hours exploring his gardens when I was a kid, searching for those splashes of surprise tucked in among the vegetables and flowers. The sculpted 'footstool' flanked by old shoes and boots sprouting succulents. And …" She stops. "Oh, Lily May, how I wished I could live here and never have to leave." Emily is suddenly crying.

Aunt Lily May waits. When Emily calms, she takes her niece in her arms and whispers, "I know. I know."

The night sounds intensify around them. They resume their walking.

"I can't understand why my mother ever left here," Emily says, "or why we couldn't visit for more than a few days at a time. She would never even unpack, and she would get all itchy and anxious until we drove away. Just down the road, I would feel her flatten out. But it wasn't that she couldn't wait to get back home. I mean, none of the places we've ever lived felt like she put any of herself into them. They were each just a group of rooms under a single roof, utilities included. That's why it was so special when you invited me to stay for the whole summer when I was nine. I couldn't believe it when she said yes. You'll never know how much that summer, and you, shaped my life. Thank you for that."

Lily May nods. "It was our pleasure. You had a bit of an impact on us as well, Sweet Pea." The fragrance of pond lilies engulfs them as they near the water's edge. Sweet. Almost too sweet for Emily to bear. Again, she lets go into soft crying.

"Your mother has seen more than her share of the dark side of things. Maybe one day she'll find a place that quiets her restless heart."

Emily is silent. "Then maybe she'll tell me her story and we'll both be released from it, whatever it is."

"Perhaps."

They circle the pond and settle on the weather-bleached cedar bench. A sliver of a moon has risen over the house, a star just off its lower point. Crickets and peepers chirp and sing around them.

"You met Margaret Meader today?" Lily May picks up a new thread, or perhaps she knows it's the old one in another guise.

"I did. Do you know her?"

"Not well. I like what I know of her, though. I'm a lot older than she is, and she lived away for many years. She only came back a couple of years ago to nurse her mother until she passed.

"She's a plain speaker. Spinach stuck in your front teeth, Margaret will tell you first thing. 'Course, people don't always want to hear the truth told. There's always someone eager to kill the messenger. So, she has her enemies, and some of the old troubles have come 'round to haunt her since she came back.

"Handles it all with grace, though. She's an original. I admire her. Next chance I get, I should tell her so. Life is just too darn short to keep a kindness to yourself. ... Unless, of course, you had a different take on her?"

"No. I liked her. She told me— Wait a minute. That's the second time I've heard there was trouble in her past. What happened, exactly?"

"You know how gossip and a poor memory can conjure more fiction than fact. So, details I can't give you. I only know she was picked on when she was young because of that canny knack of hers to know things the rest of us aren't privy to. Made her the target of a pack of petty bitches—sorry—with too much time and too little mind on their hands. Led to a downright nasty affair, but I won't dignify it by dredging it up again. It sent her away from here."

"I found that 'canny knack' a bit unsettling. I'm not sure what to think. I haven't processed all she said. Most of it felt really helpful as she said it. But later, after I left, I began to question the whole experience."

"Hmm."

"She talked about Nana."

Lily May sighs. "Oh, how your Nana Emily loved you. What she would have given to watch you grow up. You were the joy and light of her heart."

"Margaret saw a vision of Nana coming to me after she'd died.

She was trying to comfort me."

"Your nana would certainly have done that if she could."

"Margaret said some of what she saw was symbolic. She said Nana wanted to tell me something. Prepare me for something. Then I remembered I dreamed about her last night. I'd completely forgotten."

"Tell me about the dream."

"I can't remember it. I just know it was about her. But in talking to Margaret, I suddenly remembered that Nana called me Emily-Memily, Teller of Tales. She'd start telling me a story and then stop and say—"

"Make it yours!" Lily May laughs gently. "Oh, my. You've just taken me back. That's what our mother used to do. On summer nights when the wind was low and the stars were just beginning to appear, she'd light a fire in the backyard. All five of us girls—Emily, Katy, Zoe, Ruby, and me—would sit around it in our nightgowns, faces washed and teeth brushed. Mommy would build up the fire to a lovely blaze and she'd start a story. Then she'd stop and we had to continue it, each adding a part.

"Your nana was best at it. We always let her finish the stories because she had such a flair for tucking in all the stray story lines. Somehow, she would take a story full of fantastical twists and corkscrew turnings, unrelated elements, and characters and weave them into a satisfying tale." Lily May pauses in reverie, a smile on her face. "I wish we'd written them down."

"Margaret suggested that maybe that's where I come in. She thinks Nana is trying to remind me that I'm a storyteller."

"This reunion held more for you than any of us could have imagined when we were baking pies and setting out the porch chairs."

"Thank you for that. I hope you know how much I appreciate you. How much I love you." Emily searches her aunt's eyes.

"I know, Sweet Pea. I know." Lily May pats her hand.

"Margaret 'knew' that I write stories." Emily shakes her head, trying to square her experience with her niggling skepticism. "I told her they're just doodles, silly little nothings that help me get to sleep at night. They'd never qualify as real stories, as anything close to literature. I could never share them."

"If I were a girl of your age, do you know what I would never do?"

"What?"

"I'd never say never." And Lily May rises and heads back to the house.

Chapter 3

Margaret feels unsettled after the Donne girl leaves. She questions the wisdom of not telling her everything she saw. She's kept the darkest image to herself. And, as usual, she falls into second-guessing. "Who am I to decide what to impart and what to withhold?" she says aloud. "When will I ever learn?"

Hearing her own words, she realizes this uneasiness has a deeper genesis. She knows the cause. The old business is coming back around. This is not a vague feeling. She knows it. For certain. What she doesn't know is how it will end this time.

She sets the kettle on the stove and pulls the scarred and faded card table from the closet. After setting it up in the corner, she takes a wrinkled brown bag from a shelf by the door and dumps out the contents. Her hands move quickly, automatically turning puzzle pieces face up and spreading them out. Shades of gray and blue with touches of white and hints of green suggest a misty waterscape. Her inner eye drifts over the pieces. Lulled by the familiar motion of practiced hands, she settles into a dreamy state of openness. She notices with detached awareness the hues changing to a dull red or a muted orange or mottled black, until dozens of pieces with such colorings lay sprinkled among the cooler watery tones. With a sudden sharp pain to the forehead, a series of images sizzles through her mind, then stops abruptly.

Wincing, she drops into the Morris chair nearby. The images return, sizzling more loudly. She knows not to fight them. Better to breathe into them.

A contorted face. A sheet covered in blood and afterbirth. A round-cheeked, green-eyed baby. A jagged bolt of lightning. Flames pouring from an upstairs window of a once white house. ... Children playing tag, breath visible puffs against the evening air. The smell of burning leaves. The stench of burning tires. Colorful squares of cloth raining down around wide-eyed men. An overturned tractor. A slowly turning wheel. A little boy, blond hair powdered with dirt. The green-eyed baby slipping into sleep. Ches Bramwell wrenched from her arms. Dark eyes wide. Thick brows raised. Mouth open in a silent scream.

Sky. Nothing but sky. ... Plummeting through a viscous black, heart and stomach left behind.

A jolt. A shattering of bones. A swallowed scream. A ringing silence.

Margaret opens her eyes. The fire snaps in the grate. The teakettle screams. The pain in her head is gone.

She knows it's best to sit with it and then let it go—this jumble of sensory details, some drawn from memory, some prescient. Later, when one presents itself in real time, everything will slow down and something inside will say, *Here it is. Pay attention.*

She pours a cup of tea and sits back down. Slowly she sips, holding the cup in both hands, taking in its warmth. She wishes Joe were here. Aches for the comfort of his gentle, listening presence, if only for a while.

The tears come. She sits and sips and cries.

She whose gift is sight cannot see Joe's face for all her trying. When this happens, it scares her. Her attempts are as sketchy as the images she just experienced. It's as if her sensory mechanisms are blocked by a squirrelly electrical interference. To allay her fears, she summons a familiar scene, the backyard in afternoon sunshine. As she looks out over the hydrangea bushes and echinacea beds, a gray fog bank settles in around the house and yard. Along with it, a stifling sense of disquiet settles into her chest.

She sets down her cup and wills herself to yawn deeply,

exaggerating the stretching of her arms and the opening of her mouth. This is an escape route; she's had to use it often of late. Again, she yawns, and her body slumps into a state of deep weariness. She closes her eyes and sinks back into the chair. *Nothing. Think of nothing*, she tells herself. *Breathe. In and out. In … She dozes.*

The dream is lovely. A memory wrapped in a dream. She hears Joe's laughter from behind her. She is standing at the stove in their cottage in Camden. Joe is out on the porch. Sunlight streams in the open French doors along with a playful breeze. Happy. This is what happy feels like. She wants to hold on to this. Hold on tight.

The ringing of the phone wakes her, pulling her back into the now dark living room with her cold tea on the table beside her chair.

It's Annie Foss, her neighbor. "Come quick, Margaret. Oh, please, come quick."

Margaret grabs a flashlight and sweater as she runs out the back door. Calling to the dogs to join her, she heads for the path through the woods.

She reaches Annie's house minutes later and stops to slow her pulse before knocking. As the dogs settle beside the steps, the door swings open and Annie pulls her inside. Her appearance stuns Margaret. Tall and solidly built, her usual regal bearing has collapsed into the stooped and trembling posture of a frightened child.

Dark eyes wide, she gasps, struggling for breath. "It's time. I think it's time and I don't know what to do. I thought I'd know. But I don't." She curls forward into Margaret's arms.

Margaret holds her until Annie's body surrenders to the deep wave of warmth flowing between them. Then she steps back. "You're right. It's time. He's ready and you'll know what to do. I'll help you both."

Annie leads the way through a heavily curtained doorway. The hospital-style bed stands in the middle of the room. Fat flames crackle in the fireplace, radiating a near stifling heat into the close quarters. Jake lies still beneath a pile of thick quilts, his head raised on a thin pillow, his eyes closed. The bedding lifts and lowers almost imperceptibly with each raspy breath.

Margaret stands on the threshold, eyes closed, listening deeply. A fierce, frozen tautness hangs in the air. Jake appears to be asleep or in coma, but that outward calm belies an intense inner struggle for life. The magnetic pull of his focused concentration moves her to guide the immobilized Annie into the chair beside the bed.

"Trust yourself, Annie, to know what to do next. Just give yourself over to this."

Annie reaches beneath the covers and withdraws Jake's hand in both of hers. She leans in as if listening with her whole body. Quietly, she begins to sing, an old lullaby bubbling up into her mouth. As she sings, Margaret walks to the other side of the bed, her back to the fire, her eyes closed. She rests one hand on his chest, the other on his forehead.

The air around the bed vibrates and pulses with wild rhythms only Margaret can feel. Gradually, the tension smooths out, settling at last into undulating waves of liquid warmth. She removes her hands.

"He's at peace, Annie. He truly is."

"I know. I can feel it."

"You just sit here for a while and I'll go make a pot of tea. When you're ready, we'll make some calls."

୭୬

The next days are filled with the details of tending to the living while grieving and marking the passing of a well-loved man. On the third day after the funeral, Margaret straightens from her gardening and calls the dogs to accompany her once more through the woods. She finds Annie sobbing on the floor, unable to articulate in any other way the stunning impact of the sudden knowledge that Jake is never coming back. Unable to get up, Annie looks at Margaret and wails.

Margaret plops down on the floor beside her, nodding in silent acknowledgment. That's when she allows her own tears to come, and the two women, both past sixty, sit on the floor in the waning light and cry.

Finally, Annie speaks. "How did you survive the loss of Joe and still go on? And how do you keep on laughing that beautiful laugh of yours while holding the rest of us up? All these long months, ever since Jake's diagnosis, you've been there for me. For us. How do you do it, Margaret? How do you know what's coming and still do it?"

"I'm one of the lucky ones, Annie. I've been shown enough and experienced enough to trust in the process that includes, but doesn't end with, death. I think we're here to experience the good and the bad, the ordinary and the extraordinary—all of it. Joy may take us to the heights, but grief deepens our capacity for empathy and love. It cracks us open, and what we do with the light that spills out is up to each of us. I hold on to Joe's essence by making the best use of the light his passing opened me to."

Annie shakes her head. "I can't see any light."

"All in good time. Right now, it's time to rest and replenish. Give yourself this time to heal and then we'll talk some more. Indulge in a little 'light' conversation if you will."

Margaret helps Annie to her feet and over to the couch, where she covers her with a fringed woolen shawl.

"I can't believe he's gone, Margaret."

"Truth is, he's not, Annie." The next words come to her an instant before she speaks them. "He says, 'They should have sent a poet.'"

Annie stares at her, tears welling anew. After a long silence, she says, "That's a line from a movie. It became a sort of pet expression between us, one we reserved for those times when something took our breath away and there would be no words to express our awe." She wipes away tears. "Oh, my, God, Margaret ..."

"You rest now. Just rest in the comfort that's meant to bring you."

Chapter 4

Margaret rounds the corner of the house. Down the hill, a car window glints in the sun. A car door slams. The girl is back.

"I'd like to gather more flowers," Emily says without greeting. "She loved the others. Said a wildflower bouquet is her favorite thing in the world." Emily stops. "*Was* her favorite thing." She rushes her words, grasping for composure. "I was too late. I came back to be with her, but I was too late...." She bends forward, hugging herself.

Margaret moves to her, placing her hand on her back. "I'm so sorry. Lily May was a lovely person."

"Did you know? When I was here before, did you know?" There's more than a hint of anger in the question.

Margaret hesitates. "I saw loss. I didn't know it would be her."

"How do you stand it? How can you know such things and keep such secrets and ...?"

"Sometimes I can't stand it."

"What will I do without her? Even when I didn't see her for weeks, I knew she was here, and ..."

Margaret holds her, letting her cry.

When the sobbing subsides, Margaret steers her inside and eases her into a kitchen chair by the window. She pours a cup of tea, stirring in a spoonful of maple sugar. She places it in Emily's hands and seats herself across the table.

"Tell me about her."

Emily glares at her. Anger and mistrust still cloud her green eyes, but then she slumps in surrender. For the next hour she talks. She tells Margaret about her deep loneliness as a child. About her mother's restlessness and the great distance between them. Of how her mother constantly moved them from place to place. Of that glorious summer when she was nine and her mother agreed to let her stay with Lily May and Otis. How Lily May became the only anchor in her uprooted life, the one she could truly count on, come back to, call out to.

She shares her last time with her aunt in the garden. "My conversation with you that day led us to have a really deep talk that night. But I never got to say good-bye. If only I'd known. If only I'd arrived sooner."

"There are no platitudes I can offer. Your heart will hurt for a long time. Nothing I can say will make it hurt any less."

"What am I going to do?"

"*Be* in your grief. To everything there truly is a season. This is the season for grieving. As you take care of the things in your life that need to be done—and you will—you must allow room for this heaviness to be with you for a while. Don't let anyone tell you there's a time limit for when you should be 'over it.' You'll be over the deepest grieving when the time is right for you. And not before."

Margaret lets her words hang in the air. Finally, she goes on, "You've experienced a terrible loss. That's the truth of this moment. The awful, painful truth of this moment. Be in that truth for as long as you need to."

Margaret freshens her tea. As she sips the sweet liquid, Emily describes her memories to Margaret, to the dogs seated on either side of her chair, to the air around them. Aunt Lily May beside her on the cedar bench under the moon sliver, laughing; Uncle Otis staring off in the distance as if waiting for her to come walking up the path from the garden; the ticking of the old clock in the hallway; the clink of china at the Sunday table; the smell of fresh scones cooling. Lily May's hands kneading a plump round of dough. Lily

May's fingers smoothing a Band-Aid on a scraped knee, her lips kissing the hurt away. And tears slip down Emily's cheeks as the hint of a smile teases the corners of her mouth.

Margaret says nothing. Images swirl before her eyes as well. She sees Emily's mother, Janet, arrive and follow Otis into the farmhouse. She feels the woman's inner struggle; the overwhelming desire to turn and run back to her green sedan and fly down the road, eyes on the rearview mirror until the house is a speck in the distance. She feels the held breath, the monumental restraint that keeps the woman in her body and in the room. The unbearable pressure behind her eyes, the throbbing in her blood, and the numbness that spreads from her feet to her abdomen to her chest.

Finally, Margaret says, "Your mother's arrived at the house. She may not stay, but that's about her. Not you or Lily May or Otis."

"I'd better go."

Margaret reaches over to cover Emily's hand with hers. "It's not your job to take care of her, you know. This is the time to take care of yourself. Remember that. I'll help if you'll let me. Remember that too."

"Thank you." Emily rises.

"Lily May is here for you in a different way now. She and your grandmother, arm in arm, are smiling and saying, 'Make it yours. This story. This life. Make it yours.'"

As she walks to the door, Emily notices a new puzzle on a battered card table in the corner. A fiery orange piece sits off by itself, calling her attention. Absently, she picks it up and runs her thumb over the face of it. Then she places it back where she found it.

"Funny. It looked like it would be too hot to touch." And she heads out to gather wildflowers.

Margaret opens the flour bin and dusts the bread board.

Chapter 5

Emily is prepared. She knows her mother is at the farmhouse and so she is prepared. Still, the sight of the green car in the yard makes her chest tighten, her throat go dry.

"Breathe," she reminds herself aloud. "The first few minutes are the hardest. Then it will be business as usual. Let's just get through those first few."

With that, she steps out of her car and reaches back in for the flowers. As she straightens, she hears the muffled thud of the screen door. She turns to find her mother standing on the porch.

"I hope you checked for ticks. The days of wandering around in the fields willy-nilly are over, you know. I hope you remembered that and were careful. Maybe you should just leave those out here on the porch."

"Hello, Mother. I'm glad you came."

"Well, of course, I came. What do you mean, you're glad I came? Do you think I wouldn't come for my own aunt's funeral? Honestly, Emily, I don't deserve this hostility from you."

"I simply said ..." Emily stops herself. "Never mind. Let's just go inside and start this again. Okay?"

"Okay. But I still think you should leave those flowers outside. You don't want to be giving someone Lyme disease, do you? It's really very serious, Emily. These fields around here are loaded with ticks this time of year. Besides, I ordered some lovely arrangements at the local florist before I came. They'll be here anytime now, I'm sure."

"The flowers are fine, Mother. They're Lily May's favorites, and they're coming inside and going in water. And Uncle Otis and I will enjoy them, and you can keep your distance if you're worried. If I get Lyme disease, you can always say you told me so."

Damn, Emily thinks as she brushes past her mother. *Two minutes in and I've blown it already.*

"Well, what about Otis? If not me or yourself, don't you care about him?" Her mother follows her down the hall and into the kitchen. "The last thing he needs right now is Lyme disease."

Emily wants to turn around and scream, *Shut. The fuck. Up!*

She wants to. But she doesn't. Of course, she doesn't.

Otis shuffles into the kitchen from the back porch. His eyes fill as he looks upon the bundle of wildflowers Emily has placed by the sink. "Just what she woulda' picked herself." Looking at Janet, he says, "Emily picked some just like that when she came down for the reunion. Lily May was tickled pink." The memory of his smiling wife receiving that other bouquet stops him. His lower lip trembles, and he leans back against the fridge.

Janet is closest to him, and after a brief hesitation she crosses to his side. Stiffly, she pats his arm and then walks out the back door, silent.

Emily puts down the Mason jar she's taken from the shelf and walks over to her uncle. She slips easily into his arms, and together they cry.

Janet comes back in from the porch. "Things will get easier with time. You'll see. Just give it some time, Otis," she says quietly.

Her uncle straightens and pulls away from Emily. "Time will surely pass, Janet, but nothing about this is going to get easier. She was the love of my life. There's a big hole where she used to be, and won't time, nor anything else, be able to fill it." He walks past her out the back door, letting it go behind him with a soft thunk.

Emily watches as he heads down the path to the gardens. She says nothing to her mother as she goes back to arranging the flowers. There is nothing to say. When the tears come again, she lets them slide down her cheeks.

"I'm sorry, Em." Her mother comes up behind her and wraps her arms around her waist. Her cheek rests just behind Emily's ear, and she whispers, "I know how much you loved her. And Otis is right. It's going to hurt for a long time. I wish I could spare you that pain. I hope you know that."

Emily leans back against her, surrendering to this rare moment of intimacy with the mother she wishes she could call Mom or Mommy. The mother she wishes she could trust to be there beyond this moment. Just as she thinks this, her mother presses a quick kiss to her temple and pulls away. "You need to put on some weight. You're all angles and bones. And the circles under your eyes are more pronounced than ever."

Fresh tears come as her mother leaves the room, her footsteps receding down the hall and then up the stairs. Emily already knows what she'll do in her room. She'll pull the shades, lock the door, and slip under the covers. She won't come out again for hours, maybe days, and then will excuse her long absence as a migraine.

The doorbell rings. The first wave of casseroles, cakes, and condolences has arrived.

In the late afternoon, Emily and Otis put the garment bag with Lily May's plum silk dress in the backseat of Otis's car and head for the Parkinson Beane Funeral Parlor. Emily is surprised when Earl Beane hands her a pale-pink envelope containing a hand-written note. Lily May's final request is that Emily deliver her eulogy. *Keep it light. Celebrate my life, not my passing. And do it in the form of a story. It may be my story, but make it yours, Sweet Pea.*

The story begins to take form almost immediately, sending a charge of electricity through her. But as the words and phrases swirl, fear niggles at the edges of awareness. Cowed by the immensity of the challenge, she worries she may not be up to the task. This is not one of her late-night scribblings, for her eyes only. This story matters. It matters deeply.

Chapter 6

Margaret climbs into her truck. Before starting the engine, she sits back and listens to the chatter in her head until it settles and fades. When there is silence, she sits with the subtle rhythm of her heartbeat and waits, eyes closed. When it comes, the voice is barely above a whisper. She cocks her head and listens more intently, nods in affirmation, and turns the key. The old truck creaks and groans as she shifts into drive and heads down the hill. She hums the refrain from an old hymn as she drives toward town.

Otis answers the door and invites her in. She nods and heads into the kitchen.

"Wish I had some magical elixir or words of wisdom," she says, "but we both know there aren't any, not for this."

She plunks her bags and basket on the counter. She hefts the soup pot onto a back burner, and then she reaches for a large wooden salad bowl and empties a bag of freshly picked salad greens into it. Removing two pies from the basket, she puts them out on the side board, saying that she knows Otis won't feel like it, but he should try to eat a little something every few hours. "Otherwise," she warns, "I'm going to have to come back and nag you."

Emily comes in the back door and smiles when she sees Margaret. They hug, and Margaret gives her a fragrant bunch of lavender. "For your bedside table. Maybe sprinkle some under your pillow as well." Turning to include Otis, she asks if anyone is up for a walk. "I'd love to see your gardens, and I'll bet the pond is lovely this time of day."

Otis looks deeply into her eyes, then nods in agreement. "After you, ladies," he says, motioning to the door with a gallant bow.

They walk without talking. Occasionally, Margaret murmurs in admiration at Otis's handiwork. She bends to smell a flower or to brush her hand amongst the herbs, releasing the subtle aromas of thyme or mint or sage into the air. She smiles at the fork in the road and at the footstool and flowering footwear, and stops to enjoy the tinkling of a wind chime set in motion by the abrupt departure of a bird.

Emily walks on ahead, leaving her uncle and Margaret to saunter in silence. Otis stops when Margaret laughs outright at the sight of an old violin standing upright in a patch of fiddlehead ferns, its bow suspended across its middle.

"Lily May must have loved walking here, Otis. It's so full of the essence of you."

Otis smiles in spite of himself, in spite of the black heart-sized stone sitting in his chest. "That she did, Margaret. That she did." He looks off into the distance. "I remember the day I finished this. Coat after coat of spar varnish finally dry. Wires all rigged to hold the bow afloat. Had just planted it when she came along and laughed like you just did. Said something about me *cultivating surprise*." He chuckles. "Called me the steward of her heart." His voice quavers, lower lip trembling. "Said we have everything we need right here in our own backyard." With a sharp clearing of the throat, he turns and starts toward the pond.

When Margaret catches up to him, he says, "She's asked Emily to write her eulogy. Hope I can make it through without coming apart."

"Coming apart isn't the worst thing that can happen to you. Sometimes *not* coming apart is the worst thing that can happen to you."

When they reach the bench, Emily is sitting there writing in a small notebook.

"Her eulogy?" Margaret asks.

"I just think about her and words come. I have to catch them right away."

"She knew what she was doing when she asked this of you. It's a gift for both of you."

৯৵৹৻

The day of the funeral begins with a weak sun that slowly succumbs to thickening clouds. At midmorning, Emily steps out into a light drizzle and walks to the pond. Her mother has not come down from her room since the day before, and Emily hates that she's attuned to every sound from that end of the house. Hoping. Always hoping. Despite a lifetime of disappointment, she continues to give her mother this attention and this hoping.

She stands at the water's edge and removes her hood, lifting her face to the rain. Nature is mirroring her inner world, crying the tears she can't summon. She closes her eyes.

"I don't know if I can do this, Lily May," she says aloud. "Last night I thought I could, but now I'm afraid. Afraid of letting you down. Afraid my words aren't enough. This matters too much. I'm sorry. I can't do it."

The rain dampens her red hair, tightening her spiraling curls. She shivers. She knows she should go inside and opens her eyes.

Standing on the far edge of the pond, a great blue heron arrests her chattering mind. Its stillness draws her in. They stand, one on each side of the water, its surface dimpled with raindrops, looking at each other. Emily's breathing slows. Her shivering ceases. A deep sense of calm settles into her chest, radiating out through her torso and limbs. Words form into a simple sentence.

৯৵৹৻

The funeral parlor is crowded, and Earl Beane has set up chairs in the overflow room. At the front of the main room, a simple easel displays a collage of candid photos. Lily May alone. Lily May with Otis. Lily May with friends. Lily May in the center at the last family reunion.

Emily's airy bouquet, a volume of Robert Frost's poems, and a simple urn sit on a small oak table beside the easel. Behind them, flower arrangements fill the spacious central platform.

As Emily walks to the platform, she sees her mother seated near the back of the room. A mild irritation surfaces, but there is no time to give it attention. She stands beside the memorial table, her lavender linen dress set off by the brighter hues of the wildflowers. She holds a wooden object, hidden in her cupped hands, in front of her heart.

"Lily May Tyler was the still point in my life."

She looks out on the faces before her. There is a visible leaning in, a patient, listening reverence holding space for her. She knows she can take all the time she needs. They are with her in this. She sees nods of understanding ripple through the crowd.

"No matter how chaotic or unsettling my life could get, there she'd be. A centering, calming presence standing in the midst of it. This easygoing, smiling woman with the infectious laugh, animated on the outside, serene at her core.

"My mother and I moved around a lot. Sometimes I'd come home from school and find our car packed and ready to head out for a new destination. No matter how many first days at new schools I had to face. No matter how many times I lay awake at night wishing for a more rooted life or a stronger me to live it, Aunt Lily May was always my saving grace. I knew that no matter where I was, I could find her here. In the swirling maelstrom that was my life, I needed only to find that still point and I'd be home.

"I never got to say good-bye to her. I guess that's a common regret when a loved one dies unexpectedly. But the last time I was up here, I did get to tell her how much I loved and appreciated her. That gives me great solace now." Tears slip down Emily's cheeks.

"Lily May's final request was that I celebrate her life today. She asked me to keep it light and to tell it in the form of a story, in keeping with a family tradition. In that same tradition, I'd like to begin that story and then offer it up for continuation by anyone who feels moved to take up the thread."

She pauses, clearing her throat. "This is the story of a woman who lived with the love of her life." She smiles at Otis. He smiles back, his shoulders and torso shaking with his silent sobs. "They lived on a piece of land that flourished and blossomed under his hands, and amid a family that flourished and blossomed under hers. This was a woman who said often, 'I have everything I need right here in my own backyard.' And this is a woman who, if she didn't have everything she needed right in her own backyard, would set about creating it with simplicity and humor.

"Lily May told me about a woman in this town whom she greatly admired. She said of her, 'She's a plain speaker. Spinach stuck in your front teeth, she'll tell you first thing, no beating around the bush.' The fact that she admired such straightforwardness and honesty says as much about her as it does about that other woman." Emily looks at Margaret seated in the third row, blue eyes glistening. "Lily May regretted not telling this woman how much she admired her. She said to me, 'Life is too darned short to keep a kindness to yourself.' She planned to tell her the next chance she had.

"She didn't get the chance. Life was, indeed, too short.

"But we get to learn from this. I hope I'll live the rest of my life with greater openness. I hope I'll remember more often than not to pass along a compliment, to extend a kindness, and to look no further than my own backyard—wherever that may be—for all I need in this world. I hope I can become the still point in my own life. And then, one day, the still point for someone else."

She holds up the wooden figure. "Years ago, Lily May and Uncle Otis placed a bench beside the pond out back of their house. In the evenings, they would sit there together. He would whittle and she would watch as he transformed bits of wood into exquisitely detailed birds.

"Once, when I was little, I asked Lily May if I could have this one, this heron." Emily holds the delicate carving to her heart again. "For the first and only time in my life, she said no. She said, 'You are the heart of my heart, my child, but Uncle Otis made this special for me and I could never give it away. Not even to you.' With those last three words, *even to you,* she reassured me that I was, indeed, the heart of her heart.

"She told me it's the first one he ever made. The one that inspired him to make more. It's the bird who would come to visit them from time to time the first year they were here. It would stand on the far side of the water in perfect stillness, sometimes looking right at them. She said, 'The three of us would share the silence. The longer we kept that silence, the longer the heron would stay.' Its waiting stance, its delicate balance, reminded them to practice patience and to never let their lives get too filled up with busyness or stuff. To focus on what was really important and to never let a day go by without taking time to sit … be still … and listen.

"Be still and listen," Emily repeats.

All sit in silence, most with eyes turned upward, some with eyes closed.

After a long pause, Emily clears her throat and resumes. "This is the story of Lily May Tyler. This is the part *I* know. I welcome you now to share how Lily May's story and yours intersects. This part of the service will take as long as it takes. I invite you to tell us the part you know."

There is a gentle stirring of people settling back, uncrossing their legs, shifting their bodies, coughing softly.

Emily's heart quickens as her mother rises from her seat in the back. Everyone turns, and a pleasant murmur acknowledges this first one to pick up the thread.

As her mother crosses the row, excusing herself to those seated between her and the aisle, Emily steps to the side, making room for her to join her. She glances at Lily May's smiling photograph.

As she looks back, her mother reaches the center aisle, stands for a moment looking at Emily, then turns away. With her head down, she exits. The double doors swing closed.

Uncle Mert hefts his two hundred pounds up from his seat beside his wife and sons. He leans on the chair back in front of him, wheezing. Then he clears his throat and says, "Lily May could stop me in my tracks with that laugh of hers. I'd get to rantin' about something that had gotten stuck in my craw, and she'd let me go on and on for a good bit. Then she'd start smilin', and she'd lower her chin and look at me over those half-glasses of hers and laugh out loud. And all my bluster would evaporate like dew in the morning grass…"

❧

Outside on the steps after the service, Emily and Otis exchange words and hugs with friends and neighbors as they file past. Forty-three of them had stood to speak after Mert finished, each adding another episode or a string of adjectives to the narrative. And then, as if given some silent cue by the rightness of the moment, one of Lily May's closest friends stepped to the front and sang "Amazing Grace."

Margaret is the last to come through the doors. She stands behind the two until the others have descended the steps and headed for their cars. "If you need anything, call. *Anything*. Even if you're not sure what it is." She starts down the steps, then turns around. "I take my morning walks in the woods around seven, if you'd care to join me. The trees and wild creatures are good company and good listeners."

As she walks away, Emily wants to run after her, to remain in her calming presence. Instead, she takes her uncle's arm and they descend the steps together. People will be waiting at the house.

Getting into the car, Otis says, "I think you ought to go out to Margaret's woods in the morning. It'll be good for you. She will be good for you."

"And what will be good for you?"

He sits for a moment before starting the car. Then, he turns the key and looks straight ahead as he says, "Watching you live your life. That's what will be good for me. That's what Lily May would want too." He pauses. "I think Margaret can be of some help there too. Don't know why. Just do."

Chapter 7

As Emily tops the hill, Sophia and Grace bound out of the house ahead of Margaret. They circle her and then stop and sit, heads lowered. She kneels between them and pats each in turn, speaking softly to them as tears flow down her face. Margaret stands by smiling. The girls are doing the work they were born to. Fully present and accessible, they know what is needed in any given moment, especially those charged with emotions that need release.

When Emily stands, the dogs take off toward the woods, and the two women follow without a word.

An hour into their walk, they climb a slight rise and come to a patch of wild blueberry bushes. Margaret pulls two muslin sacks from her pocket and hands one to Emily, and they begin to pick. Emily takes her cue from Margaret and reaches deep into the bushes, pulling forth huge round berries, indigo frosted with lighter patches of blue. They pick in silence, then Margaret sits on a granite outcropping in a patch of sun. Emily joins her.

Margaret waits.

"I've lost my job and my apartment," Emily says. "Can you believe it? The board cut my position at the museum, and my roommate invited her boyfriend to move in. Everything's coming apart at the worst possible time. I don't know what to do."

Margaret is silent.

"Otis offered me the cottage down beyond the pond. The teacher who was renting it moved away and it's been sitting empty. It would give me time to figure things out."

"Sounds delicious."

"I've always loved that little house. I used to imagine it was mine. My 'room of one's own' with curtains in the windows. There's something about that image—curtains in the windows—that feels like home."

"Sounds to me like you've already made the move, already begun to inhabit the cottage. The sorting and transporting are practically underway. Especially the sorting."

Emily smiles for the first time. "I have the money Lily May left me and some savings. That will keep me going for a while. There's a low-residency MFA program for writers I'd like to explore. Or maybe—"

"Maybe it doesn't have to be either or. And how wonderful for Otis to have you so close. It'll be good for both of you."

"I didn't get the chance to tell my mother any of this. She left in the night. I woke to the sound of an engine starting, and when I looked out my window I saw taillights going down the drive. She left two notes. I don't know what Uncle Otis's said, but mine could have been written by a casual acquaintance."

The two women sit.

"She is a mystery you may never solve completely," Margaret says, "but you'll understand her better one day. That will be necessary to your own journey. She inhabits a section of the puzzle that is your life. You have to know some of her story to reconcile its impact on you. But now is not the time. Now is the time to *be* in this transition period. It's quite literally a time for nesting. For making this place and the cottage your home. For writing and musing and ... simply being."

"If only my mother—"

"If your mother is unable to give you what you need, you must learn to give it to yourself. To mother yourself. You must learn to love and nurture yourself from the inside out."

"I think I'm going to need some help with that." Emily is crying.

"Asking is the first step. The second is opening to receive."

Chapter 8

Margaret sits up in bed and listens. She waits for the night sounds to separate themselves from the elements of the dream that woke her. Moonlight whitens the bedcovers. A tree branch scratches at the window screen. The girls breathe in unison on the floor beside her. The voice calling her name fades. She knows this voice. Wishes it would stay.

"What is it, Mattie?" she asks aloud, but he's gone. And she can't recall his words. She knows better than to strain to remember. Best to settle against the pillow and allow herself to slip back toward sleep.

"Daddy's on a rampage, Maggie. He's slingin' paint and turpentine. Breakin' brushes. Yellin' and stompin' around. We gotta stop him, Maggie. We gotta stop him now."

She can feel her brother trembling beside her as they crouch behind the potting shed. He'd come running to find her, his eyes black with terror, his face stained with dirty tears. She hears the shattering of glass and her father's bellowed curses. Mattie is shaking violently with smothered sobs. Margaret hugs him tighter, not daring to speak out loud but desperate to reassure him that this storm is subsiding already. Mattie, so sensitive to sound, assaulted even at a distance by invisible waves, writhes in agony. And Margaret, so empathically attuned to her twin's suffering, is rendered impotent by his pain.

She feels herself rise from her body and float across the backyard to her father's studio. With practiced detachment, she looks back to the spot where she and her brother kneel. Two five-year-olds huddled together, eyes fixed in the direction of the studio. Mattie draws back farther, scraping his elbow on a nail sticking out of the wall behind him. Blood runs down his arm, and he bites down on the flesh of his other arm to keep from crying out.

She continues to float until she is inside the studio watching her father as he cries out and sweeps all the bottles and jars and paint tubes and brushes from his workbench. Bending down, he picks up a shard of glass in his left hand. He holds it up to the light, grows still and quiet, and then rips open the back of his right arm from shoulder to wrist. A blood trail follows the glass point as it slices down the length of his arm. He stops then and watches the blood flow. His body slackens, his head hanging forward, and he crumples to the floor. Picking up a brush, he dips it in the blood and begins to paint on a discarded canvas. Margaret looks out the studio's dusty window and sees her mother standing in the yard, wringing her hands in silence, her delicate face pale and drawn. Lost.

"Remember?" Mattie says. "It's time to remember. And then it will be time to wake up."

Margaret remembers. Even though she doesn't want to, she remembers it all. Squatting behind the shed with Mattie. Her father's angry bellowing and the shattering of glass. The sudden silence followed by her father's soft humming. The crack of the gunshot.

Mattie pulls away from her and races into the back field. She stands for a moment, torn, and then runs toward the studio. Her mother steps inside the house, closing the door with one hand, holding the revolver with the other. Margaret looks in the studio window. Her father sprawls on the floor on his back, a small round hole in his forehead, a thin trickle of blood running into his open right eye.

She remembers going inside and sitting beside him, laying her head on his still chest. She feels the warmth of him. She smells the paint and linseed and sweat of him. She tastes her own blood on the inside of her cheek. When they pull her from him, she can tell them nothing because she has forgotten it all.

"She's only five," says the man with the big belly who smells of cigarettes. "Probably doesn't have the vocabulary to tell us what she saw anyway, and the woman's in shock."

"Her twin brother has got to be around here somewhere," says Mrs. Adams from next door. "Delicate little thing. We better find him before it gets dark."

At this, Margaret runs toward the woods in search of Mattie.

સ્જ

The wind has risen outside her bedroom window, and Margaret awakens to Grace and Sophia staring at her from beside the bed.

"It's okay, girls," she soothes. "Come on up."

The two dogs leap up and lie down beside her, on Joe's side of the bed, the long-empty side of the bed. She stares at the ceiling and the shifting patterns of shadow and light.

Chapter 9

Emily looks around her new living space, satisfied. It's taken only two days of cleaning and three more of painting and airing the place out. She is pleased with her choices as sunshine dances on the cream-colored woodwork and the gleaming hardwood floors. The soft peach of the blowing curtains picks up the same shade in the faded floral print of the sofa and armchair. Though well-worn, the sturdy pieces anchor the room with a relaxed and welcoming ambience. The built-in shelves on either side of the fireplace hold groupings of her favorite books, some upright, some in piles.

The carved heron sits on the mantelpiece below an enormous framed print. In it, a woman stands in the desert, facing away from the viewer. Her long hair shimmers down her back, indigo-black amid the subtle twilight hues that surround her. The lingering aura of a just-set sun casts a halo around her still form. Emily breathes in the magnificence of the piece, as she has done frequently in the past several days. Then she turns to place accent pillows on the sofa and to toss a plaid one on the chair.

"Voila!" she says, enjoying the freedom of living alone and out loud.

As she heads for the kitchen area with its glass-fronted cabinets and pale-yellow countertops, a truck pulls into the yard. She sets the kettle to heat as Margaret knocks on the door.

"A home-warming gift." Margaret hands her a pitcher of yellow and white wildflowers and six peach roses.

Emily welcomes her in as she places them on the coffee table.

Margaret stands admiring the space, still holding a small box tied with garden twine. When Emily offers her a seat, she starts forward but then stops, staring at the print over the mantelpiece.

"It's amazing, isn't it?" Emily is pleased that Margaret is as moved by the painting as she is. "I still can't believe it's mine. I thought even a print would be way too much for me to afford. I've never felt this way about a painting before, and when I worked at the museum, I was surrounded by them daily. In fact, it's because of my work at the museum that I could arrange to pay for this over time."

"I'm not surprised you chose it. It's one of my favorites." Margaret walks over to the fireplace and reaches up to trace the faint signature on the lower right corner.

The teakettle hisses softly, and Emily returns to the stove, her back to Margaret. She busies herself with cups and saucers, allowing Margaret the space to be with the painting. When she turns back, Margaret is sitting in the armchair wiping her eyes. She blows her nose with a cotton handkerchief and stuffs it into her pocket.

Emily wants Margaret to tell her more about the painting but offers her tea instead. "I'm afraid I only have generic green tea."

"Green is the perfect color to go with this." Margaret hands her the box.

Nestled in a bed of wool yarn is a two-inch clay statue of a seated woman. Her face is serene, with closed almond-shaped eyes and a slight smile. At the center of her forehead is a tiny jade chip.

"She's the Tibetan Green Tara," Margaret says. "She is compassion. She is love. Always there for us. A friend of mine made her for you."

"I don't want to put her down."

"You don't have to. But when you're ready, she'll let you know where she wants to be."

Emily sinks into the sofa cushion, examining the plump statue as Margaret drinks her tea. Neither speaks.

Finally, Emily rises. "I know where she belongs." She leads Margaret through an arched doorway into a tiny room. "Excuse the yard-sale finds masquerading as furniture. It's a work in progress."

The walls are painted a sage green, softening the brightness of the sunny room. The furnishings are simple. A narrow foyer table and metal folding chair face a low window that looks out into the garden. Two stacks of wooden crates serve as storage shelves. Her printer sits on the floor.

On the makeshift desk sits Emily's laptop, a notebook with a pen clipped inside the spiral, and a silver-framed photo of Lily May and Otis, laughing. Margaret smiles as Emily sets the green figurine next to the photograph, creating a tableau of three smiling muses.

"Maybe she'll change my luck," Emily says. "I reassessed and reworked some of my 'doodlings' and sent them out. Some query letters too. … I've had two rejections already."

"Ah, the realities of the writing life. Think of them as evidence that you're fully engaged. I have a very successful friend who celebrates her rejections." Margaret laughs. "She made herself a papier-mâché party hat and glues lines from each rejection letter onto it. Then, after feeling her disappointment fully, she sends the piece right back out. She says acceptance is a part of the process and tenacity is a tool of the trade."

A truck rumbles into the yard, and Margaret winks at Emily's questioning look. "Otis has cooked up a little something, and his timing couldn't be more perfect."

Emily stands open-mouthed as Otis orders her out of the cottage. "Go for a long walk. We've got work to do."

ॐ∾∾

An hour later, she's invited back in as two men climb into their truck and drive away. Making her close her eyes, Otis guides her into her writing room.

The table, folding chair, and crates are gone. Under the window sits an oak desk with drawers down one side and a deep shelf for her printer on the other. Her personal items are precisely arranged on its polished surface, the sun glinting off the silver laptop. A matching antique office chair on wheels is tucked under the desk. Nearby stands a bookcase smelling of seasoned wood and lemon oil. Two framed Mary Oliver poems, "The Lily" and "The Journey," hang side by side on one wall. A watercolor sketch of an ancient moss-covered well, a haiku inked in graceful script beneath it, hangs opposite.

Margaret holds out the little statue of Green Tara. Emily again sets it next to Otis and Lily May on the desk, and the smiling tableau is complete once more.

Fidgeting, Otis looks on, watching his grand-niece closely.

Seeing his anxious face, she goes to him, hands shaking with emotion. "There are no words. How did you know? How ..."

"I can still see you, knee-high to a garden gnome, with your little feet dangling from the chair, and Lily May ..." He swallows, choked for a moment. "And Lily May wheeling you around. Both of you giggling."

"But it was in pretty bad shape, last I knew. I never thought...I —I love it." She hugs him hard, not wanting to let go.

"Been working on it since you said you were coming back. Now sit. Try it out. Sit." He pulls the chair out, angling it toward her.

Margaret nods. "Writing rule number one: seat of the pants to the seat of the chair." She winks and lets herself out.

Chapter 10

"That's her! That's her!" yells a little boy from behind her in the produce aisle. Margaret stiffens involuntarily. A mother's hasty, "Shush, she'll hear you," follows. "But that's her. The spooky lady. Nell told me all about her. She—"

The words are abruptly cut off, maybe by a hand clamped over a mouth or a chastening look, and the youngster is silent. Margaret imagines a questioning upturned face. She knows too well the mother's look, the look that says, *"Not another word. I'm warning you!"*

Margaret sighs. The pattern keeps repeating itself. Even when she lived away from this place, the whisperings and murmurings followed her, erupting and receding again and again. Different people, different voices, different contexts, but the same recurring themes. And in this moment in the middle of Farmer Jay's Natural Foods, she realizes that everything has been accelerating, intensifying, over the past few months. The old business is definitely coming around again.

Shaken, she leaves her cart in the aisle and walks out. In her truck, she grips the wheel and closes her eyes. She breathes in short shallow gulps. "The only way out is through," she whispers to herself. Then adds, "Easier said than done."

Exhaling loudly, she sits up with renewed resolve. She goes back inside and retrieves her abandoned grocery cart. As she rounds the end cap, she passes a woman and a little girl. Margaret smiles as the little girl looks up at the sound of her cart's squeaky wheel. Big brown eyes smile back at her.

"And she shall have music wherever she goes," the child chants, grinning. "That's what Nana says when she gets a squeaker."

Margaret laughs. "That's a very wise nana you have."

"Margaret?" the woman says. "Oh, my goodness, it *is* you!"

"Catherine? Catherine Martin!" Margaret recognizes this older but still beautiful face and the once blond shoulder-length cut. "Are you back or just visiting?"

"Catherine Riley now." She lifts her hand to cover her smile – a self-conscious gesture Margaret remembers all too well. "I'm down for a month or so spending time with my granddaughter 'til her mother gets back on her feet. This is Carly."

"Nice to meet you, Carly. You and your nana will have to come for a visit while she's here. We could have a little tea party in my garden. Do you think you could help me talk her into it?"

The girl looks up at her grandmother. "Can we, Nana? A real tea party in a real garden?"

After the briefest hesitation, Catherine responds. "We'd love to. Right now, we have to pick up a prescription and get it back to Carly's mom, but I would love a chance to sit and talk. Sooner rather than later."

"Well, let's make it sooner then. Can you make it one day this week, say Thursday noon?"

"Perfect. We'll be there."

After Carly drops a bag of oatmeal raisin cookies in their basket, they hurry off.

Margaret watches them until she is bumped from behind by a cart.

"Sorry, but you were just standing there blocking my way," says a tall man in a crisp business suit as he swings around her.

She sees him seated in a red armchair. Two women bend over him. Each holding an arm, they tug him back and forth. His face is blank, an empty hole in his chest cavity. His eyes are on a little girl seated on the floor playing with a razor.

Chapter 11

Emily looks up. The room is dark. The house is still. Lightning streaks down the sky. She waits, counting to three before thunder growls long and low. Lost in her writing, she'd missed the gradual lowering of the sky, the ominous flickerings in the distance, the dropping of the temperature.

A sudden wind whips the trees at the edge of the garden and bursts in through the open window. Fat drops splotch the glass as she rises to close it. She reaches the French doors just as a violet-white burst lights up the living room, and another wind gust sweeps a bud vase from a low table. It shatters on the hardwood floor. It takes all her strength to close and latch the doors. Another flash is topped immediately by a jarring crack of thunder. She crouches, covering her ears in involuntary response.

"Stay away from windows." She hears her mother's panicked voice. *"Don't go near the phone. Stay out of the kitchen and bathroom, don't touch anything metal."* The shrill commands bark inside her head, and she can see her mother's trembling fingers stub out cigarette after cigarette. Her mother's terrified eyes look right through her.

The next peal of thunder is less intense, lagging several beats behind the flash as the storm races away. Heavy rain continues to pummel the flower beds and rattle on the roof. Emily rises and steps out onto the screened porch. The wind is cold and carries the smell of freshly turned earth. Thunder rumbles as it rolls away, sending out a faint vibration underfoot. Slowly, the rain eases until a fine mist hangs over the backyard.

She returns to her writing desk and clicks on her laptop, praying she saved everything before shutting it down as the storm hit. She sits for another half hour writing, but the outdoors seems to be calling her to come walk in the wetness, one of her favorite conditions.

She grabs her rain jacket from the hook by the door and heads toward the pond. Mist surrounds her. Falling from the sky and rising from the steamy ground, it dampens her hair and moistens her face. The rising and falling reminds her of the phrase "as above, so below." She is both lost and at home in it—walking through a Celtic story scape, half expecting the twitter of fairy laughter. She trips over a root and smells something burning up ahead. Again, she sees her mother's dark eyes, but this time they're nearly closed, lids drooping. She smells acrid smoke, tastes it thick in her throat. Someone is calling her mother's name. Then somewhere nearby, the crack of splintering wood sears the air. A heavy thud follows, shaking the ground, and she yelps.

"Emily? That you? You all right?"

It's Uncle Otis calling. The mist lifts for a moment, and she sees a small fire at the edge of the pond and her great-uncle tending it with a long-handled shovel.

"I'm fine. Just startled." She hugs him, holding on for a moment. "What *was* that?"

"Sounded like a limb off the big pine. Must have been struck when the storm was on top of us but held on until just now. This old heart hasn't settled down yet."

"It took me back to when I was little. Thunderstorms always sent my mother into a panic, and I guess I'm wired to do the same."

"Not surprising. We almost lost the two of you in that fire. And you just a baby. Unlike this one, that storm came on us out of nowhere in the middle of the day." He stops talking, realizing that Emily is staring open-mouthed. "What is it?" He looks all around, concern building.

"What fire? What do you mean you almost lost us?"

Otis looks confused for a moment. "Oh, right. I forgot. You were never told." He pauses and looks out over her head. After a time, he makes a decision, nods to confirm it, and explains. "Your mother wanted the whole thing buried good and deep. But you're not a child anymore, and I think it's better you know your own history, the good and the bad of it. And that was something bad that turned out good. Lily May and I always thought you should be told, but we promised to honor your mother's wishes."

Otis shovels wet dirt on the smoky pile of debris he'd been burning. "Let's go inside. We'll have a nice cup of tea."

"And you'll tell me about the fire?"

"And I'll tell you about the fire."

ॐ∽

"Like I said, you were just a baby, one or two maybe. You and your mother were home at your house when the storm hit. Came on fast and fierce. Lily May and I were just sitting down to lunch when the kitchen went dark. Not a black dark, a strange greenish-yellow dark. And then came the roar of the wind, and hail stones the size of golf balls, and the most vivid lightning I've ever seen. One crack after another with no break in between. We started for the cellar when a tree crashed through the bedroom window upstairs. Sounded like all hell had broken loose up there. Then, as I reached for the cellar doorknob, it was over. Bright sunshine lit up the kitchen. Hurt my eyes for a minute.

"Then sirens wailed and the phone started ringing. It was Mert, yelling that your house was hit. It took us twenty minutes to get from here to the other side of the woods on foot, there were so many trees down. By then it was fully engulfed, most awful sight I've ever seen. Black smoke pouring out and snapping flames devouring every board and beam. Afraid it had taken the two of you, we circled the yard as closely as we could, the intense heat keeping us back. And there on the back side was Matt Griffins bending over you and Paul Edwards resuscitating your mother.

"Matt was trying to give you oxygen, and when you saw Lily

May you stopped crying just like that." He snaps his fingers. "You reached up your chubby little arms to her, and Lily May picked you up and held you while Matt put the little mask on you. And you just lay there in her arms, your green eyes wide and your little chest rattling and heaving."

Otis stops, choking on tears. "I'll never forget it, Em. The look on your little face, like …"

Emily takes his hand.

"It was like you had left us somehow. Like you'd gone into another place where we couldn't go and couldn't reach you." He looks up and away, inside the memory, his gray eyes taking on a translucent quality beneath his wiry brows. "You seemed serene, snug in the safety of Lily May's arms, but there was a distance about you. This ordeal had separated you from us in some fundamental way. Like you had seen something and now knew something we could never understand.

"I'm not expressing it very well." He runs his long fingers through his hair, leaving it sticking up in a wild white disarray. Dropping his hands to the table, he fiddles with his tea cup then lets it clatter to rest in its saucer. "I mean, you were just a baby. But I will never forget that look and this feeling I had about it. I think that's why I didn't argue too much when your mother wanted to keep it from you. I felt that on some level, you already knew more than we could imagine."

Emily sits staring past her great-uncle, thinking about the burned-out cellar hole just beyond the woods. The summer she'd stayed with Otis and Lily May when she was nine, she'd walked there often and sat on one of the foundation stones, reading or writing in her diary. She'd had no idea it had been her house and that she'd been in the fire that destroyed it. She'd thought it was old and that the fire had happened long ago.

She'd heard it referred to by the family as only the old cellar hole, with no reference to a personal connection. In fact, she recalled someone telling her to stay away from it because there might be broken glass or metal shards or something else that might hurt her.

"When your Grandmother Emily arrived at the scene," Otis goes on, "Lily May handed you over to her and you fell asleep. Your breathing evened out and your chest sounded less raspy.

"Your mother was still unconscious when the ambulance arrived, and you were both rushed to York Hospital. They let Emily ride in the back. I can still see her sitting there singing you both a lullaby, her baby and her baby's baby."

"Was that when we went to live with her? With Nana Emily?"

"Yes. You were released before your mother and went to live with your nana. When your mother was finally able to come home, you both lived there for the next few years."

"Until Nana died. And then my mother sold her house and we began the years of moving from place to place, always pretty far away from here."

Otis nods and gets up, tossing their now cold tea and making two fresh cups. Neither says a word as they let the tea steep.

Finally, Emily asks, "Was my mother hurt badly? How long did she have to stay in the hospital?"

"She took in a lot of smoke and had only minor burns. But ..." Otis seems reluctant to go on.

"But what?"

"Well, they kept her there for about a week for observation."

"Observation?"

He doesn't answer.

"Otis, you've got to tell me. My mother won't. I need to know."

"But it doesn't feel right, talking about her behind her back. She should be the one to tell you her private business, not me."

Emily blinks back sudden tears. "You're right, it shouldn't be your job. But I have so much emptiness in me and she won't open up. She should be the one to fill me in, but she won't."

"Okay," he says after a while. "She went from the hospital to a ... sort of sanitarium to rest and get help. She'd had a terrible time after you were born and never really snapped out of it. She became so fragile. So anxious. So thin. Dark circles under her eyes. Began to smoke."

"Sounds like post-partum depression."

"Yes, that's what they called it. She tried hard to rise above it and take care of you, but some days it was like she was paralyzed. She couldn't move. Couldn't make the simplest decision. It got worse as you became more mobile. And then your father, who truth to tell was never much help with anything anyway, left. That's when she seemed to really disappear inside herself."

"Did she ever try to harm herself? Oh, my God!" Emily stands up. "The fire. Did she—"

"No!" Otis bangs the table with the flat of his hand. "The fire was caused by lightning. She saved you! She managed to get almost to the door before she was forced into a corner. But she protected you with her body. She had passed out from the smoke by the time the firemen got to you."

Emily feels a strange release in her chest as the tension in her body softens and liquefies. Relief. These simple facts told to her by this loving man as they sit in Lily May's bright kitchen feel like lifelines.

"Thank you."

Chapter 12

Thursday is filled with sunshine and blue sky and a warm wind. Margaret spreads a crisp white cloth on the garden table under the oak and places pink cushions on the seats of three chairs. She sets a mason jar with freshly picked flowers in the center of the table. From a limb above it, she has hung a wrought iron chandelier. Its five curved arms hold teacups on saucers with a fat pink candle in each. Streamers of pink and green ribbon hang from the chandelier to just above the flowers. As she carries out a tray of china plates rimmed with painted violets, jelly glasses, and bundles of silverware wrapped in cloth napkins, she hears Catherine calling from the front of the house.

As soon as Carly sees the table, she squeals with delight and circles it, her head tipped up toward the fluttering ribbons and the leafy canopy overhead. "Oh, look, Nana, it's like a fairy house, inside and outside at the same time."

Just then Grace and Sophia come bounding up from the back field and sit at the edge of the garden, waiting to be invited in. When Carly spots them, Margaret nods, and they run over to sit in front of her guests.

"This is Grace and Sophia," Margaret tells Carly, "and they would love to jump up and down and wiggle all around in way of saying hello, but they're very good girls and will contain themselves so you can bend down and introduce yourself." Margaret smiles at the girls as reward for their restraint.

After pats and hugs from their new friends, the two head off, nuzzling each other's necks and cavorting like colts as they disappear around the potting shed.

The women laugh, and Margaret invites her guests to sit as she fetches the lunch tray with its platter of assorted sandwich triangles, three salads, and a tinkling pitcher of iced lemonade.

Carly claps as Margaret sets down her plate. "It's Raggedy Ann!" She giggles at the smiling face in the scoop of egg salad on a bed of bibb lettuce. With olive slices for eyes, a snippet of chive for a nose, and a pouty little cherry tomato mouth, the face is crowned with a flurry of carrot curls. Beneath the plump chin, a crescent of yellow nasturtiums forms a ruffled collar.

"Your nana assured me that you like everything on the plate, except she didn't know about the flowers. Have you ever had nasturtium blossoms before?"

"You mean you can eat them?" Carly is clearly excited by this prospect.

"Yes, this is one of the edible flowers. *But*," says Margaret, stressing the word, "you *never, never, never* eat a flower without checking with a grown-up first. Right?"

Carly laughs and looks at her grandmother. "Right. But Nana says it with two more *nevers!*"

"You might want to take a little nibble first. These have a peppery taste."

Catherine's warning comes just as Carly pops a blossom into her mouth. "Wow. Wait 'til I tell Mommy about these." She eats another. "Scrump-diddly-iscious!"

"Well, that's a new one on me," says Margaret, smiling. "Mind if I borrow it?"

"Okay, but you only use it for really special things, 'cause it's a really special word Mommy taught me."

"Promise."

Margaret pours the lemonade and they eat in silence for a bit. Then Catherine, holding her fork above her plate, clears her throat. Margaret senses a growing awkwardness.

"I'm so sorry, Margaret." She puts down her fork and leans forward, her eyes filling. "I don't know how you can be so nice to me. I—"

"Catherine." Margaret reaches across the table and takes her hand. Carly has stopped eating and watches them intently. "You have nothing to be sorry for."

"Oh, but I do. I wasn't there for you. And then I let all this time go by without making contact…. I almost couldn't bring myself to come today. I'm so ashamed." She looks away, and Margaret can see her drifting into the past.

"Catherine." Margaret's voice, like the crack of a whip, snaps Catherine's attention back to the present, back to the table under the oak tree, back to her granddaughter sitting beside her with wide, worried eyes. Margaret pats Carly's hand and then turns back to Catherine. "You have nothing to be ashamed of or sorry for. Nothing. You were my friend in spite of your parents' best efforts against it. I always knew that. And it made a huge difference for me."

Carly, seeming to sense the release of the tension that's been riding just under the surface since their arrival, goes back to eating her salad.

Catherine continues to look hard into her friend's eyes. "How did you ever make it through? I look at you now and you seem genuinely happy and calm, and I don't know how that's possible. I would be a bitter, angry person. Even being on the periphery as I was, it colored my life. It still makes me seethe with anger."

"Anger poisons us from the inside out. That's not to say I haven't felt my share, but I do my best to let it pass through me. There's an old song, 'She's more to be pitied than censured.' That's how I feel, for the most part, about those who wished me ill over the years."

"They did a lot more than wish you ill!"

Margaret sits back in her chair. "Yes. They did," she says softly. She sighs and straightens. "But as you said, I made it through. And now I am grateful for this chance to pick up where we left off as girls." She slides the flower vase to one side and places the sandwich platter between them. "Sandwich? Cucumber and chives, egg salad, hummus and green olive, shrimp with lemon butter and rosemary, and peanut butter and jelly."

The conversation ends as they fill their plates. Carly finishes first with another emphatic, "Scrump-diddly-iscious!"

"Scrump-diddly-iscious, indeed!" says her grandmother.

"Would you like me to pack up some sandwiches to take home to your mother?" Margaret asks.

"Oh, big yes!" Carly says. "But do we have to leave just now? Can I play for a while before we have to go?"

"I'm sure the girls would love a run down to the stream, if it's okay with your nana." She looks at Catherine. "They'll stay with her. They love playing 'nanny.' We can see the stream from here."

"Sounds like fun. Go ahead, love."

"Nana and I will catch up, and then we'll have some dessert." Margaret calls the girls, who have been napping in the shade of the potting shed. Handing them each a carrot, she instructs them to take Carly down to the stream and to stay with her. The three take off at a gentle run.

"We should join them and make room for that dessert you've promised," Catherine says.

Neither moves.

"I wonder if imagining we're doing it would work," Margaret says.

"Sounds like a plan to me."

Laughing, Margaret nods toward a pair of faded Adirondack chairs. They settle back into silence.

"Do people seem more enlightened these days about your way of knowing things?" Catherine asks at last.

"Some. There's more access to information now. But there's still a wall between me and most people. Many keep a safe distance, a little too big in their politeness when we come face to face."

"Sounds lonely."

"No." Margaret waves her hand as if brushing away a fly and smiles. "Actually, the number of people who accept me for who I am and treat me like any other neighbor is growing. I appreciate the ones who don't pretend I'm not different. They meet me straight on, ask me direct questions. And they come to me when they think I might be of some help."

Catherine twirls strands of her faded blond hair between her fingers, a habitual gesture from childhood. "Has your process changed over the years? Do you have more control over what comes and how it affects you?"

"I sometimes forget just how out of control it was when we were little. Gave you a scare or two, didn't I?" Margaret is pleased to see her friend smile, revealing beautiful dimples in both cheeks. Gone is the tight-lipped reserve her shaming family had forced upon her for smiling too brightly as a child.

"Scared doesn't quite describe it!"

"And yet you stuck with me. I had no clue as to what was happening to me. I had no idea my father and grandmother had been the same way. You helped me keep at least one foot on the ground. You truly were my friend, and the fact that someone like you would be my friend meant everything to me."

"I'm so sorry. I—"

"Your parents forbade you to have anything more to do with me. You couldn't do anything about that, you were just a kid. I got all your notes." Margaret stares off down the hill. "I still have some. In the tin."

Catherine looks over at Margaret, bringing her hand to her heart. "Oh, Margaret, the tin. I'd forgotten."

"What a pair we were." Margaret smiles. "No one could ever say we lacked imagination!"

"I'd write down a secret wish or question on a strip of paper and put it in the tin. Then three or four days later, you'd tell me what you'd *seen*. To me, you were filled with magic. And that tin was a place to hold some of it." Catherine is absently twirling strands of her hair again, her fingers dancing a figure eight in the air.

"I could tell you anything. And you didn't let any of it get in the way of us just being kids together. Just friends."

Her voice sweetly child-like, Catherine's excitement grows. "And we put all sorts of found objects and treasures into the tin. Remember? Four-leaf clovers and feathers and lavender pods. It smelled so good in there. Oh, … and our school pictures from the first grade!" Catherine laughs. "That awful bowl haircut of mine with the uneven bangs my mother 'trimmed.' They looked like she'd used her hedge clippers!"

"And the remnants of my black eye from my fall out of the apple tree. Mrs. Follansbee kept asking me if everything was all right at home," Margaret remembers with a sad smile.

"Dear Mrs. Follansbee. She was the sweetest teacher. She opened me up to reading since there was only one book my family read." Catherine looks up, following something in the sky. She rests her head against the back of the chair and grows quiet.

Margaret follows her gaze. High overhead, a red-tailed hawk circles slowly. Silence lengthens as they watch.

"My daughter is dying and I don't know what to do." Tears slip down Catherine's face. "She's only thirty-four."

Margaret reaches over and covers her friend's hand with her own. She doesn't speak, knowing Catherine needs to tell her story, to speak her fears out loud.

"She's so frail. The doctors say there are no more treatment options for her. They say she has a few months, maybe even just weeks, left." She pauses, shaking her head slowly. "I don't know what I'm going to do to get through this. And Carly … I don't know how—how …"

"Doctors are good at making pronouncements. In all their certainty, they forget there's a Great Mystery that surrounds our comings and our goings."

"But there comes a time when we have to surrender to their experience and accept what's happening. Right?"

Margaret sits for a moment, searching inside for confirmation of what she is about to say. "I don't see her dying. Not for a very long time. I see her thriving and laughing with her little girl."

Catherine covers her face with her hands and leans forward into her own lap. Sobbing, she gulps for air as if she hasn't taken a deep breath in a very long time. Margaret places her hand on Catherine's back between the shoulder blades and massages gently in small circular motions, radiating heat into the back of Catherine's heart. Finally, Catherine raises her head and sits up, relaxing into Margaret's hand.

"If anyone else had said that, I wouldn't dare to believe them. But I know it must be true when it comes from you."

"*Through* me. I am but an instrument."

Catherine looks at her old friend. "We were meant to come together again right now, weren't we?"

Carly and the dogs are running up the hill toward them.

"Synchronicity is definitely at play."

"Nana, Nana," Carly calls as she runs, swinging her sandals in one hand and holding what looks like a slender stick in the other. The dogs trot alongside her, barking. "Look what we found. Look what we found," she sings.

She holds out a feather.

"Hawks don't give their feathers to just anyone, you know," says Margaret. "You must be pretty special."

"Oh, it's not for me," says Carly. "It's for Mommy. It's like the healing feather in the story she read to me. Maybe it will make her better."

"I wouldn't be at all surprised," Catherine says, smiling at Margaret, her face bright, her body at ease.

Over strawberry shortcake, Margaret asks to visit Catherine's daughter, and they arrange for her to come by at six that evening, the time of day when Jenna tends to rally.

෨෴ඦ

Her hands immersed in warm water, Margaret surrenders to the rhythms of dailiness. It is amidst the ordinary that the most useful information slips through. She acknowledges the images in a lazy, hazy sort of way as they begin to flow. They continue as she places the last dish on the drying rack and rinses the dishpan.

They are still with her as she heads for the woods. Four miles in, the forest deepens, letting only occasional shafts of sunlight penetrate the canopy. The air is cool and filled with the sounds of birds and insects and the tiniest of microbes chirping and buzzing, crawling and chomping and carrying on—the sounds of the sentient world engaged in the living of life. Slowly, the images in her head fade as she becomes one with the dance. She notices the varied greens of the leaves and a bright mound of moss. She smells the earthy odor of rot as layers of pine needles, leaves, and twigs break down underfoot, returning to the forest floor as nourishment for new growth. She feels the pull of gravity, the energy of the earth grounding her.

She whispers to the woods around her, "'All shall be well, and all shall be well, and all manner of thing shall be well.'" These words of the mystic Julian of Norwich have become her healing mantra. She repeats them at full voice, sending them out into the teeming stillness.

Catherine's daughter would live. Catherine would pass on long before her, as any mother would wish it to be. Margaret is certain of these things. Smiling, she heads for home.

Chapter 13

Emily hears the ringing phone as soon as she enters her back garden and runs inside to catch it.

"Emily, this is Margaret. Something important but unsettling has happened for you, yes?"

Emily hesitates, mildly irritated at what feels like an intrusion. "Um … yes."

"I see it as a good thing. Deeply medicinal, actually. Part of a healing process. Does that make sense to you?"

Emily doesn't respond at first. Margaret's words conjure the emotional jolt of Otis's revelations about the fire. Finally, she answers, "It does make sense. I think I'm ready to write about it. Then I can be done with it."

The connection is heavy with Margaret's silence until she says, "Then I will let you get to it."

Before disconnecting, Emily blurts, "Can I call you later?"

"I'll be out until early evening. But call or come over after that if you want."

Damn. Why did I say that? Emily asks herself as she sits at her desk.

She opens a new file in her laptop, intending to write about her conversation with her uncle. She types a single sentence and stops.

She didn't want to hate her parents, but she did.

She'd intended to write a reflective piece, a journal-type entry about the fire and about her mother. But here is this line written in the third person. *Hate,* a pretty strong word. *Parents,* plural. And … what? She reaches her finger toward the backspace key but stops.

A favorite assignment in freshman English had been what her professor called "a story in a day" or a "story in an hour." Written without stopping, the main requirement was that it have a beginning, a middle, and an end. It was meant to be what Anne Lamott would call "a shitty first draft." With no time for second-guessing or judging or fine-tuning, the writer was free to let the story flow.

"A story in a day it is," she whispers, and begins to type.

Three hours later, she is done. The result: a stripped-down story with a beginning, a middle, and an end about a young woman who admits to her dark thoughts and seething anger as she rips the scabs off festering wounds, exposing them to both air and light for the first time.

Emily looks at the clock. Nearly 6:30. She shuts down her laptop. Time to eat a light supper and call Margaret. A frisson of excitement surprises her.

Chapter 14

Catherine leads Margaret into the living room where her daughter is just awakening on the couch. Margaret sets a basket of fruit and vegetables on the coffee table as Jenna props herself up weakly. Her mother plumps pillows behind and around her.

Margaret explains the relaxation work she'd like to do. "Together we can access and activate your inner resources, your body's workers and helpers. But only if that feels right to you."

Jenna nods.

Catherine is again crying as she hugs Margaret, then she starts to leave the room.

"It would be better if you stayed," Margaret says. "Carly too."

Catherine hesitates in the doorway. Jenna looks concerned and attempts to rise.

"It will be good for her," Margaret says. "This has happened to all of you. And once you've experienced the essence of the process, you can work together without me in the days to come."

Catherine nods to her daughter and calls to Carly to join them.

"Can Aunt Clarissa come too?" she asks.

Margaret is surprised to learn there's a third woman in the house and turns to meet her. Catherine leans in and whispers, "Her imaginary friend," just before Carly appears in the doorway.

"Of course," Margaret says. "The more the merrier. Welcome,

Aunt Clarissa."

She gestures for Carly and her aunt to sit on the loveseat facing the couch and motions Catherine into the overstuffed armchair. Margaret stands with her back to the fireplace opposite Catherine's chair.

As she asks them to close their eyes and breathe deeply in through the nose and out through the mouth, she watches Carly. The little girl squints at her mother and grandmother several times before settling in to the rhythm of the breathing.

Soon Margaret is guiding them through a series of progressive suggestions to relax them from head to foot. She then counts them down a beautiful staircase to a peaceful place. Using multisensory imagery, she settles them into their places and watches as each face smooths into serenity.

Addressing Jenna, she asks her to invite her inner workers and helpers to introduce themselves and begin their healing work on a cellular level. Her voice rich and resonant, she describes the subtle healing energy surrounding them. She assures them it will linger long after the session ends, bathing the household in the warmth and well-being conducive to radiant good health.

After teaching the family a process for quick and easy access to this relaxed state and instructing them to do this work daily, she counts slowly up to five and invites them to ease their awareness back into the room. She suggests they spend the evening ahead in quiet, restful pursuits following a simple supper. Smiling, she asks Aunt Clarissa to help Carly compose a little song, subtly suggesting it might include a healing feather.

As the women stretch, Carly hops down from the loveseat. Margaret has a fleeting impression of a wide-hipped woman in a bright full skirt with the long fingers of a pianist and a regal head of dark curls. As the child runs past her, a hint of vanilla stirs the air.

Leaning over, Jenna explores the basket of produce on the coffee table. She hefts a head of green cabbage and holds it to her nose. "Ahhhh." Putting it back, she runs her hand along the daikon radish, the fragrant leeks, and the gnarled ginger root before popping a plump blueberry into her mouth.

"Pure medicine," Margaret says.

Catherine laughs. "Is this my girl with the nonexistent appetite?"

"I can't help myself," Jenna says. "It looks and smells so good. I was just reading about organic foods and it sounded so bland. But everything in this basket looks amazing. Thank you."

"My pleasure. ... Any questions before I go? Anything you'd like to share?"

Jenna looks up into Margaret's face. "I have an orchestra."

Margaret smiles. "Oh?"

"First there was a cellist in a beautiful courtyard. Just her. Then, other musicians sauntered in." She laughs. "Like a flash mob! Strings, woodwinds, brass, percussion. They joined in one-by-one until there was a whole orchestra playing a symphony. It felt familiar but I couldn't name it. It filled every space inside me."

"Ah, your workers and helpers. There's a wisdom within that knows what to offer. I leave you to it."

Standing on the doorstep after Catherine closes the door behind her, Margaret looks up at the stars and mouths a silent thank you. This little family of women, and a sandy-haired man waiting in the wings, will have much to celebrate in the years ahead. Of that, she is certain.

Chapter 15

A pang of disappointment. Emily finds no truck in Margaret's dooryard. As she turns off her engine, the girls bark from inside the darkened house. Then headlights bounce up the drive behind her. Relieved, she gathers up her book bag and gets out.

Margaret climbs down from her truck and looks toward the west where the faintest remnants of light linger on the horizon. Emily is surprised to note how comfortable she is with this woman's unhurried manner. She too looks toward the western sky and catches the flash of a shooting star in her periphery, just up and to the left.

"Had a feeling there was something yet to be seen," Margaret says, and then leads the way into the house. The girls wiggle and prance around the kitchen in greeting before heading out the back door when Margaret gives permission for their evening run. She puts the kettle on, and Emily seats herself at the table. After moving a pile of books and papers and a basket of puzzle pieces, Margaret sets out two mugs, a pot of honey, and a dish of lemon slices before sitting herself. Only then does she speak again.

"Something has changed for you. Something new has come to light. Yes?"

"Oh, yes. Something that raises as many questions as it answers."

"Do you want to talk about it?"

"Yes. I've been sitting with it by myself for a couple of days now."
Emily looks around the kitchen. "I'm not sure where to begin."

"Close your eyes. Just breathe. Don't think about anything but
the air coming in and the air going out."

The teakettle whistles. Margaret shuts off the flame, and
the kettle settles slowly into silence. Then the earthy warmth of
Margaret's voice continues. "Just the in and the out of the air. Just
the sound of the water from the kettle pouring gently into the
teapot, the tone changing, deepening as the pot fills. Noticing
how the hot water sets off the fragrance of the herbs waiting to be
wetted. And meanwhile, just breathing without effort. Your body
knowing exactly what to do, how to take in the air and let out the
air. Just. Simply. Breathing."

Emily hears the creak of Margaret's chair as she seats herself
again. The ticking of the clock. The distant bark of Sophia or Grace.
She doesn't want to move, or think, or talk. She simply wants to sit
here in this kitchen in the care of this woman and breathe.

Finally, her words take shape. "Our house burned down when
I was a toddler. My mother and I were inside and nearly died in
the fire." She relates this in a monotone, her eyes distant, her voice
barely audible. "Hit by lightning." She stops and picks up her tea,
cupping the mug in both hands. Resting on her elbows, she brings
it to her mouth but doesn't drink. "I never knew any of this until
the other day."

Margaret takes a sip of her tea and waits.

"Imagine not knowing that. Imagine not knowing that the old
cellar hole on the other side of the woods from Otis and Lily May's
was our home. Imagine not knowing that we almost died in a fire.
My mother kept it all from me and forbade anyone to talk about it."

Margaret is silent for some time. "How did you find out?"

"Otis told me. The big storm that came through the other day
brought it up. He forgot for a moment that I didn't know anything
about it." She sips her tea. "When I got him to talking, I find out
that my mother went to a psychiatric hospital afterwards."

Margaret lets this sit in the middle of the room with them.
"Because of the trauma?" she asks gently.

"Depression. Long before the fire, she suffered from serious depression. It started after she had me. When she was hospitalized because of the fire, they must have diagnosed it and sent her off to be treated."

She sets her mug down. "I should have been told this. *She* should have told me. It might have helped me to understand so much about her and our life. After you called earlier today, I sat down to write about it and surprised myself with this." She pulls a folder out of her bag and hands Margaret several pages.

"Hmm." Margaret nods as she reads the first sentence: *She didn't want to hate her parents, but she did.* "Writing in the third person can make it easier to look. Your wise self made a wise choice. May I read it?"

"It's pretty angry stuff. I feel kind of guilty now. But, yes. I need to talk about it. If you don't mind?"

When she finishes, Margaret places the pages on the table and leans back in her chair. "Tell me about your father."

"He left us. And then he died."

"Oh?"

"A car crash. That's all I know. Another taboo subject."

"Any memories of him before he left?"

"No. Empty air."

"And yet this piece of writing is full of him. And it's not about hating him. It's about knowing him in some deep way and then losing him."

Emily begins to cry. "No one has ever let me talk about him. My mother said once that he's best left in that grave a hundred miles from here, and I'm best served by not thinking about him. Even Otis, who is pretty slow to say a bad word about anybody, said he was never much good or much help, or something like that."

"Your mother's wrong. You need to know about him, all about him. He was your father, no matter what. You were connected to him even though you were a baby. You do have memories of him, they're just buried too. Somewhere inside, you know the smell of him, the sound of his voice, the music of his laughter—"

Margaret stops abruptly and lets those last words linger in the air. Watching Emily closely, she sees a wisp of memory floating just up and to the left, wanting to be caught. She gets up and warms both cups of tea.

"And by the way," she adds, "you don't hate your mother any more than you hate him. You're spitting angry at them both, and you have plenty of good reason, but that's not the same as hating."

Emily nods. "I don't want to be one of those whiners who blames her mother for all her problems. I know I should get over it and get on with my life. My mother did her best. And I'll never know his story, but I'm sure he did too."

"You deserved better." Margaret's words are like a balm soothing the ragged ache she's lived with for so long.

"You deserved better, child. Better than this secrecy that's shrouded your early life and denied you your experiences and your truths. That which we don't know *can* hurt us." Margaret uncharacteristically thumps her palm down on the table. "Yes, everybody is doing the best they can with what they know, but that doesn't erase or excuse the harm they do. You were a child. Your father and mother abandoned you, each in their own way. That needs to be witnessed. You need to grieve that. You need to feel your anger. Express it! You need to be heard. You need to know the details of your own story. *Then* you can begin to heal. *Then* you can get on. And only *then*."

Suddenly, the dogs bark loudly right outside the door. Margaret hurries to open it, and they rush in. They dance around and then stand on the threshold, barking into the night. There is nothing playful in their demeanor. Margaret crosses to the door and hushes them. Both dogs sit immediately, but neither moves from the doorsill as a man's rich tenor voice calls out from the side garden.

"It's Ned, Margaret. Ned Burrows." A tall blond man of about thirty-five strides up to the doorstep.

Margaret ushers him in. "What is it?"

"A five-year-old. Lost in Tilson Woods. Missing since about five thirty. Meg and Tom Allen's boy, Joey."

Margaret looks at the clock. Nearly nine. "Did you—"

"Brought all the maps we have of the region. Can you work from here or do you want me to take you up there?"

"Let me look at the big green map, the one that shows—"

"Got it."

Emily rushes to help Margaret clear the tea things and books off the table as Ned spreads out a huge topographical map. Margaret bends over the table, places her hands on the map seemingly at random, palms flat, and closes her eyes. Emily watches her from across the table, unconsciously backing away a few steps as if to give Margaret more room in which to work. Margaret is absolutely still, her head cocked in a listening stance, her face lifted toward the ceiling, her brows furrowed in a near scowl, accentuating her pale scar. Ned has moved back toward the door, his earlier brusqueness replaced by patient watchfulness. The dogs sit straight and tall by the woodstove in uncanny silence.

The clock ticks, all breathing slows, the very air in the room waits.

"Somewhere in here." Margaret points to an area of the map heavily lined with wavy circles within circles, representing hilly terrain. "There's a hidden depression, like a bowl in the terrain here. It's filled with trees and an outcropping of black rock, and somewhere inside, there are three or more standing monoliths nearly uniform in size forming a sort of wall. Behind them, there's a stand of evergreens with a large maple tree rising up in their midst. There's something red hanging on the branch of a sapling under the maple. Searchers have come close, but they've missed the opening that reveals the flash of red. The red ... something." She shakes her head in frustration.

"When they—a woman and two men—find that red object, it will lead them to the spot. He's down in under something. Sleeping ... maybe."

Ned brightens. "Sleeping, you say?"

"I think so. I hope so. I can't tell for sure. Sorry."

"It's what came out of your mouth, so I'm taking it as truth. He's sleeping for now, and we have to get to him before that changes."

Margaret pours the rest of the tea into a thermos, and then fetches a small, plump backpack. "The girls and I had better ride up there with you. I may get something more, and they can pitch in too. Sorry, Emily."

"Is there room for me to come along?"

At Ned's curt nod, Emily scoops up her bag, and they hurry out to where his Game Warden Service SUV is parked. She hops in the back as Margaret and Ned climb in front.

"It didn't show up on the map," Margaret says, "but I'm certain there's a stream or a trickle of water nearby. Is John Longfeather out there? He knows that area. Did you call him?"

"Couldn't reach him, but I asked Carol at dispatch to keep trying."

Margaret closes her eyes. Emily slouches in the back regretting the impulse to come along.

Chapter 16

After a forty-five-minute drive, Ned pulls onto a dirt road posted with a wooden sign reading *Tilson Woods Parking.* A short distance in, the road curves around to the right and ends abruptly in a large graveled lot. The lot is filled with vehicles, including a rescue squad and ambulance. Beyond, thirty or so people mill around several six-foot tables under a huge canvas canopy. Field lamps have been set up around the periphery and strung along the frame of the canopy overhead so that the area is flooded in light. Maps, computers, and GPS equipment cover the central tables. The others hold crates of flashlights, batteries, walkie-talkies, blankets, towels, ponchos, windbreakers, flares, bug spray, and first-aid kits. Air pots of coffee with stacks of disposable cups, crates of bottled water, and cartons of energy bars sit on a picnic table at one corner with a trash barrel nearby.

The three climb down from the SUV, and Ned opens the back for Sophia and Grace. They jump out and flank Margaret as they all approach the makeshift command center.

"What the hell is she doing here?" A burly red-haired man, his scowling face flushed, stomps toward Margaret, pudgy hands fisted. "Get her the fuck outta here. Now! Goddamn witch has no place here!"

Sophia and Grace leap in front of her, growling and snapping, as

Ned intercepts the man. "We'll have none of that, Keith." The man tries to break past him. Ned grabs him with both hands and jerks him around, standing face-to-face with him, practically lifting him off the ground. "There's a little kid lost and scared out in those dark woods—woods that run on for miles in any of three directions. We're all here for the same reason. So, let's get to it."

He releases the man, who stumbles backward and again loudly declares that Margaret has no business there.

"We don't want her here. This decent family don't need that crazy bitch and her un-Christian ways."

"Keith. Enough. Do I have to ask you to leave?" There is no mistaking the authority behind Ned's voice. Keith, still scowling, steps back, glares, then walks away.

Margaret continues on to the central tables, where a small blond woman, eyes puffy and red, nearly collapses into her arms. Emily follows but hangs back.

"Margaret, I'm so glad you're here. I prayed you'd come. I know you can find him. Please find him."

Margaret embraces her and pats her back as she speaks softly into her ear. "There, there. He's going to be all right, Meg. They'll find him. I'm sure of it."

"Oh, thank God." Meg slumps in her arms, and a tall bearded man lunges to catch her. He smiles shyly at Margaret and releases a sharp breath.

"Tom." Margaret nods, conveying her concern with a soft smile. Then she turns to the wardens and others standing around the table, asking for something of the boy's for her dogs to sniff and for someone to show her on the map where the searchers are.

Henry Jacobs, Ned's immediate supervisor, greets her and points out five large areas on the map. "We have teams sweeping inward and then working up toward where the more mountainous terrain begins. Each team has one or more seasoned tracker, but this whole region gets thicker and wilder the farther you go toward the eastern slope of Mount Pennatticus. He's just a little tyke, but there's no telling how far he might have gotten. His mom says he's curious and quick."

"Any word from John Longfeather?" she asks as they survey the map. "He knows this territory like the layout of his own house."

"Can't reach h—"

The roar of a black pickup truck cuts him off as it wheels around the curve, spattering gravel in its wake. It pulls up short, and a stocky man of medium height jumps out and walks, head down, toward them. He is wearing a faded cowboy hat with a dark feather hanging from the underside of the brim, over his left ear. "Just heard. Sorry."

Margaret is relieved to see him and speaks first. "John, do you know an area with a black outcropping, a trickling bit of a stream, and some big standing stones?"

"Sounds like the Grandmothers. Tall, all in a line, a thicket behind them under the trees?"

"Yes, of course! The Grandmothers. That's what I saw. And a flash of something red hanging in the undergrowth. How quickly can you get there?"

"I'm on it," John calls over his shoulder as he heads toward the woods.

"Take the girls. And look for that flash of red." Margaret looks around to where a kneeling woman is holding out a child's backpack for the dogs to smell. "Grace. Sophia. Go with John," she commands, and they race off after him.

"You two." Warden Jacobs beckons to a couple standing at the coffee station. "Grab your packs and go with them. Keep me posted."

He turns to Margaret. "They're two of our best, Bill and Jackie Houser. The three of them will make good time even in the dark. And with the girls along, even better. Coffee?"

"No, thanks. All the pieces are in place now. Let's just hope they're in time."

Avoiding for now the dazed parents and their protective circle of relatives and friends, Margaret gets her backpack from Ned's SUV. She pulls out her thermos, pours a cup of tea, and offers another to Emily who has stayed close. Emily accepts in silence, aware that Margaret is still in a listening state, all of her being poised in receptivity. She follows as Margaret crosses the parking lot to the place where John and the dogs walked into the woods.

The two women stand at the edge of the light, peering into the blackness beyond. Emily tries not to go where Margaret willingly travels. She is afraid to feel what the little boy might be feeling. Afraid to imagine the terror of being five years old and alone in the dark woods. Afraid to let the night sounds register—the sighing of the wind, the creaking of branches, the scratchings of nocturnal prowlers. She wonders, not for the first time, how Margaret can stand it.

Margaret begins to pace slowly, fluidly, her head bent toward the ground. Emily moves with her. Soon, she can sense Margaret's next turn to retrace her steps just before it happens. An easy rhythm develops, taking her out of her head and into her body. She is totally immersed in lifting her foot and placing it down, then lifting the other. She notices her breath moving evenly in and then out. She doesn't notice the passage of an hour and a half as she accompanies Margaret in her silent pacing.

Suddenly Margaret stops, releasing a long sigh. Her body slackens as she hurries to the huddled gathering around the parents. "They have him. I'm certain of it. He was asleep in a hollowed-out root pocket of a fallen pine."

Meg Allen cries out, hugging herself and falling to her knees. It is a primal, haunted sound followed by total silence in and around the clearing. Numb from holding so much tension in his body for so long, her young husband drops beside her, sobbing. Quiet mumblings of gratitude, audible sighs, and brittle coughs punctuate the air around them. An elderly couple bends over the two, lifting them and guiding them to a bench. Everyone in the family's circle is suddenly stricken by exhaustion, sinking or slumping into nearby chairs and stools.

"Wait a damn minute!" the red-haired Keith erupts, storming toward Margaret. "You evil hag." He punches the air beside her left ear. "Making them think their boy's all right when he's probably lying hurt or dying, maybe even dead. What kind of nasty devil-worshipping piece of crap are you?" Spittle flies in Margaret's face as he leans in toward her.

Suddenly, Ned Burrows grabs him from behind and spins him around. "That's it! Back off, you ignorant fuck. He's been found," he shouts into Keith's startled face. He turns to Meg and Tom Allen. "They have him. They're bringing him in. He's all right."

He turns back to Margaret but speaks to the group. "Margaret was right. Right on the mark." He enfolds her in strong arms. "Sorry about the language just now."

As she watches this strong but gentle man embracing Margaret, a sudden warmth flushes Emily's cheeks, and she turns away, focusing on the now jubilant Allen family. She carefully avoids Ned's eyes as he turns toward her.

"She had something to do with this," Keith blusters. He points his stubby finger at each member of the stunned family. "She put some sort of spell on all of you. She's trying to get you to follow in her witch ways."

The crowd turns away from him in disgust. Thus dismissed, he loses himself in indignation, ramping up the volume and sputtering nonsense until he finds his words again. "She used your boy to do it." He heads toward Tom Allen, bellowing now and gesticulating wildly. "Sent him out in the woods to be lost and hurt and heaven knows what. And you don't give a shit because, lo and behold, she magically helps to find him, sending you all into a mindless fucking state of fucking adoration. You turned your back on God for the sake of a fucking godless witch, you worthless pieces of shi—"

Keith grunts as he's knocked to the ground. Struggling to get up from under the weight of his attacker, he flails his heavy arms. Blinded by the red rage of righteousness, he fails to see the bony fist before it slams into his face.

Ned and Henry Jacobs rush to pull Tom Allen's father off Keith. "Hey, Old Tom, easy there. You all right?" Both men bend to examine the elder gentleman for injuries or, worse, broken bones. Finding none, they struggle to suppress smirks as they escort him to a chair.

"That's assault," Keith yells as he rolls over and scrambles to his feet. One hand over his left eye, he pulls a soiled bandana from his back pocket and swipes at his bleeding nose. "You all saw that. You're all witnesses to assault and—"

He finally looks up and sees the old man who tackled and punched him being helped to a chair. He stops, reddens, and then stalks off. Without turning on his headlights, he throws his truck into gear and roars away, peppering the parking lot with loose gravel.

Without a word, the crowd turns back to Meg and Tom. As Ned begins to speak, there's a loud crash from the direction of Keith's departure. Then silence.

"Guess we'd better go see what happened," Ned says to Henry Jacobs, who nods in reluctant agreement. As they start to move, there's the sound of grinding gears, then the screech of tires and a roaring engine. The familiar whine of Keith's truck tells them he's again on his way. "Guess he must be okay."

Margaret turns toward the wood's darkness at the sound of barking. Grace is the first to gallop into the light, followed closely by Sophia. Both dogs leap and twirl around Margaret's feet, rush over to the Allens, and then back to Margaret.

A few minutes later, a party of three comes into the light, one carrying the little boy. The waiting EMTs throw open the ambulance doors as Tom and Meg run to meet the searchers. Soon the crowd surrounds the weeping mother as she clings to her son, shaking and rocking, walking round and round in a tight circle. Tom tries several times to embrace them, but then steps back to allow his wife time and space to comfort their little one, who is now whimpering. Tears glisten on his face as he watches her, his lips moving in silent prayers. The elder Allens hang back, holding each other in stoic silence.

Warden Jacobs speaks at last. "Bring him this way, Meg. Let's let the EMTs have a look at him."

She hesitates and then slowly makes her way toward the brightly lit vehicle, shielding her son's eyes by pressing his face against her chest and keeping her palm cupped at the back of his head, as if he were an infant again. The crowd shrinks back as she passes, silenced by the sight of his cradled body and dangling legs blotched with bug bites and streaked with dirt and bright red scratches.

As they reach the rear of the ambulance, the boy suddenly cries out and struggles to escape his mother's arms. Meg, looking wounded, looks to her husband for help. But Joey screams at the sight of his father too, kicking and flailing until Meg nearly drops him. Just as suddenly as he began, though, the child stops, his gaze resting on Margaret standing at the edge of the crowd. He reaches his arms out toward her.

"Nana Maggie," he whispers. "Nana Maggie. You came. You came."

Everyone but Margaret is stunned. She joins mother and child and smiles down at the boy, her blue eyes softened by moisture. "There, there, Joey. Mommy and Daddy are here. You're all right now. Everything's all right. Just rest your eyes. This is Sam and Elizabeth, and they're going to take care of you. You let them take good care of you. Okay? You're safe now. Everything's all right now."

Margaret's voice is like warm honey, and her breathing is noticeably slow and even. Joey's breathing settles into the same easy rhythm. Everyone visibly, and some audibly, relaxes. Margaret smiles and nods at both parents. When they respond with weak but certain smiles, she steps back.

As the EMTs begin examining him, Joey doesn't make a sound. The crowd slowly disperses, men and women gathering up the equipment, gear, and food. Henry Jacobs and Ned busy themselves giving directions and pitching in with the cleanup. As maps are stowed and the tables are folded, Margaret moves off to the edge of the clearing and looks up into the night sky.

Emily approaches quietly. She can sense a change in Margaret. It's deeper than fatigue, more like a switch has been turned off. No longer open and listening, Margaret seems to have withdrawn into herself, shut down. Emily is about to speak when she sees John Longfeather walking toward them.

John stops beside Margaret and stands with his hands in his pockets. Emily turns to walk away.

"Emily, this is John. John, Emily." Margaret brings her back with her words.

"Sorry about Lily May," John says, his voice deep. "A good lady."

"Thanks." Emily recalls him standing at the back of the room at Lily May's crowded memorial service.

"Right where you said he'd be."

It takes Emily a moment to realize he's speaking to Margaret about the little boy.

"Between the Grandmothers, I saw the flash of red in the trees behind them. Would have missed it if not for you. Led us past the Mother spring to a little gully with a trickling of a stream. We found him tucked up under the root ball of a big old pine tree sound asleep. Barely made a sound when Jackie gave him a quick check and I picked him up to carry him out."

"And the red? What was it? I just couldn't place it."

"Bloodspot bush."

"Ah, yes!" Margaret drops her head back, nodding. "Bloodspot. Haven't seen one in years."

"Yeah. Real rare. Sacred to the People. Not surprising to find one near the Grandmothers, though. Ceremonial grounds. Lucky that leaf was on the outward side toward the opening between them."

Still facing skyward, Margaret is transported to a clearing in a wood. She is standing in a memory under a full moon. Her cloth blindfold is removed. The air is filled with low chanting, and around her dancers circle slowly, lifting and planting each foot deliberately to the beat of a drum. Three small fires flicker inside circles of stones. The fires form a triangle, and at the center is a young tree. Its slender branches are thick with green foliage but for a single bright-red leaf fluttering in the evening breeze.

She is a young woman again. John's grandmother and aunts have brought her to this sacred spot. Having witnessed from afar her tumultuous childhood and difficult teen years, they have come to acknowledge and honor her gifts. They offer themselves as teachers and welcome her into their circle, a rite reserved for Native women.

"Good thing." John's voice pulls her back to the present.

She looks up at him. "It's reminded me of your grandmother and aunts and the debt I owe their memories. I need to go up there, John, at the next full moon. Can you tell me the way?"

"Do better than that. I'll take you there. I didn't have time to properly do my prayers up there tonight. I'll bring Grandmother's bag."

"Perfect." Margaret gazes into his eyes, shadowed under the

brim of his hat. "Thank you."

"Go well until then." John touches his hat in salute and starts to walk away, but then he turns back. "When he first opened his eyes, the little guy asked where Nana Maggie went. Didn't think anybody called you Maggie anymore."

"They don't. And no one's ever called me nana."

They both smile.

"There was a strong male spirit in the woods keeping watch, good and gentle. I will thank him when we go back." John walks to his truck and drives away.

"Ready to head out?" Ned calls to Margaret and Emily. "I'm done here."

They join him at his truck. As Margaret steps up into the front seat, she is flooded with a bone-deep weariness.

"You all right?" Ned asks, staring over at her. "You better drink this down." He hands her a bottle of water. "Hydrate. You've worked long and hard tonight. Put out more energy than the searchers, I suspect. Drink and then sleep."

Margaret doesn't argue.

"How about you?" He looks back at Emily as if fully aware of her for the first time. "Sorry to have left you out of things tonight. Shouldn't have dragged you out here in the first place. You okay?"

Emily feels self-conscious under his gaze. "I'm fine. I would have been on edge all night back at home. It was easier to be in the midst of it, and a relief to witness his return to his parents. Besides, I wasn't your responsibility. You had enough to deal with." She realizes her tone is bordering on snippy. "I appreciate you letting me come."

Rambling, her inner voice chides. *Shut up before you make a complete fool of yourself.*

He starts the engine, and they ride in silence for several miles. Margaret drinks her water and listens to the crackling in the air around them. "Emily's moved into the cottage out behind Otis's place. He's her great-uncle. She's decided to settle here for a while, haven't you, Emily?"

"Yes."

"Doesn't know many young people around here yet."

No one speaks.

"She's a writer. A good one."

"Really?" Ned picks up the ball. "What kind of writer?"

The last thing Emily wants to talk about is herself. She glares at the back of Margaret's seat. "I'm still figuring that out. I prefer writing short fiction. Stories. So, I'm taking time to give that some serious attention. My great-aunt died and … Well, you don't need to know the boring details of my life. Suffice it to say, I'm taking some time off to see just what kind of a writer I am. Margaret is premature in praising me."

Shut up. Shut up. And for the last time, shut up! the inner critic scolds again. *Why don't you just bore the poor guy to tears? He's trapped in this truck with you and here you go, rambling again.*

"She's good," Margaret says.

Ned laughs. "Well, if Margaret says it's so, it must be so. Maybe it's time to own it."

She laughs too. "You're right. If Saint Margaret says it, I guess there's no fighting it."

"Saint!" Margaret exclaims. "That's a good one. Don't think I've ever been called that before. The devil. Satan's daughter. Witch. Witch with a *b*. Demon in a skirt. But never *saint*."

"Well, you'd better beware, Margaret," Emily says. "You know what they say about hanging around with writers. You may become fodder for their mill. Imagine opening my bestselling novel to find a character named Saint Margaret prancing around on the page in black and white, witch's warts and all."

Chapter 17

Emily awakens earlier than usual, a hint of light on the horizon. The wispy tail of a dream hangs in the dimness just beyond the bed. She understands the importance of not tugging at it, the futility of trying to force it into fullness. She understands, but still she has to work to make herself lie back and wait.

It comes like a kite slowly descending, tail first, then papery thin body wafting downward. A man on a hill bends to one knee and reaches out his arms. A child appears over the crest running toward him. She leaps and throws herself into his arms. He swings her in the air as he turns in circles. Heads back, they laugh as they whirl.

Emily slides inside the girl's body. Dizziness forces her eyes closed. Queasiness sours her stomach. A slight sting in her glands warns her she may throw up. Strong arms pull her against a hard chest, thrumming from within. The twirling slows, then stops. She opens her eyes. Green eyes look deeply into hers, tears slipping down his too-white cheeks. She opens her mouth to speak. Ned Burrows's voice shushes her. The face in front of her becomes his. His pale-blue eyes are wide with concern and a question. "How can I help?" he asks. "Where do you need to go?" With that, the dream collapses in on itself, and she is left staring up at the ceiling.

She knows what she must do today. Dressing quickly in khaki

shorts and a faded orange T-shirt, she finger combs her hair and throws it into a low ponytail. She downs a cup of instant coffee, fills her water bottle, and grabs a donut on her way out the door. As she pulls out of the drive, the sun is wholly visible above the horizon. When she eases onto the highway fifteen minutes later, she puts on her sunglasses and lowers the visor. Settling back in the seat, she calculates that it will take well over an hour.

The final ten miles are slow going on a little-used road in need of repair. It becomes narrower as she passes a faded sign reading *Whispering Waters Cemetery*. Her chest tightens as she passes through an ever-darkening tunnel formed by dense overarching branches. Finally, she can see a brightening up ahead and accelerates in a burst of panic. As she comes out into the sunlight, she is momentarily blinded and stomps on the brake. Her heartbeat, her entire body, is racing as she presses her forehead to the steering wheel without lifting her foot off the brake pedal. Slowly, she opens her eyes and allows them to adjust as her breathing slows. She lifts her foot and eases forward on the gas. The road has become dirt with wisps of tall grass in the center strip. Up ahead on the right stands a wrought iron gate flanked by stone walls. She drives through the gateway and several yards down a grass-covered central aisle. A series of lanes bisect this main aisle, and she can see that the entire cemetery is an enclosed square bordered by tumbling stone walls and thick woods.

Emily gets out of the car and surveys the uneven rows of headstones. Some lean precariously, darkened by age. Others stand straight and tall, gleaming whitely in the sun. She has no idea which is his. No sense of familiarity suggests she's ever been here before. But then, she reminds herself that much of her past is buried beyond conscious memory. She pulls her bag from the car and slings it across her shoulder. Pocketing her keys, she walks the center aisle, surveying each row as she passes.

As she approaches the rear of the cemetery, she looks across two bisecting lanes and spots a lone gravestone in the far-right corner lot. The name *DONNE* is etched thickly into it. Shaded by the overhanging branches of a huge maple, it is centered in a large grassy plot. Even though it is what she has been looking for, the sight stops her midstep. A single pot of red geraniums, striking in their brightness against the stone, stands in front of it.

For a moment, she cannot move. Then she is turning away and taking a step toward her car. Then she is stopping. She can still see the image, though it's behind her now. The stone. The grass. The red flowers. The name carved there. Her name. Carved in granite.

Suddenly she is on her knees weeping. Shaking. Sobbing. Clutching herself as if she could hold herself together. Knowing on every level that she can't.

"Daddy!" she calls out. Out into the sun-washed morning. Out into the woods beyond. Out into the air suddenly bereft of bird song. Only that one word. No thoughts to go along with it. Just that one word. Over and over and over again.

She crumples onto the sparse grass in the narrow lane. Outside of time, she remains there on the ground until her convulsing ebbs and her body settles into stillness.

Spent, she rolls onto her back, gazing at the blue sky and floating clumps of clouds. Tricklings of sweat ripple along her scalp and down her forehead. She is aware of minute sensations everywhere that her skin touches the earth. She is aware of the faint itch spreading across her left ankle bone and the piercing sting of a jagged rock trapped under her right buttock. She is aware and yet she is numb, detached from it all.

Slowly, she rolls to her side and pushes herself up to sitting. She fumbles in her bag for her water bottle and drinks. Turning around without rising, she rests her forearms on bent knees and looks across two rows of graves to the lone grave in the far corner.

Sunlight flickers through the maple leaves onto the stone and dances around the grass on a fresh breeze. "Oh, Daddy," she whispers.

She hefts herself up and swings her bag over her shoulder. Both feet feel weighted. Her eyes focus on the uneven ground ahead as she walks, until she is standing before the lichen-encrusted stone. She reads the inscription aloud.

"'DANIEL HARRISON DONNE, Beloved Son—Taken too soon. May your music play on.'

"Daddy. It's me. Emily." She looks down at a cluster of nearly round blooms of crinkly blue-green lichen clinging to the stone just above his name.

"Symbiosis." She says it aloud, this word that has just come into her mind. Then she remembers coming across it in a biography of Beatrix Potter, struck by the word, savoring its meaning and its message from the natural world. "Lichen is an example of two organisms of different species coming together, living together, in a way that is beneficial to both and harmful to neither. Symbiotic mutualism. Did you know that, Daddy?"

She runs her fingers across the lichen blossoms and then looks up, taking in the scent of pine, the raspy call of a distant crow, the snap of a branch as a squirrel skitters up a nearby tree.

She lowers herself to sit on the soft fragrant earth. Her gaze rests on the tiny blood-red petals that make up each round head of the geranium plant. She stretches and looks around at the other graves. Scattered throughout the cemetery are cans of cut flowers, a few potted annuals, and a pair of heavy urns at the main gate cascading with purple and white perennials. Otherwise, the graves are bare or sprinkled with wildflowers. She turns back to her father's stone and the terra cotta pot with its heavily blossomed plant. She touches the soil with her fingertips. Damp. The grounds haven't seen rain in days. Maybe even weeks.

"I wish I had known you, Daddy. I hope you hated to leave me, but I'll never know. If you left without a thought, if you never cared, if you were glad to be rid of me … I'm glad I'll never know."

She catches a flash of red. A cardinal sweeps down from a pine tree and lands on the branch of a sapling just behind the stone wall across the lane. It stays only for a moment and then lifts off, leaving the branch trembling.

Emily sits in the quiet, drifting past thought and merging with the peaceful rhythms of this place. After a while, she lies down on her back in front of the stone. She looks up through the layers and layers of green undersides of leaves overhead to the bright blue bits of sky winking in the wind.

"Not a bad place to visit. For either of us," she says, knowing that he is not in the ground here, forever stuck in stasis. Certain that he is here now because she is here. "Guess I get to make you up as I go along. Guess I get to have the daddy I need." She sits up. "Yes, I get to have the daddy who loves me and listens and is here whenever I need him to be."

Emily gets up and turns back toward the headstone. "Hello, Daddy."

In the same moment the words come out, she's being lifted high in the air, buoyed by a laughing male voice. *Well, if it isn't my little Emily!*

At long last. A memory. She hadn't dared hope.

Chapter 18

Margaret sits up with a start, the book in her lap falling to the floor. It's dark in the sitting room, and the girls scramble to either side of her, placing their noses on the arms of her chair.

"Did it again, didn't I?" Margaret shakes her head as she pushes up out of the deep-cushioned chair. Her body protests, stiff all over, as she stretches her arms overhead and bends to touch the floor. She notes the familiar dull ache in her right hip. Straightening, she rolls her head in a slow circle. Her vertebrae crackle in protest. "I feel like I'm ninety!"

She laughs as she reaches to turn on the nearby table lamp. It casts a soft circle of light. She looks to the mantel clock. Midnight.

"I've got to stop falling asleep in the chair," she half mutters as she heads for the bathroom off the kitchen. "I suppose you have to go too?" she asks the dogs, opening the back door on her way by. A waxing moon brightens the backyard and fields and casts a silvery whiteness over Sophia's and Grace's golden backs as they race down the hill toward the stream. Full moon soon, she thinks, reminded of John Longfeather's promise.

After washing up, she opens the door again just as the girls hit the doorstep. "Enjoy your little moon bath, did you? Okay, up we go. This time it's the bed and not the chair."

They follow her up the wooden stairs to the loft, where they take their time circling and settling down on their beds as she changes into pajama bottoms and tank top. She accordion folds the quilt at the bottom of the bed and slips under a sheet and light blanket. A gentle night breeze riffles the sheer curtains on the windows. A muffled grunt from one of the girls makes her smile as she goes off to sleep.

"Damned witch! Think you'll get away with it, bitch? Not as long as I'm around."

Keith Kennedy's swollen face bobs like an oversized balloon, blocking out all but its bitter self. Thick with grease, his red hair is darkened to a deep brown against his pale skin. Raised blotches dot his cheeks, looking hot to the touch. His eyes are oddly colorless, reminding Margaret of her mother's passing—of how she'd watched her mother's hazel eyes dissolve until they looked like twin pools of well water.

"Daughter of darkness! You're gonna' get it—"

"You're dreaming, Maggie. You can wake up. Just think it and you can wake up."

Mattie's voice freezes the image before her. Tiny crackling lines spread across Keith's face, fracturing it into a thousand pieces. The pieces hold together for a breath, then drop away in a shower of colored glass.

"Mattie?" Margaret smiles at the thought of her little twin. "Don't leave. Let's keep dreaming for a while."

No answer.

"Mattie? Don't go." She starts to sit up …

"Bet I can beat you to the old elm on the hill."

She takes off laughing, chasing her brother's fleeing back. She catches up to him just as he circles the tree and heads down the other side toward the woods.

"Not there, Mattie. Let's not go there," she pleads. "Let's have fun and not go there."

But he laughs and runs faster, getting farther and farther out of reach. She wants to stop him and hold him and hug him and feel him hugging her back. But her body is too old, too slow, too sore. And he's such a little boy.

Margaret sits up sobbing. The bedroom is cold. The curtains are blowing straight out in a now hard wind. She wraps herself in her own arms, clutching her shoulders and rocking.

A sudden surge of energy jolts her fully awake, and she slides from the bed and runs to the window. A flickering of light grabs her attention down at the corner of the garden shed—her workshop. Her mind speeds up. Wind—fire—go—

She races down the stairs and out the back door, leaving it standing open behind her, the girls at her heels. She twists the spigot at the rear of the house and grabs the hose. It spins off the wheel that holds it in coiled readiness and snakes behind her across the yard. Fanned by the wind, the flames are climbing up the back side of the structure. She hits them with a blast of water. They crackle and hiss and sizzle and continue to blaze. She waves the nozzle side to side and up and down, wetting the untouched cedar shingles as well as the flames.

"Grace, get my bag," she commands.

Grace returns with the bag clutched in her teeth. "Good girl," she yells as she bends and fishes the phone out of the bag with her free hand. She dials 911, then Ned Burrows's cell, then tosses the phone and bag out of range of the fire. She is forced to step back again and again as more of the wall is engulfed. The fire is growing faster than a single garden hose can handle.

Barking wildly, Sophia and Grace circle her, nudging her farther away from the fire. She orders them back, assuring them she's okay. Despite the stinging heat and lunging flames, Margaret refuses to retreat. Steam and smoke rise as water and fire meet. Suddenly Ned is at her side with an oversized fire extinguisher. She moves around to the side of the little building where the flames have begun to gnaw at that wall. In the distance, she hears sirens. Soon she is surrounded by a dozen men and women. One takes the hose from her and orders her out of the way. It's then she turns to see Otis and Emily rounding the house.

Emily runs to her. "Margaret. Thank God you're all right!"

"We come as soon as I heard the call on the scanner." Otis is panting. "Thank God it's just the shed and not the house. Maybe they'll be able to save some of it."

Crying her name, Annie Foss approaches from the field, having come up through the woods on the run.

"Here, Annie," Margaret calls out against the wind. "Over here."

Annie grabs her friend in a fierce embrace, rocking them both side to side. "Thank God, you're all right."

God's got nothing to do with her! The devil saved the bitch. She does the devil's work, that one.

Margaret looks around to see who is speaking. Ned and the volunteer firefighters are thoroughly engaged in fighting the flames, and the group gathering around her is made up of friends and neighbors. She's sure of that.

Annie's cheek is badly scratched. "You're bleeding. Let me get you something." Inside the house, she pulls on a knee-length cardigan before getting her first-aid kit and dampening a cloth. As she starts out the door again—

Thought you got away with it all these years, did you? Well, you've got another think coming. The next generation is primed and ready. As you sow, witch. As you sow …

Margaret shakes herself free and heads out to the widening circle of concerned neighbors. She sits Annie down on a backyard chair and dabs a thick yellow ointment from an unlabeled jar over the red slashes across Annie's sharp cheekbone. As it sinks in and disappears, the redness begins to pale.

"I'm fine, Margaret. Just some branches in the woods. It's you who needs tending."

"I'm fine," Margaret asserts. "No need to make a fuss."

"Damn it, Margaret." Everyone turns to Otis, shocked at the sharpness of his tone. "Let somebody else take care of you for a change. You don't want to deny us the chance to feel all gooey inside, do you?" He winks at Margaret, and everyone laughs, releasing some of the night's tensions.

"Well, now that you mention it, I do feel a bit wobbly on my feet. Adrenaline's wearing off, I guess. Thank God help arrived when it did or I might have lost more than the shed. This wind could well have meant the house."

Margaret shivers in spite of the thick woolen sweater. The group clusters closer around her as the fire chief joins them.

"Fire's under control, Ms. Meader. A couple of us are going to stick around and make sure no sparks or embers rekindle. 'Fraid the back section of the shed and pretty much everything inside is ruined. The smoke and water damage will mean a real mess and a total loss. Looks like it was your workshop? I'm sorry. Lost some beautiful stuff."

"I appreciate you getting out here so quickly. It's a long way. I'm just grateful no one was hurt and the house didn't catch."

"I suggest you get yourself inside and deal with this tomorrow. Nothing you can do in the dark. As I said, we'll keep an eye on things until we're certain it's safe to leave."

"Let me make you some tea th—"

"No thanks, ma'am. Got a thermos full of strong black coffee in the truck. Now, let these fine folks take care of you."

"For a change," Otis says. "Like I said."

The chief starts to leave, turns back. "I'll be by tomorrow afternoon to check on things and get your input for my report. Until then, get some rest." Two steps away, he turns again. "Oh, and don't do any cleanup. Not until we talk, okay?"

A deep weariness has settled into her limbs, and she wonders if she can walk back to the house without help.

Fuckin' bitch. How does it feel to get a taste of hell?

Again, she looks around but knows she won't see anyone. Again, she shivers and is grateful when two strong pairs of arms escort her into the kitchen and ease her into the Morris chair in the corner. Annie has already put the kettle on and steeped a pot of fragrant chamomile tea.

"This, and then it's to bed with you," she says.

"The warrior queen is back I see." She smiles up at her friend. "But the girls need—"

"We'll take care of whatever the girls may need," Ned assures her, bending over her protectively.

"It was set," she whispers into his ear before he has a chance to rise.

He hovers just above her. "I know. We'll talk about it tomorrow."

"But—"

"The chief knows too. Get some rest."

Chapter 19

"Is she asleep?" Emily asks as Annie Foss comes down the stairs carrying a teacup and saucer.

Annie nods. "Wish she'd sleep 'til noon, but she'll be up with the sun." She looks at her watch. "Which won't be long now!

"It was good of you to stay, but you can go along now and get some sleep. I'll stay put and be here when she comes down. I've no reason to rush home to an empty house. I'm glad to have a chance to keep her company like she did me when my Jake was dying and after …" Annie's gaze drifts downward and away.

"Well, I rode over with Uncle Otis and sent him on his way, so—"

"I'm ready anytime you are, Annie," Ned interrupts, gently knocking as he comes through the back door.

"Oh, thanks, Ned, but I'm staying on. I appreciate the offer, though. The woods are pretty dark now that the moon's moved on." She turns toward Emily. "Oh, but Emily could use a ride home. She's without a car, and there's no need for both of us to stay."

Emily stifles a yawn as she starts to protest. "I wouldn't want you to have to go out of your way. I'm fine, really."

"Not out of my way at all. I go right by your place. The cottage beyond Otis's place, right?"

As Emily climbs up into Ned's truck, she is aware of a rising panic. Her cheeks burn with self-consciousness at being alone with him in his SUV. She's glad for the darkness until he turns the key, and then she's sure the dashboard lights illuminate her discomfort.

Stop it! her inner critic chides. *He's just giving you a lift home because he's a nice guy, so stop going all high school here.*

Trying for a safe subject to get them through the ride, she says, "You've known Margaret a long time?"

"I grew up here. So, I've always known about her. When she moved back here after her time away, she helped out with our searches a number of times. The happy-ending cases like Joey Allen's have sadly been outnumbered by those that have turned out badly. In those other cases, Margaret was a godsend to the searchers involved, present company in particular." He falls silent, eyes directed at the road ahead.

Emily doesn't try to engage him, understanding that he has slipped into a space of private reflection. As the silence in the truck deepens, she realizes she's perfectly comfortable with it. She realizes also that there was a time when she would have felt the need to fill it with inane conversation. *Is this what it's like to be a grown-up?* she wonders with a smile.

After a couple of miles, Ned says, "She can usually tell when it's not going to turn out well and prepares us as best she can. Then, afterwards, she makes herself available to talk and listen. Mostly to listen." Again, he lapses into silence.

Again, Emily waits.

"Nobody has to ask her to. She isn't paid or anything. She's just there when we need her, like the wise grandmother you never had and never knew you needed until your first sit with her. She's pretty remarkable."

"That she is."

Emily hopes he'll continue this time. She wants to know what he knows about Margaret. And she's also thoroughly enjoying the sound of his pleasant voice. As they turn onto her road, she's not surprised at the disappointment she feels. The ride she had dreaded has turned out to be far too short, and she wonders when and how she will see him again.

"Were you aware of her, um, *unusual* skills of perception before you joined us on the search?" he asks as they pull into Otis's driveway.

She points to the right, to a break in the trees bordering the narrow lane to her cottage. "You can pull down in there. It's wide enough to turn back around at the end."

As he eases down the lane, she answers his question. "My uncles hinted about them before I met her. And then when we did meet, she said some things that really ... It was ... Well, as you said earlier, pretty remarkable."

Ned stops outside her cottage, shifts into park, and turns to look at her in the dash-light glow. "The first time she joined us on a search, I was shocked. I couldn't believe Henry—Warden Jacobs—had asked her. I'd grown up hearing stories about her. Then when she came back, I heard even wilder tales. So, I was more than a bit irked. I figured our team was trained for search and rescue and she would just be in the way. Maybe even get herself in trouble and need rescuing. I resented her, and I'm embarrassed at how badly I behaved. All full of myself and my own expertise."

"Sounds understandable to me. I'm sure Margaret didn't take it—"

"Oh, don't get me wrong. She quickly put my objections to rest and sobered me right up. We've since laughed about it many times over. She was used to people like my younger self going off half-cocked when it came to her otherly wisdom."

"*Otherly wisdom.* I like that. Well put."

"It's what my grandmother Hancock used to call it. She said Margaret's father had it too. But his took him in a whole different direction. More like madness than wisdom in his case, I guess. Very sad story."

Although curious, Emily tries to steer him back to Margaret's story. "How did she settle your objections on that first search?"

"As soon as we arrived at the PLS—the place last seen—before the two women disappeared, Margaret got out of Henry's truck and stopped short. She turned a ghastly white and nearly dropped to the ground. He and I grabbed her and helped her to a boulder. She couldn't speak. She couldn't look at either of us and kept wringing her hands as if in pain.

"Finally, she said in a hoarse voice, 'I'm afraid they're both dead. They're in a ravine near a pile of rotting logs about ten miles that way.' And she pointed off to the left. Then she said, 'Tell your people to prepare themselves for a grisly scene.'

"As Henry started away, she said, 'And watch out for animal traps. It's a trapper's territory. Not related to the killings.'"

"And she was right."

"Right."

Again, the silence.

Emily knows he's reliving the experience. The precision of his words in quoting Margaret, the distant expression on what she can see of his face in the dimness, his haunted tone of voice all tell her he's back there in the woods again.

"I'm so sorry." She lays her hand on his, which rests on the seat between them. In sharp contrast to the images he's evoked, his hand is warm beneath hers.

He closes his eyes and breathes deeply. Neither moves. Finally, he speaks again.

"One of the searchers nearly stepped in a trap along the way, but Margaret's warning had everybody on high vigilance, and he spotted it just in time. Then, when we got to the bodies, I understood Margaret's reaction. I don't know how she does it, how she doesn't go crazy seeing the things she sees, knowing the things she knows.…

"Anyway, when it was over, she got us through the aftermath. Looking much more composed when we returned, she coaxed us into talking about what we'd found and how it had felt. Guided us through the story. It didn't take away the horror, but it started us on the path to dealing with it and the emotions churning inside us. In the past, I would have gone off by myself and bottled it up inside. Now, I go to Margaret and we talk, and sometimes we even find our way to laughter in spite of it all."

He smiles at Emily. Her hand is still on his. He turns his upward so that his thumb encloses hers. He squeezes gently.

Emily looks down, unable to meet his eyes. She leaves her hand in his, savoring this strange yet comfortable intimacy. She doesn't want to move. Doesn't want him to move. Doesn't want anything to spoil or change this moment.

Finally, she lifts her head and looks at him. He's closer than she'd realized. He's leaning in toward her, his eyes unreadable in the darkness. She wants him to kiss her. She wants him to want to kiss her.

And then he's kissing her. A soft, sweet kiss. And then he's pulling away. She can see his eyes now. They're glistening in the dashboard light with a look of mild surprise.

"Okay?" he asks.

"Definitely okay," she says.

He kisses her again. This time it's a longer, slower kiss. She leans in closer. She presses her lips more deeply into his, parting them slightly, enjoying the taste of him.

They pull apart as if in slow motion and stare at each other. No words seem appropriate. Emily realizes she is truly in a place beyond words, a place of simplicity and pure awareness. She smiles. He smiles back.

His cell phone rings. He seems unaware. She's barely aware. It rings again. He stirs but without urgency. She feels a shift in the space between them. He reaches for the phone on the third ring.

"I can be there in an hour," he says after listening briefly. He ends the call and turns to her.

"But you've had no rest," she protests, feeling suddenly protective of him.

"Comes with the job sometimes. Besides, I did get some sleep before Margaret called me. I'd gone to bed unusually early for me. In my line, you learn to get sleep when you can."

"Can you take time for some coffee or tea? Or to fill a thermos?"

"Sorry. Got to get up to Brownsfield. I'll swing by a drive-through if I need to. Thanks for the offer, though."

She starts to get out, but Ned turns her back toward him. "I'm really sorry about this. Can I call you tomorrow?"

"I'd like that."

"And can I ..." He leans in for another kiss.

"I'd like that too."

But he surprises her by pulling away. "Wait."

He jumps out the driver's door and comes around to the passenger side to lift her down. Then, without letting her go, he bends down for a long, deep kiss as she reaches her arms up around his neck.

Finally, he pulls away and walks her to her door. Another kiss, and she feels his reluctance to leave. She wants to pull him close and not let go.

"I'll call you tomorrow," he says.

"You mean later today?"

They both look up, noticing the dawn has begun to lighten the world around them.

"Later today, then," he says. He looks into her eyes for a long moment before turning to go.

Chapter 20

Margaret awakens to the sound of Sophia and Grace barking in the distance. She sits up in bed, surprised to see a late-morning sun angled across the covers. She pulls on her robe and crosses to the window, where she smiles at the sight of the girls racing up from the creek toward the house. Then she looks down into the trampled yard and the charred remains of her workshop.

She hurries downstairs to find Annie pulling a covered baking dish from the oven.

"Good morning," Annie says, motioning for Margaret to sit at the table. She sets a teacup in front of her and pours a lavender- and honey-scented brew into it. "I'm so glad you were able to sleep until now. I was afraid you'd be up at first light. I've whipped up a little egg and veggie scramble and some sourdough biscuits, and I won't take no for an answer. Unless of course you're allergic or something. You're not allergic, are you? 'Cause if you are, I could —"

Margaret laughs. "Sounds delicious, but you shouldn't have gone to so much trouble."

"Just listen to me. I'm babbling on, I know. It was just such a night last night. And I'm so happy to be able to do something for you for a change. And you know I love to cook and I only have myself these days." She sets a steaming plate in front of Margaret and a cloth-covered basket between them. Finally, she sits and pours another cup of tea and helps herself to a fragrant biscuit.

"Actually, I'm famished. You better be careful. I could get used to being spoiled like this."

They eat in pleasant silence until a truck rumbles into the side yard. A heavy metal door slams shut, and Annie jumps up, ordering Margaret to stay put. She heads out the back door as another truck approaches. Margaret is surprised that she feels no inclination to follow. She is content to sit and savor the food set before her. As the warmth of the tea settles in, she realizes how incredibly weary she is and how deeply she appreciates her friend's ministrations.

Voices near the back door, and she leans back in her chair, readying for what she knows will now come. Sophia and Grace slip in the door past Annie as she enters, followed by the fire chief, Paul Edwards, and a police officer Margaret doesn't know. Margaret turns to them as the girls settle in under the table by her feet.

The officer opens his mouth to speak, but Margaret stops him with her raised hand. "The boy you picked up is the victim of his family's animosity toward me, I'm afraid. He's been told that I've done his family harm and that I'm still a threat to them, so he burned my shed."

"So, you know him?" Chief Edwards says. "You saw him set the fire then?"

"No. I didn't see him."

"How do you even know we've picked someone up, ma'am?" The young officer moves closer until he's standing over her chair looking down at her. "And how do you know he's the one who set the fire?" There is a barely concealed accusation in his tone.

Margaret leans her head against the back of her chair and closes her eyes. Suddenly overcome by a debilitating fatigue, she stifles a sigh. She is unable to speak or think.

She hears movement and opens her eyes. The young officer is looming closer, but Annie has stepped forward.

"That's not easy to explain, Officer," she says

"Why don't we step out back, Dave?" says the Chief. "I'll

show you around the scene. Point out the evidence that makes it a definite case of arson. I don't think Ms. Meader is feeling quite herself today, and it's little wonder after her ordeal last night."

The officer frowns at Chief Edwards. "It's important we get her statement as soon after the fact as possible. You know that. And I want to know how she knows our suspect. Something doesn't feel right here, and I'm going to get to the bottom of it."

Margaret winces at the stabbing pain behind her left eye and closes her eyes again. The field of darkness behind her closed lids is awash with red and orange and yellow. In the distance, she can hear Annie's voice speaking her name, but the sound of rushing water tumbles the word over and around itself until it merges with a swelling turbulence inside. The vibrant colors swirl dizzyingly, shifting to blues and purples and greens until everything is dark and silent and still.

"Well, if it isn't my little Magpie."

"Father?"

"Himself."

She can feel her heart beating in her ears. It nearly drowns out the sound of her words as she whispers, "I haven't heard your voice since—"

"I know, Magpie. I'm sorry."

"Why? Why did—"

"It was too hard, Magpie. It was just too hard."

"But …"

"No buts about it, Maggie mine. You and Mattie were the only reasons I stayed as long as I did."

"But …"

"I wasn't strong like you. They didn't call me Mad Maxwell for nothing. Forgive me, my brave little girl. It was just too hard."

Silence closes in around her. Darkness. Stillness.

"Father?"

Silence.

"Father?"

Silence. Darkness.

"Father? I'm not strong. I'm not brave.… I'm scared."

Silence. Darkness.

"And I'm tired. Can I stay here?"

"No! You need to go back. But first, you need to rest. Then all will be well. You'll see. All manner of thing shall be well."

Suspended in a warm liquid, she is floating. Breathing with ease. Drifting.

The pieces are brown and green, rust and tan, ivory and peach. They move sluggishly around her, suspended in the thick air. Beautifully carved with their loops and sockets, tabs and slots, they dance and twirl as the air lightens and lifts. Pieces interlock and disengage rhythmically, like dance partners coming together and moving apart.

Certain pieces shimmer, highlighted as if by shafts of sudden sunlight. Paint, applied with thick brush strokes and burnished by the light, glistens. The brightened pieces are drawn magnetically to their shadowy mates and interlock. Larger and larger segments of the emerging puzzle fill the air. The music swells—a half-remembered waltz from somewhere long ago.

She is back on the wooden chair, fidgeting. She wants to be outside but she wants even more to be good. Mattie is out there somewhere in the sunshine, running. She tries not to think about that, but the chair is so hard and the air is so close and her father is lost in his looking—at his palette … at the canvas … at her. Her body settles into sitting, settles into being still. For him. For her father.

His long hair is the color hers will become with age, chestnut streaked with silver. It flies around his head in thick, unruly waves, as hers will always do. His eyes, a brilliant blue, look into and beyond her. His left hand wields the brush, thick with paint, in wide, sweeping strokes. At times it slows to stab at the canvas with short, staccato jabs, then resumes the broad swirls and flourishes. His arm and brush arc upward and then back. Again and again. Margaret hears the music he must hear inside his head, the waltz.

That's when the vision comes. A sharp sizzle in the center of her forehead. A starburst of vivid colors, more brilliant than the fireworks she's always loved but hated at the same time. A deeper-than-black darkness fills her mind, backdrop to flickering images, like on a movie screen. Repelled yet mesmerized, she stares as they flash, her pulse quickening. As one image fades to be replaced by another, it leaves a ghostly impression that lingers before dissolving into the next.

A woman's face in the water, eyes staring up from the blurry depths, white hair floating around her. A mermaid etched with age. Her mother's face turning away from her, blue-black hair streaming over her shoulders. A girl's face, the skin along her hairline stained like an ugly bruise, her hair the color of ripened grapes. Mattie running through woods, tripping over tangled roots. Her father sprawled on the floor, his empty eyes not looking anymore.

These stand out in bas-relief amidst dozens of faces she's never seen and places she's never known. A landscape keeps appearing, each time dressed in a new season. Green with spring. Sun-soaked in summer. Russet and gold. White with winter. The blue sky is ever empty but for a single heron in flight.

She tries to close her eyes, but they are already shut. She tries to call out to her father, but no sound escapes her open mouth. She tries to find her way back to the hardness of the chair by the window, back to her father's studio, back to the moment before the visions exploded in her head. And suddenly she's looking into her father's terrified eyes.

He is kneeling in front of her, his hands on her upper arms. He is squeezing them much tighter than she's sure he intends. His face is frozen in an anguished mask.

"No!" he moans. "Not her too. Not my little Magpie. Not my precious darling girl!"

Then, he is gone, rushing out of the studio, leaving her alone.

Slowly, she rises and walks to the canvas on the easel. Nearly finished, the painting is of her and yet not her. The child's face is framed by windblown waves of her own brown hair streaked with coppery highlights. Her dimpled chin is turned upward, her lips slightly parted. The peach tones of her round cheeks glow. Her blue eyes, the same bright shade as his, glisten. Sitting in the sun on the bank of a bubbling stream, she is dressed in a simple slip. This child is a creature of the natural world. Mostly wild, with sun-bronzed skin under a faint layer of dirt, she must surely sleep on a bed of moss beneath a tree, under the moon and stars.

Margaret marvels at the way her father has painted away the chair and the window and the heavy indoor air teeming with dust motes. She wonders at how he removed her stiffly laundered dress, her once white socks, and her Sunday shoes. She imagines herself dressed in the lightness of that tissue-soft slip. Her toes stretch and wriggle inside her shoes. She relishes the thought of standing barefoot in the cool grass and dipping her feet in the giggling brook.

As she stands before the painting, she is drawn again and again to the eyes of the wild creature who is her and yet not her. They glisten with moisture, as if the child is deeply moved. They are alight with both sunshine and some luminous inner source. Her brilliant father, known to the world as Mad Maxwell Meader, has captured the essence of wonder in a child's eyes. Her own blue eyes.

Young Margaret stares at her other self and then at the surrounding landscape. Water droplets flung up from the frothy depths sparkle in the sun as the wind catches them. Beyond the stream, a gnarled tangle of undergrowth gives way to the purple darkness of the nearby woods. Behind the child, a field of wildflowers spreads up a steepening hill to a stand of birches silhouetted against the sky. In the nearest tree, a lone bird sits. A magpie. Another bird, strong wings beating at the wild wind, approaches from above.

Young Margaret stoops and absently picks up her father's palette lying facedown on the floor. He must have dropped it when he came to kneel before her, she thinks. When he realized what was happening to her. When he realized she had inherited more than the colors of his hair and eyes. He must have dropped it then, she thinks. She sets the palette on his workbench and rights the jar of brushes.

"Margaret?"

"Father?" She whirls around, holding her breath.

"Margaret? It's me, Annie."

Disappointment seeps into her awakening body. Feeling unbearably heavy, she takes in a deep breath and opens her eyes. "I'm all right, Annie. Just give me a moment."

"Oh, thank God, Margaret. Oh, my God, you had me so worried. I—"

"A moment, Annie. Please."

Annie sinks into a nearby chair, watching Margaret closely. Then she goes to prepare a fresh pot of tea.

The colors, the darkness, the visions and memories, have all receded, like figures swallowed by a thick fog. A profound sadness fills the emptiness left behind. Tears slip down her cheeks. She makes no attempt to wipe them away.

Her father could offer no help or advice as she struggled with her emerging clairvoyance. Beyond that moment of recognition in his studio, he couldn't even tell her that he too had the sight. He left her to suffer the aftermath of her first experience—the fear, and the confusion—alone. But now she understands why. She can see it from his perspective. He was so deeply empathetic, so exquisitely sensitive, he suffered as much in that moment as he probably ever had in his life. He knew what she would go through, his little daughter whom he loved more than anything except Mattie, and it paralyzed him. She knows that with a certainty she wouldn't have thought possible.

That big strong man, that brilliant man, couldn't help her. He couldn't help himself. The visions drove him into madness at times. The rest of the time, he barely managed to straddle the border between normalcy and what the world called eccentricity. Because he was such a gifted artist, the quality of otherness in him was written off as artistic temperament, and his works sold well. He spent long hours alone in his studio, and invitations to visit him there were prized by her and her twin brother. She knows now that he struggled mightily to keep himself afloat, until it became too hard, too much. And then he shot himself.

"Oh, Father," she says softly, shaking her head.

Annie seems to understand that these words are not meant for her to hear and continues to prepare the tea tray.

"Where's that irritating young man?"

Annie's back is turned, and she whirls around in relief. "The chief, bless his heart, ushered him out of here. He won't be back to bother you today. But the chief will be back when he's through making his preliminary investigation. Now, let's get some hot tea into you."

"Thank you, Annie. For being here."

Annie beams with pleasure. "I'll be here until you shoo me away." She sets Margaret's rinsed and empty cup back in front of her. "Had one of your visions, I presume? I still say I don't know how you can see what you see and not go to pieces. Was it a bad one? If you wish to talk about it, I can be a pretty good ear."

Margaret takes a sip of the mellow tea. Then another. "It was a mixture of visions and memories. Some neutral. Some not so pleasant. Lots to sort through before I can talk about it. Some of it, I'll probably never figure out."

"How do you live with that?"

"Without going to pieces? I think I've shown today and last night that I sometimes do just that. I'm not exactly holding myself together very well at the moment." She smiles.

Annie places her hand on top of Margaret's. "Talk to me."

"I'm not sure why, but something has really stirred things up. Brought the past into the present. Guess I didn't realize how much has been passed along to a new generation. That youngster who set the fire is only acting on things he's been told. It's not his fault. He truly believes I'm to blame for his family's tragic history."

"You mean the Kennedys and the Larsons and all that long-ago nastiness?"

Margaret nods slowly.

"Jake told me a bit about it shortly after I first met you. Coming from away, I was confused by some comments made by Elaine Barker and her cousin Ethel. They referred to you and what they called your 'troubles,' and it made Jake really mad. He said it was time they stopped bringing up all that old nonsense and put their good minds to better use. He fixed them with a fearsome stare when he said it. He was such a kind man and it was so unlike him.

I can still see them hurrying off like a couple of chastised pups."

"Jake was like an older brother before he left to go in the service." Margaret leans forward and pours herself more tea from the pot on the table.

They sit in silence, Margaret sipping tea and Annie smiling at an image of her late husband as a young man, dressed in his uniform.

"Maybe it's time I had a talk with Ruth or Agnes. Or both," Margaret says at last.

"I wouldn't approach either one of them without someone to watch your back. As far as I can tell, they haven't changed over the years."

"Maybe there's a chink or two in that old armor. Maybe a little reason and goodwill can get in now. Worth a try."

"Let me come with you, at least. They've never tried to intimidate me like they do so many others around here. Something about me not sharing a common history, I guess. I didn't know them back when they could bully everybody with body weight and family reputation. Of course, my height doesn't hurt. The two of us would make a pretty formidable pair."

Margaret laughs. "Mutt and Jeff! Thanks. But I think I need to do this alone. Maybe they'll listen for the sake of the youngster who's now in trouble with the law. I'll go see them after I've had a chance to clean up this mess out back."

"That'll be the easier mess to clean up, I'm afraid."

Margaret smiles and resumes sipping her tea as Chief Edwards taps lightly on the door.

Chapter 21

Three o'clock. Emily sits up, disoriented by the brightness of the room. It's not three in the morning, it's late afternoon. On the verge of chastising herself, she remembers.

Ned. The kisses. The sun coming up. Writing in her journal until she could no longer keep her eyes open. Tossing her clothes on the chair in the corner and sliding under the covers.

Ned. She smiles, plumping her pillow and propping it behind her as she leans back against the cushioned headboard. She smiles at the thought of him looking down at her with those soft blue eyes. She smiles at the memory of his sweet tenderness as he leaned in to kiss her, and of the eternity the kiss seemed to last, and of the warmth of his breath on her face. She stops smiling as she recalls the catch in her own breath and the unpleasant quickening in her chest as he left.

She knows very little about him, and she smiles again at the thought of getting to know him better—of how much time it will take, how many long hours together they will need. She walks to the bathroom without dressing and steps into the shower. As the warm water runs down her body, her thoughts become more explicit, and she keeps smiling.

He calls shortly after four to say he will be tied up for a while longer. She closes her eyes and listens with her whole body to the sound of his voice. His rich, masculine voice. Like the warm water of her shower, washing over her. Lost in the sound, she travels beyond the meanings of words.

"Is that okay? Emily? Are you there?"

Jolted by his urgency, she says quickly, "Yes. I'm here. Sorry." And then she does something she's never allowed herself to do before. She speaks the truth to him. "I'm glad you called. I was afraid you might not. What with the light of day and all …" Always so careful at the beginning of a new relationship, she's held herself aloof until she's sure it's safe to open up, and then only a tiny bit at a time. She forces out a light laugh even though she suddenly feels heavy, constricted.

"Does that mean the answer is yes?" he asks. "It's okay to call later?"

"Yes. I'd love it."

"Good."

"And maybe you could come by when you get back? If it's not too late." She holds her breath. Has she gone too far? Pushed too hard?

"What would be too late?"

She exhales softly. "I just slept most of the day away. You're the one who's worked since the fire. You must be exhausted. So, let's make it your call." Before he has a chance to answer, she adds, "You can always have a rain check."

"I'll call you when I'm on my way."

"Good." She's smiling. "How about a late supper? Something simple. No matter how late."

"Sounds perfect."

She can hear the static and bleats of his service radio and knows she has to let him go. But she doesn't want to break the connection. "You probably better go."

"Yeah, I probably should."

They stay on the line for seconds more.

"I'll call you."

"I'll be here."

She is still smiling as she hangs up.

❧

When the phone rings at seven, Emily answers on the second ring. "On your way?"

"Afraid I'm not the one you're hoping for."

"Oh, Margaret. Hi."

"Sorry I didn't get back to you sooner. A bit hectic around here. What can I do for you?"

It takes Emily a moment to remember that she'd left a message for Margaret earlier in the day. "I was calling to check on you. I intended to stop over, but I slept most of the day. Sorry."

"Not surprising. You were here most of the night. Annie says you didn't leave until she insisted just before dawn."

"Well, as long—"

"With Ned," Margaret adds. Emily imagines the impish smile on the older woman's face.

"He was going to take Annie home, but she begged off and suggested—"

"Doesn't matter how it came about, so long as it did. No sense wasting time getting things started. You two kids had a 'I'd like to get to you know you better but I'm afraid to make the first move' look written all over yourselves. I'm glad Annie had the good sense to push things along."

"Okay, Saint Margaret." Emily laughs. "I want you to keep any visions of the future to yourself—good or bad. If, and I'm saying *if*, anything is developing between Ned and me, I don't want to know what's ahead."

"Don't worry. I haven't seen a thing. Except what was right in front of my eyes in the here and now." Margaret is laughing outright, and Emily finds it irresistibly contagious. As she joins in, her phone signals a call coming in.

"Can you hold for a minute, Margaret. I have—"

"Speak of the devil. You can call me back tomorrow. Enjoy your evening." And Margaret clicks off.

This is no devil, Emily thinks as she switches over to Ned. "Hi."

"Hi. I'm on the road. Should be there in another hour. Still okay?"

"Very okay. See you then."

Before she can put the phone down, it rings again.

"Yes?" she says in a somewhat sultry tone.

"Emily, it's Otis. Think you can come over?" His voice sounds faint and raspy.

"Are you all right?"

"Don't know. Feeling kind of—"

Dialing 911 as she goes, Emily heads out the front door at a run. As she approaches Otis's house, she sees only two dim lights on inside: the night light in the kitchen and a lamp in the upstairs bedroom. The house is locked, and she fumbles for her key, calling out to Otis. Finally, she finds the right one and throws the door open. Silence inside. She races up the stairs.

Otis is lying facedown on the floor by his bed. She turns him over, and her heart lurches. His face is a pasty white and covered in a sheen of sweat. His breath is shallow, his pulse rapid. As she bends over him, she smells a fruity odor. In a panic, she slaps his cheeks lightly and shouts his name.

Otis mumbles and starts to struggle against her. "Leave me 'lone. Get Lily May," he says, followed by some garbled syllables Emily cannot make out.

"Otis! Otis! It's me. Emily." She slaps his cheeks several times.

"Lily knows ... Lily May ..."

Emily hears a siren in the distance. "Help is coming. Help is on the way. Otis? Otis, can you hear me?"

He stops struggling and mumbling and goes limp, sinking into unconsciousness in her arms. "Help him. Oh, God, help him," she cries, pulling his upper body into her lap and rocking him like a child.

The sirens are deafening as the rescue squad pulls up to the open front door, its flashing lights pulsating in the stairwell. The pounding of her heart matches their frantic rhythm. "Here!" she shouts. "We're up here."

Footsteps on the stairs, then two EMTs rush into the room. She gasps in relief at the sight of them, and then everything slows down. The woman of the pair addresses her sharply, enunciating her words: "You have to let go and let us help him. You have to let go now."

At that, Emily releases him, sidling out of the way until she's sitting with her back against the wall, watching as if from a distance.

Terrified, she tries to understand what they're saying and doing, but everything seems garbled. She feels totally alone, cut off, separated from her uncle and those working on him by an invisible yet impenetrable wall. When a young man bends over her and helps her to her feet, she mutely accepts his assistance. When he wraps a thin blanket over her shoulders, she looks up into his kind eyes but can form no words.

"We're going to transport him to the hospital," he says. "He's suffering from insulin shock but we've stabilized him. Is there someone you can call? You shouldn't be driving right now."

"Can't I ride with him? I don't want him to be alone."

"You can ride up front, yes. But you should call someone to be with you once we get there."

He helps her gather the spilled contents of her purse, which has been kicked into the corner on the floor, then guides her into the hallway and down the stairs.

Her first thought is to call Margaret, but she quickly rejects that because of all the older woman has just been through. Before forming the next thought, she's calling Ned. When he answers on the second ring, the sound of his voice overwhelms her and she begins to cry.

"Emily? What is it? What's wrong?"

She forces herself to speak through her tears, mustering a composure she does not feel but knows he deserves. "It's Uncle Otis. Insulin shock. He's stable but we're on our way to the hospital by ambulance. I've left my car—"

"I'll be there as soon as I can."

Her heart slows for the first time since Otis's call. She takes in a shuddering breath. Her shoulders and chest soften. "Thank you," she whispers, and hangs up.

৵৵

After a flurry of filling out forms and answering questions, Emily is allowed into the curtained cubicle in the emergency room where Otis lies on the gurney, eyes closed. Machines beep behind him, and a clear liquid drips intermittently from a suspended bag on an IV pole. A hint of color has returned to his pale face, and she prays it's a good sign that he's been left unattended. She can't allow herself to think about possibilities. She *won't* think beyond this moment of relative peace and quiet. She takes his hand in both of hers. It is limp but warm.

"I love you," she says, although she's sure he can't hear her. Again, she begins to cry.

A hand on her shoulder squeezes lightly. Warm. Strong. Comforting.

"How is he?" Ned's voice is gentle. She thinks for a moment she's imagined it. Then she's on her feet, reaching up to hold him and pressing herself into the warmth of him. Silent sobs rock her body in convulsive waves as his arms gather her in.

"What's an old man got to do to get some attention around here?"

Emily drops back into her chair, snatching up her great-uncle's hand. Her breath catches at the sight of his smiling face. "You had me so scared."

"I can see that." He winks at her and grins up at Ned.

Emily feels herself pinkening. "We came in by ambulance and I have no car here. So, Ned—"

"Thanks, young man. Didn't mean to scare you, Emily. Almost didn't call you, but—"

"If you hadn't called me, you'd still be lying on your bedroom floor." She stands. "No one would have known until morning. You might have died!" Her voice rises, becoming shrill.

Ned's hands are on her shoulders. Applying a gentle pressure, he guides her back into the chair as Otis looks momentarily stricken.

"Sorry, little one. Just didn't want to cause a fuss. I thought it was a touch of the flu or something I ate. Thought it would pass. I was afraid I'd feel silly if I got you all the way over to my place for nothing."

"I love you. You call me anytime, for anything. Do you hear me? How many times have you told me, 'We're here to take care of each other'? Well, that's a two-way street. Right?"

"Well, I don't like to make a fuss—"

"Am I right?" Her voice is raised again as she cuts him off, but she's smiling this time, playfully. As their usual easy banter settles into place, she sighs and leans back against the chair, back into Ned's calming presence behind her.

A tall man in a white coat pushes through the curtains surrounding them. His eyes are on the clipboard he's writing on as he begins to speak. "Who is the responsible party for the patient… ah …" He hesitates as he flips to the front page of his paperwork. "Mr. Otis W. Tyler?" At last, he looks up and around the room. "Would that be you?" he says to Ned.

"I would be the responsible party for Mr. Otis W. Tyler," Otis says, attempting to rise up taller on the gurney.

Emily eases him back against the pillow. "And I'm his grand-niece, Emily Donne, and his closest neighbor."

"And I am a friend," Ned adds, a mild rebuke in his tone.

The young doctor addresses Otis. "Well, Mr. Tyler, we're going to admit you so we can get your diabetes under control. You were in insulin shock, and you're lucky you were found when you were. Did you forget to eat or did you exert yourself too much and forget to check your glucose levels?"

"All of the above, I'm afraid. Guess I overdid it when I chopped and stacked some wood earlier today. Then I wasn't feeling well and didn't have much appetite, so I thought I'd just go to bed early. Figured I'd feel better in the morning."

"But you'd taken your insulin for the day as usual?"

"Yeah. Guess I wasn't thinking when I didn't eat after all that activity. My wife always kept a close eye on my sugars. Guess I'm still not used to doing it on my own."

"Maybe you shouldn't be living on your own, Mr. Tyler. Maybe it's time—"

"I'm perfectly capable of living on my own." Grasping the rails of the gurney, Otis pulls himself up to a full sitting position. His cheeks are back to their usual strong color. His voice is strong as well. "I'm not some feeble old idiot who can't take care of himself. I just had a bad day, and Lily May wasn't here, and—"

"It's okay, Uncle Otis. We'll work this out together. We'll work it all out." Emily lowers the railing and sits on the bed beside him. When she puts her arms around him, he slumps forward, burying his head in her neck. She can feel his silent tears on her skin. "You're coming home to your own home when you're released, and that's where you're going to stay. We're in this together, remember? We take care of one another. We'll get your diabetes back under control, and you'll come home. Okay? Sound good?"

"Sounds good."

She coaxes him back down onto the thin mattress. "Funny, the way things work out for the best. How life falls into place if we just let it. Here I am, all settled in at the cottage, and now my home is a stone's throw from yours. In this together."

Otis relaxes, his muscles settling into rest after his brief exertion. The lines on his face smooth out as his breathing slows.

Emily stands and faces the doctor. "Why don't you admit him, and then you can fill me in on what we need to do when he comes home."

Chapter 22

It's nearly midmorning. Having gone out early, Margaret walked well into the woods, circling the largest of three terraced waterfalls. Sitting on the mossy ground, she lost track of time, leaving behind the words of Chief Edwards and the images of charred remains and blackened glass. Her face and hair glistening with beads of mist from the tumbling waters, she watched her thoughts float by like clouds in a clear sky. But now she's back. Ready to face the reality of her situation. Ready to assess peripheral events as they work their way in toward the center of her life.

She stops at the harvest table against the wall, drawn by the half-finished puzzle surrounded by dozens of scattered pieces. She begins snugging them into place with a rapidity she seldom experiences. As her hands work, her eyes scan the emerging picture and her mind empties of all but the image before her and its component shapes, colors, and patterns. The wind picks up outside, gusting against the house in sudden bursts. She is hazily aware of the room darkening but doesn't stop, her hands in continual motion.

A midwestern farmhouse, three stories high, stands alone against a sky unbroken by bird or cloud or any moving thing. Its clapboards are weathered to a vague red. A bright sun glares off a field of golden grain spreading out behind. The absence of shadows indicates it's straight up noon. Her fingers place together a cluster of pieces, creating a patch of variegated rust and brown. Slowly, what lies beyond the rearmost corner of the house registers.

Two wooden doors with rusted hinges lie side by side, nearly flat against the ground. Raised slightly at their farthest ends, they slope downward, ending at a rough-hewn threshold. At its base, a hollowed patch of bare ground attests to years of use.

The air is suddenly thick and black around her. Panic seizes her. Her heart pounds, her pulse gallops. She gasps for breath, dust swirling around her. Cobwebs cling to her skin and hair. She struggles with her bindings, writhing in the dirt. The coarse twine sears the bruised and bloodied skin of her wrists and ankles as she thrashes. Her face is soaked with sweat and snot and tears.

Her arms and legs sting hotly where her attackers burned her flesh. Their taunts echo in her head. She remembers being twirled around, her head covered by a burlap bag, her hands bound. They poked and punched and jabbed at her with their flaming sticks. The burlap scratched her tender skin as she thrashed her head from side to side, trying desperately to anticipate each strike.

A sudden blow knocked her off her feet and into the small fire they'd built for their hateful work. She screamed and flailed, her right thigh seething with pain. Then someone, mercifully, pulled the sack off her head and beat at the fire with it. Others, their faces blurred, grabbed handfuls of sand and threw them on her and the scattered fire. Someone pulled her roughly to her feet and shoved her toward the storm cellar's gaping doors. She pleaded, fighting them as best she could and digging in her heels. Panicked beyond thought, she screamed for them to stop, to please not put her in there. At the threshold, a pair of tanned and calloused hands looped bailing twine around her ankles and pushed her down the stairs into the shallow cellar. Her head smacked against a wooden beam and nausea welled up in her throat before the darkness sloshed in around her.

With immense force of will, Margaret pulls herself back into her now-dark kitchen. Thunder rumbles overhead as fat raindrops splat against the windows. She is grateful for the sounds and smells of this summer storm, giving her something to focus on as she shakes loose the remnants of the childhood memory.

She moves to the old Morris chair and sits, seeking the sturdiness of its solid frame and the comfort of its cushioned seat. Leaning back, resting her arms on the chair's wide arms, staring out the window at the rain, she lets herself revisit those dark days.

Three days and nights, she lay trapped in that cellar—burned, bruised, and bloodied. Three days and nights, she floated between empty sleep and pain-soaked semi-consciousness, her prison alive with dark rustlings and scratchings. For two days and nights, she waited to be found. On the last night and day, she begged for it to end. Only nine years old and face-to-face with mortality, she wondered what death would feel like when it finally came. She tried to call out so it could find her, but the searing pain in her head sent her into vomiting spasms, and she slipped into unconsciousness.

The rain is heavy now, running down the windowpanes, blurring the world outside. Sophia and Grace have come to sit on either side of her chair, watchful, wary.

"It's okay, girls," she says softly. "I'm all right. Just need to let this come."

At that, the two lie down, settling like bookends flanking her chair.

"Just kids being kids," the chief of police said. "No need to ruin their young lives just because they took things too far. No need to get the law involved at all." She'd heard him talking to her mother and the doctor in the hall outside her bedroom. "We make a big deal about it and they'll pick on her again, keep on picking on her. You don't want that for her, do you? Best for her if we just leave them to their parents and you keep a closer eye on her."

Her mother came into her room, and they both heard the chief say to the doctor, "Kids have been picking on the strange ones since the beginning of time and will go on doing it 'til hell freezes. Best to teach her to keep her mouth shut and keep out of sight. Nothing we can do. It's just the way things are."

When her mother sat down beside her, her fragile frame barely jostled the bed springs. She lay her hand on Margaret's forehead. "I'm so sorry, my sweet. I'm so sorry they hurt you." She kissed her daughter's cheek and quietly wept. "Three days. I was worried sick." Then, suddenly, she straightened, wiped her face with both hands, and said firmly, "Best to put it behind us, Maggie. Best to forget about it. Best to forget all about it."

And that had been that.

Nine years old, bullied and battered and left locked in a root cellar for three days by a group of kids who were bigger and older than she was ... and that was that.

Tears slip down Margaret's cheeks. "Sweet child," she says aloud. "Nobody was there for you. Nobody was able to be there for you." She pauses. "But I'm here for you now."

With these words, she holds her child-self in her arms, a treasured lullaby pouring from her. Sophia and Grace rise to rest their golden heads on her lap. A boom of thunder reverberates through the ground, followed quickly by another. Lightning brightens the walls around her in a series of intermittent flashes. A sharp crack splits the air, but neither she nor her companions move.

"'Sweet, sweet, sweet be your slumbers. Peace, peace, peace fill your heart. I am here. I am near. Holding you. Loving you. I am here. Never fear. For never shall we part.'"

The phone rings, and the answering machine clicks on. As she sings the final refrain, John Longfeather's unhurried voice wafts out of the machine and into the room. "Full moon tomorrow night. Pick you up at six."

Margaret smiles as wind and rain lash at the windows and the outer walls creak with each watery gust.

Chapter 23

Emily awakens to a jarring crack of thunder. Lightning flickers dimly around her bedroom despite the drawn curtains. She scowls at the glowing red digits on the clock as the events of yesterday wash back into her mind.

"Otis," she says aloud as she sits up. Then she remembers he's safely in a hospital bed with a promised full recovery.

Heavy and sluggish, her body is slow to waken. Another thunder crack quickens her heartbeat, and she fights the urge to burrow beneath the covers until the storm passes. Instead, she gets out of bed and pads barefooted toward the kitchen. Thunder again crashes, followed by twin flashes of lightning that dance around eerily, as if chasing one another in the semidarkness of the living room and kitchen. Ten thirty on a late August morning, and the sky outside is nearly black. She turns on a table lamp and draws the drapes over the French doors. As she heads for the kitchen windows to close the curtains there, she hears a car pull into the yard. A moment's hope that it might be Ned is dashed by the realization that it's the sound of a small car's engine and not his rugged SUV. He'd left her off in the wee hours and raced away on a rescue call. He said he wouldn't be back in touch before dark. As she looks out the window, she says to herself, "Real dark, that is."

A green car sits in the yard. "Shit." Emily ducks down. "No. Please. Not her. Not now!"

She backs away from the window. Her mother probably didn't see her with all the rain and wind, she reasons. She reaches for the doorknob to make sure it's locked. A bolt of lightning zigzags down the blackened sky as another violent crack stops her in midcrouch. Out the window of the door, the entire yard and driveway are lit by a too-white brightness. Inside the car, her mother's face is turned toward her, a grotesque mask of stark panic. Emily rushes out. Squinting against the driving rain, she splashes through deepening puddles of muddy water. She tugs at the passenger side door handle as her body lunges to jump inside, but the handle doesn't give and the door doesn't budge. She slams against the side of the car. Through the rain-blurred window, she can make out the outline of her mother's frozen face, her hands gripping the steering wheel.

"It's locked, Mother. Let me in."

Her mother doesn't move.

"Mother. Let me in."

Still, no movement.

"Unlock the door. Let me in. Or slide over here and we can run inside the house together. Mother!"

She's shouting, her voice sharp and commanding. She jiggles the door handle up and down. Her mother's head shakes back and forth in a frenzied no. She says something Emily can't make out.

Thunder booms and the yard lights up in a purple whiteness. Emily jumps.

"Mom!" she screams. "Let me in."

She flicks the door handle up and down again, and hears a thudded click as the door comes open in her hand. She's nearly knocked off balance by the suddenness. She jumps into the seat and slams the door.

"You're soaking wet." Her mother's voice is tinged with hysteria, yet there's a note of reprimand in the statement.

Emily bristles, but catches herself. She understands her mother's heightened state and chooses not to react defensively. Instead, she laughs good-naturedly and says, "So I am. I guess I won't need a morning shower now."

Her mother's shoulders lower slightly as her mouth opens to respond, then closes.

The air inside the car is thick. Emily's tightly sprung curls drip heavily down her chest and back, onto her sodden T-shirt and cotton shorts. Goose bumps rise along her arms and mud-spattered legs as a chill ripples through her body.

"You're shivering," her mother says. She cranks up the heat until it's blasting on them both. In the steamy interior, sweat blossoms and flushes both their faces. The outside world feels distant and muffled. "You're dripping all over my seat cover. You'll—"

"The seat cover will survive, Mother. Would you rather I'd left you out here alone?" More gently, she adds, "I know how you feel about thunderstorms."

Her mother again closes her mouth and settles back against the seat, looking at the rain-blurred windshield. "The safest place, they say, is inside a car." She repeats the words, as if this mantra might settle her frenzied nerves.

They sit in stifling silence until Emily speaks.

"I now know why you feel the way you do about them." It's almost a whisper, but even with the sound of the heater, her mother straightens and looks over at her.

"What do you think you know?" There's a hard note of defiance in her voice, a dangerous challenge.

Emily hesitates then plunges forward. "I know about the fire. I know everything."

The rain suddenly stops. They both lean forward, peering out the windshield and up at the gray but brightening sky. The wind still whips the trees wildly as retreating thunderclouds race away and lightning flashes in the distance. A soft rumbling sends waves of shimmering vibrations back through the ground.

"You know nothing," her mother finally says as she turns off the ignition. She climbs out of the car, slamming the door, and walks quickly toward Emily's front door.

Emily sits for a moment in the sticky, heavy air, then gets out and follows her mother inside.

Janet has removed her shoes and coat and is slowly circling the living area, taking in every detail from furniture to wall color to the painting over the fireplace. There, she stops briefly, studying it. She touches the little heron beneath it on the mantelpiece, then walks around the sofa toward the French doors. Without asking, she yanks back the drapes and looks out onto the porch and garden beyond.

After wiping her feet with a dishtowel, Emily puts on the kettle and crosses the small cottage to her bedroom. In the adjoining bathroom, she drops her wet clothes into the tub and then changes into a dry tank top and loose linen pants. Her mind sinks into a blank stupor. As she slips her feet into a pair of sandals, she gently blots her hair with a thick bath towel. She straightens the bedcovers and folds the clothes she dropped in the corner before crawling into bed at two in the morning. She's stalling, avoiding going back out into the stony silence that awaits her in the living room. The whistling teakettle screams, *Get out here and deal, if not with her, then with me!*

"The place looks nice." Her mother's raised voice, pitched above the whining kettle, startles her as she crosses to the kitchen. That it's a compliment is even more surprising.

Before she can respond, her mother says, "Putting your inheritance to good use. Who'd you have do it?"

Ah, the rub, Emily thinks but doesn't say aloud. Instead, she tends to the kettle with a clattering of cups and saucers and spoons. She rattles around in a drawer for a knife and slices an apple and a lemon. She divides the apple wedges into two bowls and sprinkles them with lemon juice and cinnamon. She gives a handful of almonds a rough chop and tosses them on top. Placing both bowls, an open jar of granola, and a carton of yogurt on the counter, she plops down serving spoons between them. She fans lemon slices on a saucer and sets out a jar of honey and a tin of assorted tea bags. After pouring hot water into both cups, she walks around to the other side of the counter and sits on one of the bar stools.

"Tea?" is all she says as she dips a tea ball of jasmine green in her cup. She knows her mother never eats breakfast and usually lives for most of the day on black coffee, but it's close enough to noon that she might agree to have a little something.

As her mother makes no move to join her, Emily realizes with interest and a hint of satisfaction that it doesn't matter, one way or the other, whether or not her mother chooses to eat.

"Well, maybe just a bite or two," she says. "You know I don't eat much before dinnertime." Her mother slides onto the farthest stool, leaving one between them, and reaches for her bowl and cup. "No coffee?"

"Instant." Emily starts eating without looking at her.

Her mother fingers through the selection of tea bags and chooses a packet. As she rips open the foil wrapper and bobs the tea bag in the steaming water, she looks over at her daughter. "Not your usual gooey donut or slathered bagel for breakfast?"

"Nope." Emily stifles the urge to engage.

"The place really does look good. You've always had a knack. No matter where we ended up, you always managed to spruce it up. You remember how I used to call you my Little Susie Homemaker?"

The words sting. She does remember the nickname. And she remembers the stab of criticism hidden beneath her mother's laughing delivery every time she said those words. The true message was always clearly conveyed by her tone.

She sets her spoon in her bowl and looks at her mother, who has picked up an apple wedge tipped with yogurt. "I remember. And I remember that you never meant it as a compliment."

"Oh, for goodness sakes, Emily. Why must you take everything I say and make an issue of it? I can't say anything without you giving me one of your sour looks and a gross misinterpretation of my intent. Can't we have a simple conversation? Just once?" Shaking her head, she turns toward the kitchen window.

"You're right. We need to have a conversation. But it needs to be much deeper than superficial chitchat." She pauses, considering her words. "Don't get me wrong, I like that you like my place." Another pause. She suddenly feels small and vulnerable. "You're my mother and that matters to me. But there's all this forbidden territory we're not allowed to enter. We need to go there, Mother. *I* need to go there."

"Oh, Em. There's no need to go all melodramatic on me. Why can't we have a peaceful visit without you getting emotional?"

Tears burn. Her lower lip quivers as she struggles to regain her sense of self. Although her heartbeat quickens and her mouth goes dry, she plunges forward. "For once in my life, could you please not shut down the conversation with dismissive comments like that? I'm not being melodramatic. Wanting to know things about my own past from my own mother is not unreasonable. Yes, I have emotions, and I wish you'd stop trying to make me feel like that's a bad thing. A weakness!" Emily allows the tears to flow. "I deserve to know my own history. This is emotional territory."

A renewal of her earlier resolve spreads through her as she speaks, and she sits up taller. As her mother turns back toward her, Emily looks boldly into her gray eyes. For a flicker of an instant, she thinks she sees resignation there before her mother turns away again.

"What you think of as 'your' history is my personal business."

Emily stares at the back of her mother's head, noting absently the fine streaks of gray within the black. "I need to know the parts that are mine. I need to know everything that pertains directly to me. That's my personal business. Can't you see that?"

Her mother sighs but doesn't answer.

Expecting no further response, Emily plows ahead. "I didn't even know that the cellar hole across the woods was our house. I didn't know about the fire that almost killed us. Or that a thunderstorm caused it. I didn't know about your—"

"Stop it, Emily Jane. I'm not going there with you. Not now. Not ever. If you're trying to humiliate me, it's not going to work." Her mother slides off the stool and circles into the living room.

"Humiliate you? What makes you—"

Janet whirls to face her. "Enough! I don't know what that old man has been telling you, but it's nobody's business but mine. When I get my hands on … When … He agreed not to—"

"Don't try to turn this into something about Otis and some

unreasonable promise you exacted from him and Lily May way back when. He didn't mean to tell me. It slipped out. And I had to coax him to go on. He was torn. He didn't want to betray you, but he couldn't leave me hanging with questions when he knew the answers. For the first time in my life, some things started to make sense. But—"

"He had no right." Her mother is screaming now, her hands shaking, her face reddening. "I came here because I thought he might need me. That you might need help. But, silly me, I see you have everything under control. You and he are all kinds of cozy and sharing little intimacies at my expense."

"Oh, come on! You make it sound like—"

Emily's cell phone rings. She grabs it from the counter, planning to send the call to voice mail. But it's Ned. She stops. It rings again in her hand. She's frozen, trapped in this moment between her need to engage with her mother and her desire to hear his voice.

"Take your call." Her mother heads for the door, snatching her coat and purse from the row of wall hooks.

"No. We need to finish this." The phone keeps ringing in her hand. "Don't leave like this. Again!"

Her mother stops just as she's opened the door. She stands with her back to Emily, her coat thrown over her arm. The phone stops ringing.

"Please," Emily says, her voice barely audible. As she sets the phone back on the counter, a tinkling sound tells her there's a voice-mail message waiting.

Her mother straightens but remains with her back toward her daughter. "What's your plan for Otis?" She turns, her demeanor polite but distant. "I planned on staying for a week or so, no need to change that now."

"My plan was to shop for groceries after I check the garden and see what's ready to be picked. He should be released tomorrow, so I have meetings scheduled at the hospital with the diabetes educator and the visiting nurse coordinator for this afternoon at 3:30 and 4:30."

"All right. I'm going to put my things away in the spare room over there and then I'll go to the hospital to see him."

"Please don't—"

"I won't say anything. He'll never know I know."

"I don't think more secret keeping will—"

"Emily. Quit while you're ahead. I'm staying. I'm not going to give Otis a hard time. Let's leave it at that, shall we?"

"Okay."

"I'll be back to clean, and I'll come to the appointments as well. Then we'll both know what to expect and what to do. It may be time for a nursing home."

"No!" Emily takes a breath and softens her tone. "It's not, I assure you."

There will be no relief from their impasse anytime soon, but she recognizes a mild sense of accomplishment. She didn't back down when things got tense. She stayed engaged in the face of her greatest challenge—confrontation. She said some things out loud that she'd never imagined she could. And the walls hadn't fallen down around them.

"Truce?" her mother says unexpectedly.

They stand looking at each other.

"Truce."

Each nods and turns away.

"For now," her mother adds, and closes the door behind her.

Looking at the statue of the blue heron on the mantelpiece, Emily takes another deep breath, then she carries her phone to the sofa and settles in to listen to Ned's message. As she's hoped, he's on his way home from the rescue site. She calls, and he answers on the second ring. She leans back into the sofa cushions as substitute for the comfort of his actual presence.

"How you doing?" he asks.

"Good now. I'm glad to hear your rescue had a happy ending."

"Did you get some sleep?"

"I'd still be sleeping if a thunderstorm hadn't woken me."

"You needed it. First, the shock with Otis and then a late night at the hospital."

"Speaking of which, you were there too and then had to run

off to work. This is becoming the pattern. Maybe you need to stay away from me. I'm a jinx or something."

"Are you trying to get rid of me and let me down easy?"

"Don't even think that. But your life would be a lot more restful if you hadn't met me."

"But so much less interesting!"

Emily is smiling. "Interesting is good. Yes?"

"Interesting is very good." He laughs. "So, will you be at the hospital tonight or can I take you to dinner? A friend of mine just opened a restaurant in York. Her seafood dishes are pretty much food for the gods."

"I'd love to go. My mother showed up today and plans on helping me get everything ready for Otis's homecoming. So, I can't think of anything I'd like better than an evening out."

"You sure? You wouldn't rather spend time with your mother?"

"God, no!" It's out before she realizes what she's saying. Her next thought is, *What will he think of me?* "Long story, but we're better off staying out of each other's way just now," she offers in explanation.

"Seven good for you?"

"Perfect." She clicks off and stretches. "Thank God for your appearance in my life at this moment, Ned Burrows. If I could, I'd be whistling right now!"

Chapter 24

Margaret steps out into the backyard as the storm rumbles off toward the south. The girls slip past her and run down the hill. Strands of gray hang from the belly-heavy clouds racing away. Sunshine breaks free of a cloud mass shaped like a woman's head with billowing hair. She smiles. It reminds her of one of her father's paintings—an ordinary old woman, her deeply pocked face a spiderweb of wrinkles. Her dark eyes held the weight and wisdom of the world. Her gray hair fell loosely, concealing her torso but for a simple neckline of coarse cloth. Backlit by a setting sun, the woman was transformed by her father's brush into an iconic figure.

How she missed that face, now hidden away in a private collection. She'd wanted to keep all his works to herself—to have her father's brilliance if not his presence around her always. But she had grown to realize they belonged in museums for everyone's pleasure.

The idea for a philanthropic foundation had come to her on just such a day as this—perhaps on this very spot. She'd allowed a few paintings to sell and was amazed at the staggering sums they fetched. That money had funded the Vivien & Maxwell Meader Foundation.

"Margaret? Yoo-hoo." A high-pitched voice rounds the corner of the house just before a trio of women in boots and bright rain slickers appears. Margaret waves them over.

"Oh, Margaret," says Betsy Frank, town clerk and distant neighbor. She stands appraising the remains of the shed, nodding her head and clucking with concern. "When I heard about this, I was so upset! Did you lose everything?"

"Pretty much, I'm afraid."

"All your lovely work. I'm so sorry. They should throw the book at the kid who did it. I know your pieces are prized in Boston and New York. His whole family could never make restitution for that kind of loss. Your art, your time, your materials. It's a crying shame."

"I had just sent off a couple of shipments, so there wasn't as much here as might have been."

"Yes, but there's your materials. I know you gather all year long for the wood and plant dyes for your frames."

"Well, Mother Nature will continue to provide. There's no end to her generous supply."

"Of course, you'd look at it like that. Some things never change." Betsy laughs, a musical sound, and turns to her two companions. "This woman has put up with more grief from some of the folks around here than any soul should have to. Unflappable is the word for her."

She looks back at Margaret. "This is my sister Liz and our friend Donna. We were down to the flea markets in Barnstead yesterday, and there was a psychic there who was phonier than a three-dollar bill. Complete charlatan! I told the girls that I know someone who's truly psychic. Then, as we drove past your road on our way into town, I thought we might stop in and check out the fire damage and see if maybe you would give one or all of us a *real* reading." She stops and takes in a breath. "Figure it's best to come right out and ask. Nothing to lose. Living up to my last name. Frank!"

Margaret chuckles. "That you are, Betsy, and it's refreshing. But, you know I don't do what you'd call 'readings.' Sometimes I can answer a question or two when we're talking, but I can't conjure information. No tarot cards or crystal balls here. And what does come to me is often not what people are looking to find out." She gives Betsy an earnest look.

"We understand," says Liz, her voice sounding just like her sister's. "But if you don't mind spending a little time with us, maybe something helpful will come up that you can share?"

Betsy laughs again. "No pressure, of course."

"Well, since you're dressed for it, would you like to take a walk? We can talk as we go." Feeling pleasantly open, Margaret puts her hands into the pockets of her windbreaker and starts down the hill. "My dogs are out on a romp, so don't be surprised if a pair of goldens comes bounding out of nowhere. The storms always get them a little on edge, and so they love a good run afterwards."

She notices Donna slip in between her two friends and pull her open slicker closer around her body. Images tumble: a flash of black and tan fur, a threatening snarl, bared fangs under curled lips. A German shepherd leaps a fence, knocking down a small boy. Blood and spittle fly as the child screams.

She decides not to say anything but knows what she'll do when the dogs show up.

As they walk, Liz says, "I have a question, or rather a situation that has me uptight, and I would like to know your thoughts if you get any. Or maybe it's best to say your 'feelings' on the matter."

As they reach the stream at the bottom of the hill, Margaret stops and picks up a handful of stones. She plops one after the other into the water. The last and largest of them sinks with a hefty *plunk*. Out of the momentary silence that follows, she speaks softly as if to each one privately. "And what if it's not what you want to hear? Are you prepared for that? For honesty?"

Liz is silent. She looks into the swiftly running water and then steps in. It comes up to the rim of her boots and splashes her pant legs. She stares down at her bright yellow feet, blurred and wobbled by the rushing water, transformed into the dancing feet of a child.

"My partner and I are looking at a house," she says. "We've been saving and searching for a long time, and I think this is it. Perfect location. Perfect bones. A little more than perfect price. And even though that price scares me, I want it so badly, I can't stand it. I'm so on edge, I can't sleep. I know there are more pressing issues in the world, but this is what's on my heart right now. If you can offer anything, any help at all … And, yes, I want honesty."

"Is it gray? Stone steps with a floral design on the stair fronts?"

"Yes! That's it. The owner is an artist and built it himself. The steps have tiles along the fronts with alternating yellow and white rose patterns."

"I'm sorry. I don't see you there."

"Oh." Liz remains standing in the water looking at her feet, her animation of a moment ago gone.

Margaret gives her a moment to digest the news, then begins. "There are major problems with the house. Something in the basement, in the foundation, and in the water system. Buying this house would be a dangerous mistake."

Liz looks at her, her eyes registering both her amazement and her deep disappointment.

"Actually, I see you in another house, and I see it happening soon and wrapping up quickly. It's pale yellow with lots of light inside. And … there's a secret passageway your little girl is going to love."

Liz looks as if she's been slapped. Recovering, she says, "I don't have a little girl."

Margaret looks off toward the woods. "Sorry. Sometimes I'm wrong. She must be connected to the house somehow. She literally danced into view. Perhaps she lived there once. Little Rose Marie."

Liz stumbles out of the water toward Margaret. "That's the name I always said I'd give my little girl. Ever since I was little, I've said that." She turns to her sister, who nods vigorously.

"And I always wanted Charlotte," Betsy says. "Rose Marie and Charlotte would be the best of cousins, we always said."

Liz turns back to Margaret. "But I can't have children." Tears slide down her cheeks.

"I am sorry." Margaret looks away.

"I *do* like what you saw, whatever it means. A yellow house?" She starts up the hill toward the woods, then turns back. "No matter what happens, I feel positive now. Hopeful. Thank you."

"Tell your real estate agent to warn the owner. There are serious health hazards lurking in that other house. He should know about them." She looks off to the right and adds, "Though maybe he already does."

"Is it always like this for you?" Donna asks. "So specific?"

"Sometimes. Sometimes not so much." Margaret smiles, then laughs. "Actually, mostly not so much."

They are halfway up the hill when Grace and Sophia appear at the edge of the woods off to their right. Margaret gives a subtle signal with her hand, palm facing downward, and they slow to a gentle prance and approach the women in a wide arc. Margaret hooks her arm through Donna's and moves between her and the dogs. "They will keep their distance. You're safe, don't worry."

When the girls are within ten feet, they lie down in the grass and Margaret introduces them.

Betsy and Liz crouch to pat the girls. Donna remains at Margaret's side. "I can't," she whispers.

"I know. It's all right. Shall we move a bit farther away?"

"Yes, please."

"Grace, Sophia," she says in a conversational tone, pointing toward the house. "Go on home and stay until I get back."

The girls rise up and turn toward the house. With one look back at Margaret, they move away, picking up speed as they go.

Margaret turns to Donna. "Your brother?"

Donna's surprise settles into acceptance. "Yes. Sammie. When he was four. It left him with horrific scars, but I was the one who grew up with a fear of dogs. I feel so foolish. My rational mind can see that your dogs are harmless, but …" Her body is trembling, her breathing fast and shallow.

Still linked arm and arm, Margaret pats the younger woman's hand. She walks at a leisurely pace, maneuvering Donna to match her easy stride and the slow rhythm of her own breath.

"You witnessed a vicious attack on your little brother when you were very small yourself. Of course, it stays with you. Your reaction just now was visceral. That response resides in your body, waiting to be triggered by the sight of a dog coming toward you. Today it was two dogs. It's your body's wisdom at work protecting you."

They walk for a while in silence. Up ahead, Liz stops and points at the sky to the west. "A rainbow."

"It's a double rainbow!" Betsy cries out. "Double good luck."

"Then maybe it's time I asked you my question." Donna looks toward the fading rainbows, then back at Margaret. She opens her mouth, closes it, then opens it again. "It's about Sammie."

Margaret waits.

"He disappeared seventeen years ago. He was twenty-three. By then we called him Sam. After graduate school, he decided to see the country from the back of a motorcycle, documenting his travels as he went. He took off with a backpack, a bedroll, a camera, and a journal." Donna again stops, her already fragile reserves dissolving.

"For the first few months, we received postcards and a few letters with photos enclosed. Then they stopped abruptly. The last one came from New Mexico. My folks didn't get concerned for a while. He was a grown man with a thirst for adventure. But when four more months passed, they began searching. They even hired a detective after a year. But he could find no trace."

Margaret feels nothing. No images come. No words form in her mouth. Nothing.

"Anything you can give me. Anything," Donna says, her words barely audible.

Margaret is about to tell her the stark empty truth. But as she opens her mouth, a sharp pain sizzles through her head, followed by a blinding image. Like an overexposed photograph, a scene presents itself.

Clean white bones lie scattered in the sand. A half-buried skull juts out beside a prickly pear cactus bright with desert blooms. Beyond it, a sheer wall of red rock rises up into an unbroken blue sky. At its base, the sun glints off the silver chrome of a fender wedged beneath a boulder.

"What does your heart tell you?" she asks softly.

"That he's not coming back." Tears wet Donna's cheeks. "That

… he's dead." She speaks strongly for the first time.

"The heart knows. Saying it out loud is the beginning of healing."

Donna straightens, her eyes searching the sky. "Can you tell me what you've seen?" She speaks without looking at Margaret.

Margaret watches her closely, until the tension in the younger woman's body resolves into a lightness of being. Now she's ready to hear what Margaret has to tell her.

"It was an accident. He was there and then he was gone. He was happy. Doing what he wanted to do."

"So, he didn't suffer?"

"No. But you and your family have. For all these years, you've carried this unbearable grief, each in your own way. This not knowing has taken a toll, and it's time for the suffering to end. He would want that for you. Don't you think?"

"Yes."

They have reached the edge of the woods, and as they step inside, their world turns lush and green. The sun filters down through still dripping branches. A flickering of bird wings and snippets of song accompany them as they move deeper into the natural world. Liz's and Betsy's voices, just up ahead, drift back to them.

"He's in Arizona," Margaret says. "I can tell you where to go."

"What will I find?"

"His bones and his bike and belongings."

They walk a ways in silence.

"Somehow that isn't what I expected you to say. I don't know what I thought."

"It's beautiful there. Desert. Red rocks and earth. He loved it. You can bring him home or have a ceremony there. Or both. You'll know what to do."

"I'll go to my mom and dad's tonight and tell them in person."

"Will you tell them how you know? Will they be able to accept this?"

"I don't know how they'll take it. I had a brief thought not to tell them until I go out and find him. But that wouldn't be fair. They're strong. Even if they're skeptical, they'll want to be there with me. For me. And for him."

Liz's and Betsy's voices rise in excitement above the sound of splashing waters.

Donna stops abruptly and hugs Margaret. "I don't know how to thank you. You don't know what this means to me. Or maybe you do." For the first time, Donna laughs as she squeezes Margaret tighter. "What's up ahead?"

"They've found the smallest of three waterfalls in these woods. I think you'll find it quite enchanting."

Donna hurries forward, leaving Margaret momentarily alone. The forest around her is fragrant and alive. She closes her eyes and listens.

"Margaret!" Betsy calls out as she rounds the curve in the path. She's come back for Margaret. "I've never been up here before. It's like a fantasy world. I half expect to see fairies peeking out from behind the rocks and ferns." Her cheeks are pink and shining. When she reaches Margaret, she turns and they walk together toward the sound of water.

"Thank you, Margaret. My sister and my friend are both floating. I couldn't have asked for anything more of this day."

They stop when the falls come into view, and Betsy looks carefully at Margaret. "Are you okay? I would think it must be tiring—exhausting, really—doing what you do."

"It can be, but I'm fine." As Betsy turns back to the falls, Margaret adds, "Thanks for asking, though."

"Look at the two of them. They look so serene." Betsy takes a step toward the others but halts abruptly. "Other wise. That's what you are. The phrase is perfect for you on so many levels. Unflappable and other wise!"

"Interesting." Margaret takes both of Betsy's hands in hers. "And the answer to *your* question—the one you didn't ask—is yes."

"What?"

"Yes, Carl will get a clean bill of health next visit. All clear. No cancer."

"Oh, my God! Margaret!" Betsy bends forward, hugging herself and weeping.

Margaret places her hand between Betsy's shoulder blades.

"I couldn't keep a thing like that to myself, now, could I?" She is grinning.

"I wouldn't have dared ask that one. I wouldn't put you on the spot to have to break that kind of news if it were bad."

"I know. Another reason I'm glad I'm able to tell you. You've both been through enough. Maybe now you'll do some of those 'someday' things you've been putting off."

"Yes. If there's any gift in cancer, it's that—a reminder that life is to be lived fully. Now."

A shaft of sunlight shifts and widens, illuminating the entire basin at the foot of the falls. The water cascades down a series of terraced embankments, tumbling over successive boulders before emptying into this clear bowl of sparkling liquid light. A fine mist rises off the surface in a dance of shimmering rainbows.

The four women gather together and fall silent, each immersed in her own moment of grace.

Chapter 25

At 6:25, Emily steps out of the shower and listens. Nothing. Her imagination, she decides, piqued by anticipation for her dinner date with Ned.

She removes her shower cap and shakes loose her auburn curls. The steam in the room can only improve upon them, and so she takes her time patting her body dry. She walks naked into her bedroom and opens her closet door. As she pulls out the simple peach sundress she intends to wear, the full skirt of the green one hanging beside it flairs out with a dramatic swoosh. She holds it up appraisingly. Thin straps. Fitted scoop-neck bodice. Voluminous skirt with attached petticoat. The perfect shade of green to complement her coloring. In spite of its price tag, she'd bought it before leaving Boston as a naughty indulgence to tuck away for a special occasion.

She carries it to the full-length mirror and holds it up in front of her. Smiling, she knows she wants Ned to see her in it. Frowning, she gives her practical side its head. *You have no idea what this restaurant is like. You don't want to overdress and make him uncomfortable, do you?*

She grabs her phone to find that an online critique of the

restaurant describes it as "on the upscale side of casual."

"Well, little green dress. Looks like you're on." She laughs at herself as she tosses it onto the bed. As another thought strikes her, she rushes back into the closet and rummages through her shoeboxes. "Yes!" she yelps as she pulls out the sandals she bought at the end of last summer. Flat, strappy, feminine sandals in turquoise and green. The perfect green! Serendipity.

Feeling almost giddy, Emily hums as she dresses and applies a touch of makeup—eyes, cheeks, and lips.

Pulling out a small clutch purse, she drops her phone inside and heads to the kitchen.

"Well, look at you!"

Emily nearly drops the purse at the sound of her mother's voice. Sitting in an armchair, Janet Donne looks over her daughter's attire with an approving nod.

"What are—" Emily twirls toward the kitchen window at the sound of Ned's SUV pulling into the drive.

"Looks like I'm going to get to meet someone special."

"We're going out to dinner. He's—"

Emily is cut off by the knock on the door. She opens it and remains standing on the threshold so Ned can't see inside. "Hi." For a moment, she stays where she is, looking into his handsome face and blue eyes, unable to move. Then, all awkwardness and embarrassment, she regains herself and steps back, beckoning him in with the sweep of her arm. "Almost ready," she finally manages. "This is my mother, Janet Donne. This is Ned, Mother. Ned Burrows."

"Hello, Mrs. Donne. Nice to meet you." Ned takes several long strides across the room, holding out his hand to shake hers.

Janet stays where she is, offering her hand at the last moment as he reaches her. "I'm afraid I've interrupted the beginnings of a date. And a rather special one, I'd say, from the look of my daughter. Emily, you didn't mention you were going out tonight."

Emily says nothing, expecting her mother to leave. But Janet stays where she is.

Though it lasts only seconds, the silence builds to a crescendo in

Emily's mind. Having her mother in the same room with Ned and their blossoming relationship is too much. Beyond disconcerting, it feels debilitating, and this realization has her flushing with embarrassment. She turns toward the kitchen counter, picking up her everyday bag and fumbling inside it for what she needs. She can feel herself closing down—the tunnel vision setting in, the sensation of being underwater taking over, expanding. And then Margaret's words flow into her mind, the words she spoke on the night Emily met Ned. The night the little boy was lost in the woods.

Close your eyes. Just breathe. Don't think about anything but the air coming in and the air going out. Your body knowing exactly what to do, how to take in the air and let out the air. Just. Simply. Breathing.

Margaret's soothing voice is inside her head, her easy breathing showing her the way, filling up and emptying, until Emily knows she can open her eyes and she'll find herself standing steadily on both feet, able to carry on.

"I'm sorry, Mother. I thought I told you earlier today when you said you were going to bed early." She transfers her wallet and lipstick from her everyday bag to the bright yellow clutch and then turns around.

Mercifully, Ned asks after Otis, and Janet fills him in. Emily excuses herself and hurries to her room. Standing with her back against the closed door, she hears her mother call out that she's leaving and will see her in the morning. As the front door closes, Emily straightens and walks to the mirror. She smiles in surprise. "None the worse for wear," she says under her breath. Her outward appearance reveals no hint of her inner turmoil of moments ago. With a final smoothing of her skirt and pat of her hair, she joins Ned in the living room.

As he stands looking at her, lips slightly parted in a pleasant smile, she has a chance to take in the totality of him. A shock of blond hair grazes his forehead just above those pale-blue eyes. His face is deeply tanned, open, and handsome. He's wearing a short-sleeved shirt of cerulean blue and a pair of cream-colored slacks. The silence in the room now feels comfortable, absolutely right.

OTHER WISE   141

"You look ..." He lets out a long breath. "Really nice." His face reddens slightly as if he's not sure he's said the right thing. "I mean, you look beautiful. You really do."

"Thank you. You look ... rather nice yourself." She smiles, feeling at once shy and self-assured in assessing their mutual attraction.

"Ready?" he asks.

"Just one thing," she says, as she again runs into the bedroom. As she scoops up a light turquoise shawl, she glances one last time at the mirror, pleased at the radiant glow to her cheeks. Tapping the closet door closed, she quickly surveys her room and snaps on the bedside lamp.

Ned nods at the shawl over her arm, "Good idea, there's bound to be a sea breeze."

He opens the door and then guides her to his SUV, his fingertips placed gently on the small of her back.

Though famished, she wonders if she'll be able to eat. Inside and outside, she's smiling.

ॐॐ

Over wine and a shared appetizer of crab cakes on a bed of mixed spring greens, Emily and Ned discuss the restaurant and his friend Jacquie's swift rise to local fame as a chef and entrepreneur. Emily is secretly relieved to learn that the two grew up together, their mothers being best of friends. She laughs at herself, aware that it's been a long time since she's felt even an inkling of competitiveness or mild jealousy over a man. A couple of passing waitresses dip by to say hello to Ned. One kisses him lightly on the cheek. He laughs easily with them, and Emily feels a twinge of satisfaction at being the one at his table. *Silly schoolgirl,* she says to herself. *What are you, seventeen?* After a moment's inner silence, she answers herself. *Feels like I very well could be. And I don't mind the feeling one bit, thank you very much.*

"Are you laughing at me?"

She realizes she's grinning again. "No, at myself. Inside joke.

Literally."

During their main course, Jacquie slips out of the kitchen to say hello and see that all is well with their meals. A tall, plain woman with short dark hair and brown eyes, she has an easy, self-possessed air and keen sense of humor. Emily likes her instantly.

"The salmon, everything, is fabulous." She tips her glass at Jacquie. "And your aesthetic is stunning. Elegant simplicity. Perfection. You must be very proud."

"Thank you. I am feeling pretty good. Everything's happened so fast, though, I have to remind myself to pause and take in big gulps of these incredible moments."

"You're closed on Monday, right?" Ned asks. At her nod, he suggests they get together and celebrate her spectacular triumph. "Have a little ritual fire on the beach at my place? Reflect and savor?"

As he says *we,* his gaze includes Emily, and she prays he's inviting her as well. Then, as if to avoid any chance of misunderstanding, he adds, "Is Monday good for you, Emily?" She relaxes her shoulders and says yes.

Ned turns back to Jacquie. "Leave everything to me. You are to do nothing but bring yourself." After a beat, he adds, "And Brian too, of course."

As Jacquie walks away, Emily notes a look of concern flicker across his face. She laughs as her college roommate's words, bounce back to her. *So, what's wrong with him? There's gotta be something wrong. He's too good to be true!*

"What?" Ned asks, laughing as well. "Here you go again, laughing at me, I fear."

"Truth?" she says.

"Yes. I think," he says with a light-hearted smirk.

"My old roommate's words just came back to me. She would say, 'Run, Emmy, run! He's too good to be true!'"

"And? Will you?"

"Run? No. I'm not going anywhere anytime soon."

"Except to the beach Monday night for a fire circle with a few new friends?"

"Except for that."

She looks across the table at him. His eyes shine in the light of the single candle on the table, perfectly set off by the blue of his shirt. They finish eating without another word. Her senses sharpened, Emily is lost in the experience of the moment. The taste of the food. The sounds of murmured voices around them. The soft clatter of silverware on plates and the clink of glasses. The salt air scented with garlic and herbs. The roar of the waves out the window. The subtle darkening of the room as evening waxes. And all the while, with their feet lightly touching under the table, she's acutely aware of him.

Over coffee and a shared chocolate confection, he asks if she'd care to take a walk on the beach. Wanting to say, *no let's go right home*, she says, "Yes, that would be lovely."

Ned leaves a generous tip, and she's sure he would do so even if the owner and waitstaff were all strangers. Taking a moment in the restroom, she looks at herself in the mirror and nods. "Life," she says aloud. "Take a big bite."

∽⬧∾

After walking for a mile in silence, they turn to find a nearly full moon rising up out of the water. They stop, and Ned puts his arms around her, pulling her close against him. Then he's kissing her deeply, slowly. Finally, they draw back. She looks up into his face and whispers, "Take me home and stay the night."

He answers by leaning down and kissing her again, this time more hungrily, his right hand finding her left breast. Then he pulls slowly away and straightens. "You sure?"

"I'm sure."

They take their time, now that the formality of an invitation and its acceptance has cleared the air of any questions. Knowing where they're headed frees them to drift and savor and linger, exploring the sensation of anticipation. They continue walking up the beach, stopping from time to time to gaze at the swiftly rising moon. With each sensual pause, they venture further with their hands and mouths.

Emily is grateful for the short ride home. Their proximity in his truck is almost too much to bear. Her breasts feel heavy and full inside the confines of her dress. The wetness between her legs is thick and warm. She wants him more than she's ever wanted a man, and the feeling exhilarates her.

He pulls into the yard and hurries to open her door. As he lifts her down and into his arms, she wraps her legs around him. He carries her into the house, kissing her as he goes, and then presses her against the door as he closes it. Their kisses become primal, his hands clutching her buttocks, hers grasping his head and neck and running up and down his back as their bodies press and rub together wildly.

She unwinds her legs and slides down him. Taking his hands in hers, their lips never separate as she leads him into the bedroom and shuts the door. He unzips her dress and lets it slip to the floor as she unbuttons his shirt. As they step out of their clothes, their kissing slows and they move to the bed. For a moment, they separate. Emily pulls back the covers and climbs onto the bed on her knees. Still in bra and underwear, she pulls him to her. He reaches around and unhooks her bra. The look on his face as he takes in her breasts makes her smile with pleasure. She arches forward, offering them to him, and he leans down and takes a nipple in his mouth, gently pressing her back against the pillows.

She loses herself in the wet hot fire of his mouth on her body and wraps her legs around his naked waist. As his hardness touches her tender inner skin, her body shudders, thrusting to be closer. He enters her, and she reaches up to receive him. Soon their bodies are undulating to a natural pulsing rhythm. Sensation only— flesh against flesh, hardness against softness, warmth and sweet stickiness spreading one to the other and back again. Together they journey down and down and up and up and on into a place of shared forgetfulness and deep remembering. And then ... silence. Total, impenetrable silence.

She's floating. Floating in the darkness and the silence. Her whole body is smiling. Her heart is smiling. Something bigger and wider than this body of hers is smiling. She is no longer this body. She is the smiling. She is the floating. She is the silence.

"Emily." It's not a question. It's the simple calling of her name.

"Ned."

A line comes to mind she once memorized: *How wonderful that I have found the one I wanted, the one I called.*

They lie intertwined, their bodies moist and warm. The dim light of her bedside lamp casts shadows on the walls. Out the window, the moon whitens the woods beyond the house.

Emily rolls on top of him, straddling him, marveling at how comfortable her body feels with this man she's known only a matter of days. Smiling at how unselfconscious she feels with him here in her bed for the very first time, she kisses him softly. He hardens in response. She kisses him again. Raising herself slightly, supporting her body with her hands on either side of him, she looks into his eyes, enjoying the pleasure she sees there. She lowers onto him. As he enters her, she sits up, back arched, hips rocking gently.

This time they take their time. This time they look into each other's eyes. This time there is a lightness, a playfulness to their lovemaking. This time, when it's over, there is no silence or floating or blackness, no deep sense of return. This time, Emily can recall every moment, every movement, as they settle back against the sheets and lie contentedly in each other's arms.

"I probably should go," he says. "You have a full day tomorrow with Otis."

"Not so fast, mister! If you think you're going to sneak out of here now that you've had your way with me ..."

He laughs. "Oh, I haven't even begun to have my way with you. I just don't want to overstay my welcome."

"I would love it if you stayed the night. But ..."

"Nothing could make me want to leave this bed right now. Nothing."

"Not even an emergency call?"

"Phone's off. Got all my 'do not disturb' signs out. I'm all yours."

"How about some wine then? We could go out onto porch and enjoy the moonlight on the garden."

"Sounds delicious."

"Here, just wrap yourself up in this comforter. I'll get the wine and glasses."

Emily slips on a light robe and goes to the kitchen to make up a tray of wine and cheese. When she steps out onto the porch, Ned is standing in the garden with the comforter wrapped loosely around him and up over one shoulder like a toga. A surge of desire ripples through her body.

You've got it bad, girl, she tells herself.

And ain't it a kick! she responds with a wicked grin. She sets the tray on the small porch table and drops her robe as she approaches him. He opens out one arm and pulls her against him, wrapping the comforter around them both.

All heat and hunger again, they lie down on a bed of thyme under the white moon.

Chapter 26

Margaret awakens to the liminal light that sits between deep night and earliest morning. As she swings her legs over the side of the bed, a vivid image startles her. Three contorted faces—features pinched, eyes flashing fire, mouths spewing spittle-laced curses. Then they're gone.

She sighs heavily, giving in to dread. Before John Longfeather picks her up later in the day, there's something she must do. This necessary preamble to the night's ceremony is nonnegotiable. It's time to face them, forgive them, and finish with them once and for all. Or to at least begin that process.

Two hours later, invigorated and fortified by a simple breakfast and a walk in the woods, Margaret climbs into the truck. Pushing resistance aside, she heads for the cluster of outlying farms unofficially known by locals as the Kennedy Compound.

As she turns up the long drive to Agnes Kennedy's house, three mixed-breed dogs dash out of the bordering trees and race along beside her, barking. The driveway ends several feet from the front steps. Five women are seated at a table on the deep front porch.

She assesses the threat level of the dogs and decides that the only true menace here comes from the occupants of the porch. Or rather, from three of the occupants. The other two appear to be in their eighties and seem only curious. As she climbs down from the truck, the dogs back away but keep barking. Agnes Kennedy rises and walks to the top of the steps, glaring down at her.

"Got a lot of nerve coming here. What do you want?" Agnes's voice is nasal and sharply pitched.

Margaret's heart pounds, and every primitive instinct in her body urges her to turn around and put some major distance between this woman and herself. Outwardly, she stands firmly grounded, appearing steady and unafraid. *Unflappable,* she thinks, remembering Betsy's word for her. She smiles inwardly, knowing her stance and demeanor reflect calm assurance and neutrality.

Before she can respond, Ruth Larson, all edges and angles, stomps over to stand beside Agnes, her body rigid, fists clenched. "Yeah. What the hell are you doing here? You gotta know you're not welcome."

Margaret notes how thin she's grown, how gaunt her features.

A third woman crosses to them but hangs back, not speaking. Margaret recognizes her as Nancy Pill, always the quiet one of the group but somehow just as menacing, with a cold, unreadable stare. Her father, Jacob Pill, had famously and frequently called for the town's council to condemn the Meader family as devil worshippers and to run them out of town. He'd proclaimed Margaret's gift of sight the Evil Eye and encouraged the kids of his extended family in their bullying of her.

As she stands in the drive looking up at them, images flicker across her inner eye. She tries to concentrate, to remain present and focused, and not let the images distract her.

"I've come to talk. One of your kids is in serious trouble. Together we can save him a lot of grief. In fact, we can save this whole next generation."

Ruth comes down a step. "We don't trust you as far as we could throw you. I wouldn't be surprised if you didn't burn that building down your own self. You've been doing us dirty, hexing us, since we were kids. You have a lot to answer for, lady. So, you might as well climb your ass back on your broomstick and fly back to where you came from. Which isn't far enough, if you ask me. Nobody here wants to hear anything you have to say."

Margaret centers herself and continues in a strong, clear voice. "A youngster, a mere boy, is looking at juvenile detention. That won't serve anyone any good, least of all him. He was only doing what he thought you'd want him to do. He's paying a high price for acting out of a hate that was passed down to him." Margaret looks straight at Agnes as she says this, aware of the bond between the woman and the grandson who set the fire. "Let's see what we can do to work this out. Let's—"

"Get the fuck out of here! You're up to something, but it ain't gonna' work." Ruth has come down another step and is screaming now, shaking her fist. Agnes takes hold of her arm, but she shakes her off. "And the next time something catches on fire, I hope to God you're inside it!"

Margaret continues to look into Agnes's eyes. She sees a hint of softening there before Agnes turns away at the sound of a feeble voice. "Aggie? Isn't that the Meader girl? She's the one kept me from drowning all those years ago. You shouldn't be yelling at her, Ruthie. Come on up here, girl. Let me look at you."

The seated woman waves a stick-thin arm, beckoning Margaret toward her.

Margaret takes a step toward the porch.

"Shut up, Ma," Ruth snaps. "You're mixed up in your head again. She's not getting anywhere near you. People tend to end up dead around her." She turns back to Margaret, her eyes narrowed. "Her daddy. Her twin. Ches!" She spits out the name. "Her husband from away. What was his name? Joe?" She lets her stinging words hang in the air. "Now get the hell out of here."

The words pierce her, but Margaret maintains the mask of calm and looks again at the woman with a grandson at stake.

Agnes avoids her eyes. "I think you should leave now," she says quietly.

Margaret straightens to her full height. "One of these days we will sit across a table, you and I. We will not become friends but we will settle our differences. We will never have to speak again, and the next generation will be freed from the burdens of a past they didn't create."

"Shut your trap right now!" Ruth turns from Margaret to Agnes. "Don't look her in the eye. She's putting a damn spell on you."

With a renewed sense of strength, Margaret looks hard at Agnes and notes the slight nod of her head. She acknowledges it with her eyes and climbs back into the truck. As she heads down the drive and out onto the blacktop, she feels light, buoyant. She welcomes the flood of warm energy filling her. Smiling, she turns on the radio, and Iris Dement's quirky voice fills the cab, choosing with a delightful twang to "… let the mystery be." Margaret joins in, singing loudly until the last note drops off into a momentary silence. She clicks off the radio and lets the silence sit. Into the space thus created, she says aloud, "A beginning. Face them, forgive them, and be finished with them."

While she realizes the physical work will take time, she knows she has already faced and finished with them energetically. The forgiveness part will take longer. But it only takes one on the other side of the equation to begin the healing process. Agnes Kennedy has everything to gain; her grandson will be the immediate beneficiary. Grandmother love will surely bring her around.

She pulls into the parking lot between the art supply store and Farmer Jay's and sits for a moment in thought. This short trip to the Kennedy place was a necessary prologue to the long journey she will take that night. Before undergoing an honoring ceremony, a purification process has to take place, usually supervised by tribal elders. Margaret realizes she has been guided to walk the forgiveness path as part of this purification. In so doing, she has started to unravel entanglements that bind her to the past. Tonight, she will thank the women of the Longfeather ancestry for their part in this. And she will ask for their continued help with the most difficult part—the forgiveness part.

Faint spots dot the windshield, and as she gets out of the truck, a downpour lets loose on her. As the hard rain hits the hot pavement, it bounces back up. Icy drops splotch the shoulders and back of her shirt as she dashes through the storm. She ducks under an awning and takes in the smell that only a sudden summer rain carries. She is pleased that the showers have begun and hopeful they will run their course by evening, as predicted. With the fire danger already low and the woods well soaked, it will be safe to build a blazing fire when the moon reaches its zenith tonight.

Headed home once her errands are completed, Margaret makes a sudden decision as she passes the road to Emily's cottage. As she makes the right at the fork in the driveway, she can see Ned's vehicle through the trees, parked in front of the cottage. She pulls in beside it, smiling.

Ned answers the door, leaning down to give her a welcome hug.

"I hear Otis is coming home today," she says to Emily as she enters.

"Yes. He's been chomping at the bit to get home and out into his gardens."

"It'll do him a world of good."

"My mother is here, and between the two of us we'll see to his sugars and make sure he doesn't overdo."

Margaret notes the sliver of irritation in Emily's tone as she mentions her mother. She also notes that Ned's presence keeps it a sliver. "I'd like to come by in a few days to see him, but I'll call first. In the meantime, tonight's my visit to Tilson Woods with John. I stopped to see if you have something to include in the honoring bundle for your grandmothers."

Emily looks at her with an odd expression.

"I left a message that I'd be going—"

"Yes. I remember. It's just that you said 'grandmothers,' plural. I don't think about having another grandmother because I never knew my dad's family."

"That's right, we never finished talking about his family that night. We were interrupted." She smiles at Ned and then turns back to Emily. "Why don't you come over in a day or so and we'll talk more?"

Emily hesitates a beat and then says, "That would be nice."

"In the meantime, I'll say a prayer tonight to all the grandmothers, known and unknown, named and unnamed, whether or not they were able to 'grandmother' us. They're in our blood, our DNA. We came through them."

Emily goes to her desk and returns with a small envelope. "I wrote this letter for Grandma Emily and Lily May. And I thought ..." She blushes, looking down and away. "I thought you could place these somewhere up there too." She drops a heart-shaped stone, a seashell, and an acorn into Margaret's palm.

"Good for you. I know this isn't something you're used to or comfortable with."

Emily nods, clearing her throat.

As Margaret turns to go, Ned asks if she got the go ahead to clear up the shed debris and offers his help.

"Yes, but I'll be up all night tonight, so tomorrow is a down day."

"I'll come by day after tomorrow."

"Only for an hour or so. I'll send you packing if you look like you're gonna pitch a tent in the backyard." Laughing, she heads out the door.

Chapter 27

"Okay, okay, I guess I'm outnumbered." Otis agrees good-naturedly to sit at the kitchen table and wait for Janet and Emily to finish preparing lunch.

"You'll get out to that garden soon enough," Janet says, "but you're going to have a proper lunch first. Your sugars look good, and we're going to keep it that way."

"Okay, okay. But I won't be treated like some useless old invalid. I got a bit off track for a while there, but I'm back on now."

Emily bends to look in his eyes. "No one thinks of you as useless or an invalid," she says, her tone firm. "We just think you should ease back into things, that's all. You've been in bed more in the past few days than you probably have in your whole *old* life." She laughs as she stresses the word. "So, humor us and take your time building up to full-blown Otis mode."

Janet sets in front of him a bowl of vegetable soup and a plate with a mound of tuna fish salad surrounded by thick tomato wedges on a bed of mixed greens. "Here you go, *old* man."

"All right, you two, I give up." He slurps a spoonful of soup. "For now."

"Sit," Janet says to Emily, waving at a chair. "I'll serve."

Emily sits. How odd to see her mother smiling and sharing in the banter. How strange to have her here with them at all, and even more so to have her behaving like a storybook version of a mother, serving food to her little family. Emily almost comments but keeps silent instead. Better to enjoy the moment. Better not to think about the next.

"So, what you up to these days, little one, besides taking care of your old uncle?" Otis asks between bites.

"Writing mostly."

"Among other things—" Janet begins.

"Writing what, mostly?" Otis interrupts.

"Yes, what are you writing about, Em?"

"Right now, I have a short story in the works, and a couple of blog posts I—"

"A couple of what?" Otis laughs.

"Blog posts. A blog is a—"

"Blog! Sounds like something decidedly unappetizing."

"It's a contraction of the words *web* and *log*. It's a column, like for a newspaper or magazine, but online. Or as you like to say, 'On the line.' My old boss—that's *old* as in *ex*, not *old* as in *ancient*—asked me if I would post weekly on the museum's website for a small stipend. And that led me to explore blogging. My favorite project is a personal blog for and about writers.

"I'm also checking out MFA programs, but I may just take a more hands-on experiential route for now. I recently attended an artist talk, and the woman said she sought out the best teachers and created her own self-study curriculum. I'd like to apply to a writers' retreat or artist community like the MacDowell Colony, or—" She looks up from her salad to see her mother and uncle sharing a look of amusement. "What?"

"It's just such a treat to see you excited about all this," Otis says.

"That, *and* a new love interest. My, my."

"New love interest?" Otis gives Emily a wink. "Do tell."

"Mother!" Emily flushes.

"I repeat, love interest?" Otis says.

"*New* is the operative word here. So, I'd appreciate not going there right now."

"Ned! Is it Ned?" Otis beams at the thought.

"Okay. I'm going to say this once and then we're going to change the subject. Ned and I have begun seeing each other. I like him and he seems to like me. The rest is yet to be written. That's it."

"Ned's a fine boy. No need to go all hush hush about it. … Oh! I get it. Don't want to jinx things. Okay. Mum's the word." Laughing, he gestures as if zipping his lips.

Emily shakes her head in mock disgust. "He's not a secret. I just don't want to make a big deal about it, that's all." She gives her mother a pointed look and takes her dishes to the sink. "And no acting all weird in front of him or grilling him with questions or, heaven forbid, trying to make clever jokes around him."

"No promises," Otis says, "but I'll do my best." He finishes his soup, his spoon clattering into the empty bowl. "I had no idea what was percolating over there in the cottage, but to watch your eyes light up when you talk about writing, I'd say you're on to something. You never looked that way when you talked about the museum, though you seemed to like it well enough."

He carries his dishes to the sink and turns back to them. "Now, I'll be headed out, if none of my prison guards object." He raises his hand as Janet opens her mouth to speak. "I have to gather some things, and then I'll be right back in to check my sugars. Then, after I work up a sweat in the gardens, I'll check them again. I have no intention of getting all off-balance again. Too little time left on this planet to be spending it in a damn hospital!"

He grabs his hat off the hook by the door and heads outside.

"He's going to be fine," Janet says as she clears the table. "That scare was probably a blessing in disguise."

"I'll get this." Emily takes the salad bowl from her mother's hands. "I'll be heading home in an hour or so to get some work done, so you might as well take this time for yourself."

Instead, Janet takes a cloth and begins to wipe down the table. "I'm glad you're back to your writing. Ever since you could hold a pencil, you've been scribbling your little stories when you weren't nose deep in a book. They say the seeds to who we really are and what we're meant to do can be found in our childhood."

Emily doesn't say anything as she fills the dishpan with soapy water.

"Your eulogy for Lily May brought that all back to me. All your spiral notebooks and the loose-leaf binders you stored them in. I was tempted to read them, but they were your private business, like a diary, so I left them be."

"I wouldn't have minded," Emily says, mustering an air of nonchalance as she plunks the dishes and silverware into the dishpan.

"Well, I didn't know that."

"Well, if you'd just asked—"

"Ifs and buts, Emily. You know what they say about ifs and buts." Janet walks back over to the table.

Emily stiffens. The tone that could always stop a conversation in its tracks.

As if in apology, her mother adds, "*If* it's any consolation, I regret what I did and didn't do to you as a child. And *if* it's any consolation, I wish I could go back and make different choices. Choices that wouldn't have brought another unhappy child into the world."

The plate in Emily's hand slips back into the water. She straightens, resting her wrists on the edge of the dishpan. "Are you saying you regret having me?"

"No, Emily! That's not what I'm saying." Janet sighs. "That didn't come out right, as usual." She takes a breath. "No. I'm saying ... I'm saying I would make choices that would have given you a happier life. I'm saying I know I was a lousy mother."

Emily grips the edge of the counter, steadying herself, taking in the words before turning toward her mother. "I wasn't saying—"

But her mother is gone. The screen door closes with a soft thunk.

Emily leans back against the sink, looking at the door. "Okay, Emily," she says aloud, "speaking of choices, you have two of them here."

Otis pulls open the door and comes in. "Reporting as promised, ma'am." He gives a smart salute. "Do you know where my meter got to?"

As Emily finds the small zippered bag that holds his glucose meter and supplies, Otis sits at the table. "You and your mother make a pretty good team. It's nice to have you together again, even if it's only for a while. I don't know how long she's planning to stick around, but we'll make the most of it while she's here, shall we?"

"I'd like nothing better." She watches as Otis checks his blood sugar level. "What's it say?"

He rises and tosses the test strip and lancet into the trash bin. "Bingo. Right in target range. I'll check it again later, but I'm sure it'll be good. Headed back out, want to join me?"

"I'm going to finish up the dishes. Then I'll be out."

As she watches him stride out the door, his gait that of a much younger man, the thought that she almost lost him hits her again. Dear Otis. Losing Lily May had devastated them both. She isn't ready to let him go too.

As she puts the last dish away in the cupboard, she decides not to go home. Her plans for the afternoon can wait. Otis time is too precious. She grabs her hat and slips her phone in her back pocket.

She finds them down by the water, seated on the bench. Janet turns to her as she approaches. "We were just reminiscing. Remembering back to the very beginnings of these gardens, when this area around the pond was a tangle of invasive weeds."

"Your mother spent day and night out here as a kid, helping me clear and dig and plant and transplant. My constant companion, covered in dirt, head to foot. Toasted to a nice golden brown by the sun, and soaked to the skin and slicked with mud in the rain. A natural little gardener. Until the day she discovered boys! Or maybe I should say they discovered her." Otis chuckles.

"Don't look so surprised, Emily. I was a pretty normal kid, once upon a time. And I loved digging in the dirt. There's nothing like the smell of freshly turned earth." She breathes in deeply, letting her head drop back, and then turns to Otis. "I look forward to helping with the garden for the next few weeks, if you'll have me."

"Nothing would please me more, Chiclet." They both laugh at

the resurrection of this nickname Emily's never heard before.

"Give her a trowel and a box of Chiclets gum," Otis explains, "and she was one happy kid."

Emily wanders to the edge of the water and then wades in slowly, lulled by the sound of their voices tripping over each other in dynamic conversation, with sudden bursts of laughter and gaps of companionable silence filled with the echoes of shared memories. She closes her eyes and is a child again, listening to the voices of the grown-ups in the other room as she falls asleep on the big green sofa in Grandma Emily's living room in the house around the corner that now belongs to strangers.

She opens her eyes, a young woman again, standing in water up to her knees. Was that her father's voice she heard in the mix just now?

She turns around to face them. "What was he like? My father."

Janet's smile disappears. "Oh, Emily. Can't we just …" She stops herself and looks over at Otis, who nods almost imperceptibly, giving her a gentle smile.

She takes a breath and shrugs. "He was handsome as all get out. A movie-star smile, gorgeous green eyes, and that easygoing laugh. Easygoing everything, actually."

"Hmmm," Otis grunts in agreement, grimacing as he looks down at the ground.

"And then, of course, there was his music. When your grandmother gave me 'the talk,'—which truth to tell, really wasn't much of a talk at all—she forgot to say, 'Don't ever fall for a musician.' And, boy, did I fall! Hook, line, and sinker." She pauses before suddenly adding, "Please tell me Ned is tone deaf." Though she laughs as she says this, it's a self-deprecating laugh.

Otis leans forward and rests his forearms on his thighs, his fingers clasped. "He was a good person, Em. A fun-loving, charming-as-all-get-out kid who just couldn't face the hard stuff when it came. The only son of a family who never asked him to take any kind of responsibility." He looks over at Janet before continuing.

"He was never meant to be a family man, but no one can tell that until they're knee-deep into it. He just wasn't equipped. He couldn't be there for Janet, though he loved you both like crazy."

"He loved you," Janet says softly, nodding. "And he tried, for your sake. He *did* try. I'll say that for him."

Emily knows it has taken a lot for her mother to say this. She can see the pain in her gray eyes, the tears welling.

"I'm sorry to make you remember what I know you'd rather not."

"Well, then, why don't we just leave it be?" Janet rises from the bench and turns as if to go.

"Don't, Janet." Otis stops her with his voice. "You've opened the door. Why not walk all the way through? Your daughter needs to know some things about her father. Maybe the telling of it will be of some use to you as well."

"Damn it, Otis! Why do you have to go all wise and sensible?" She punctuates this with a half-hearted laugh.

Emily has never seen her so soft, so vulnerable. So open.

Her mother turns back toward her. "I'll tell you as much as I'm able to right now. And for right now, I'm asking you not to press or question me. I'll do my best to fill in what you need to know over the next few weeks."

"You're not going to take off in the middle of the night, are you? I need to know you're not going to disappear."

Janet opens her mouth, an angry expression flitting across her face and then disappearing. "I suppose I had that coming." She pauses, her lips quivering slightly, her eyes downcast. "All I can say is, I'll do my best to stay put. That's all I can promise."

Emily notes her trembling, her shallow breathiness, her hunched shoulders. "Okay. That's all I can ask."

Janet releases a slight gasp. Of relief? Resignation? Emily is not sure.

Otis rises. "I'm heading up to the house to get a basket. Why don't you two take a little walk? Then you can come back and help me gather up something from the garden for supper." He goes off without waiting for a response.

As they start to walk the path around the pond, Emily's phone signals a message. Torn, she ignores it.

"Take it. It might be Ned. It's okay."

Emily reads the text. "Damn!"

"What?"

"He's been called up north. He'll be gone for two or three days. That's one of the not happy parts of his job. It takes him away at a moment's notice. Game wardens cover a lot of territory here in Maine."

"I suppose saying absence makes the heart grow fonder isn't any help." Again, her mother's tone and manner are soft, available.

"Not hardly, Mother." Emily gives her a half smile. "It's a little too new for that to be a benefit."

"Why don't you give him a call? I'll wait."

"No. He says he'll call later when he can, so he must be tied up."

They walk on without speaking, Emily trying to push aside her disbelief and mistrust. This is not the mother she knows walking beside her. Though not exactly warm, the cold wall is down. But can she trust this mother to stick around? Is this a moment of grace that must be met with blind trust? Or is this one more trap designed to snap shut in the very moment she dares to let go?

Trust. She hears the word as if spoken aloud by someone standing right beside her. The voice sounds like a blending of Margaret's resonant tone and the higher-pitched voice of Grandmother Emily.

"So. How did you meet Dad?"

"College. He was a friend of my roommate's cousin and played on weekends at one of the downtown hangouts."

"What did he play?"

"Lead guitar, keyboard, sometimes drums. He was multitalented. And he had a great voice too. You got your voice from him."

Emily is silent, not wanting to interrupt the dream-like delivery of her mother's story.

"Frankly, I was like a giddy teen around him. I was shocked that he picked me to talk to when he could have had any girl in the room, even those attached to steady boyfriends." She stops talking for a moment. "Like I said, don't ever fall for a musician.

"I dropped out of school when I got pregnant, something I immediately regretted. It took me years to get my degree, one or two courses at a time fit in between work and being a … not-so-terrific mother." Again, she pauses, and Emily keeps her eyes on the path ahead.

"Things began to fall apart when your brother died. We—"

"My brother?" Emily stops, stunned by her mother's words. "I had a brother?"

"Look, Emily. I'm going to keep on walking and keep on talking because that's the only way I can do this. I'm sorry. But it's the only way I can do this."

Janet quickens her pace, head down, hands in her pockets. Emily falls in beside her. Her mind is listening as her mother continues, but she's also hearing the words—*when your brother died*—again and again.

"We named him Jonathan after my dad, and he was almost a year old. He died in his crib right beside our bed while I was sleeping," She delivers this in a monotone. "Danny was out playing a gig, or playing with his …" She stops and shakes her head. "Anyway, I woke to find him …" She stops talking but continues walking. Emily keeps pace without a word.

Suddenly, Janet stops. She turns away from Emily, out toward the water. "SIDS. Sudden Infant Death Syndrome. Healthy and happy. Then gone. Just like that."

As Emily opens her mouth to speak, her mother raises her hand to stop her. "Then there were two miscarriages. And then there was you. And I came apart. And he went away. And the house burned down around us and we went to live with your grandmother and he died in a fiery crash. And that's all I can say about any of it right now."

They stand looking out at the water. Tears slip down Janet's face as Emily stands mute and motionless beside her. A subtle movement off to their right catches her attention. She turns. Across the water, a great blue heron stands looking back at her. Her breath catches in her throat as her own tears come.

Chapter 28

The girls race out to greet John as he pulls into the yard. He drops the tailgate of his truck, and they hop aboard as Margaret sets her backpack in the truck bed.

"All set?" John offers in greeting.

"All set," she responds, knowing they are now entering a time of silence.

The sun is sitting low in the sky when they approach Tilson Woods. John drives past the entrance to the public parking area. About ten miles beyond it, he turns right onto a barely visible single-lane road overgrown with tall grasses, weeds, and scattered saplings. After bouncing along for a couple of miles, a fallen tree blocks farther access, and he stops the truck.

John takes a blanket roll and knapsack from the truck bed as Margret straps on her backpack and bends to tighten her boot laces. Then they head off into the woods, the dogs running ahead of them, noses to the ground.

As they crest the fifth in a succession of steep hills, John stops and Margaret comes up to stand beside him. They are looking down into a deep bowl-shaped hollow as they stand on its tree-lined western rim. The sloping sides are strewn with rocks and lichen-covered boulders, and layered with creeping ground cover and patches of moss. As the bowl bottoms out, a thick grove of trees, too dense to see into, stands like a separate, smaller wood. Thousands of yellow wildflowers form a ring around the perimeter, their heads dancing in the light wind.

John looks at her as if searching her eyes for something, then nods toward the left and begins walking the rim. She follows as they circle the hollow. They reach the eastern side, where the rim dips gently toward the woods at its center.

As they enter the thick stand, the scent of pine mingles with the rich earthiness of the forest floor. They make their way through thick branches until the trees thin out and three massive stones rise up, towering over them a few feet ahead. The Grandmothers. Margaret realizes she would never have found them on her own.

Between each upright stone, there's a two-foot space through which Margaret can see a thicket of smaller trees and tangled undergrowth. John signals for her to step between the centermost Grandmother and the one on the left as he walks to the right. As she does so, she feels as though she's stepping through a veil of silken threads, like cobwebs. She shivers and closes her eyes, and a pair of strong hands come to rest on her shoulders, warming her. For a moment, she thinks John has moved around behind her, but she realizes he is on the other side of the center stone. An ethereal voice fills her mind.

Nana Maggie. The boy child has much to do in this lifetime. You helped to keep him here. I, Mettah-Wa'-Ba-Na, watched over him until you came. I and the Grandmothers send you blessings and grant you deep mahet'maha'twa.

The hands lift. The warmth remains. She opens her eyes and looks up. The spreading branches of a huge maple ahead of her radiate a golden warmth. The air around it tingles visibly with a vibration she can only describe as loving. Her gaze runs down its trunk to the tiny bush standing at its base. One crimson leaf flickers like a flame in the crackling air.

Sophia and Grace stand on either side of her, heads cocked, ears perked, bodies taut. She kneels between them, nuzzling each in turn until they relax their wary stance. Then they circle back to the central Stone and lie down, one on each side.

To the right of the maple, a fan-shaped cluster of dangling roots and clinging clumps of earth thrusts upward from the base of a fallen pine. It forms a hollowed pocket in the earth. She remembers seeing Joey Allen huddled inside it on the night of the search; remembers telling him, "They're coming for you," and then singing the old lullaby. "Sweet, sweet, sweet be your slumbers. Peace, peace, peace fill your heart ..."

Margaret spreads her woven prayer blanket a few feet away from the bloodspot bush smoothing the wrinkles with care. Time has shifted. Time as measured by clocks has dissolved into an unhurried, immeasurable realm of timelessness.

Sitting cross-legged on the blanket, she opens her prayer bundle and lifts the journal she has prepared with poems and prayers, and into which she has placed Emily's envelope. She holds it to her heart and then bows her head and closes her eyes, waiting for John to begin.

She senses movement to her right as he spreads his blanket. Then, the snap of a match, a sharpness in her nostrils, an acrid taste on her tongue. A mingling of lavender, sweet grass, and sage fills the air. A wreath of drifting smoke teases her nose.

She listens as John walks the perimeter, carrying his smudging stick. The forest is alive with sound until the first notes from his flute lift hauntingly into the evening air. All other sounds cease, and she opens her eyes as the purple twilight deepens into an indigo darkness.

Bird chatter resumes, mingling with the rhythmic peep and croak of night songs. John's flute melts into the background, subtly underscoring nature's symphony. She closes her eyes again.

As the final note of the flute hangs in the air, she senses a presence. Then another and another, until the air is alive with murmuring. She smells woodsmoke as crackling, snapping sounds separate themselves out from the cacophony.

She opens her eyes. John smiles at her from across a blazing fire. She follows his gaze upward to meet the round white moon sitting overhead.

"They're here," he says as he lowers himself onto his blanket. "It's time.

"Grandmothers and mothers, sisters, aunts, and daughters. Women through whom I came to walk this walk, I honor you. I thank you.

"I bring Margaret. One you have much blessed, having shared your wisdom ways.

"May we be heard. May we be welcomed. May we be blessed."

The hoot of an owl is accompanied by a warm gush of wind. It swirls and is gone.

John speaks again. "When last I came, it was to find the boy, and there was no time to properly pay respects to you and to the Grandfather Spirit. I have returned to do so with humble heart and true intent.

"May I never give you cause to curse my name. May I be heard. May I be welcomed. May I be blessed. May I be granted deep mahet'maha'twa."

Margaret gazes at the spiraling snakes of light that twist up from the center of the fire into the darkness, her mind oddly empty. A sudden fluttering overhead pulls her gaze upward. Three mottled feathers float down, dance around John's head, and land on his blanket. He gathers them and tucks them into the beaded stitching along the neck of the pouch that hangs at his chest. He nods at her. It's her turn.

"Women of the Long Feather, I thank you. You took me as a young woman into your arms and hearts and taught me much. I am humbled by your generosity of spirit.

"We discovered together that the plants don't sing for me as they do for you. But you showed me that my gifts lay elsewhere."

Margaret smiles as she steps briefly into a memory. An elder speaks as she dips her finger into a bowl of ashes and herbs and then presses it against Margaret's forehead, between the eyes. "Your gifts rest here. Don't hide your special knowing from searching hearts. Trust your sight."

Stepping back into the present, she rises and circles the fire, her feet touching down toe first with each deliberate step. As she begins to chant, John joins her—the masculine answering the call of the feminine. Night sounds swell and diminish, swell and diminish around them.

"And so it is," she calls out as she returns to her blanket.

"And so it must be," John responds.

Margaret holds out an earthen bowl in cupped hands. "Formed from the clay of this good land and fashioned on the wheel by the hands of a friend, I offer you this bowl. In keeping with the tradition of your people, may this empty vessel hold the space into which new energy may flow. May this sacred ground, these ancient roots, this simple bush be ever nourished and enriched by the gifts of Spirit. I keep the gift in motion as it is meant to be."

She kneels before the bush and sets the bowl beneath its umbrella-like canopy of heart-shaped leaves, all green but one. Bending forward, she lifts the solitary blood-red leaf and rubs her cheek along its velvety surface. A stinging vibration buzzes along her cheek. Laughter echoes through and around her.

"Remember, Maggie? Remember the first time?"

She turns in time to see Mattie's back as he runs away. His loose shirt is untucked, rippling out behind him. His bare feet are stained green and caked with mud. Giggling, he darts behind an oak. She blinks and he's back in view, weaving in and out among the mottled trunks of white birch, their hanging curls of bark fluttering in the breeze from his passing. Then he's galloping waist-deep in a patch of ferns.

She follows, calling to him to wait for her. But he keeps on running, laughing and turning back to check her progress.

His blue eyes shining, spittle at the corners of his mouth, a sheen of sweat on his cheeks, a rim of wetness along his tawny hairline, he calls to her, "Remember, Maggie? Remember the first time we ever saw the bush?" He stops running, flushed with excitement. "Remember how you touched it with your cheek like you did just now and then you saw? You saw me. You saw this. Remember, Maggie? Remember how you knew right then what was going to happen?"

Margaret drops to her knees, a terrible aching *no!* forming in her mouth as he turns and runs headlong down the curve of the earth and out of sight.

Tears running down her face, heart thumping, she walks forward. Past the stand of birches. Past the fern-filled clearing. Past the soft and pulpy stump caving in upon itself. And on to the edge of the drop-off.

He's there. A crumpled little heap. His shirt rippling in the breeze. One dirty foot showing, the other tucked up underneath him. His face turned away from her, cradled in the crook of a folded arm. A rivulet of red running down his freckled neck.

Stillness all around.

Then movement along the periphery. Silently they come. The women, encircling him. The grandmothers, chanting an ancient song full of sorrow and loss, redolent with a promise of hope. The eldest kneels, taking up the child in her arms. The others surround her and walk as one toward the woods, a soft lullaby wafting among the trees.

Margaret follows them with her eyes and then looks back to where her brother's broken body still lies upon the ground. A hand squeezes her left shoulder and she looks up. Blinded by the sun, she cannot make out the face of the figure standing over her.

"We'll stay with you until someone comes. We'll be with you through all the days ahead."

Margaret topples forward, screaming out her brother's name.

"There, there, Little One." The voice of a Grandmother, slow in cadence, careful … tender … familiar. "There's nothing you could have done. It was his path to walk."

"Maggie?" It is Mattie's voice and yet not Mattie's voice. Her brother. Her twin. Speaking now in a deep and soothing baritone. A voice equal to her own, balancing her own—the masculine side to her feminine self.

"Yes, Mattie."

"I'm with you still, but now I have a broader view." He laughs, a deep and comforting laugh. "We're so much energy, you know. Think of me as operating on a higher frequency now, but still operating. I was there the night you found Joey Allen. My heart sang for you. You couldn't change my path, Maggie, but you put that little boy back on his. It's time to let go of the guilt. I'm sorry, Maggie mine. Forgive me."

Margaret sits up. "Of course, I forgive you. You were just a little boy."

"Goes both ways, Maggie. If you look at it like that for me, you have to forgive yourself on the same grounds."

"We're a pair, aren't we?"

"That's what Momma used to say. Even when she was so very sad. 'You're a pair, you two. A proper pair of rascals.' Remember, Maggie?"

"I remember."

Margaret senses him pulling away and calls out to him.

She opens her eyes. She is still kneeling by the bush, its red leaf still resting on her palm. Blinking, she looks around. John is deep in prayer. The fire crackles, sending sparks into the darkness. The cool air hints of autumn. Her chest feels light and spacious. And she is smiling.

She returns to her blanket and pulls out the creamy envelope containing Emily's letter and tosses it into the fire. The paper curls and wrinkles, glowing orange and blue as it is consumed.

In a clear strong voice, she recites the poems she's written for the Grandmothers, known and unknown. Then she walks to the edge of the circle where a tiny nest rests on a mossy patch of ground. She places Emily's stone, seashell, and acorn into it, then walks to the fire and lays her handmade journal into the flames.

As she settles back on her blanket, the owl returns to the branch overhead with a fluttering of wings and a soft hoot. A moment later, its call is answered.

Margaret tips her head back, listening to the forest. Then, as if pushed, she falls backward into a velvety blackness, arms and legs flailing.

Just as suddenly, all is still and she is floating in a lavender mist, a delicious warmth enveloping her.

"There, there, sweet Margaret," a gentle voice soothes. "Time to rest."

She wants to speak but can't open her mouth. She tries to open her eyes, but they are too heavy. So deeply tired, she surrenders to the depth of her weariness.

"This is not idleness. This is nourishment—necessity. You must fill your empty cup. Otherwise, you will do more harm than good. Be still now. Rest." The voice, soft and feminine, drifts away beyond hearing.

She dreams she is standing at the top of a hill under an empty sky, looking down into a dusty crater littered with blackened boulders. Beyond it, a series of distant mountains rise toward a far horizon backlit by a setting sun. She picks up a white pebble and tosses it out in front of her. As it arcs downward, the crater becomes a lake of deep-blue water, and the pebble plops in the center, sending rippling rings toward the outer edges.

When the water settles back into stillness, she sees her home reflected in its fathomless depths. A charming outbuilding stands in the place of her burned-out shed, its natural cedar shakes darkening to a weathered gray as she watches. Solar panels on the roof make her smile, a longtime dream fulfilled. Sophia and Grace sleep in the shade just outside the door.

"Hey, Nana Maggie."

She turns to see a slender teen standing in her kitchen garden, crunching on a cucumber. "Best pickling cukes in the state of Maine."

Her heart lifts at the sight of him. "Joey!" She opens her arms wide. Joey Allen is still child enough to linger in her embrace. She breathes in the fact of him, noting the shift—the once distinctive aroma of child sweat now more akin to musk. A reminder that life is long. And then it's short.

And she floats inside the lavender mist.

"There now." The gentle voice returns. "Remember to nourish this precious body you have been given for this Earth walk. Teach this to all who seek you. First is self-care. Then is love."

Like a water droplet plopping into a pond, a single note from John's flute lands in the empty air. Then a chorus of voices, female and male, speaks.

"You have been heard. You have been welcomed. You have been blessed. You have been granted deep mahet'maha'twa. Go back into the world and give your gifts away and away and away."

A cool morning breeze brushes her upturned face, and a feeling of deep belonging warms her.

Head bowed, watching where she places each foot, Margaret follows John out of the woods. The dogs lope along beside them, subdued. The path becomes easier to see as dawn broadens into early morning light.

Chapter 29

Emily grabs up her laptop and phone and heads out for Margaret's. Smiling as she turns onto the main road, she thinks of Ned, hoping he'll be back soon. She's surprised at how much she misses him. She can't recall ever feeling this way.

A disturbing thought niggles. *What if he hasn't missed me? What if he's had a chance to rethink this relationship? What if—*

As she rounds a sharp curve, a red pickup truck straddling the yellow line barrels toward her. She swerves, nearly losing control.

Trembling, she pulls over.

There on the side of the road, she starts to cry. Once started, she can't stop. She cries and shakes and catches her breath and cries some more. No words accompany this crying. No thoughts. No storyline. Just sounds and sensation. Hiccuping spasms. Quick. Sharp. Painful.

Her phone chimes, signaling a text. As she picks it up, the phone rings. She jumps. The display tells her it's Margaret. After a moment's hesitation, she answers with a choked, "Hello."

"Take a deep breath."

"What?"

"Something's just happened. I can hear it in your voice."

"Oh." Emily tamps down the irritation she knows Margaret will hear if she says more. She takes an audible breath into the phone.

"Good. See you soon."

Emily hangs up without responding and notes the red number *1* on her message icon.

Bracing herself, she taps the screen to read Ned's text.

Should be done here tomorrow. Will let you know when I'm heading home. Hope you're missing me 'cuz I'm sure missing you. N

A shivering intake of breath, and she's crying again.

∻⸙

Margaret is waiting in her dooryard, truck keys in hand. "Come on. Let's go for a ride."

Mutely, Emily climbs into the truck.

"Got blindsided, did you?" Margaret asks as they head onto the highway at the edge of town.

"More like a near head-on collision. The damn truck was half on my side of the road, right on that wicked curve before you get to the Granger place."

"That too. But I'm talking about the deluge on the side of the road. All caught up to you at once, didn't it? Blindsided you."

Emily is silent.

"I suspect you've had some heavy stuff coming at you. Both good and bad. But even the good leaves a mark, and you suddenly find yourself in overwhelm."

Emily remains silent. For a moment, she's experiencing it again—the red flash of the pickup truck screaming past her window, the thumping of her tires as they skimmed the raw edge of the ditch, the shimmying of her car skidding along the curve, the thudding of her heart slamming against her ribs. Then, she's back in the awful silence on the side of the road just before the dam burst.

Margaret drives. Silence fills the cab, cocooning them from the world at large. Emily settles against the seat and closes her eyes.

She hears the blinking of the turn signal and feels the truck slow as it makes a definite turn to the left. She must have dozed, and now she can't open her heavy lids. Then the truck bounces and jiggles as it transitions to a bumpier terrain, and Margaret slows further.

Her head jostling from left to right, Emily gives up her attempts to slip back into sleep and opens her eyes. They're passing under a canopy of overhanging branches that form a deeply shadowed tunnel, and she sits forward in recognition. She looks at Margaret, expecting an explanation, but the older woman simply smiles and doesn't take her eyes off the road.

"Drawn here for some reason I'm not yet sure of," she finally says as they emerge from the tunnel into bright sunshine. "This is for both of us, but mostly you."

She turns in between the wrought iron gates and drives up the central lane of the Whispering Waters Cemetery.

"He's over there." Emily points to the right. At the intersection of crumbling stone walls that form the back corner of the large square that is the cemetery, the stone stands dappled in sunlight under overhanging trees.

Margaret pulls up behind a dark-green sedan and an orange Jeep parked just off the lane and looks around. Two lanes over to the left, three people are gathered around a gleaming white stone set at the head of a grave mounded with fresh loam and a sparse array of floral arrangements. She gets out and reaches in the truck bed for a large canvas bag.

"Time for a little tea and quiet conversation." She nods at the graveside gathering. "We'll be far enough away not to disturb them over there."

Without waiting for Emily, she heads for the solitary stone.

తైం

When Emily catches up, Margaret has already spread her blanket on the grassy lane bordering the plot. Seated on it, she is removing a thermos and two mugs from her bag. Emily kneels at her father's gravestone.

"Hi Daddy. Me again. And this." She turns and gestures. "This is Margaret."

She touches the bright red petals and velvety leaves of the potted geranium centered in front of the stone. The ground around her is dry; the soil in the flowerpot is damp. Noting the grass clippings along the base of the stone, she looks at the adjoining plot. No clippings.

"Someone's tending this regularly," she says aloud.

"There must surely be family." Margaret doesn't look up as she pours tea into both mugs. "*Your* family."

"That sounds so strange. I know nothing about them, yet they've always known about me. Why would they make no effort to ..." Her voice trails off and she shrugs, adopting an air of nonchalance.

"Sit. Have some tea." Margaret pats the blanket beside her.

As she places her hands on the ground to push herself up, Emily feels something sharp in the grass. Digging carefully around it, she pulls out a half-buried triangle of plastic with rounded corners.

"A guitar pick." She sits on the blanket and shows Margaret. "My mother opened up to me the other day." She rubs her thumb and forefinger around and around the pick as she continues. "She's still holding back, but she gave me more than I expected. I know it was hard for her." Emily smiles. "She also told me never to fall for a musician." She sips her tea, an earthy blend akin to the deep flavor of roasted coffee.

In a flash of red, a cardinal swoops between them and lands on Daniel Donne's gravestone. Emily stares at the bird and after a moment says without blinking, "I had a brother."

"Oh?"

"He died before I was born. SIDS. There were two miscarriages between him and me."

"Jonathan," Margaret whispers, nodding as if something has fallen into place.

"How do you live with that?" Emily looks hard at her. "The loss of a baby? In his crib beside you. While you slept. How do you do that? How did she do that?"

Margaret shakes her head. "It amazes me. What the human

heart can … must … endure."

"It's no wonder she came apart. First Jonathan, then two more babies before they were even born, and then the postpartum depression after me. And my dad running away and leaving her alone with it all." Tears slip down Emily's cheeks. "I can't imagine."

"And yet you can, because you are a sensitive, empathetic being. I'm glad she told you. Nothing is served by silence. Now you can both hold space for what might have been but was not."

The sound of laughter stops her, and Margaret looks beyond Emily's left shoulder, squinting. Something in her expression makes Emily turn.

Not far from where the truck is parked, two older women are climbing over the stone wall that runs along the back edge of the cemetery. One passes a small bucket to the other as she balances herself on a crumbling pile of rocks. She crawls over with an exaggerated swing of her leg and laughs loudly as she stumbles, catches herself, and stumbles again. Her companion reaches out to catch her, misses, and trips on a root. In a comedic show in slow motion, she tucks and tumbles to the grass. The two lie on the ground laughing.

Margaret and Emily turn back to their tea, smiling, feeling lighter.

"I never thought I'd feel sorry for my mother. I've always thought, 'poor me.'" Emily takes on a whiny self-mocking tone. "'My mother's so mean. She's such a lousy mother.' Now I feel guilty."

"Ah, guilt! Such a waste of time and breath. But don't we all indulge. We beat our—"

"What do you think you're doing?" a woman screams at them.

Margaret and Emily rise to face her. It is one of the pair who was on the ground laughing just moments before.

"This is somebody's grave! You can't picnic on somebody's grave!"

Emily looks into flashing green eyes as the woman's next words sink into her startled mind.

"That's my Danny's grave, and I'll ask you to show some respect.

Go sit on your own son's grave if you have to sit on—" The woman's eyes widen. "And what do you think you're doing with that?"

She is staring at Emily's right hand and then looks back up into Emily's eyes. Her mouth opens, then snaps shut. She looks at her companion, who has caught up to her. Then she turns slowly back to Emily.

In the silence that follows, Emily looks at the woman's wrinkled face, a round-cheeked face framed by shoulder-length hair, faded red and streaked heavily with gray. She watches a series of disparate emotions flicker across this face until her vision blurs. Pain wells in her chest. As if wounded, she staggers back and looks away.

Margaret puts her arms around Emily and looks straight into the green eyes of the now silent woman. "Once you've recovered yourself, perhaps you'll want to begin again. This time graced with the understanding that you are a grandmother meeting the granddaughter who can't recall ever having known you."

The woman takes a step back.

"I'd like to go now," Emily says softly. "Please." It's barely a whisper.

The other woman makes no move, no sound.

Margaret guides Emily over to the gravestone. "Let me just gather our things."

Emily places the guitar pick on top of the stone. Did he hold it in his fingers? she wonders. Or, did someone leave it here as a tribute? Beyond these questions, her mind is blank, her body numb.

Margaret sets the canvas tote down and pulls Emily into a full embrace. "Be in these feelings," she whispers. "Feel them fully. It's the only way. The only way out is through. This is the truth of this moment."

She picks up her bag and guides Emily back down the lane toward the truck. As she reaches for the door handle, a voice calls out, asking them to wait. She opens the door for Emily to climb up into the cab and then turns. In the distance, Emily's grandmother stands at the gravestone looking off into the woods. Her companion has followed them to the truck.

"She's in shock," the woman says. "You have to understand. She never expected to see you here." She looks past Margaret, directing this to Emily. Emily sits looking straight ahead, out the windshield.

A gap. Silence. Then Emily turns to the woman but says nothing.

"She wants you to have this." The woman is holding out the guitar pick. "*If* you want it, of course."

Emily looks at the pick and then into the woman's dark eyes. "Why?" she finally says.

"You were his daughter."

When Emily doesn't answer, she goes on. "It was his favorite. She kept it here on his stone. She'd thought it was lost. But you found it. She thinks you should have it. *Hopes* you might want it."

Emily looks at Margaret, then at the woman, then at the pick.

"Thank you." She accepts the offering.

His favorite. The words resound in her head as she rolls the pick between her thumb and forefinger. Green flecks shimmer from inside the scratched surface of black plastic.

"You were his daughter. She is your grandmother."

A spark of anger sends Emily leaning toward the woman. "I *am* his daughter. That baby she must surely remember isn't lost somewhere in the past. *I* am that baby all grown up. I went on to live a life. Without him. Without her in it. She needs to acknowledge that."

"I know. *She* knows." The woman looks down, wringing her hands. "Please forgive her. She needs time to take this in."

"Where was she? Why was she no part of my life? Why didn't she look me up? Connect in some significant way?" Emily is crying again. "I'm sorry," she says, taking a deep breath. "You're not the one I should be saying this to."

The woman doesn't look away. "I'm Rosalie. I'm your great aunt. I hope you can forgive me too. You're right. We should have made an effort. It was just so …" She shrugs. "It was complicated."

Margaret steps forward. "Perhaps you could take Emily's address for when you're ready to uncomplicate things?"

"Yes, that would be good. Yes. That would be perfect."

"But tell her not to waste any more precious time." Margaret's eyes are hard, matching the flinty timbre of her voice, "Life is too darned short, and you never know what's— Well, let's just say, you never know."

Emily hands Rosalie a piece of paper with her mailing address. Rosalie looks at it. "Oh, you're not still living away then?"

Something in these words prickles Emily with an odd sliver of comfort.

Margaret holds out her hand, "I'm Margaret." An odd look crosses her face, then she continues. "Tell her the misplaced packet is in a metal box in the linen closet."

Wrinkling her brow, Rosalie looks at her but says nothing. She starts away and then stops. She turns back to Emily. "We'll be in touch." Her eyes fill with tears. "I promise. And I'm sorry."

Margaret closes Emily's door and starts around the back of the truck to the driver's side. As she rounds the tailgate, she calls to Rosalie, "And tell her that knowing Emily, even briefly, will go a long way to taming those nightmares that have started up again. But time's a'wasting. Tell her to get to it."

Rosalie's eyes brighten. She gestures as if tipping her hat to Margaret. "Thank you."

As Margaret turns the truck around and heads back down to the gate, Emily's phone chimes. "Maybe Ned's on his way early," she says as she touches the screen to read the text.

"Damn. He's been called out on a rescue farther up in the mountains. Just when the other job was winding down." She lays her head back against the seat. "Maybe I'd be better off if he *were* a musician."

As Margaret turns onto the highway, a disquieting ache in her left shoulder spreads down into her chest. It slowly intensifies as she heads toward home.

Chapter 30

Margaret awakens to the light of a waning moon barely reaching across the room. The dream again. The same one every night for three nights. Falling. Falling. Falling. A sudden impact. A crunch and a pop. Then nothing. No further sound. No pain. No sensation of any kind. Just deep silence and total blackness.

Barefoot, she pads down the stairs and into the kitchen. She fills the kettle without turning on a light—a familiar ritual in a comfortable semidarkness. As she crosses to the back door, the girls follow her out into the yard. She shivers as she steps into wet grass and remembers awakening to the sound of pounding rain and distant thunder in the night.

The girls hang by her side until she reassures them with a flick of her hand that all is well. "Go on. It's okay." And they race off down the hill.

"Okay. What are you trying to tell me?" she says, looking up through scudding wisps of clouds at the early morning stars.

The first sputterings of the teakettle draw her back inside, and she switches off the flame just as they build to a sharp whistle. She notes the nagging ache in her left shoulder as she lifts the kettle off the burner. Slowly, she pours the steaming water over the loose herbs in the pot, focusing all her attention on the sound of the water, the heft of the kettle, the aroma rising with the steam. Deep in thought, she hooks her fingers around the handle of a mug, her thumb pressed against the dragonfly imprinted in the clay, and waits for the tea to steep.

"May I join you?"

Half rising, she turns toward the door at the sound of Ned's voice.

She is alone in the kitchen. She is alone in the house.

Her heart quickens as she bends forward and drops her head between her knees, a wave of nausea rising in her throat. Her glands zing a warning, and she reaches for the basin under the sink. A stabbing pain in her head settles into an ache at the base of her skull. She lurches forward, gagging into a series of dry heaves. Each spasm sends snakes of light sizzling along her brow bones to burst behind her eyes.

Then, as quickly as they arrived, the pain, the nausea, the weakness disappear.

"Ned," she says aloud as she paws through her bag for her cell phone. She taps his number, but her call goes straight to voice mail. She leaves a message.

She hangs up and paces. She calls Warden Jacobs. Again, voice mail. She leaves a second message.

A truck rumbles into the dooryard, and she sighs in relief. "Ned?" she calls as she throws on a sweater and rushes out the front door. Her mind is just registering the fact that it's barely four o'clock and Ned always drives around to the back.

The fire chief runs across the yard. "We need your help," Paul Edwards shouts. "A couple of rock climbers got caught in a slide up near White Face above the Ledges. We sent out a team of rescuers and—"

"Ned? Is he all right?"

"That's just it. We've lost contact with him. Can you come with me to the search site? We'll have to chopper you in from the helipad behind the station, and I can't say when you'd be back."

"Let me grab my bag and put the girls in."

ཉ⊷

An hour later, the helicopter sets down in a small clearing three-quarters of the way up the north side of Mount Pennatticus. Above, a sheer rock face rises, its surface gleaming white in the early-morning light. At the edge of the clearing, a large canopy snaps as it lifts and lowers in a rising breeze. Under it, a rectangle of collapsible tables covered in maps and equipment is surrounded by men and women, some dressed in climbing gear, others in uniforms of varying colors and descriptions. Margaret recognizes many of the faces.

"Marcus," Chief Edwards says to a tall, rugged man in a state trooper's uniform. "I'd like you to meet—"

"You must be Ms. Meader, the psychic everybody's talking about. I'm Captain Raymond." He extends a hand the size of a bear's paw, but there is no warmth or welcome in his pale blue eyes. She's seen that look too often to take it personally, and she takes his hand in the spirit in which it's offered: professionalism. Time was when she wouldn't have been given the courtesy. "Someone will be with you momentarily, ma'am." He gives a curt tap to the brim of his hat and turns away.

Without waiting, Margaret walks toward a path that weaves through a narrow opening in the trees. Before she reaches it, a new wave of nausea hits her, sending her stumbling forward, hugging her stomach.

"Oh, for God's sake! We have to put up with theatrics now?" The voice is unmistakable. She has lived up to the captain's expectations.

Past caring what he or anyone else thinks, Margaret drops to a squat as a cold sweat coats her body. The nausea intensifies, and an ominous certainty fills her. Ned is very close to death. His head injury must be treated soon.

The nausea eases for a moment, and she crumples to her knees. Feeling the presence of others on either side of her, she whispers, "Just give me a moment. Just let me be for a moment."

They pull back but remain near.

For a moment, she panics. Her body is shaking. Her mind is steeped in a thick fog. She's never felt so frightened when working before. She doesn't know how to summon the visions needed to find him before he …

Stillness spreads over her like a coverlet. It slips around her shivering shoulders, enveloping her body—calming, warming, soothing her—as words form in her head.

Ned. Help is coming. I'm going to tell you how to let me see through you.

She waits. Then goes on.

Listen to the sound of my voice and only to the sound of my voice. Think of my voice as a tether and allow yourself to rise above the landscape. Show me where you are, what's around you, and who's with you. Stay connected to the sound of my voice. Rise and show me.

This is new to her. She's never worked in this way before. But this is Ned, dear Ned, and she's his lifeline now. He will die if this doesn't work. Of that she is certain. She keeps talking to keep him tethered to the earth and to keep the other thoughts, the frightening thoughts, from getting inside.

For a while, there is only darkness and the sound of her voice and the sensation of pain in her head. Then an image flickers and disappears. Too quick for her to catch and hold it before all is dark again. Then she sees boulders and rocks and debris piled against the base of a smooth wall. A jagged crack, two feet wide at its top, tapers to mere inches as it runs down the rock face. It ends in a spiderweb of tiny lines that reach outward in a circular pattern just above the rock pile. Above and to the right of the crack, faint symbols and figures run parallel down its length. A scattering of these petroglyphs fades off along the left as well, disappearing into the crack itself halfway down the wall. A pair of tiny brown birds hop from rock to boulder to nearby tree, chattering frantically.

As she kneels and listens, Margaret senses the series of subterranean hollows behind and below the rock pile. A musty odor and thick cloud of dust hang in the air. Four bodies lie scattered and broken among the rocks. A single ray of light pierces the darkness, shining on Ned's bloody shirt.

Okay, Ned. Rest and breathe gently. Emily is waiting. She needs you to hold on, to come back to her. Let your mind rest in that. All is well and all shall be well.

She turns to those around her and describes the location. "I see all four of them. Ned is seriously injured. Another one is unconscious and barely breathing." She pauses. "I'm afraid the other two are dead."

There is a collective intake of breath and a rush of activity around her. Radios bleat and squawk, helicopter rotors begin to turn, and men and women take off on foot up the path nearest Margaret.

"If you're fucking faking it, lady, I'll see you pay," Captain Raymond mumbles before loping away.

Stay with me, Ned. Listen to the sound of my voice. Rest and float and stay.

Gentle hands try to lift her from the ground.

"I'm fine," she says. "I just need to stay here for a while. If I could have a chair and be alone for a while."

"Anything you need, anything at all." Paul Edwards guides her up and into a camp chair and then places a light blanket over her still-shivering shoulders. "You just do what you need to do, Ms. Meader. Someone will be nearby if you need anything."

Gratefully, Margaret settles back into the stream of comforting words flowing through her to the young man she cares for so deeply. Time evaporates into a mist then liquifies into a gentle flow. Minutes slip into an eternity. Then, the ragged breathing of another person pulls her back. It's the one lying not far from Ned. Guilt stabs at her for having ignored him.

Softly, she sends comforting words, calling him Gordon. Images flit by her. A small boy in a red jacket flopping on his back in the snow, sticking out his tongue to catch fat flakes. A flash of pink fluttering in the wind. A teenager in cap and gown standing between two smiling adults. A lean but muscled young man diving into a quarry. Joy emanates from every image.

A presence hovers near him in the cave. Intense warmth fills her as she watches him rise and step up onto a threshold. His back is to her, his body silhouetted by a brightness beyond.

Suddenly, another kind of brightness fills the chamber. It spills onto Ned's still form wedged among jagged rocks, dust covered and bloody. Gordon turns back toward Ned and his own crumpled body. Indecision clouds his face. Then everything goes black.

Margaret slumps forward in her chair with a groan. Strong hands grasp her upper arms, keeping her from falling to the ground. A heaviness settles into her body, and her head aches dully. Her mind is a vast black emptiness.

"They've got them." The words float around in her head, attaching themselves at last to a voice. Paul Edwards's voice penetrates the darkness, circling down into her heart. "You were right on. Ned and Gordon Willoughby are being treated on the spot. The other two hikers are, as you already know, dead."

Margaret whispers two prayers—one of condolence, one of gratitude—and struggles to get up. Her legs nearly give way as the terrible weakness she's come to know too well takes root in her exhausted body.

"Let me help." The chief eases her back into the chair. "You're pretty pale." He lifts his head and shouts, "Someone get some water and something to eat over here."

"We'll get you back home," he says to Margaret. "There are plenty of people freed up now to drive you." He takes both of her hands in his. "I don't know how to thank you. I don't think we'd have found them in time without you."

"Any word on how they are?"

"Ned is critical but stable enough for transport. As to Gordon …" He shakes his head. "They had to revive him. Heart stopped. Still touch and go with him, but they're almost ready to airlift them out. They're in good hands with these guys."

"Have their families been notified? I have to call a friend of Ned's and tell her."

"Someone's job is notification, and I believe that's been done. I'll check and find out."

"I need my cell phone and don't know where my bag ended up."

"It's right over here on the ground. You dropped it when you fell." He hands her the bag and leaves her, calling to someone else.

As Margaret digs in her bag, the helicopter suddenly rises up, the sun glinting off its whirling blades and bubbled windshield. It hovers for a moment, rocking slightly, then sweeps off to the left, down and away.

Chapter 31

Lost in her story, her fingers flying over the keyboard, Emily is dimly aware of a dull thumping. *Thump, thump, thump.* Pause. *Thump, thump, thump.* Pause.

It grows in intensity until it is a sharp banging she can no longer ignore.

"Damn."

Bang. Bang. Bang. Accompanied, she realizes now, by a muffled voice.

She crosses to the living room, muttering, "The door is locked for a reason. Trying to write here! Guess I have to add a 'do not disturb' sign." She yanks the door open.

"Emily—"

"Mother? What's wrong? Is it Otis?" Her heart thuds in her chest.

"No, it's that Margaret woman."

"Margaret?" Emily's heart rate kicks up even further. "Is she—"

"She called." Janet pushes past her into the kitchen, then stops to catch her breath.

"And?" Emily's mind fires off a flurry of potential emergencies.

"And ..." Again her mother bends forward, hand to her chest, breathing heavily.

"Damn it, Mother, what is it? What's happened?"

"Don't you listen to your messages? Why is your phone not on? You're—"

"What the fuck's happened?"

Her mother straightens up, looking as if she's been slapped. "She's been trying to reach you. She's left messages. Finally, she called over to Otis's."

"That's it? I just need to check my messages? Jesus, Mother, I thought something terrible had happened." Emily heads for her study to get her phone.

"She said it was urgent. I think something *has* happened."

Emily's heart slams her ribcage again. She grabs her phone from her desk and turns it on. A flashing number *3* on the message icon. All three from Margaret. The first two voice mails are the same: "Margaret here. Call me, please." The third: "Emily, please call me as soon as you get this. It's important. I need to reach you."

She hits the call button. Margaret picks up on the first ring.

"He's all right. *Ned* is all right. You need to hear that first." Margaret pauses. "He's had an accident and he's being flown to Maine Medical by helicopter. They lifted off a half hour ago."

"What happened?" Emily gathers her purse and laptop and rushes into the kitchen. She continues talking as she fills her water bottle and throws an apple and some granola bars into her backpack.

"A rock slide on a rescue. He's in critical condition. Beyond that, I'm not sure. But I *am* sure he's going to recover. He's going to be all right. They will just make you wait in the waiting area at the hospital, so there's no need to rush to get there. You must drive safely and arrive safely. Do. You. Hear. Me?"

Emily looks around the house, checking to see if there's anything else she'll need.

"Do you hear me, Emily?" Margaret says again, her voice curt.

"Yes, I will. I'll drive safely. Will you be there?"

"I'm on my way. I've gotten a ride with one of the rescue team. I'll meet you there."

Emily runs out to her car. "You were there at the scene? How did he look? Did he say anything to you?"

"I was at the search center, not at the site of the slide. I didn't actually see him but I was in touch with him. He's getting the best possible care. He's not in pain, I assure you. And he's going to be all right."

"I'm on my way."

"Where are you going?" Emily's mother has followed her out to her car. "What is that woman on about now?"

"It's Ned. He's been hurt and I'm going to Maine Medical." Emily slips the car in gear.

"Oh! Okay. I'll close up here. Call me—"

"Don't tell Otis unless he hears about it somehow. Tell him Margaret says Ned's going to be all right, but only if he hears about it."

"But—"

Emily pulls away, leaving her mother standing in the drive.

An hour and a half later, she runs into the hospital lobby. The reception desk is empty. A passing nurse indicates a crowded waiting area and bustles away. Reluctantly, Emily sits, facing the desk. Every time someone in scrubs appears, she rises, only to have them hurry on through. Light-headed, she lowers her head between her knees. Too aware of the cacophony around her, she can't find her way back to her breath.

She looks up to see Margaret and a young woman in a SEARCH & RESCUE T-shirt come through the lobby doors. Margaret sees Emily and rushes to her.

❧

As they sit in a smaller, more intimate waiting room with a dozen others fresh from the rescue site, Emily suddenly thinks of Jacquie. Ned's best friend must be told. She shouldn't hear this on the news.

Following Margaret's example, she first tells Jacquie that Ned will be all right. Then she explains the situation and offers what comfort she can.

"You said he's going to be all right. How can you know that if—"

"He's in good hands, and a friend in whom I have absolute faith says he's going to be all right. She's —"

"Do you mean Margaret?"

"Yes."

"She's there?"

"She's the reason they found him."

"Thank God! And Emily? I'm so glad he has you in his life."

Emily hangs up smiling. Then she looks over at Margaret and is shocked at how drawn and pale she looks. "We need to get you something to eat and a quiet place to rest."

Margaret doesn't argue. She only sighs and gives Emily a wan smile as Paul Edwards sits down on her other side, placing his hand on hers.

"Why don't I get you a hot meal and arrange a ride home?" he says. "Nothing any of us can do here but wait. Let me see if I can scare up something hearty."

He leaves the room, and Emily turns back to Margaret.

"I hope you're going to take him up on it and then go home and rest. I'd take you myself, but ..."

"I wouldn't hear of it. You need to be here. For your sake as well as his." Margaret takes Emily's hand in both of hers. "It matters to him, you know. Even in his present state. *Especially* in his present state. Your being here matters."

Emily looks toward the empty doorway. Ned is somewhere in the hospital, unreachable. "I feel like I should be doing something. Something more."

"Your presence is enough. But if you want to feel even closer to him, you can get out that laptop and write. Write as if you're talking directly to him. The energy of such a focus is deeply powerful."

Emily looks into Margaret's eyes and sees pure loving-kindness. She also sees fatigue and strain. "Some hot food for you, and then you go home to rest. Okay?"

As Margaret nods wearily, a middle-aged couple is escorted into the waiting room. Both are in their late fifties. She is tall and slender with blond hair fashionably cut to just above her shoulders. Her hazel eyes behind rimless glasses sweep the room. The man, an inch or two taller, is also blond and when she sees his pale-blue eyes, Emily knows these are Ned's parents.

Mr. Burrows steps forward and clears his throat. The room quiets.

"I'm Howard Burrows, and this is my wife Natalie. We're Ned's parents. We want to thank everyone involved in his rescue and evacuation. Gordon Willoughby's parents are on their way here from New Mexico, and I'm sure they'll want to thank you as well. We've just talked to the doctors." He stops and runs both hands through his hair before continuing. "Ned's still in surgery. He has head and chest injuries, a fractured clavicle and breaks in his left arm and shoulder, and internal …" His voice quavers. His wife tucks herself under his right shoulder, sliding her arm around his waist. Taking a deep breath, he finishes, "And internal injuries. They don't know the extent of those as yet."

Emily sits stunned, replaying the list of injuries to Ned's beautiful body one by one. Each one feels like a punch.

Natalie Burrows, still holding onto her husband, speaks in a clear bright voice. "He's strong and the doctors are optimistic, and so are we." She surveys the room, looking at each of them.

"We will keep you informed as we are informed, but we've been told there will be no visiting him until tomorrow. We appreciate you staying as long as you can but understand that you have lives and loved ones that need your attention as well. Ned understands that too. So, stay or leave, but do what you must." She lowers her head, then lifts it and says, "And give your loved ones an extra hug today. And let them hug you back, long and hard."

The room is silent.

Margaret straightens in her chair and grips Emily's hand. "Send him your love right now. Right now! Envelop him in love. Tell him to stay."

Without thought, Emily looks at the round clock on the wall.

1:38 p.m. Silently, she calls out to Ned. *I love you. Please stay. I'm here. Waiting. I love you. … Stay. Please stay.* As she concentrates on the words she's sending to him, another part of her mind floats inches from her body, witnessing what's happening around her with an odd detachment. Voices filter in.

"Ms. Meader? Margaret Meader?"

Ned's parents are coming closer. His mother sits down on the other side of Margaret, taking her hands.

Margaret says, "I'm so sorry."

"We can't thank you enough—" Natalie bows her head and softly sobs. Ned's father bends over her, his shoulders shaking with silent crying.

Everyone in the room is still. Some look away while others stare openly, their eyes shining and wet and full of sympathy.

Margaret speaks to them both. "I feel strongly that he's going to be all right."

Natalie looks into Margaret's eyes, searching them. Howard's head remains lowered, but his body is now perfectly still. "When you say you 'feel,'" Natalie says, "do you mean … I don't how to ask this. I mean, he talks about you, about how you know things."

Margaret squeezes Natalie's hands. "I don't know why I 'know' the things I do, but I've learned to trust what comes. And what's come to me now is assurance that your son will be all right. The long road ahead will be hard, but he will be all right."

Taking an audible breath, Natalie rises to stand with her husband.

"I'd like you to meet Emily Donne," Margaret says, startling Emily out of her comfortable anonymity beside her. "She and Ned are—"

"Emily?" Natalie turns to her, fresh tears filling her eyes. "*The* Emily we've been hearing about? We are so pleased to meet you."

Emily flushes. She doesn't know what to say and smiles up at them shyly.

"I'm sorry to put you on the spot like that. Forgive me." Natalie extends her hand. "We had dinner the other night with Ned at Jacquie's restaurant, and the two of them talked about you—a lot."

She smiles. "I wondered when I'd finally get to meet you."

Suddenly, her face registers the stark realization of the situation that has brought about the meeting she'd looked forward to. She turns from Emily to her husband, whose face is a pale mask, and dissolves. "Oh, God. I'm sorry," she says to no one in particular.

Emily stands. "I can't imagine what this is like for you." She looks down at Margaret, who smiles encouragement. "Please know that I'm here to help Ned through his recovery in every way I can."

"Here we go," Chief Edwards announces as he returns to the room, carrying a tray of covered cartons and bulging brown bags. "I have soup and sandwiches." He walks directly to Margaret first and then notices the Burrowses. "Oh, I'm interrupting. I'm sorry." He nods and steps back.

"Not at all, Paul," Howard says. "Glad to see you're looking after everybody as usual. Question is: Who's looking after you?"

"Oh, don't worry about me." He clears his throat, clearly uncomfortable with the focus on himself. He nods toward Margaret. "You know Margaret's responsible for us finding Ned and Gordon when we did? Saved their lives, I'd say. Certainly Gordon's."

"Well, let's get some food into you, Margaret." Howard is suddenly animated as he points to a doorway. "There's a table and chairs in that little room over there. Shall we?"

Emily stands in a daze as Ned's parents help Margaret up and escort her out of the room. Some of the others in the room grab food from the tray, and then Paul follows the Burrowses and Margaret into the other room. Emily slumps back into her chair, vulnerable and alone. She closes her eyes and lets the tears come.

"Aren't you joining us?" Natalie's voice is close to her ear. So quiet, so pleasant, so warm.

Emily looks up into moist hazel eyes behind the chic rimless glasses and is unable to speak.

"Unless, of course, you'd rather be alone? I don't want to pressure you." Natalie sits down beside her. "Forgive me if I'm being inappropriate. I feel like I'm moving around in a fog."

Emily hesitates for just a moment and then takes her hand. "Yes. The fog. This must be what they mean when they say something feels surreal. My brain keeps saying this can't be happening."

"Come on." Natalie gets up and pulls Emily with her. "Let's get some food into us. Ned's brought us together, and he'll need us to be well nourished and strong."

Margaret's eyes are half closed, her face is even paler than before, as Emily sits down beside her. Leaning in, she quietly urges Margaret to eat.

Margaret smiles at her. "I will if you will."

"Deal." Emily opens a carton of soup and blows on a heaping spoonful before tasting it.

Natalie refuses the chief's food offerings, and Emily looks at her with eyebrows raised. "Remember what you said to me a few minutes ago? Ned needs us to be nourished and strong?"

Both parents begin to eat mechanically, without relish but without stopping.

Margaret manages three bites of a sandwich. "Someone is driving me home soon. Please keep me posted."

"By all means," Natalie and Howard say in unison.

Howard yields to his wife with a gesture, and she continues for both of them. "We can't say thank you enough. We ..."

"No need. If I had a grandson, I'd want him to be just like Ned. He's a sweet, kind boy. I take very selfish comfort in knowing I could help in some small way."

"In some huge way," Howard corrects her.

Margaret rises and takes up her bag. "The crisis point is past. There was a moment ... but it's over now."

As she turns to leave, a man in green surgical scrubs steps into the room. "Mr. and Mrs. Burrows?"

They nod.

"Your son is out of surgery. His condition is still critical, but all signs are good that he's out of immediate danger." Everyone in the room expels a collective breath. "Once he's settled into the critical care unit, we'll let the two of you in for a few minutes."

"That'll be the three of us," Natalie says, putting her arm around Emily.

Tears prickle Emily's eyes. Margaret smiles at her.

"By all means, Mrs. Burrows," the surgeon says. "Your daughter can come in too. But I have to warn you, he won't be conscious for a while yet and your visit will need to be brief." He pauses, looking into the eyes of each in turn before resuming. "I have to be honest and tell you there was a critical moment in surgery when it could have gone either way. Thankfully, he came through it. He's young and in excellent condition. Both factors were on his side and will serve him well as he recovers."

"And Gordon Willoughby?" Howard asks. "Can you tell us about his condition?"

"I'm afraid I can't share any information with nonrelatives." He starts to turn away, glances back. "Someone will come out and get you when you can see your son." And he is gone.

Margaret puts her arms around Emily. "I'm leaving now. He knows you're here," she whispers.

She turns to Ned's parents. "He's deep in a restful place where there's no pain right now, but he'll know you're there when you go in. He'll feel the lightness of your presence. So, talk to him. Send loving thoughts until then. It matters. Love always makes a difference."

As Margaret leaves, Emily remembers her promise to Jacquie. "I have to call Jacquie back. I promised to keep her informed."

Natalie smiles. "How thoughtful of you to contact her. She and Ned go back to childhood, and yet I never thought to call her." Her lower lip is quivering as she takes Emily by the shoulders. "I'm so glad you've come into Ned's life. Into our lives."

Chapter 32

Margaret awakens disoriented. The room is dark, the drapes drawn. She feels her way over to the window and parts the curtains. A feeble light tells her it's early morning, but her mind's a blank as to which day. She stretches and settles into the only moment she can be sure of.

The girls clatter down the stairs ahead of her as she makes her way to the kitchen and out into the stillness of the backyard.

As she stands on the hill, eyes closed, three simple lines come to her.

> *mingling dark and light*
> *predawn, neither day nor night*
> *drinking stillness in*

An image of Ned slides into her mind, carrying the full memory of yesterday's ordeal. She shivers and offers a prayer of gratitude, ending with her usual request. "May I be of service today. May I interact with open heart and mind with all who cross my path."

As she steps back inside, a gauzy image slithers along the periphery of her consciousness, just out of reach. She closes her eyes. A radiant afterimage remains. And a sensation akin to joy.

She lights a flame under the kettle and goes into the sitting room. Puzzle pieces are scattered on a large baking tray on the coffee table. She kneels and runs her fingers over them, rapidly scanning for the blues. *Blue. Blue. Blue.* The word keeps repeating in her head. She snugs the blue ones together, forming small units, seeing connections in sudden spurts. Her fingers swirl the units into an expanding mass of blue.

Water. Starbursts of sunlight glinting off its surface. And down in the corner, a small patch of yellow. She'd begun laying out the pieces three days ago before being drawn away to complete a different puzzle. A round one—an intricate mandala, such as those created by monks sifting fine, colored sands through curled fingers. A mandala that would be swept away moments after completion.

∾∾

Two hours later, Margaret is deep in the woods, following a barely visible trail she hasn't walked in years. Fallen trees and thick underbrush slow her progress, but she is compelled to keep moving. When she stops for a drink of water, she realizes she's wandered off the path completely and is standing in an unfamiliar stretch of beeches, birch, and pine. A tumbling stone wall wends its way into the undergrowth.

"Ah," she says aloud. "'Something there is that doesn't love a wall, that wants it down …'" She smiles, remembering the face of the old poet, as craggy as the wall beside her.

The girls have circled back, heads cocked as she talks. She laughs. "Okay, lead on." And they race off along the crumbling wall.

She follows, stepping over it and back again as it winds and twists through the trees, around boulders and outcroppings of granite. At times, it ends abruptly in a pile of scattered stones only to reappear a few feet away. As her foot slips on a moss-covered rock, her ankle twists sharply. She carefully lifts and lowers the foot, easing her weight back onto it. No twinge of discomfort. Relieved, she proceeds more slowly than before.

"No point in pushing your luck when you're lost in the woods and you'd like to live to see sixty-three, old girl."

She hears a crackling nearby—the snap of a twig underfoot. She scans the woods, her whole body listening. She wills the girls to stay put wherever they are.

Lowering herself to sit atop the wall, she slides off her small pack and pulls out an apple and sheathed paring knife. She slices the apple in quarters and tosses three of them. They land silently in a cushion of pine needles and moss. Her back itches, but she doesn't move to scratch it. A snap, then a rustling. A small doe appears. Her nose is in the air, her nostrils flared. Her body is taut, ready to flee. Minutes pass before she lowers her head and eats the first apple wedge. Two spotted fawns step out of the bushes behind her to stand just beyond her hindquarters. Margaret remains motionless. The mother steps closer and scoops up a second piece.

After a long eye-to-eye pause, the doe comes forward for the third. Margaret extends her hand, cupping the remaining piece. The two babies venture up along their mother's left flank, eyes and pointed ears toward Margaret. The mother bends her head back toward them as if to tell them to stay put and then steps forward. One tentative step at a time, she approaches Margaret's outstretched hand, her nose twitching. Margaret flattens her palm so that the apple is perched for easy plucking. The doe takes it, the rough texture of her tongue in sharp contrast to the liquid pools of her brown eyes.

Suddenly, the doe's head and tail lift, and she springs around, sending her twins scampering away. With a flash of white tail, she dashes off into the woods.

Distant yelps pierce the quiet. Margaret swings her pack to her shoulders and heads off. Sophia and Grace burst around a long curve in the wall and dance around her, paws muddy, coats dripping.

"You found yourselves some water, did you?"

In tandem, the two dogs crouch and shake, spattering her with muddy drops. Laughing, she sends them off to show her the way.

After ten minutes, they leave the remains of the stone wall, which has disintegrated into random piles of rocks and pebbles. Behind a cluster of birches and pines, a jagged outcropping slants up and back along hilly terrain. A faint splashing of water emanates from within. Flirting just beneath the heavy smell of pine and the pungent odor of humus underfoot is a sweet, light scent. Easing around a sharp-edged section of black rock that juts from the grayer expanse, she reaches out for support. Surprised at the coolness of the rock, she pulls her hand away, her fingertips wet. The splashing is louder now.

She leans into the shadowy crevice. Just inside, a recessed opening deepens and widens. She tugs at some branches and vines clinging overhead. The opening is tall and wide enough for her to step into it. Expecting darkness, she is surprised to find it light inside; and what appeared to be a mere niche is, in fact, a cave.

The dogs scramble past her, disappearing around a corner in the passageway. She follows, her body alive with curiosity. The sweetness in the air is stronger now, the smell of pine lost in it. The splashing is louder. The downward slope levels off as she goes.

At a fork, two tunnels curve off to the left and right. The sounds of the dogs and water mingle now with lively bird chatter, rebounding off walls and ceilings, circling, echoing, obliterating her usually strong sense of direction. She stands in the notch between the tunnels and closes her eyes. The sounds are coming from the right and swirling up and away toward the left.

She turns right and steps into a massive cavern with a domed ceiling. She looks up through the huge hole in its center into blue sky. Framed by leafy branches from overhanging trees on the hillside above, clouds float overhead. Ten feet below this skylight, a glistening waterfall tumbles from a hole in the wall into a deep crater. Wild rosebushes heavy with blossoms surround the pond on three sides, and slanting rays of a midmorning sun sparkle on the surface of the water.

On her right, above a patch of grassy ground, three white birches rise from a single root ball, their leaves shivering in the breeze. Birds flit from the trees to the bushes and out the opening into the sky. She turns in a full circle, scanning the curved expanse of stone that forms the cavern. Faint marks and drawings cover the upper stretches of the walls.

Margaret removes her shoes and eases her feet into the water. It's not the icy cold she expects, but pleasantly cool. She yelps as the girls gallop past her into the water, and her surprised laughter echoes round and round.

Cautious as always around unknown water, she strips off her clothes and slips in. She gauges the changing depth by taking shallow dives. Swimming through the tumbling waterfall, she explores behind it, then deep dives to the other end of the pool. Floating on her back in a wide circle, she looks up at the patch of sky, her heart beat thrumming in her ears. The girls climb out, their shaggy coats dragging heavily as they rise. They shake off and settle on the shore, eyes fixed on Margaret and the rippling circles spreading out around her.

Refreshed, she swims to shore and stands in a circle of sunlight, face upturned. Slowly, she turns, feeling a deep kinship with those whose hands etched the markings on the upper walls so very long ago.

Clouds float on the surface of the water. Reflected tree branches reach from its depths. No unwanted images. No disrupting visions. No inquiries from without or niggling from within. A sense of floating and being still at the same time. Smiling, she remembers Joe's gentle admonishments whenever she let herself get too busy, too wrapped up in others, too much in the world. He would take her in his arms and recite an old Spanish proverb: *How wonderful it is to do nothing and afterwards to rest.*

She tosses a carrot to each girl and crunches one of her own, noting the clean crispness of it in her mouth. "It doesn't get any better than this, girls," she says as she walks to the patch of grass beneath the tree. Stretching lazily, she lies down, propping her folded shirt under her head. Sophia and Grace settle on either side of her. "I'm just going to rest my eyes for a moment. Wake me if I drift too far," she instructs them with a yawn.

The dream is gentle, filtering in like wisps of smoke. The air is sweet with roses and sunshine. She is being rocked as someone sings a lullaby.

We are here. Always near. Safely sleep. Rest, my dear.

The voice is lovely, clear and sweet as the air. The pleasure of being rocked soothes and quiets, lifts and lightens.

Rest. Nourish and renew. Look to the care of your physical self. Attend. This is a lesson you came here to teach.

Something tickles her cheek. Twitching her nose, she tries to lift her hand, but it won't respond. Her lids are heavy, her brain sluggish. A soft snuffling sound from Sophia and a mild yip from Grace prompt her to open her eyes as a butterfly lifts off her cheek. It flutters to a nearby bush and lights on a rose. Pale yellow resting on pink.

She rolls to her side and pushes herself up. The sun is now shining on her. An hour or more has passed. The girls wiggle and prance in place.

"Give me a minute," she tells them. "Go take a final swim and we'll head out."

The breeze riffles her naked body as she slips on her clothes. Her senses are acutely attuned to her surroundings. The colors are bolder, the sounds sharper, the smells brighter, the sensations stronger.

As the girls race up the tunnel ahead of her, Margaret turns back for a final look. Her heart leaps as a pair of goldfinches bursts from the tree. They dance in the air, bright flashes of yellow twirling around. They dip in and out of the hole in the ceiling as a red-tailed hawk glides overhead. Then, just as she's about to turn away, a flurry of pale yellow wings lifts off from the rosebushes and rises into the afternoon air. Margaret smiles up into the circle of sky, the mandala spread above her.

≈•≈

Head down, lost in a reverie, Margaret stumbles into him. She lurches forward and he catches her by the shoulders. They do an awkward sort of dance, clinging to each other as they right themselves on the rocky path. She looks up into eyes the color of coastal waters on a calm day. His open face is framed by wildly curling gray hair.

"So sorry!" he says. "Guess I lost myself in my mental meanderings. You all right?"

"Totally my doing," she says, steady on her feet at last. "I'm the one lost in 'mental meanderings.' What a perfect description." She smiles, and he responds with a wide grin, a dimple flashing and then disappearing in his left cheek.

"You sure you're all right? I startled you pretty good there. I was coming down from up there"—he points up to the ridge top—"moving crosswise to the path. You certainly had the right of way, if there is such a thing way out here."

"I'm fine. Really. I was so relaxed, I might as well have been sleepwalking."

"These woods will do that for you. Nothing like the balm of nature. She'll cure whatever ails you, that's for sure. As long as some lunkhead doesn't come lumbering by and knock you for a loop."

His laugh is deep, layered with rich undertones. Hers joins his easily, comfortably. Suddenly, they are surrounded by barking dogs, two goldens and two black labs.

"Sophia! Grace!"

"Maxie! Gulliver!"

Ignoring their shouted names, the four dogs clamber around the two people, leaping and bumping and wagging. Margaret and her companion look into each other's eyes and shrug helplessly. They stand thus, nearly chest to chest, until the dogs begin to settle.

"Sophia. Grace. Sit!" Margaret commands curtly.

All four dogs sit in unison.

Raising her brows, Margaret shakes her head and laughs.

"Guess yours is the voice of authority. I'm Kenneth. Kenneth Chisholm. And you are …?"

"Margaret." She extends her hand, again noting the soft sea green of his eyes.

"Well, Margaret. I must apologize for the …" He looks down at the dogs and exaggerates the next word as if for their benefit. "The *wicked* antics of these very *naughty* boys."

Tails thump as four sets of dark eyes are fixed on the man with the teasing voice and flashing dimple.

"And I must apologize as well for these misbehaving miscreants." She looks down at Sophia and Grace, scowling with mock disapproval and shaking her head. The girls look away.

Margaret stoops to pet the labs as Kenneth does the same with her goldens. Maxie is the younger of the two, maybe two or three. Gulliver is larger, no more than five. Both are sleek and solid with shiny coats and bright eyes.

"Time we were headed home," Margaret says to the dogs, her way of breaking away before the conversation can become awkward. She rises and reaches out to shake hands. "Nice meeting you, Kenneth. Hopefully if we bump into each other again, it won't be so literal."

He takes her hand in a firm shake. Laugh lines ripple from the corners of his eyes. His dimple remains visible as he smiles down at her until her cheeks begin to warm. When he drops his hand and looks away, she feels a shiver of disappointment.

"Well, we're headed that way," he says, and points downhill through thick trees, saplings, and scrub.

If either of them had come a few minutes earlier or later, she thinks, they never would have met. They would have literally crossed paths without knowing it.

"'Bye," she says simply. She snaps her fingers and signals for Sophia and Grace to take the lead, and they head off along the faintly visible path toward home.

"Margaret?" he calls after her.

"Yes?"

"Margaret what?"

"Meader," she says, scanning his face for a sign of recognition and recoil, for a change of expression or an intake of breath.

"Until next time then, Margaret Meader." He smiles and turns away with a wave.

She catches up to her dogs and whispers, "Remember when I said it doesn't get any better than this, girls? Seems I might have been wrong!"

Head down again, her step is livelier than before, her stride longer. She realizes she is smiling—broadly. Lean and strong, she is a girl again, at home in her body, in sync with her surroundings, at one with these woods teeming with multilayers of life. And again, she feels her cheeks warming, the blood rushing to the surface in a subtle blush. Her grin softens to a hint of a smile as a lovely daydream blossoms.

Chapter 33

Hugging herself, her chin tucked to her chest, Emily stands under the showerhead. The hot water prickles her skin, and soon she is enveloped in a steamy cocoon. She dissolves into wracking sobs.

Mechanically, she soaps her body and shampoos her hair. Tears mingle with the soapy water running down her body. Tilting her head back, she lets the water wash over her until she's standing in a clear, swirling puddle.

When she steps out of the shower stall, she hears muffled sounds coming from her living area. She wraps her head in a towel and slips on a fluffy robe, and then flops down on her bed. She doesn't want to see anyone. She doesn't want to talk to anyone. She doesn't want to move.

"Emily?" Her mother's voice.

Emily turns on her side, curling her knees to her chest. "Go away," she mumbles into the comforter. "Leave me alone."

The door opens, and she hears her mother walk into the room. "I didn't want to startle you," Janet says. "It's just me. I heard your car." She sits down on the bed.

Emily turns her head deeper into the comforter, the towel wrapped around her hair spreading like a veil. She tucks herself into an even tighter ball.

Her mother remains silent and makes no move to leave.

A wave of sobs again convulses Emily's exhausted body. No words or thoughts attach themselves to the sobbing. Her body is simply immersed in sensation. In stark, unadulterated pain.

After a while, the spasms subside, and she lies limp on the bed. Still, her mother waits without speaking or moving.

"He was so pale," Emily says. "So broken, so …" She twists her torso so that her back is flat on the bed, her knees still drawn up to one side. "So not there. His body was on the bed, but he wasn't there. There was an emptiness, a distance I couldn't reach across."

Janet places her hand on her daughter's knee.

"Margaret says he's going to be all right," Emily continues. "She told me to talk to him. She said he would hear me. But I couldn't feel him there. Just this empty body, so bruised and damaged, connected to machines by tubes and wires in a stark white room. Mechanical beeps and blurts and watery swishing sounds all around." Her voice fades to meet her mother's silence.

Janet lifts her to a seated position. She unwraps the towel around her daughter's head and gently blots her damp hair. "I have no doubt he could hear you. No doubt at all."

"So, you think Margaret was right?"

"I … think she said what anyone would say who understood the circumstances."

Janet goes into the bathroom and returns with a comb. "Here. Sit on the floor." When Emily slides down to the floor and sits cross-legged in front of her, Janet runs the wide-toothed comb through her thick curls, gently untangling them with her free hand.

Emily is transported to another time and place. She sits on a footstool cradling a rag doll. Her mother sits behind her in a chair, her legs straddling Emily's child self. She hums softly as her fingers run from Emily's scalp through her hair, loosening tangles and separating strands of just-washed curls. The sweetness of baby shampoo and lilacs floats in the air. A shaft of sunlight brightens a bouquet of purple blossoms in a milk-glass pitcher on a nearby table.

A ritual she's not remembered in years floods back. A weekly respite from the daily tension of trying to bridge the distance between them, of trying to find a way in.

Emily's head lolls back as she gives in to the moment and the memory. As she settles into her mother's cupped palms, her thank you is barely audible. Janet's fingers respond with a subtle circular motion.

"He's going to be all right, and so are you. What you need right now is nourishment and a good long sleep. I have some tomato soup heating on the stove, and your favorite summer sandwich ready to be grilled—cheese with basil and a thick slice of tomato fresh from Otis's garden. So, let's move you to the porch. I just saw three hummingbirds at your feeders and a bluebird on the garden post."

Reluctantly, Emily lets herself be led out to the screen porch that overlooks the garden. She settles heavily into the cushions of the wicker settee, her terry robe loosely fluffed around her. Hummingbirds hover around her butterfly bushes and bee balm, their tiny wings soft blurs, their slender beaks dipping in and out of bright blossoms. Tears slip down her cheeks as she remembers her night in the garden with Ned.

☞⋅✌

Emily opens her eyes in the semidarkness of her bedroom. She stretches deliciously and settles back on the pillows, wondering what day it is. An image arises of a woman standing on a deserted beach, wind riffling her long black hair. It's a scene from the story she's been working on. The woman's name is Ned and—

"Oh my God!" She sits up.

It all rushes back. Her mother banging on her door. The trip to Portland. Her few minutes with Ned, lying in the ICU, battered and unconscious.

She can't get it out of her head. Ned on the bed, machines beeping and whirring around him. His devastated parents clinging to each other and then to her. The doctor, brittle and aloof, wearing a white coat over his scrubs, saying, "Only time will tell how complete his recovery will be. We'll keep him sedated if he wakes up, let his body heal. Go home and rest."

Rest. All the way home, she wondered how she could ever rest again, sleep again. Then her mother— her mother—sitting on her bed as she cried. Her mother giving her space and time to empty herself. Combing her hair. Leading her through the French doors and onto the porch. Feeding her. Handing her tissues as the steaming soup flushed her nasal passages of fluid she thought she'd surely released. And then her mother tucking her into bed, drawing the drapes, and leaving as quietly as she had come.

A sudden panic seizes her. Did she *leave* leave? Just when the walls were starting to come down, did she walk out again? Was the combing and comforting another way of saying good-bye?

Emily sits with her arms wrapped around bent knees, her chin resting there. No point in getting up. Either her mother has left or she's stayed, and no jumping out of bed to check will change things. "But I hope you've stayed," she says to the darkened room.

She reaches for her phone on the bedside table. Her last memory was of putting it in her backpack, so she assumes her mother put it there. A red 5 lights the message icon. She pauses and takes a breath before clicking to read her messages. She scrolls through them. As she scans the first three—two from her former boss and one from a magazine editor she had queried about one of her stories—she wonders how the ordinary world can keep rolling along when her portion of it has collapsed.

The last two messages are from Jacquie and Margaret. Jacquie's is a quick thank you and Margaret's reads: *Call me when you can.*

She climbs out of bed and heads for the kitchen. A note sticks out from under her empty mug on the counter by the stove. *Be back later.* She lets out her breath and then shakes her head, irked at herself for letting it matter so much that her mother is staying.

She calls Margaret. "Margaret? This is Emily."

"'Fraid not, dear. It's Annie. Annie Foss. Margaret took some vegetables over to Jim Cain. He's been ordered off his feet with some swollen ankles and, frankly, I think he's got a touch of the …

Oh, forgive me, dear. What is it you young people say, TMI? Too much information! Suffice it to say, she'll be back in a bit."

Emily thanks her and clicks off, feeling empty and alone. She nearly drops the phone when it rings in her hand.

"Can you use a little company, or would you rather be alone?" Margaret's voice seeps into her weary body like warm liquid.

"I don't want to be alone."

"I'll be there in half an hour."

As she hangs up, her mother walks through the kitchen door carrying a brown bag and two large Starbucks coffees. "Croissants from that lovely new bakery downtown. And these at a little stand by the road." She pulls two large peaches from her pockets. "I've missed the way people here leave produce out by the road with a cash box on the honor system."

As she sits, Emily's phone rings again. Her heart bumps up as Natalie Burrows's name appears on the screen.

"Good morning, Emily," Natalie says when she answers. "There's been no change with Ned, but the doctor says no change is good. His body is repairing, and this is best done in the unconscious state. We were allowed in for ten minutes a while ago, but the next visit won't be until late this afternoon. If you want to come up for that, we'll give you some time alone with him. That is, if you'd like that?"

"Yes. I'd like that. Thank you."

"Four o'clock?"

"Yes. Thanks."

"Jacquie's coming up later too. Maybe you could travel together. And would you call Margaret and fill her in?"

"Margaret's on her way over here. I'll tell her."

Her mother is looking at her as she hangs up, then returns her attention to the food. She sets a plate with a croissant and a quartered pitted peach in front of Emily. "Margaret's coming over?"

"Yes."

"Then I'll head back over to the house."

"Why do—"

"Otis is chomping at the bit to go get lumber for a project, and I think it's best if I drive him."

Emily watches her mother go out the door, then calls Jacquie and arranges for them to go visit Ned together.

She hangs up and takes a bite of the peach, sweetness exploding in her mouth, juice squirting down her chin.

"Mail," her mother announces as she comes back through the door, sifting through the pile in her hands. "Junk, junk, junk, and more—" She stops mid-sort. "What the hell?" She holds up a pale-pink envelope, tossing the rest onto the counter.

"What?" Emily asks. When her mother fails to answer, she asks again, "What?"

"This." Janet's voice is like a child's, her eyes questioning.

Emily takes the letter. Her name and address are neatly written in a hand she does not recognize. There is no return address. "It must be one of those advertisements that looks like a personal letter to get you to open it. It—"

"No! It's from her. How long have you been corresponding?" The words are clipped. Her eyes glisten with tears.

"Who?"

"Danny's mother! Your—"

Emily looks at the envelope and then at her mother, her mouth open in disbelief. "I ... we ... We haven't been. Margaret and I went to the cemetery and she was there. We were—"

"Margaret again! Is there no end to her meddling in your life? What's that about anyway? How did you even get involved with her? She's trouble, Emily. How did she wheedle her way into your life?"

"Mother! She's been a good friend and—"

"She's too old to be your friend. She's after something. I've been hearing about her since I was a kid. She's trouble. Dangerous even. And I won't have her latching onto my daughter."

"Latching on? Really, Mother. Meddling? Wheedling? Do you think I'm stupid? Gullible? An easy mark for some—"

A truck pulls into the driveway. Emily can see through the window that it's Margaret.

"That I'm incapable of having friends who like me for me?"

"That woman has stirred up a regular hornet's nest of ugly

memories since Lily May died. Playing Madame Psychic. Bringing up things best left in the past. What's she doing now, calling in people who deserted you long ago?" Janet is screaming now. "Something's in it for her. She's a parasite. She has a history. She was even involved in a—"

"Stop it. Please." Emily can see Margaret stop on her way to the door. She lowers her voice. "Margaret's here. Please be civil to my friend. You could stay and get to know the real her and not some invention of the gossip mill, or … you're welcome to leave."

Emily walks past her mother and opens the door, calling a greeting. Margaret hesitates and then continues toward her. She carries a pie basket, a potted plant, and an insulated lunch bag.

Janet moves back into the kitchen to give Margaret room to enter. Margaret nods to her. "Good to see you, Janet. What a gift for Otis to have you here while he gets back on his feet. And how perfect for you and Emily."

"I was just on my way out, so I'll leave you two to visit." Janet refuses to make eye contact as she sidles around Margaret to the door.

"Sure you can't stay for a bit?"

"No. I already told Emily that Otis and I have supplies to pick up." Janet is looking everywhere but at Margaret.

"Well, maybe next time. I know we share a deep concern for your daughter and her young man."

Janet's eyes flit up to meet Margaret's. "Otis is waiting. I'd better go." Head down, she hurries out.

Margaret watches through the sheer curtains as Janet retreats. "If you still harbor doubts that she loves you fiercely, take a good look. She's in Momma Bear mode. She wouldn't care one way or the other about me if she weren't desperately concerned about you."

"I'm sorry."

"No need to be." Margaret moves into the kitchen and sets the basket, bag, and plant on the counter. "She knows you're in a vulnerable place right now. She wants to protect you."

"I don't need protecting." Emily rounds the counter and plunks herself down on a stool on the living room side. "And certainly not from you. Suddenly she wants to play mother?"

"Admit it, Emily. She's been making an effort. She's been showing you in small ways in ordinary moments that she wants to be better at it.

"It's only until she takes off again."

"That may be true, but while she's here, why not surrender to this opportunity? Let yourself be open to a new way of being with her." Margaret is unpacking the insulated bag as she speaks. She sets a fat glass jar and a tall bottle of milky liquid on the counter. "Here's a batch of my vegetable barley soup, very hearty and strengthening. Now, don't go zapping it in a microwave, you'll change its molecular structure. Heat it slowly over a low flame. And this is a protein shake. Drink it as is or add fruit or ground flax seeds—whatever appeals to you that's plant-based."

She reaches into the basket. "And be sure to indulge in a little blueberry decadence. We're coming up on the last good ones of the season. The bushes are thinning out and the leaves are turning red." She presents the small pie with a beautifully fluted crust and thick purple syrup oozing from slits in the golden top. "Even if you don't feel like it, you must eat."

"Thank you." Emily circles around behind her to dump her coffee in the sink and light the stove under the kettle.

"So, tell me." Margaret says as she pulls out a stool. "How is our Ned doing?"

Without trying to stop the tears, Emily sits beside her and describes her visit to the ICU and recounts her phone conversation with Natalie. Margaret does not speak, offering instead her total presence. When Emily is done, they sit in silence for a while.

"What can I do to help?"

"You've just done it. You listened. You didn't try to fix it or me. You didn't walk away."

As the kettle whistles, Margaret gets up and prepares two cups of tea. "Here. Drink. Eat."

Emily finishes her peach and then takes a few bites of her croissant. "It's not the most nutritious choice, but it's one of those small offerings from my mother you talked about. An ordinary croissant that's not so ordinary after all."

"I call that extraordinarily nutritious. Nourishing yourself in every sense of the word. Perfect."

"And this?" Emily nods at the potted plant with its burst of long fleshy leaves with serrated edges, thick at the bottom and tapering to slender points. "Is it an aloe?"

"It is a variety of aloe, yes. My Native teachers say it's good medicine to have in your home. You apply some of its gel to a burn or sting, and it will soothe as it heals. And like all plants, it oxygenates your home. Whenever you look at it, let it remind you to breathe. We women tend to be shallow breathers. Other than that, let it be a silent, healing presence."

"I know just the place for it." As Emily pushes back her stool and gets up, her arm sweeps the discarded pink envelope off the counter onto the floor. "Oh. I forgot about this." She stoops and picks it up. "It's what set my mother off just before you arrived. She says it's from my dad's mother. The one we met …" She sets the plant down and stares at her name written on the envelope in her grandmother's handwriting. Bold swirling letters in blue ink on the pale-pink paper. If she never opens it, she can't be disappointed.

"Would you like to be alone with it?"

"No!" Emily looks up at her. "I'm not sure I want to open it. Now or ever."

"Ah."

"No insights as to what might be inside? No inklings?"

"Sorry. Not a one."

Emily tosses it back on the counter. "I don't think I can handle this right now. I mean, what incredible timing. I …" Again, the tears come.

Margaret embraces her, patting her back. "There, there. You don't have to do anything right now. Nothing at all."

"I think I'd like to take a shower."

"Just let the water wash everything down the drain until you feel like stepping into the next moment, and then the next, and so on through the day. I'll clean up the dishes and put things away. Then I'll stay or go, whichever serves you best."

As Margaret wipes the counter down, she stares at the envelope. She picks it up and studies the handwriting, tracing it with her forefinger. Her chest tightens and her gut contracts. A wave of sorrow nearly overwhelms her, and she is forced to sit on a nearby stool. Such pain. Such regret. Such grief. And underneath it all, such naked hope.

"Margaret?" Emily stands in the doorway of her bedroom wrapped in a towel, her damp hair pulled up in a top knot. "It's bad, isn't it? I knew I shouldn't read it."

"No. I think you should read it. I think it might help."

"Now?"

"Especially now." Margaret hands her the envelope.

Emily walks around the couch and sits. Carefully, she opens the envelope, pulls out several sheets of folded paper, and reads.

Dear Emily,

I'm not sure how to begin. You are my only child's child—my only grandchild—and I failed you and I am deeply sorry. In hopes that you will read this, I want you to know that your daddy loved you with all his heart.

Your grandfather and I spoiled your dad. We failed him in important ways. He wanted to be a good dad but he wasn't ready to be a father. He was too much of a child himself and we own the blame for that.

I know your mother felt that we blamed her for their hardships, and we did nothing to disprove that. All we could see from our myopic perspective was a beautiful young woman who bedazzled our boy and saddled him with children he couldn't father and a load of grief he couldn't handle. Writing this makes me cringe. We saw everything through the lens of overindulgent parents unable to admit how ill-prepared our son was for life. We were not kind

*to your mother or helpful when she faced tragedy.
We are deeply ashamed. None of this is easy to
admit. But truth is truth.*

*Our boy loved her and that should have been
enough. We should have seen how good she was
for him. We should have welcomed her and treated
her as our daughter. He once told me that he didn't
feel worthy of her love and faith in him and so he
went about destroying both. (Not intentionally, of
course.)*

*We enjoyed our time with you before things fell
apart. Your dad lit up around you, and you filled
him with song. You were such a bright little thing,
and we missed you when he didn't bring you by. I
honestly don't know why we didn't make an effort
to see you on our own. Your grandmother Emily
would have included us happily.*

*Then our Danny died and our hearts shattered.
When we could finally walk around in the world,
we couldn't bear the thought of seeing you. Of
seeing your beautiful red curls and those green eyes
and Danny's bright smile. We couldn't see past our
own selfishness to tend to what you needed. That is
my lasting regret.*

*I say 'we,' but I'm sorry to say your grandfather
suffers from dementia. When I saw you at Danny's
grave, I flew off the handle. When I realized it was
you, I was stunned. When I came back to myself,
you were leaving and shame flooded in and I froze.*

*I understand if you don't want to see me and I
don't expect forgiveness. But I had to tell you that I
am sorry and that I'm glad you have his guitar pick.
I've kept it at the base of the stone all these years,
burying it a little each winter to protect it. Then this
year I couldn't find it. It's appropriate that you were
the one to discover it.*

*I've enclosed copies of some of his songs. I have
the originals and will give them to you. I didn't
want to send them through the mail, in case you
tossed this letter unread and the music with it. But
they belong to you.*

*Please know I am happy to answer any questions
you have about this side of your family tree. (Suffice
it to say it's filled with music and stories.) You
deserved better than what we gave, and you have a
right to know about the sweet, sensitive man from
whom you came.*

Sincerely,
Kathleen Fitzgerald Donne,
your paternal grandmother

Emily sets the letter aside and, her breath catching, looks at the other pages. Musical staves are marked with handwritten notes and lyrics. Scrawled notations in thick pencil fill the margins. At the top of the first page, in swirling cursive, is the title: *Family Man*. She shuffles to the next page. *For Janet* in the same handwriting. At the top of the third sheet: *Emily's Song*.

She pulls the pages to her chest. Margaret sits beside her but says nothing.

Finally, Emily turns to her. She separates out the pages of the letter and hands them to Margaret. "You were right. It helps. Go ahead. Read it."

When she finishes, Margaret looks up at her, smiling. "No matter how you feel about this or her, it's a beginning. A shift has taken place, and nothing about you will ever be quite the same. No matter what your small self is thinking, your soul is dancing."

"To my father's music. And my father is singing. I can almost hear his voice in these lyrics. Lyrics he wrote for my mother and me. I don't know if it's memory or wishful thinking, and I don't care. I can hear my father singing."

Margaret smiles. "And his timing could not be more perfect."

Chapter 34

In the late afternoon, Margaret gathers summer squash and cucumbers and a fat heirloom tomato for supper, and then snips parsley, basil, and dill as she passes the herb garden. When she returns to the kitchen, the message light is blinking on her phone. She fills the sink with cold water and plunges the sun-warmed vegetables in for a rinse before hitting the playback button.

The first message is from Ben Hardwick, the carpenter she's called about rebuilding her workshop. His raspy voice apologizes that he's away for a month. He suggests a man in York Harbor and leaves the number. The second message is from Annie Foss, asking her to call.

She sighs and dials the number Ben left. It rings five times before a woman answers, sounding winded. "Yes?"

"Hello, I'm calling on the recommendation of Ben Hardwick. I'm looking for a carpenter with design skills. Have I the right number?"

There is a hesitation, then, "You want my dad. He's not in right now. Can I take a message?"

Margaret lays out what she needs, and the woman promises a call back.

Impatience sizzling, Margaret hangs up with a sigh. "Fingers crossed, girls. I was really hoping for Ben on this."

Annie Foss answers on the second ring. "Oh, Margaret, I had an interesting encounter in the pharmacy today. An elderly lady asked if I was Jake's widow. That word just stopped me in my tracks, let me tell you! *Widow.* I still can't get used to it." Annie's voice seems to fade.

"That's a hard one. I know."

"Sorry." Annie's voice comes back stronger. "I got sidetracked. What I wanted to tell you is that this old woman, eighty if she was a day, was a teacher and remembered Jake fondly. She admired the way he looked out for everyone. She told me I was a lucky lady to have married such a good man."

"How sweet for you to hear that. And how right she was."

"She asked if I knew you too. When I said I did, she said she always worried about you and was relieved when you went off to art school and later moved to Camden. She said that mess with the Kennedy gang was heartbreaking, and she regretted not being able to do anything to help you."

Margaret smiles. She knows exactly who Annie is talking about. "Oh, but she did help. Miss Miranda Welks was a blessing, kindness itself. She was my ninth-grade English teacher and she introduced me to haiku. She and poetry saved my life."

"Well, she doesn't seem to know that, Margaret."

"Thank you for saying that. I'm ashamed to say I haven't seen her in a long time."

"Well, you told me that the old business is coming back around again. Sounds like Miss Miranda Welks is a part of that."

"A very positive part. A light in a dark business. What would I do without you, my friend? Thanks again."

"Happy to be able to give a little back."

"See you tomorrow night at Hilda and Bryce's August Supper?"

"Definitely."

Margaret is smiling as she hangs up, pleased that Annie is feeling less indebted to her. Pleased that their friendship is finally coming into balance.

As she slips her hands into the sink and gently rubs the vegetables free of garden soil, a series of images swims before her. A handsome new building stands in her backyard. A man, his back to her, is balanced on a tall ladder, attaching something beneath the window at the peak of the roof. She senses, but cannot see, another male figure—much younger—standing below.

Inside the building are rows of shelves holding dyes and inks and paints, pens and brushes. Rolls of thick paper and lengths of wood, foraged limbs, and branches stick up from bins on the floor. A workbench holds her jigsaw, table saw, and miter box. A vice attached to the edge of the bench gleams dully, its movable jaws standing open. A multi-drawer cabinet sits to the left of the bench, filled with hand tools and clamps.

A huge worktable dominates the center of the room, and a smaller wooden table stands by a south-facing wall of windows. The table is draped with a linen tablecloth and set with a tea service for two. She hears a dry crackling laugh. *It's about time you sat and aired things out.*

With the chiming of her cell phone, the visions vanish. She dries her hands and picks up.

"Hello," a man says. "My daughter left a message to call this number, but I'm afraid she didn't leave a name. Something about rebuilding a workshop that burned down?"

"Yes. Ben Hardwick gave me your number. I'm Margaret Meader over in the Berwicks and—"

"Margaret? This is a pleasant surprise. Kenneth Chisholm here. We ran into each other in the woods the other day. Literally."

"Oh, my. Kenneth. I had no idea. What an interesting coincidence."

"So, you need a carpenter?"

"I do. But I also need someone who can work with my design ideas and help with the cleanup from the fire." Margaret keeps talking, afraid to stop and give him a chance to say he can't do it. "What I have in mind is a bit larger and more involved than the shed I lost." Finally, she stops and holds her breath.

"Well, I'm finishing up a job this week, and my next scheduled client just got transferred to California and had to cancel a huge project. What do you say I come by in a day or so and assess the situation and give you an estimate? If it looks like we're on the same page, I could start as early as next week."

Margaret is silent for a moment.

Kenneth jumps in to fill the gap. "You aren't obliged to take it any further than the look-see, of course. You want to get the right guy for something as personal and important as your workshop. I can give you some names if it doesn't work out. No problem."

As she speaks, a glimpse of her earlier vision returns. "Do you want to set a date now or call me when you have some time?"

"How's tomorrow for you? I could come by around four."

"I have an evening obligation, but four should give us plenty of time."

After giving him directions and hanging up, Margaret prepares a savory garden supper and carries a tray to the outdoor table. The girls run up the hill and sit on either side of her chair.

"Tomorrow morning, I'll check in with Emily about Ned," she says aloud, "then I'll visit Miss Welks." The girls cock their heads as if party to a conversation. "Then tomorrow afternoon, I'll go over my workshop sketches and prepare something for the August Supper." She takes a few bites of her dinner, enjoying the explosion of earthy flavors in her mouth. "And late tomorrow afternoon …" She smiles. "Kenneth will come over."

The girls sit up taller at the sound of this name. "Ah. You remember Kenneth. And maybe he'll bring Gulliver and Maxie?" At this, the dogs are up and prancing in place. "No promises. But maybe." She laughs and finishes her meal, and then suggests a walk before dark.

By the time they return home, long shadows have crept across the backyard and darkness has seeped inside the house. Margaret plunks her supper tray down beside the sink.

Suddenly bone tired, she heads up stairs. As she climbs into bed, she realizes she's left her phone downstairs. Too exhausted to retrieve it, she is asleep within minutes.

༃

Her dreams are filled with him. Tall. Smiling. Standing over a drawing table, a pencil behind his ear. Bumping into her in the woods, looking startled and then delighted. The coarse feel of his linen shirtsleeve beneath her hand. Sea-green eyes. Disappearing dimple. Curling gray hair ruffled by a steady wind. A sense of familiarity, of recognition.

As she shifts toward waking, Joe is standing on the porch of their Camden cottage, nodding. Margaret sits up, tears just behind her eyes, the ache that lives always in her heart more pronounced than usual. She lets the quiet tears come, lets the ache be what it is.

"Oh, Joe," she says aloud. "I miss you so."

She allows herself to go back. Back to Camden. Back to that day. The police car stops out front. Two young officers, eyes downcast, backs stiff with the solemnity of the duty before them, walk toward the porch steps. They are too young to be doing this, too young to have seen what they've seen. She knows what they have come to say. Not because she had a precognition. She simply knows as they step out of their cruiser that they've come to tell her Joe is gone.

She no longer tortures herself with questions and regrets. No longer wracks her memory to see if she missed something that had been sent as foreshadowing.

Sitting on her bed, a cool morning breeze fluttering the curtains, she thanks the two young officers for carrying the burden of knowing until the very last moment. And she thanks Joe for loving her and giving her those years of peace, treating her like an ordinary woman. She laughs at the memory of his words when he first got to know her. "Okay, so you're a woman with some rather interesting talents. Any chance we can conjure a winning Megabucks ticket?"

She hears his laughter. She sees the happy scene captured by Joe's words days before his death.

"Freeze this moment," he said. "Freeze it, and we can take it out anytime we need it and live it again."

That moment she had been standing at the stove in the kitchen and he'd been on the porch setting the table, and their love hung in the air around them, insulating them from the world at large. The gulls swooped and cried out in the harbor, and the ocean lay blue and serene, glistening in the morning sunshine. He'd read her mind in that moment, and now she can take it out and savor it whenever the ache grows too big to be contained.

"I love you, Joe."

The girls nuzzle the bedcovers.

"I know. I know. Time to step into this beautiful day."

They scramble ahead of her down the stairs.

Chapter 35

A petite nurse in lavender scrubs shows Emily into the intensive care unit. "You can stay for ten minutes. Sorry it can't be longer, but that's hospital policy. You can hold his hand if you'd like. He probably won't feel it, but you never know. I'll let you know when the time is up."

Emily closes her eyes as the nurse leaves and then reopens them as she adjusts to being alone with the whirring, wheezing sounds. The still form on the bed looks pale and small and not at all like Ned. Hesitantly, she steps closer and reaches for his hand. His skin is cool, his hand limp as she slides hers under it. She is holding her breath. She lets it out and draws in deeply of the sterile air.

"Ned. It's Emily. I'm here."

Was that movement? Did he just move his hand? Again, she holds her breath, placing her whole attention on the feel of his hand in hers, scanning for a ripple of movement just beneath the surface. But there is nothing, and she lets the breath slip softly through her lips.

"Oh, Ned," she says with a smile. "Here I am imagining something because I want it so much. Here I am thinking you'll wake up at the very moment I've come. Well, don't mind me. It's just that I'm not very patient when it comes to you. I can't wait to look into those blue eyes and tell you how much you mean to me. I can't wait to hear you laugh again. I can sit in silence as long as you need me to, as long as I know you're coming back. Take all the time you need to heal, and then come back to me."

The nurse in lavender returns and signals that it's time for her to go.

"I love you, Ned." She bends and lightly kisses his hand. She wants to kiss his face, but there are tubes and wires and equipment in the way. "Know that I love you and I'll be here for you when you come back." She squeezes his hand and follows the nurse back out into the waiting area.

Ned's parents and Jacquie greet her with warm hugs when she emerges.

"It's a little less awful the second time around, yes?" Natalie says.

"Yes." Emily's voice is barely beyond a whisper. "A little."

"The doctors are particularly optimistic today for reasons I can't fathom," Ned's dad says. "They seem to think he's shifted into a different level of unconsciousness. They say it's good for the healing process, a protective mechanism that keeps the pain at bay while the deeper healing gets underway." He smiles at the women, looking for a moment like a boy. "Or something like that."

"But then," his wife says, "they've said such things before, Howard. Let's not get our hopes up too high."

"I thought his hand moved in mine," Emily says. Ned's parents brighten. "Wishful thinking, I know. I just wanted it so badly." She avoids eye contact, feeling like she might start to cry again and this time not be able to stop.

"Maybe not," Natalie says. "Maybe you were hypersensitive to it because you care so much. Maybe he really did move. Or maybe it was some natural muscular twitching that goes on all the time, and we're all just attaching meaning where it doesn't belong."

Emily understands Natalie's need to keep a tight rein on her hopes. She understands the human need to prepare for the worst while secretly hoping for the best, and the superstition of not daring to say aloud anything that could seem too hopeful.

The hallway door opens and a tall doctor in blue scrubs enters. "Ned has regained consciousness," he states without preamble. "He's opened his eyes and I'm about to examine him. I thought you'd want to know. As soon as I'm done, you may be able to see him for a very few minutes." With that, he strides past them and into the ICU.

The four recipients of this news stand in stunned silence, watching the door swing closed behind the doctor.

Jacquie is the first to speak. "Oh, my God! Oh, my God! I can't believe it. All this time we've waited for this news, and I can't believe it. Did he really just say what I think he just said?" She is crying and laughing at the same time.

Natalie pulls her in for a hug. "Yes. He said it. Ned is awake. Our boy is awake." She wipes her eyes and leans back against her husband.

Jacquie turns to Emily. "You felt it. You did. He *did* move his hand. Oh, Emily, I'm so glad he met you." She throws her arms around Emily.

The wait seems interminable, and the foursome sits in silence, exhausted from the explosion of emotions.

Finally, the door swings open again and the doctor stands before them, softer in manner, less abrupt. "He's awake, and I think seeing you would be very good for him. He can't talk because of his breathing tube. I want to give that a little more time. Maybe by tomorrow. I've told him as much as I think he can hear right now. The basics of time and place, and the fact that he's suffered some injuries from a rescue accident. So, don't throw too much at him. Mainly, let him see and touch you. Then he'll probably slip into sleep, and you should go and get some rest. He's going to need a healthy team around him in the months ahead."

Natalie speaks first. "We'd all like to go in together. We promise not to overwhelm him. In fact, we'll be silent if that's best. But he needs to see all four of us."

The doctor looks at her for a long moment and then nods. "All right. You don't have to be silent but limit your words. Speak one at a time, and give him time to adjust his focus with each new speaker. Got it?"

"Got it," Howard says with a grin.

The nurse goes in ahead of them and tells Ned in a deliberate manner that he has some visitors coming in. When he attempts to lift his head, she gently settles him back down with a hand on his forehead. She reminds him that he's hooked up to some equipment and must let it and her do all the work. "Just lie back and enjoy your family's visit."

Natalie and Howard lead the way into the tiny room, followed by Jacquie and then Emily. When he sees them, Ned lifts his hand and tries to speak. Natalie rushes to his bedside and lovingly strokes his hand, getting him to focus on her face by leaning down and reminding him not to try to speak. "We're here, Ned. Mom. Dad. Jacquie. And Emily."

At the sound of Emily's name, Ned's eyes brighten and search the room. Natalie pulls Emily forward and steps out of the way.

Emily leans close, smiling, relieved to see life in his eyes again. Relieved to find the awful stillness gone. Relieved even to see the shadow of pain in those pale-blue eyes. "We're here, Ned. We're all here." She takes his hand in hers, kisses it, then holds it to her cheek. "And now we want you to rest and get well. We love you."

She starts to move away to let Jacquie and Howard come forward, but he squeezes her hand weakly and holds on. She leans close again, tears slipping down her face. "I love you. I'll be back. I promise."

A slight squeeze again, and then he releases her hand.

ॐ

As she eases her car onto the Maine Turnpike, Emily's thoughts tumble. *I said I love you! I never should have said that. It's way too early. I've put him on the spot. Idiot!*

Jacquie, silent until now, says, "He's going to be all right. He's going to be Ned again before we know it. Today was huge. And you were a big part of that."

"We all were. But mostly him. He's so strong. I just wish we could skip over the next few weeks. It breaks my heart to think of him suffering."

"He can take it, Emily. I've known him all my life, and if anybody can take it, Ned can. Especially with you at his side. Really. I don't mean to go all sappy or anything, but you and he were meant for each other. I know Nat and Howard see that too. And it's a pretty big deal when the parents of a son like the girlfriend. Believe me, I know what I'm talking about. Brian's parents like to pretend I don't exist or that I'm just a passing phase. You know, the old 'no one's good enough for their baby boy' type." She laughs.

"You? A five-star chef with her own twelve-star restaurant? Brains. Looks. Talent. What do they want?"

"I don't think they know. But it's definitely not me!"

"Their loss." Emily is smiling. It feels good to feel this light. To be able to laugh with a girlfriend and not have the next moment drop her into a chasm of despair. The chasm may still be open and in the vicinity, but it's less of a threat than it was a few hours ago.

They ride the rest of the way in chatty conversation punctuated by bursts of laughter.

After dropping Jacquie at her restaurant, Emily calls Margaret and leaves a happy message on her voice mail.

Back home, she heads toward her uncle's gardens and finds him sitting on the bench in the gathering dusk. She hurries over, eager to share the news. "He's awake! He woke up."

Otis rises and opens his arms. "I knew he would. He had good reason to." He kisses her on the forehead and embraces her. "Glad to hear he did it while you were up there."

"I'd just left his room when the doctor told us he'd opened his eyes, and I got to see him again. His parents and his friend Jacquie and I went in together for a brief visit. He couldn't talk because of the breathing apparatus, but he knew us. He knew me."

"Then the worst is over, the scary part when you don't know if he'll be himself or not. It may take a while, but he'll be back on his feet and chomping at the bit in no time."

"Emily? Is that you?" Her mother's voice comes at them through the trees.

Emily turns to see her mother skirting the back side of the pond. She seems ethereal as she steps from the deepening dark of the woods and walks through the ground fog hanging just above the path.

"A fey creature, your mother," Otis says. "A wood sprite come to pay us a visit."

Emily turns back to him, surprised. "You read my mind."

"Hardly, my dear. On evenings like this when the night sounds arise and the fog is in the hollow and the conditions are just right, we can see her most clearly. If we choose to use our heart's eyes or we're caught unawares."

"You are a poet, Uncle Otis. Dear, dear Uncle Otis." Emily hugs him.

"Emily has some good news," he calls to Janet.

"Oh?" She's closer now, almost to the bench.

"Ned woke up." Emily is guarded as she says this, her shields up since their last encounter.

Janet sits on the other side of Otis. "What do the doctors say?"

"They're optimistic. They're relieved that he's conscious. They hope to remove the breathing tube tomorrow and then go from there. His surgical wounds all look good, and they're counting on his natural state of good health and the good shape he was in before this. His parents are beside themselves with happiness."

"Don't get your hopes up too soon. Life has a nasty way of pulling the rug out. Did you get to see him?"

"Twice. He was still unconscious when I went in alone. Then we all went in together after he opened his eyes."

"All of you? Who was 'all of you'?"

"His parents and his friend Jacquie and me. He knew us. He squeezed my hand."

Her mother frowns. "And his parents didn't mind you being there? Didn't they want some time alone with their son?"

Emily barely stops herself from snapping at her mother in response to the underlying censure she perceives in her voice. "They welcomed me in and insisted I be included. They've been nothing but kind to me. Some people are like that. They even told me they're glad I'm in Ned's life."

"No need to sound defensive, Emily. I was merely surprised that a nonrelative would be allowed in at such a delicate moment. You said he'd just awakened. Usually hospitals don't allow that. I was just surprised."

"He squeezed my hand. It mattered to him that I was there."

"I'm sure it did. I give his parents a lot of credit in the midst of their grief. I'm glad for you. Really."

Emily suppresses a sharp retort. "Thank you. That means a lot."

The three sit in silence as the evening closes in and the air hums.

Finally, Otis stirs. "Summer in all her glory. Not much left to her, though. Almost September. Got to savor her while she's here. Anyone for a cup of tea before I take myself off to bed?"

"As long as it's herbal," Janet says. "Join us, Emily?"

Emily is quiet for a moment, taking in what Otis just said. As much as she wants to get to the other side of Ned's recovery, she wants to savor this time too. She wants to savor the heat of the days and the cool of the nights and the loveliness of evenings like this one, tinged with purple and steeped in otherworldliness.

"I think I'd like to sit for a few more minutes. Savor, as you say. I'll be along in a while."

"Suit yourself," Otis says. "I'll put the kettle on."

She sits listening to the beginning strains of the symphony of the night as her mother and uncle wend their way up the path. Her heart is light, her mind at peace. She allows her thoughts to drift without purpose or destination, and they keep touching down on the same remembered images and sensations. Ned's eyes wide, searching the room at the sound of her name. Those same eyes finding hers and locking on with an intensity that belied the notion that he might be trapped in a haze of confusion as he resurfaced. His hand in hers. The slight squeeze as she started to leave.

He knew her. He sought her. He relaxed when he found her. He squeezed her hand to let her know, *I'm here. I'm back.* Maybe it was a good thing she said she loved him.

She lets the tears come. She feels no need to wipe her cheeks. The moist evening air mingles with the wetness there and dampens her curly hair. She drops her head back and looks up into the first glimmerings of stars in the sky.

"Oh, Ned. We're going to be all right. I think we're going to be all right."

The rhythmic chirps and peeps of crickets and frogs pulse like a heartbeat, growing louder as the light fades. Emily immerses herself in the coming of night, in the series of plops at the edge of the pond and the something slithering through the grass and slipping into the water. In the distance, an owl hoots. She gets up and turns toward the house.

Janet and Otis sit at the kitchen table stirring hot mugs of tea. A third cup sits at Emily's place.

Otis looks up at her. "Janet tells me you got a letter from Danny's mother, Kathleen?"

Janet sighs and rolls her eyes at Otis.

"Now, Janet, no sense waiting for the two of you to get to it. Let's make an agreement to talk about things and not pretend they're not there. So." He turns back to Emily. "How long have the two of you been writing back and forth?"

"There's no back and forth about it. I received my first letter from her today."

"What brought that about? All these years go by and now she decides to write to you?"

"We ran into her at the cemetery—"

"We?"

"Emily and that woman," Janet interrupts. "That Margaret person."

"If you're going to start up with that again," Emily says, "I'm not going to talk about anything." She rises.

"Now wait just a minute, missy," Otis says. "This is what I'm talking about. Sit down and talk about this out in the open. Please. Humor an old man, will you?"

Emily sits. "Oh, so you're going to play the old man card, are you?" She hesitates, then sighs. "Okay." She looks across at her mother, waiting until she is willing to look back and not turn away. "Mother, I know you have issues with Margaret. But I would like for you to put them aside for now. We can talk about them later."

When Janet doesn't answer, Emily says, "Please. This is important to me."

Janet sighs. "All right. I'll put them aside. But—"

"No *buts,* Janet." Otis raises his brows as he questions her with his eyes.

"I was just going to say, I *do* want to talk about this at some time.'"

"Agreed." Emily looks from one to the other. "Now. I went to my Dad's grave for the first time not long ago. Then the other day, out of concern for me and because she sensed there was something to be resolved there, Margaret took me back to the cemetery. While we were there, his mother and her sister Rosalie saw us sitting by the grave. She got angry and confronted us."

"What a lot of nerve!" Janet exclaims.

"Please, let me finish."

Janet is chewing on the corner of her mouth, hands clenched, but she nods for Emily to continue.

"She thought we were strangers, but when she recognized who I was, she went mute. Margaret was very protective of me. She really put her in her place. She was curt but she did it with grace." Emily pauses to give her mother a chance to take in what she's saying. "As we were leaving, Rosalie came over and gave me this." She pulls the guitar pick from her pocket. "It's Dad's. She said my grandmother—"

"Your *grandmother?* Hah!" Janet practically spits out the word.

"I'm sorry, Mother. It's just the easiest way to tell this without saying *she* and *her.*"

"Well, it's hard to hear you call her that after—"

"I know. I *do* know. I'm just trying to tell you what happened. I know she was no grandmother to me. I know she was no friend to you. She was unkind and unsupportive. I know that, believe me."

Emily gives her mother a moment to sit with this, praying she hears her, really hears her. Janet looks across the table at her and then seems to deflate, her shoulders rounded, her face impassive.

"It was a peace offering of sorts. A gesture. Then Rosalie took my address. The letter arrived today, and you happened to be the one who brought it in from the mailbox."

"What did she say in it?" Otis looks concerned. "What could she possibly have to say after all this time?"

Emily looks back and forth between them. "I know this is painful for you, Mother, and I'm sorry. But I'm glad she wrote. It doesn't mean I want her to *be* in my life, but she did shed light on some things, and she apologized for failing both of us. She's ashamed and full of regret."

"What does she want from you?" Janet asks without trying to hide her bitterness.

"Understanding, I guess. And forgiveness, though she said she doesn't expect it. And she wants to tell me about my father and his side of the family."

"And how do you feel about it all?" Otis asks, placing his hand on hers.

"I'm still processing it. I had my mind on Ned and going to the hospital, so I put the letter away. But, Mother." She waits for Janet to look at her. "There's something else you need to know about the letter."

"Which is?" Janet looks wary.

"Which is that she included three of Dad's songs. … One is for you."

Janet sucks in a breath with a quivering sigh. Her gaze drops to the table.

Otis reaches over and places his free hand on hers.

"And the other two?" Janet asks.

"One is for me and the other is called 'Family Man.'"

Janet blows out a breath in disgust, shaking her head.

Emily rushes to continue. "It's about how much he *wasn't* one. About how much he wanted to but wasn't able to be. It's a beautifully written lament."

Janet sits in silence, her gray eyes welling with tears. "I don't think I can do this. I can't go back and revisit this." She is looking at her daughter now.

Otis pats both their hands. "You *can* and *must* do this, Chiclet.

For both your sakes." He smiles. "Hell, for *all* our sakes."

"I'd like to share the songs and the letter with you when you've had a chance to digest this."

Shaking her head, Janet starts to get up. Otis grasps her hand, and Emily rushes on, "I really think it'll help. All of us. Maybe especially you."

Janet drops back into her chair. "Emily. I know you think you're doing the right thing here, but you can't know what you're asking of me. You can't—" Her breath catches. "You can't possibly know."

Emily sighs and sits back. "I'm sorry. You're right. I can't. I just … I can't."

The three sit, eyes downcast, studying the intricate lines and whorls of the wood grain on the old tabletop. Otis still loosely covers the hands of his niece and grandniece with his own. No one moves. The night sounds filter in through the screen door.

Finally, Janet pushes back her chair, slips her hand out from under Otis's, and stands. The rhythms of the late summer night have taken on a bittersweet quality. All three are aware of it and the melancholy that has seeped into the room with them.

"I'm going to bed. I'm sorry."

"Will you …" Emily can't finish the question.

"I'm not going anywhere but to bed."

The sadness, the regret, the pain is palpable, and Emily feels both guilty and oddly relieved.

When they are alone, she turns to Otis. "I'm sorry I brought all this up."

"Au contraire, Little One. I have a good feeling about what happened here tonight. The only way out of this quagmire of old issues is to go into it. To wallow right through to the other side. We waded in tonight. Up to our hips, at least. You done good, kiddo. You done good."

Emily smiles. "You have such a way with words, Old Man." She gets up and goes over to him, kissing him on the forehead. "I think you may be right. I think we're at a … a sort of crossroads. At least, I hope we are."

"No doubt in my mind. And I think Lily May is smiling to beat the band."

"Oh, she definitely had a hand in it." She looks up. "Thank you, Aunt Lily May." Looking into her uncle's now moist eyes, she adds, "And now she's telling me to clean up these mugs and let you get off to bed. Looks like there's a heavily ripening harvest out there that'll need tending tomorrow."

"Not to mention the new addition on the potting shed that needs some serious attention." He gets up. "Good night, Sweet Pea. And never mind these dishes. They can wait until morning. You've had quite the day for yourself." He takes her in his arms. "That young man of yours will be up and about in no time, but he'll need you. So off to bed with you too."

ॐॐ

After washing up, Otis goes to Janet's bedroom door and knocks. Janet flings the door open. "What's wrong? Are you all right?"

"I'm fine. I'm fine." He pats the air in front of him as if tamping down a blaze. "Didn't mean to scare you."

"Oh, Otis. You had me going there for a minute." She has her hand to her heart.

"Just wanted to say something before you go to bed. Something for you to sleep on. You have a rare chance for a do-over here, Janet." He fixes her with a serious gaze. "Now don't blow it!"

Chapter 36

The early morning sun promises another hot day. Joe is with her again as she hums his favorite song. "Ah, yes," she says aloud. "A bright blessed day. Let's be in it, girls. Time for a good long walk."

An hour later, Margaret puts the kettle on and checks her phone. Three messages. She jumps to the one from Emily and smiles as she listens. Ned is awake.

She plays the message from Paul Edwards to find the same information about Ned and new news about Gordon Willoughby, the injured climber. He's still in critical condition, his prognosis is less hopeful, and his parents, in from New Mexico, would like to meet with Margaret. Paul leaves their contact information but no other details. The final message is from Hilda Hanson, her neighbor and friend, checking in about the August Supper that evening.

Margaret calls Emily, but she doesn't answer. She leaves a brief message and then dials Paul Edwards. Again, she gets voice mail. Unwilling to call the Willoughbys cold, she leaves a message for the chief to call her back. When she calls Miranda Welks, a warm human voice greets her.

Miss Welks happily accepts her spur-of-the-moment invitation to lunch at the Harrison House Gardens, and Margaret arranges to pick her up at 11:45.

Smiling, she prepares a breakfast salad of leftover quinoa, nuts, and blueberries. Stray lyrics still swirl in her head, and she sings loudly, "'I see friends shaking hands …'"

A colorful scene flashes before her. Bright bouquets of field flowers in mason jars on long tables with fluttering checked cloths. Heaping bowls and platters of food. Groups of neighbors talking, listening, laughing …

"'They're really saying I love you.'" Her strong alto voice rises. "'I—'"

A sharp knock on the door stops her. Embarrassment quickly gives way to curiosity as she opens it.

"I'm sorry to come by unannounced." Chief Paul Edwards stands on the mat twisting his hat in his hands, his eyes anxious. "Gordon Willoughby's parents followed me here. I didn't realize it was them behind me until I started up your drive. They're pretty distraught. Some of the hospital staff told them about you in more fanciful detail than was warranted. I tried to explain that to them."

"It's okay. I'll go get them." Margaret indicates the table and chairs in the backyard. "Why don't you join us for a few minutes, then you can slip away."

A car has stopped beside Paul's truck, a couple getting out of it. A tall thin man in his fifties puts out his hand as he approaches her. "Frank Willoughby." His eyes look toward but not at her, as if he's focused on something just beyond her right shoulder. "Gordon's dad. And this is my wife, Eileen." The woman nods.

Margaret shakes his hand and reaches out for Eileen's. The woman wraps her arms around herself and nods curtly again. Margaret lowers her hand and leads them out to the backyard table. "Let me get the tea things."

Paul leaps up. "Let me help you," he says, and follows her into the kitchen. Once inside, he apologizes. "I find it hard to be around that woman. I feel like I should be saying something, but I haven't a clue what would do."

"I know. Do you think he's the one who wants to be here and she's too timid to object?"

"I was hoping you'd know." He grins at her, looking for a moment like a teenage boy.

"Not a clue. Guess we'll figure it out as we go." She quickly fills a wooden tray with a pot of tea and the breakfast salad she made for herself. She hands the tray to Paul, and they go out to the guests who look like the last thing they want is herbal tea and breakfast.

Without asking, she pours four cups of tea. Then she places a spoon and bowl of breakfast salad in front of each of them.

She seats herself and lets the silence settle. She lifts her mug and blows on the steaming tea, inhaling the scents of lavender and mint. Paul follows her lead, taking a careful sip.

Frank Willoughby plunges his spoon into the bowl, but it never reaches his mouth. He looks at his wife hunched in the chair beside him and drops the spoon. Berries roll across the table as he props his elbows and rests his forehead on clenched fists. His words are barely audible. "We're at the end of our rope. They say you have some sort of power. That you can heal our boy. They say you saved the other one because you know him. That you focused on him and not our son."

Paul starts to rise. "Now wait a minute, Mr. Willoughby."

"It's okay, Paul." Margaret puts out her hand to stay him. "Mr. Willoughby—Frank. I helped to find the boys, but that's all I did. That's all I was able to do. Ned's recovery has nothing to do with me. The nature of his injuries was different from your son's. Believe me, if there was anything I could do for Gordon, I would—"

"Witch!" Eileen Willoughby suddenly stands, knocking her chair over and slamming her hands on the table. "Why won't you help him? He's just a boy. He's a good boy. Our only child."

Paul is up and around the table. He retrieves the overturned chair and firmly guides the woman back into it. "I know you're suffering terribly, but Margaret Meader is not the cause of your son's accident or his condition. If not for her, we might never have found him. Now please, Mrs. Willoughby. You owe this woman an apology."

Margaret turns to Eileen. "I understand your frustration. There are those who don't understand what I do but love to talk about me. They honestly think I'm a witch. But they are wrong."

Paul remains standing. "I'm sorry, but I have to be going. And since I'm responsible for you finding your way here, I must ask you to follow me out."

"Please, just a few minutes." The anguish in Frank's voice sears Margaret's chest. "Please?"

"I'm sorry." It is spoken so quietly, so meekly, they all nearly miss it. Then Eileen clears her throat and speaks more loudly. "The woman at the hospital was so convincing. She said you have the power to make terrible things happen to people and to heal them afterwards for money. I thought it sounded far-fetched, but one of the nurses said you're psychic and that Ned Burrows is a friend. Then Ned woke up and Gordon may not and ..." She stops.

"This is not who we are," Frank says, taking his wife's hand in his. "We're just so afraid."

"It's okay, Paul," Margaret says. "We'll be fine here."

After giving Margaret a long questioning look, he excuses himself, nodding curtly to the couple.

Sophia and Grace come to settle on either side of Margaret's chair.

Margaret starts to explain. "Sometimes when I look at a topographical map or go to a search area, I can find missing people. I can't explain it, it just happens. That's what they asked me to do the day of the landslide, and I found the cavern and sensed the presence of both Ned and Gordon. Sadly, the other two were no longer alive. But your boy and Ned were holding on to life. It's true that I know Ned and I honed in on him in order to find the exact spot."

She watches their faces, trying to gauge if she should venture further. Tears run down Eileen's cheeks. Frank's face is a mask of neutrality. His breath is thin and shallow, the movement of his chest barely perceptible.

He picks up his mug and drinks. Then Eileen sits forward and does the same. "There's more," Frank says, looking at Margaret over the rim of his mug. "I know there's more. Please."

A butterfly cuts a jagged path through the air between them, and a jay screeches as it leaps into flight from a nearby maple.

Margaret looks from one to the other. "Just before the rescuers broke through, I sensed Gordon rise from his body to stand on a sort of threshold, silhouetted by a brilliant light behind him. Then I saw some scenes from his life and felt joy."

"What scenes?" Franks asks.

Margaret closes her eyes. "I saw him in cap and gown, beaming as he stood between the two of you." She pauses. "And him as a little boy in a red snowsuit and a thick knitted scarf—a pink one— laughing and catching snowflakes on his tongue. And him as a teenager, diving."

"Into the quarry." Tears run down Frank's face. "We used to worry that he'd break his darn fool neck. That's what I would say to him. 'You're gonna' break your darn fool neck!' But he loved taking chances and being outside. Once he discovered climbing, there was no rock face he didn't want to try."

Eileen grabs her husband's arm. "Oh! The pink scarf!" She smiles for the first time, suddenly looking very young. "He wore it home from school one day. He'd traded with one of his classmates. I worried that Frank would take a fit seeing his boy in a girl's color. But he just smiled and asked if he could have a turn wearing it. Later, the two of them went sledding on the back hill, and Frank *did* wear it, and Gordon laughed so hard, he nearly fell off the sled. I can still see him, his cheeks all red and blotchy."

They settle into silence as their smiles fade.

"Then what?" Frank looks hard into Margaret's eyes. "You say you saw him rise?"

She clears her throat. "He was getting ready to leave. I'm sure of it. But then the rescuers broke through. He looked back at Ned and beyond Ned to the rescuers, a look of indecision on his face. Then my vision went blank. But he obviously chose to come back."

"The doctors said they had to resuscitate him twice before getting him to the hospital. Now they say he may never come back to us. He may stay in a sort of limbo. We can't live like that. We want him back or we want him there, on the other side. When that doctor said 'a permanent vegetative state,' I thought my heart would stop. I wanted my heart to stop. I'd gladly let my heart stop if his would keep beating."

"Don't, Frank. Don't talk like that. I can't bear to hear you talk like that."

"Can you see anything now?" Frank looks down at his hands.

Margaret sits in perfect stillness, listening, waiting. "I'm sorry. I wish I could make myself see what you want me to see."

Frank lifts his head. "Ah. Well. I had to ask."

With a shake of her head, Margaret dismisses the tiny voice that wants her to make something up to give these parents solace. The voice she's heard before in difficult situations when her inner movie screen has gone white.

"I truly am sorry."

Again, a voice speaks in her head, but this time it's different. *"Somebody needs what I no longer need. Somebody's little boy."* Margaret holds up a finger to the couple across from her, telling them with her listening posture that something's happening.

"Tell them I'll hold on until this afternoon, but then I have to go. A little boy's laugh will let them know I'm okay. Tell them I love them. Tell them—" His voice fades. Then, in a crackling burst of energy, *"Tell them it's an incredible climb!"*

She lets his voice resolve into silence and then looks into the searching eyes of his parents. "I have a message from him that is both beautiful and difficult to hear."

A soft gasp escapes Eileen as she grips her husband's hand, but both nod for Margaret to continue.

"He has to go. But first, he's asking something of you. He says somebody's little boy needs what he no longer needs. That's why he stayed."

The stricken couple lean toward her, anguish on their faces. Frank speaks for them both. "What little boy? What does he mean?"

Margaret takes a breath and plunges on. "Has anyone talked to you about organ donation?"

"I told them I didn't want to even think about that!" Eileen starts to rise. "I told them …" She looks at Margaret's face and drops back into her seat, her voice softening. "Yes. They asked us if we would consider that."

"*That's* what he's asking for. He says he'll hold on until this afternoon so you can be there, but then he has to go. He also says he won't really be gone. He asks you to listen. He says the boy's laugh will let you know he's okay." She looks at Frank. "He says to tell you it's an incredible climb!" She says it with the same exuberance he showed. "Most important, he says, 'Tell them I love them.'"

Both parents drop their heads to their hands, tears overwhelming them. Then, as if on cue, both look up at Margaret. Her chest tightens. She's taken a huge risk in blurting it out so matter-of-factly to two people already on the edge.

"Thank you." Frank takes his wife's hand and stands. "That woman at the hospital was dead wrong about you. And you were wrong about you too. You *do* have the power to heal. There's a lot more to it than saving someone from dying." He holds out his hand. "You've given us as much peace of mind as two parents can possibly have in the midst of the worst tragedy of our lives. And some other set of parents is about to get the best gift of their lives— the gift of Gordon."

"You really did see him!" A look of wonder brightens Eileen's drawn face. "I mean, nobody could make up that pink scarf." She smiles through her tears. "And now I must go and say good-bye to my precious boy and sign forms that will save someone else's child."

After they've gone, she calls Paul. "They've left. Their son is going to pass today, and they're as ready as parents can ever be. I thought you should know and be prepared yourself."

He thanks her, emotion heavy in his curt response.

Back in the kitchen, she answers her cell phone to Emily's chirping voice, "Oh, Margaret. I feel like I'm floating. Ned is going to be all right. But then, you knew that all along."

"And you got to be there at the time. You were touched by grace." One of the dogs leaps up and runs over to her. Margaret laughs and ruffles her head. "Not you. The other grace." Turning back to her phone, she invites Emily to come for lunch the next day.

"Sounds great. I'll be by at noon."

"Before you go, I feel I must tell you some sad news. Gordon Willoughby will pass away today. I'm telling you because you may see his parents at the hospital. They know it's coming, but that doesn't mean they're ready. We never know what we'll really do once a thing moves from being a concept understood by the head to a reality experienced by the heart."

Emily is quiet, fully aware of the contrast between what's happening for her and Ned's parents and what's about to happen for Gordon Willoughby's. "Thank you for telling me."

As she puts down her phone, an uneasy feeling passes through Margaret. A plume of darkness sits just over her left shoulder and behind her. She turns quickly, but it is gone. She pauses for a moment, takes a breath, and goes upstairs to shower and dress for lunch with Miss Welks.

As she steps out of the shower, she again feels the darkness hanging just behind her. As she wipes the fogged-up mirror, a kaleidoscopic burst flickers in the upper right corner, then is gone. Hand to her heart, she hears a snatch of a song rise and fall away. *Oh, my darling, oh my darling ...* Silence follows. She slips on her robe and grabs a towel.

In the backyard, she towel dries her hair in the sun. As she turns to head inside, her robe slipping off her shoulder, she stops. A man is standing at the corner of the house. A stranger.

The girls bound up from the stream, barking. They stand in front of her, growling uncharacteristically. She doesn't quiet them as she pulls her robe around her and tightens the sash.

"You wanna hush those bitches up?" he says without moving.

Margaret stiffens. "You wanna tell me what your business is here?" Her voice is firm, imparting much more authority than she feels.

"No harm meant. Heard there's a woman of a certain ... reputation living in these parts. Heard that might be you. And I thought—"

"This is private property. These 'bitches' belong here, and they've made it clear that you're not welcome. I'll thank you to leave." She stands as tall as she can, despite feeling vulnerable in her light robe and bare feet.

He steps toward her, his hands hidden in his pockets. Alarm sizzles up her body as the girls ramp up their agitated barking.

"Hey, Margaret."

The stranger turns at the sound of a male voice at his back.

John Longfeather stands a few feet behind him. "Everything all right? The girls seem a mite upset."

The stranger turns back toward Margaret. "The *girls* have no reason to fear me." He pulls his hands from his pockets and splays his open palms at his sides. "I'm just a simple traveler looking to meet someone I've been hearing about. Started off on the wrong foot is all." He starts to walk away but turns back abruptly. "My grandmother had the sight. She had reason to be wary too, especially when they tried to burn her out. You can imagine how unsettling that might be." As he walks past John, he touches the bill of his rumpled baseball cap in a brief salute.

John follows him around the house and then comes back. "Saw him heading up your drive on my way to deliver some ice and hay bales to the Hansons' for tonight."

"I'm glad you did. I have to admit, I was damned uncomfortable when I turned to find him here. As you could see, so were the girls." She pets them both. "What was he driving, anyway? I never heard him come up the hill."

"On foot. One of the reasons he didn't feel right to me. What's a guy doing on foot way out here? I'll make sure he continues on his way when I leave. Might even give him a lift to wherever he's headed."

"Thank you, John."

"What did he say he wanted?"

"The first thing he did was ask me to 'hush those bitches up.' Then, in so many words, he said he was looking for me. I asked him to leave and then you miraculously appeared. I don't know what I would have done next. He didn't appear ready to go on his own."

"Sounded like a veiled threat, the bit about the burning. After your shed, I think it's worth checking him out."

"I hate to give the whole thing power by expending energy on it, but …"

"I'm heading out now. I'll check on his whereabouts. Let you know what I find."

"Will you be at the supper tonight?"

"Planning on it. But then, you never know."

"Good title for a book, *You Never Know*. Mind if I borrow it?"

"Consider it yours."

&-&

Margaret pulls up to the Harrison House on the river and the old truck's engine sputters into silence. Time to give the old girl a tune-up, she reminds herself. She chuckles, realizing the same need not be said for the woman seated beside her. Then she hurries to catch up as her former teacher hops down from the cab and heads up the walkway.

As the two walk arm in arm into the grand foyer of the mansion, they step back into another age. They pass through gleaming French doors as cool air off the river greets them on the covered terrace. Below the beautifully appointed tables, formal gardens dotted with fountains and statuary spread to the banks of the tidal river.

After ordering, Margaret looks across the table at her companion. Olive-skinned beneath a mass of white curls, her face is barely wrinkled. Her black eyes glisten with curiosity as Margaret hesitates, gathering her thoughts.

"What is it, my dear? You're looking so serious. I hope nothing's wrong."

"Sorry. I'm just at a loss for words at the moment."

"You're a poet, Margaret. I trust you'll find them." The older woman's light laughter lifts off into the air.

"I want you to know how much …" Margaret's throat catches, her eyes fill.

"What is it, my dear?" Miss Welks reaches across the table and takes her hand.

"Thank you. I want to say thank you."

"For what?"

"For being there for me in the darkest time of my life."

"I was your teacher. That's what I was there for."

"You saved my life. I should have told you long ago."

The older woman doesn't dismiss her words—her truth. She meets Margaret's gaze, squeezing her hand.

"You were always a beautiful being of light, Margaret Meader. Fear of that light turned people into monsters. I could do nothing about that back then, and that is my one regret."

"But you did do something. You showed me that I was worthy of the care and concern of Miss Miranda Welks. And you gave me literature and poetry. My way through it all."

Their server arrives with two bowls of cucumber soup topped with sprinklings of fresh dill and clipped spikes of chive. With a mild flourish, he offers freshly ground pepper to both, bows with a mischievous smile, and leaves.

They eat their soup in silence, and when their sandwiches arrive, Margaret takes up a lighter thread. "We should make this a habit. A monthly luncheon date that is sacrosanct."

"I would *love* that! Let's schedule our next one right now." With this, the eighty-something-year-old Miss Welks pulls out a smart phone in a bejeweled hot-pink case and opens to her calendar.

Margaret smiles. "If someone had told me years ago I'd be walking around with a palm-sized phone that would replace my datebook, address book, and camera and could connect me to anything from a thesaurus to a tide chart, I'd have called it sci-fi nonsense."

"Since I have at least twenty years on you, imagine what I've seen! But have we advanced as a human race? I'd like to hope you'd be treated with more understanding if you were coming up today, but I'm not sure."

"I have to believe there will always be people like you that kids can look to for help and hope. I'd like to be one of those people myself. To pay it forward, as the expression goes."

"Something tells me you do that every day with your special

gifts and kind ways." She pauses, fixing Margaret with a serious gaze. "Maybe that's why you had to suffer so growing into those gifts. The terrible abuse from your classmates, the tragic loss of that brilliant father of yours, and then dear little Mattie ..." Miss Welks sits back, overcome.

Margaret recalls the division that erupted within the community when Mattie died—some neighbors sending condolences, food, and comfort; others praising their god for visiting a just punishment on a wicked family.

"Mattie comes to me sometimes," Margaret says softly. "He wants to help me find my way to forgiveness. But I'm still pretty attached to my anger."

"Forgiveness is a hard one. Your anger is understandable. So much harm was done to you. But I'm sure you'll find your way there. And a heavy burden will be lifted from your heart."

"That's what Mattie keeps trying to tell me." She smiles at the thought of him. "He helps me with my work too."

"Makes my heart smile just thinking of his sensitive little face and wild laughter."

"He was too sweet for this world. But on some level, his sweet energy lives on." Margaret laughs again. "You're one of the few people I can say such things to."

"'There are more things in heaven and earth, Horatio, than are dreamt of in your philosophy.'"

"Ah, the Bard understood such matters. I wonder who his guides and invisible means of support were."

Miss Welks laughs brightly. "Well worth pondering."

Their waiter clears their dishes and asks if they'd like to see the dessert menu. Margaret catches the look of hopeful anticipation that flickers across her companion's face and nods to him.

"May I suggest you order and then take a brief walk before I bring it out? The Trust wants our guests to have a dining experience, and that includes a walk about the gardens. What more perfect time than between the entrée and the dessert?"

"Oh, Margaret, this day just gets more and more delicious. We should make our reservation for our next visit before we leave."

ॐॐ

As Margaret places food for the community supper into the refrigerator, movement outside the kitchen window catches her eye. Her heartbeat quickens, and she shudders at the memory of the disheveled man who appeared earlier.

"Damn him. He's not going to make me afraid in my own house," she says aloud, and tosses her apron over a kitchen chair. She steps out the back door to find John Longfeather looking out over the hills. Sophia and Grace sit on either side of him, backs straight and tall.

Margaret smiles at the tableau. "So much for my guard dogs."

John nods. "Had a talk with your visitor. He's down by Old Creek in one of those all-in-one camper trucks. Not quite sure what to think of him. Odd duck. I'll keep checking on him. My cousins too."

John continues to look off toward the woods as he speaks again. "He has a name for his truck. Rocinante."

"Cervantes or Steinbeck, I wonder?"

"Beg pardon?"

"Rocinante. The camper John Steinbeck had specially built to travel across the country—"

"Oh, right. Named it after Don Quixote's horse. Wanted to get back in touch with America. Wrote a book about it."

"*Travels with Charley.*"

"I remember reading it in high school. He called the trip Operation Windmills or some such. I knew that word felt familiar when I saw it on his camper. Went right over my head at the time. Might have given me some insight into him during our conversation."

"Well, I appreciate your talking to him at all."

"I also thought since my truck's empty, I'd take a load of this shed debris to the transfer station. Going right by it anyway."

"Again, I thank you. I have a carpenter coming by shortly to discuss rebuilding. I want him to clean up the rest of the mess as well as build the replacement."

"That be Ben Hardwick?"

"No. Couldn't get him. He recommended this man from York Harbor. Turned out to be someone I had just met out on one of the old trails in the woods. His name—"

She is interrupted by the sound of a truck in the driveway out front. "That must be him now."

The girls leap up as two black labs gallop around the corner of the house. The four dogs meet in a frenzy of barking and sniffing and dancing about the yard.

"Sorry!" Kenneth Chisholm appears, holding up two leashes. "Afraid they got away before I realized what was happening. You're going to think I have the two worst-behaved dogs in the county."

"The four worst-behaved dogs," Margaret says with a laugh as the dogs head off down the hill. They stop briefly to splash in the stream at the bottom before chasing each other 'round and 'round on the farther hillside.

"Maybe they'll tire themselves out." Kenneth grins, extending his hand to Margaret. "Good to see you again."

"This is John Longfeather. John was just offering to take a load of this debris away."

"Kenneth Chisholm." the older man offers his hand.

"Your reputation precedes you," John says. "I admire your design aesthetic, Mr. Chisholm."

"So, you know Kenneth's work?" Margaret looks from John to Kenneth.

John nods. "The Prescott Peabody Award for green design is the most recent award, I believe. The Whetherling Retreat Complex is an extraordinary example of what a truly 'green' community of buildings can be. I tip my hat to you, sir." John touches the brim of his hat.

Margaret stands with eyebrows raised, mouth open. Then she reddens. "Well, this is embarrassing. Here I am, asking you to build a little backyard shed."

"A *workshop*, I believe you said. Designing and building an artist's workshop is no insignificant task. It's a most worthy undertaking. If you still want to consider me?"

She laughs, and both men smile at the warmth and richness of it. "I am many things, but I am no fool. Consider yourself considered."

"Well," John says, moving away. "I'm going to pull my truck around and start filling it up."

Margaret offers to help, but John shakes his head. "You have some serious business to discuss. Besides, you can't be mucking about in the blackened debris and then be getting yourself off to the party on time, now can you? Some people wouldn't be missed over there, but you certainly would be."

Margaret smiles her thanks and guides Kenneth over to the site of her burned-out workshop. Together they survey the footprint of the building and discuss enlarging it and including all the features Margaret has in mind. She then takes Kenneth into the house and lays out her drawings on the harvest table, on top of two unfinished puzzles.

"These are beautiful." Kenneth speaks in the near whisper of reverence. "Margaret, these must be framed and hung in the shop as soon as it's completed." He smiles down at her, and she finds herself wanting to reach out and touch the deep dimple in his cheek. She nearly does.

A soft knock on the door, then John sticks his head in. "I'm on my way, Margaret."

"Wait," Kenneth calls out to him. "Have you seen these?" He motions to John to join them.

"Now you're going to embarrass me again." Margaret moves back so John can get in past her.

Looking down at the drawings, he sucks in his breath and shakes his head.

"Amazing, right? I want to move right into this *shed*"—Kenneth gently mocks Margaret with the word—"and never come out again."

John nods. "That's Margaret's work, all right. Though her watercolors are usually more sketchy and accompanied by her even sketchier poems. As to framing ..."

"Oh, my God," Kenneth nearly shouts. "I know your work! You're the artist who signs her work with an *M* and a dash. Your work is only available through a handful of galleries in Boston and New York. Now who's embarrassed?"

He rushes on, caught up in a frenzy of artistic excitement she recognizes. "As a designer, you don't really need me. I can see exactly what you envision in these, and I can work out the necessary specs easily. I also have some suggestions for materials and a new brand of windows I think would be stunning as well as practical and energy efficient. And—"

"And you really have the time for a small job like this?"

"I can't think of anything I'd rather be doing. I haven't felt this excited about a project since ... Well, for a very long time. Reminds me of how I felt when I first started out.

"Of course, I realize I have to work up an estimate you can live with, but I'm beginning to see the finished building in my mind already. And that's always a good sign."

"It does include some dirty work, as John just discovered. The cleanup ..."

"A welcome part of the job. Not to get too schmaltzy here, but I'm reminded of the phoenix rising out of the ashes. I like to see and handle the ashes, which in this case are literal. In fact, at the risk of getting deeply schmaltzy, I wonder if you might not want to retrieve something from the rubble to incorporate into the new building. Maybe mix it into the foundation, or bury it beneath the building, or have a ceremony of some kind."

Kenneth looks suddenly uneasy, as if he's gone too far.

"You're hired," Margaret says.

"If she didn't say it, I was going to." John touches the brim of his hat and leaves.

☙❧

A half hour later, Kenneth says he's taken enough of her time and knows she has an engagement that night.

"Would you care to join me? Us? My neighbors, Hilda and Bryce

Hanson, throw an annual August Supper. Their organic produce is beyond belief. Everyone brings something. A local family provides the music. It's always a good time and … You have to eat, right?"

He hesitates.

Embarrassed at acting on an impulse, she quickly adds, "You can bring a guest, of course. Your wife or … The more the merrier."

"If you're sure it's okay, I would love to go. There's just me. Would wine be an acceptable contribution?"

"Excellent." His words, *There's just me,* sing in her mind.

"How about I go change and come back and pick you up?" He starts out but returns to the drawings. "May I take these?"

She nods, and as he strides to his truck, a red-haired woman in a pale green dress reaches for his hand. He is suddenly younger, his shaggy hair darker and longer, just touching his shoulders. Margaret watches as they walk away, hand in hand, laughing.

Chapter 37

Emily awakens to the muffled clatter of dishes and the aroma of brewing coffee. She looks at her phone. One p.m. The tension of the past days has kept her awake into the early hours again. Irked with herself for sleeping so late, she throws a denim shirt on over her tank top and shorts and heads for the kitchen.

"'Morning," her mother says. She lifts the kettle off the burner just as it begins to whistle.

"Morning?" Emily recognizes the mild buzzing sensation in her chest as wariness and decides to be quiet and wait. The last time they were together, she'd tried to talk about her dad's music and her need to know more about him but Janet had shut her down. And though Otis had assured her she had a right to pursue the issue, she had left feeling frustrated and guilty.

"Morning, noon, or night, breakfast food always boosts the spirits. Hearts or smilies?"

Emily stares at her mother's back, then laughs. "Both. And blueberry syrup."

Janet turns to her. "I may not be the world's best cook, but give me a boxed mix and a couple of eggs, and I'm a whizz at good old-fashioned pancakes."

"I'd even call for butter on them, if I had any. All yellow and melting on top and dripping down the sides."

"Voila!" Her mother presents her with a stick of butter on a crystal butter dish. "And I won't take no for an answer. I know you're turning all healthy these days, but a little comfort food can do a world of good. Besides, I've whipped up a fruit and veggie smoothie à la Otis. Fresh from his garden, that is." She sets a glass of thick green liquid in front of Emily along with a small vase of yellow nasturtiums and then turns back to the stove.

Emily loses herself in a memory. The sun is streaming through curtainless windows in a drab little apartment kitchen. She's sitting at a table just big enough for two, and her mother sets a plate in front of her. A stack of pancakes drips with butter and maple syrup. A jelly glass of orange juice glistens in the sunlight. Her mother's voice, tight and strained just moments before, softens into a familiar song. At nine years old, Emily decides to accept the peace offering, choosing to swim around in it for as long as it lasts.

On the plate now before her sit two plump pancakes with tiny holes peppering their crisp edges like bubbles in a golden sea. Without thought, she places a pat of butter on the smiling circle sitting atop a huge heart and watches it melt into a translucent puddle. After drizzling thick blueberry syrup over it, she picks up her fork and sings, "'You've got to S-M-I-L-E to be H-A-double P-Y!'"

Her mother turns from the stove, her shoulders relaxing. "I'd forgotten about that."

"I'll always remember it."

Her mother returns to her cooking, and there is silence in the kitchen for a few minutes. When Janet turns back toward the counter with a bowl of fluffy scrambled eggs and a bottle of hot sauce, Emily laughs. "Oh, wow. Scrambled hotsy too?"

"Comfort food. Sometimes *it* says what a buttoned-up mother can't." She sprinkles chopped scallions on top of the eggs. "So, eat."

Janet joins her daughter at the counter with a mug of coffee and her own bowl of eggs covered in scallion curls. She reaches for the hot sauce, shakes out an orangey-red blob, and mixes it into the eggs. She takes a bite, frowns, and shakes out another dollop. Neither speaks as Emily reaches for the sauce.

Finally, Emily pushes her empty plate and bowl away. She drinks a portion of the smoothie and pushes that aside as well. "I'm going to have to save the rest of this for later. Delicious, but way too filling on top of this feast." She looks directly into her mother's gray eyes. "Thanks. I needed that."

"What's your plan for the day?"

"I'll be leaving for the hospital around five. Ned' parents told me he can't have day visitors. They're doing some tests. Hopefully they're removing some of his paraphernalia too."

"And before that? I hope you're planning on resting or getting outside."

"I'm back to running again and I'm going out for a run in the woods as soon as I check on the time for my lunch date tomorrow. And then—"

"With her? With Margaret?"

"Yes. With Margaret."

Janet sighs. Emily tenses.

"Well," Janet says, "since you've brought her up, perhaps it's time to talk about her."

For a moment, Emily doesn't respond. Her mind, ready to defend her friendship, is caught off guard.

Janet continues, "For reasons I can't quite articulate, I worry that she's taking advantage of you." She shrugs.

"She's helped me a lot," Emily says. "And she and Ned have a long-standing friendship. If you'd just get to know her ..."

Janet picks up Emily's dishes and takes them to the sink. Standing with her back to her daughter, she says, "I've heard weird things about her all my life, Emily. Dark weird. And it still seems odd to me that she would strike up a friendship with someone so young. Maybe it's because she had no friends growing up. Maybe it's some sort of arrested development. Or—"

"*I'm* the one who sought *her* out. At the family reunion, which you conveniently missed, Otis and Mert called her a real 'puzzler.' I was curious, so I went up there."

"And?"

"And she knew things about me. She helped me remember that Nana Emily called me Emily-Memily, Teller of Tales. She *knew* about the stories I write."

"In your notebooks."

"And on my computer. She knew things were about to change in my life and encouraged me to take myself seriously as a writer. For a while after I left her house, I resisted accepting it all. I rationalized it away." Emily pauses, reflecting on her initial unease with Margaret's revelations. "Then, later that night, Lily May confirmed something Margaret had seen. She told me about her mother. She told me how Great Nana would start a story and Nana and Lily May and their sisters would have to add to it? And Nana Emily was best at weaving all the loose threads together. She described just what Margaret had seen. That was ... that was our last talk before she died. We wouldn't have had it if not for my visit with Margaret."

Janet comes back around the counter and sits. "Why didn't Margaret *see* Lily May's death coming?"

The question stings. "She saw something, but not in a way that could have made a difference. She doesn't see everything."

Janet shakes her head. "Sounds like she's playing at being grandmother to you. And what's her relationship with Ned about?"

Emily notes the distaste on her mother's tone. "She helps the rescue squad with searches. That's how I met Ned." Emily smiles, remembering. "I was at her place when he came to get her. A five-year-old boy was lost in the woods." Her smile grows. "It was an amazing night! If you could have seen the child's parents and grandparents when the searchers brought him in."

"To lose and then find your little boy must ..." Janet's voice fades into silence as a wave of sadness washes over her face.

Knowing where this has taken her, Emily reaches out and rests her hand on her mother's. Trying to ease her back, she says, "I'd love for you to get to know Margaret. She saved that child. I—"

"She blamed me for the baby's death."

"Margaret?" Emily says, shocked.

"Kathleen." Janet's head droops. "She said it was my fault."

Stunned, Emily is speechless.

"Later she said it was a blessing. A blessing! My little boy died, her own grandbaby, and she called his death a blessing."

Emily slides off her stool and enfolds her mother in her arms. She is surprised Janet doesn't shrug her off.

Finally, Janet straightens and digs in her pocket for a tissue. Wiping her nose and eyes, she shakes off the moment. Emily sits back down.

"Well," her mother says rising to clear the rest of the dishes. "Look at me, still holding on to that after all these years."

"You'd have to be made of stone not to. How unbelievably cruel of her." Emily's voice rises with each word. She joins her mother at the sink. "I'm not going to make contact with her."

Janet turns to face her daughter. "No. Don't cut her off because of *my* experience of her. This is about *you*. *Your* history. *Your* story. Remember?" Instead of turning away, Janet looks into Emily's eyes. "How can you make it yours if you don't have all the threads? She's one of those threads. As you weave them together, you'll need *hers*. I see that now."

"But you—"

"Like I said, it isn't about me. I am a thread in your story too, but it's *your* story, Em."

In the softness with which her mother uses this familiar nickname, Emily hears Margaret's words on the night of their first meeting, *She loves you both gently and fiercely, Em.*

They turn back to the sink full of dishes. Janet washes and Emily dries as they settle into the familiar thrum and clatter of dailiness.

"I'd like to see the music," Janet says as she hands Emily the last dish.

Emily stifles the impulse to respond. Instead, she places the last dish on the stack on the shelf, hangs the dish towel, and walks to her study. She returns with her father's songs.

Janet joins her on the couch, placing a mug of steaming coffee on the table. She takes in a deep breath and puts out her hand.

"Do you want to see all three or—"

"All three."

Emily hands them to her and then looks out the French doors at the gray day. Many of the plants in her garden need deadheading and the bushes need pruning. She tries to keep her mind on these matters as her mother reads in silence. Finally, she gives up trying, rests her head on the cushion, and turns to watch her.

Her mother is back to her old, unreadable self. Her body is taut, her posture erect. Quietly, she slides the top sheet to the bottom and continues reading without any change in her shallow breathing. After a while, she again slips the top page to the bottom and reads the last song without any sign of emotion. Finally, she lowers the pages to her lap.

Emily's phone buzzes in the bedroom. She ignores it. A simple chime tells her there is a message. She ignores it.

"That might be about Ned," her mother says.

"I'm sure it can wait."

"Please. Go and see."

Emily hauls herself up and goes for her phone. She listens to the message from Jacquie about going to the hospital together, texts a pick-up time, and mutes the phone. She returns to the couch and waits in silence.

"Damn him," her mother says, but her voice is soft. Dreamy.

Emily waits for her to continue, but Janet hands back the songs and reaches for her mug. She rises and walks to the French doors, where she stands sipping her coffee.

"I'm sorry," Emily says. "I didn't mean for them to make you angry."

"Angry?" Janet turns back toward her. "No. Not angry. It was more of a 'damn him' for taking me back to that place and time with his beautiful words, his poetry. And for reminding me of how sweet he could be, how incredibly sweet and naive and infuriating he could be."

Emily lets her mother's words linger in the air around them, then speaks. "His words tell me that he wanted to be better. To us. For us. Or was he just using us as material for his music?"

"No!" Her mother's response is surprisingly sharp. "Don't ever think that. His life always made its way into his music, but he would never have used us." She comes back to the couch and sits. "What he says in these songs was his truth. And that's why I said, 'Damn him.' Damn him for reminding me how much he loved us and how devastating it was to lose him twice—first when he left us, and then when he died."

Emily stares at her mother. Her eyes are shining and a calmness has descended upon her. "He loved us, Em. He loved you wildly. Earnestly. Deeply. You were his absolute joy." Her voice grows stronger and more resonant.

"Why did he go?"

"He couldn't handle what love asked of him. He was too damned sensitive and totally unprepared. As one thing after another went wrong for us, he couldn't make everything all better with a smile and a guitar case full of good intentions. And I was a pathetic, needy creature clinging to him, needing more than he was equipped to give. So, he retreated. But here, in these simple words on these scribbled pages, I see him again – the Danny we loved and who loved us back."

Emily leans in, touching her mother's knee. "I'm sorry for opening this up for you again. Maybe you should treat that wounded young woman with the same compassion you give that lost young man."

Janet looks down at her hands. "How did you get to be so wise at your age? I guess I do have to thank Kathleen for sending these."

"And Margaret?"

"Oh, Emily." Janet gets up. "One thing at a time. I don't think she's the innocent you'd like her to be." She walks to the French doors. "Like I said, when I was growing up, I heard terrible stories about her. There was even talk of time in jail. For …" Turning to meet Emily's angry eyes, she stops. "Maybe that's something you need to learn about on your own.

"Look." Janet begins to pace as she talks. "People like her are adept at reading situations. They pick up cues. They get you to reveal things without you even realizing it. Next thing you know, you're convinced they're the genuine article. A little skepticism is not a bad thing. Okay? But I guess maybe she does deserve some thanks for helping you. And so does Otis."

"Otis?"

"Suffice it to say, he delivered one of his pithy directives. Something about a do-over."

"In that spirit, why don't you reconsider coming to lunch with me tomorrow?"

The moment the invitation is out of her mouth, Emily knows she's just shut down the conversation. She's taken it that one step too far.

Janet walks to the kitchen and sets her mug in the sink. "I can't possibly tomorrow. I have errands to run and a dentist appointment."

"It's okay."

"Maybe if you'd given me more notice. Time to adjust."

Emily picks up the songs from the couch. "Would you like me to make copies of these for you before you go?"

"No." Janet shakes her head. "They're yours, meant for you." She pauses and turns back to her daughter. "Actually … I would like that."

Emily nods. "It will only take a minute."

Chapter 38

Kenneth raps lightly on her door, and she waves him into the kitchen, noting the twinge in her chest at the sight of him in his red shirt, black vest, and comfortable jeans. His hair is damp, curling up along his collar, and he smells of soap and a mild spice she can't quite identify.

He stands watching her as she places mint leaves and thin slices of lemon drizzled with honey into two glass jugs of tea. She gives each jug a quick stir and adds ice cubes before screwing on their covers and setting them in a sectioned wooden crate.

From the fridge, she pulls two containers of summer salads and places them in a sturdy canvas bag, then tucks a bottle of dressing into the deep interior pocket. On top of the containers, she sets a covered pan of golden corn bread and tosses a bag of roasted kale chips on top.

Kenneth moves in to take the crate and bag to the car as the girls dance around their feet. "I'm ready to go," she says, "but I have to let the girls out for a last go 'round before we leave. It'll only take a few minutes."

He returns from the car and joins her. The backyard shadows lengthen as the girls run down the hill, splash through the stream, circle back to drink noisily, and race toward the darkening woods. Margaret enjoys his proximity, his easy laugh, his relaxed manner. Sighing happily, she feels both remarkably light and solidly grounded.

᠃᠃᠃

Bryce Hanson and Paul Edwards help with Margaret's crate and bag and then come back for the two cases of wine Kenneth has brought. As they lug them to the dining area under the huge canopy strung with twinkling lights, curious eyes look on.

Margaret retrieves her pie carrier from the car, and Kenneth reaches to take it from her. A sudden image flashes before her, and she nearly drops the basket. Again, it's the red-haired woman— this time throwing her head back in a ripple of laughter. Liza. The name comes to her as if carried on the wind. Liza bends to take off her shoes, turns to Kenneth with a teasing grin, and runs off barefoot, her laughter trailing behind her. Kenneth smiles as he watches her go.

"Where would you like this?"

The sound of his voice brings her back.

She points to the dessert table and then introduces Kenneth to Paul, Bryce, and Hilda, who has joined them. She's aware of the many heads turning toward them.

She and Hilda leave the men in animated conversation. They transfer the tea into glass pitchers and set them, tinkling with ice, out on the long dining tables before arranging the food on the buffet.

"Margaret!"

She turns to see Meg, Tom, and the elder Allens heading toward her.

"Nana Maggie," a child calls out, and little Joey bursts through from behind his grandparents. "Nana Maggie!" He leaps, and she bends to catch him in her arms. He wraps his legs around her waist and squeezes her around the neck. "I been missing you. I been missing you," he squeals, his blonde hair curling around his face, his blue eyes sparkling. "Sweet, sweet, sweet be your bumbles," he sings, and kisses her wetly on the cheek.

Margaret's tears surprise her. The sound of his child's voice singing his version of the old lullaby touches a deep and usually closed-off part of her. A flood of emotion burbles up as soft laughter wet with tears.

Everyone in the small circle around her is smiling, touched by this little boy's exuberance and this seasoned woman's response to its call.

Kenneth, in particular, is smiling broadly as he witnesses this moment of intimacy. His eyes ask questions but he remains silent, standing back slightly to allow the Allen family in around Margaret.

"Oh, Margaret, it's so good to see you," Joey's mom says. "Not a day goes by but what your name comes up. You brought our little guy back to us and he's always asking after you."

"Well, he's welcome to come visit me anytime. I could use a little more kid energy in my days."

"We wouldn't want to bother you," Tom says with a shy smile.

His father, Old Tom, puts out his hand and gives her a shake. "We know you like your privacy. And with good reason."

"I would love to have all of you come by anytime. You would never be intruding."

"You might regret saying that." Sally Allen, Joey's grandmother, laughs robustly. "You're a kind of saint in our eyes, and you might find our adoring stares a mite disconcerting after a while."

"Not to mention downright irritating," Old Tom adds.

Margaret laughs. "I'm far from saintly, but better to be called that than the names I'm used to."

Old Tom turns to Kenneth and holds out his hand. "Tom Allen, senior. Most call me Old Tom. And you are?"

"I'm sorry." Margaret steps back, including Kenneth more directly in the circle. "This is Kenneth. Kenneth Chisholm." She hesitates a moment before going on, rather enjoying the curiosity buzzing around them. *Margaret Meader brought a man?* "Kenneth is going to rebuild my workshop."

"Nasty business, that," Old Tom says. "I was furious when I

heard what they'd done. They could have burned your whole place down, and you and the dogs inside!" He shakes his head in disgust, clenching both fists.

Sally pats his arm. "We were heartsick when we heard. There's no excuse for that kind of small-mindedness."

"What happened?" Kenneth asks. Then he quickly adds, "If you don't mind my asking?" He is looking down at Margaret with deep concern.

Before she can brush off the matter, Paul Edwards addresses it full-on. "Someone burned that building down deliberately. Someone who comes from a family that has long feared Margaret for her ..." He hesitates, glancing at Margaret, obviously not sure if she wishes to share her story with this new acquaintance or not. She nods resignedly, giving him a small smile, and he continues. "For her special way of knowing things the rest of us don't."

Meg takes her now fidgeting son from Margaret and sends him off to run with the other kids in the nearby field. She leans in to Kenneth. "Margaret saved our boy's life when he wandered off in Tilson Woods. He was lost for hours, well into the night. Then they brought Margaret in and they found him right where she said they would. It was the worst night of our lives."

"And then the best." As he speaks, Margaret notes how Tom has positioned himself to watch the kids at play, his eyes never leaving his son.

"She helped us again a few days ago," Paul says, "when two of our young wardens were caught in a landslide on a rescue mission for two hikers. Our own Ned Burrows is the only survivor, and he wouldn't be alive today if not for Margaret."

"I heard the other boy just died this afternoon," Old Tom says. "The Willoughby kid. A real shame." He gives Paul a sympathetic nod.

"Gordon Willoughby," Paul says. "Twenty-six years old. His parents were with him when he died." He looks at Margaret. "They were amazingly calm, and I suspect it had a lot to do with a conversation they had with you this morning."

Kenneth is looking at her too, and she can't read his expression.

Surprise, certainly, but is there something else mixed in there? Wariness, perhaps? Judgment? Skepticism? She searches his eyes, his serious expression, his pinched brows.

"Information comes to me," she tells him. "Mostly unbidden. Has all my life. There are many terms for what I am. I prefer the word *intuitive*, especially over *witch* or *crazy lady*." She gives a small laugh. "Some of the older folks say I have 'the sight.' But whatever you call it, it usually stirs a reaction." She breathes deeply, sensing relief at having it out in the open. "I probably should have told you it was arson at the outset. I understand if you don't want to take on a project steeped in that kind of negativity."

He stares at her without responding for a long while, his mouth slightly open. She stares back, holding her breath, still not sure what she sees in his sea green eyes.

"My God, Margaret! You could have been killed!" He turns to Paul and the others. "What's being done about it? Did you catch whoever did it?"

"The police got him," Sally Allen explains. "He's just a kid. His family has been filling his mind with lies and crazy stories about Margaret all his life. It's all on them, but he'll pay the price."

"Margaret's working on that," Annie Foss says as she joins them. "She went to see the real witches of southern Maine." She pauses. "Sorry, not nice. But maybe that hard-headed, narrow-minded family is ready to listen and work with her with their boy facing jail time."

"That would be a miracle," Old Tom mumbles. "But if anyone could work one ..." He grins and raises two fingers to his forehead in a smart salute to Margaret.

"Oh, yes, Saint Margaret!" She laughs, and the others join her, lightening the mood just as the Bellows family begins tuning their instruments.

Hilda Hanson nods to her husband Bryce. "Guess as hosts, we'd best get to it." She gives Margaret a quick and uncharacteristic hug, and then the pair walk off to join the musicians.

All turn to the makeshift stage as the microphone screeches at Hilda's attempt to speak to the crowd. As she adjusts it and makes her welcoming announcements, Kenneth and Margaret drift toward the field.

"I really am sorry I didn't tell you about the fire. It wasn't intentional. I guess I've adjusted too well to the fact." She doesn't look at him as she talks. Instead, she watches the children run to join their parents, little Joey red-cheeked and happy in their midst.

"No need to apologize. It doesn't change anything. It just piques my concern for you and the girls. I'm sorry to hear you've had to live with that kind of malice."

"I try—" She cuts herself off from finishing the thought. "Thank you. This community"—she sweeps her arm to encompass the gathering—"is filled with friends and people who don't give a thought one way or the other about who or what I am. Those others have their reasons for their beliefs."

"Sounds like both a gift and a burden, this 'sight' of yours. And you say you've had it all your life?"

"As far back as I can remember. My father had it too, but I never knew that until just before he died. He saw it as a terrible burden, but I know it informed his work. It pained him to know I had it too. I remember the day he realized it. He was shattered." She realizes as she talks that she hasn't shared this with anyone, not even Joe. She realizes too how easy it is to talk to this man she barely knows. She listens for any intuitive warnings against it. All is quiet inside.

"You say it informed his work? How was that?"

"He was …" She hesitates for the briefest beat. "… a painter." She turns toward him, again searching his face as she speaks. "It's hard to explain. His paintings were known for their multidimensional imagery. His style was representational on the surface, but his figures and landscapes possessed a depth that transcended usual levels of perception. It was as if you could see into and into and into them, and touch something like the soul beneath." For a moment, she is lost in the labyrinthian journey she's describing. "Sorry. I ramble. He was my father. I was in awe of him."

"Mad Max." Kenneth looks horrified. Not at the sudden recognition of Margaret's famous father, but at his own careless use of the infamous nickname. "I'm sorry."

"Actually, he enjoyed being called that. Laughed at it. Thought of it as part of his mystique, I think."

"I'm proud to say I own a Maxwell Meader. A gift. I love that painting. It reminds me of my daughter, and I didn't realize why until now. It *is* like looking into her soul. I used to call her my little wild child."

They stand quietly, the murmuring conversations and sudden bursts of laughter behind them a distant backdrop, although just a few feet away. A single fiddle playing a sweet and simple melody stirs Kenneth. "What is that tune?"

"An original piece. They call it 'Maine Morning.'"

"Yes, I can hear that." He smiles as he looks out across the field, then he turns to look at her again. "I'm keeping you from your friends and your dinner."

"Hey, Margaret, Kenneth, we've got two seats here with your names on them." Bryce Hanson, standing at his place at the head of a nearby table, calls to them. He spreads both hands like a conductor and indicates two seats facing each other just down the table from him, his wife, and Annie Foss, and just up from where the Allens are seating themselves.

When Joey sees Margaret pull out her chair, he clambers up on the one next to her. "I'm gonna sit by Nana Maggie. My seat. My seat."

She turns to Kenneth. "Speaking of a little wild child!" As she repeats his words, a sudden realization makes her smile. She knows the painting Kenneth is referring to. She remembers sitting for it all those years ago.

Chapter 39

When Emily knocks at the front door, Margaret calls from the backyard for her to come on through. In the kitchen, two unfinished puzzles sit, one on each end of the harvest table against the wall.

Drawn to the one on the left, she stands over it. It is complete enough for her to make out the long curves and gleaming wood of a stringed instrument and the button-like keys of a silver flute. Against a heavily shadowed background, the corner of a page of sheet music is just being revealed as the puzzle comes together.

As she looks over the scattering of unused pieces, she's aware of the other puzzle, shimmering on her periphery. She leans over it. The dizzying swirls of primary colors agitate and repulse her. She turns away, feeling mildly nauseated.

"What did you see?" Margaret is standing beside her.

"Confusion. Chaos." Emily winces. "Anger. Definitely anger."

"And this other one?"

"Refuge." She smiles, relaxing.

"Hmm. Interesting. Worth thinking about."

"The angry one isn't finished. Maybe I'd feel differently if I saw the whole picture?"

"I think we fill in the empty spaces with what we need to see.

Puzzling is about process. The journey is the teacher. At least, that's how it feels to me. Sometimes, by the time I put the final piece into place, there's a sense of disappointment. All the energy has dissipated through the act of putting it together."

"You think I *needed* to look into anger? To what end? It's unsettling, and I'd rather not go there."

"Ah, there's the rub. Anger was your word. It's what you saw in that riot of bright colors. Someone else might see joy. Exuberance. Creative energy. Juiciness."

Margaret pauses before continuing. "Maybe just acknowledging that you don't want to go there is enough. Or, it might be an invitation for self-reflection through journaling? You are a writer, after all." She smiles.

"And what are you, Margaret?" Emily asks, and laughs.

"An old woman who talks too much." Margaret walks away, leading her out to the backyard table, already set with their lunch.

They eat in silence for a while, and then Margaret asks about Ned.

Emily lowers her fork and grins. "Oh, Margaret it was so amazing." As she describes being in the ICU and having him recognize her, Emily becomes more and more animated.

Margaret nods and smiles and doesn't mention the sudden image that flashes between them. Emily in an ivory-colored wedding gown holding a bouquet of wildflowers. Ned in a gray suit with an ivory vest and tie. They stand on the far side of the pond. Behind them, a great blue heron.

With a click like the shutter on a camera, a new scene slides into view. Ned is lying on a hardwood floor, grimacing in pain. Emily leans over him, but he barks at her to go. She reels at the rejection and backs away. Ned rolls onto his back, alone, surrendering to a wave of despair. A gray-haired woman enters the scene. She waits. When his great heaving gasps ease into quiet breathing, she bends down. "I think that's enough for today. Good work."

Another click of the camera, and she sees a storage room. A woman in a white coat lies unconscious on the floor, her eye blackened, her lip bleeding. She is covered in white dust.

Margaret lurches forward and stops Emily midsentence with the look on her face.

"What is it?" Emily says.

"Your friend. The chef. Describe her to me."

"Tall, athletic, short dark hair. Olive skin, brown eyes."

"Is there someone violent in her life?"

"I don't know." Emily leans across the table. "She has a boyfriend, but …"

"What do you know about him?"

"I know his parents feel no one is good enough for him, but …"

Margaret doesn't hesitate. "She's in danger. Is she at her restaurant?"

"I'm picking her up there later to go to the hospital."

"Call her now. Make sure there are people around her."

Emily dials Jacquie's cell. It goes to voice mail. She texts and then calls the restaurant. A recording clicks on. She looks up at Margaret. "I can't reach her."

࿇

Jacquie's car is parked by the back door of the restaurant. The rest of the lot is empty. They run through the unlocked door and call out her name. No answer. Margaret leads them through a narrow passageway into a large kitchen. The lights are on, and every surface shines. Again, they call out to Jacquie. Again, silence.

To the right is a closed door next to the steel walk-in refrigerator. On the opposite wall, swinging double doors lead to the dining room. The wall to their left is lined with shelves stacked with pots, pans, bowls, and assorted equipment, all gleaming stainless steel and glass.

Margaret turns to the door next to the walk-in. "Jacquie?" she calls. She motions Emily behind her and thrusts the door open, swinging her leg around to hold it with her heel. She scans the storeroom. Jacquie lies unconscious on the floor, covered in a thin layer of flour from the broken sack behind her.

Emily is dialing 911 as the two women rush to her side. Jacquie moans as they kneel beside her.

As Margaret leans over her, Jacquie lurches upward with a start. "It's okay, Jacquie. I'm Margaret. Lie still. Help is on the way. Just breathe with me. Nice and easy. There you go."

"What happened?" Jacquie whispers. "Where …"

"You're in the storeroom of your restaurant. You've been hurt."

"Brian!" Jacquie's eyes flutter open. One is red and quickly swelling. Her body tenses as she tries to rise.

Margaret applies gentle pressure to keep her in place. "Don't move or try to talk. Just close your eyes and breathe with me."

Emily slides her hand into Jacquie's and whispers, "Emily here. We've got you."

As the wail of sirens grows closer, Jacquie tries to open her eyes, but her right one is now swollen shut. With her left, she looks up at Margaret. "I didn't see it coming. I never saw it coming."

A cacophony of sound fills the room as EMTs and police flow in. Margaret and Emily are ordered into the kitchen.

Finally, a young officer joins them there. He flips open a notepad and looks at Margaret. His brow wrinkles, as if he's trying to place her.

"The fire!" he says as recognition kicks in. "Some kid burned your shed down. My folks say you're like that television medium. Only better. Sorry about the shed."

"Thank you."

"So?" He continues in a more serious tone, straightening and squaring his shoulders as if putting on his professional face. "What happened here?"

He takes notes as Margaret and Emily describe finding Jacquie, but then suddenly looks up. "I get it. You had a premonition? Isn't that what they call it—a premonition?"

Margaret shrugs. "That's what they call it. Yes."

The young man grins, his freckled face coloring with pride at having deduced this interesting twist in a routine investigation. "So, tell me about it." For a moment, his professional policeman's demeanor drops, and he's a kid who's found himself in the midst of a cool story. "What, exactly, was this premonition like? Did you see who did it? What can you tell me about—"

"Whoa, Johnson. One question at a time." A tall man in a suit and tie walks over to them.

The young officer looks abashed at the reprimand but quickly recovers. "These women came upon the scene because of a premonition by Miss Meader here, sir." He points at Margaret.

"Yes. Miss Meader." His smile extends into his eyes as he holds out his hand. "Margaret. Good to see you again."

"Detective Horner. I was just telling this officer how we found Jacquie. He has treated me with the utmost courtesy and professionalism. As you know, I am not always treated thus." She pauses for a moment before smiling and winking at him.

"Will I never live that down?" He smiles, shaking his head. "You have to admit, your story was a hard nut to swallow on that case." He turns to the blushing young officer. "Continue. I'll be back in a minute."

Margaret describes her "premonition." "I 'saw' her lying on the floor, injured and covered in white dust. That's all I saw. I was with Emily." She points to her companion.

"What is the victim's full name, do you know?" He looks at both women.

"Jacqueline LaBelle," Emily answers. "She prefers Jacquie."

"A friend?"

"The best friend of a friend of mine."

"Oh? A male friend?" he asks, raising his eyebrows.

"Shall we get on to pertinent issues, please?" Margaret says with a stern look.

For a moment, Officer Johnson looks as though he'd prefer to find out about this male friend. But Detective Horner returns and assigns him to accompany the hospital transport. With a moment of hesitation, Officer Johnson does as he's asked.

Detective Horner takes over the questioning. Margaret tells him that when Jacquie first regained consciousness, she said the name Brian. Later she said, "I didn't see it coming. I never saw it coming."

"But that's all she said to us," Margaret finishes. "Of course, I *did* tell her not to talk."

"That was the right thing to do. Tell me about the vision. Any useful details we won't find here at the scene?"

Margaret is silent for a while, going back over it as best she can. Finally, she sighs and shakes her head.

Emily looks at Margaret. "Before we left your house, you asked if there was someone violent in her life. Remember? And I told you about her boyfriend's parents—"

"Her boyfriend?" the detective interrupts. "Who's her boyfriend? Do you know him?"

"No. Jacquie's a childhood friend of Ned, my ... new boyfriend. She was happy that his parents like me. She said her boyfriend's parents didn't approve of her. She called it the 'no-one's-good-enough-for-our-boy syndrome' and laughed about it. But it was the first thing I thought of when Margaret asked if she had anyone violent in her life. I guess that's not very nice of me."

"I rely on instincts. Intuition. Being nice doesn't get us far in a police investigation." Horner writes in his notebook. "Is he the Brian she spoke of?"

"Yes."

Horner looks to Margaret. "Anything?"

She lowers her head and listens for a moment. "Afraid not."

"Well, call me if you remember any details at all." He hands Margaret his card. "Good to see you again. I'll be in touch. We may need your prints for elimination purposes, but you can go now."

Emily stops on their way out. "Detective Horner, Ned was injured in a rescue a few days ago."

"Ned Burrows? He's your boyfriend? Oh. I'm sorry. Such a tragedy."

"He's awake now, and I'd like to let his parents know about Jacquie. Is that all right?"

"I guess it would be better for them to hear it from you. But ask them to call me. I have questions they may be able to answer."

✿❦✿

In the car on the way to the hospital, Emily begins to shake as the shock wears off. Margaret reaches over to pat her hands. "You've taken another jolt to the nervous system. Lay your head back and close your eyes."

Emily is aware of Margaret's breathing and of her own body slowing to match her rhythm. As the truck slides into a parking space and rattles to a stop, Emily doesn't open her eyes or lift her head.

"I know an amazing massage therapist," Margaret says, "and I'm calling her right now. Body work will help you de-stress."

While Margaret makes the call, Emily slips into a daydream. She is walking hand and hand with Ned, laughing. His blond hair shines in the sun. His pale eyes smile deeply into hers. Their easy banter is comfortable, familiar. Yet there is a sense of discovery in every moment.

The slamming of a car door jerks her back into the cab of Margaret's old pickup.

"A client just canceled. Beth has a two-hour slot at 2:30. The universe is on our side! I'll take you over after we check in on Jacquie and then pick you up afterwards."

Jacquie is awake and propped on a gurney in a curtained cubicle in the emergency room. She is pale and dazed. The swelling around her eye has worsened, and a nasty bruise has blossomed on her neck. Her words are disjointed—"How could he? I never thought …"—as she shakes her head and cries, looking for an explanation for the last thing she ever expected to happen.

A tall, slender woman in a white coat enters the cubicle. Her demeanor softens as she looks at the three of them. "Jacqueline LaBelle?" Her voice is like liquid—thick, sweet amber liquid. Emily is surprised by this simile that slips into her mind. The writer in her alert and taking notes even in the midst of crisis.

Jacquie croaks out a yes.

"I'm Dr. Barker. I'll have to ask your visitors to leave while we talk. Okay?"

Jacquie looks stricken for a moment but nods.

Assuring her they will be right outside, they leave.

A dark-haired woman bursts past them in the hallway, whips back the curtain, and loudly announces herself as *Doctor* Marie LaBelle.

When they are allowed back in, Jacquie, even paler than before, is sleeping. Dispassionately, her mother fills them in on her daughter's condition. "A likely concussion, a possible orbital fracture, a fractured wrist, and multiple contusions. It's difficult to tell at this point if she'll have permanent damage to the eye itself." As she finishes, she sways slightly and leans against the gurney. She stiffens as Margaret slides a chair over to her.

She sits, but her dark eyes bore into Margaret's as she says, "We're fine now. I'll see to my daughter's needs. You can go."

Margaret and Emily leave in silence, but as they climb into the truck, Emily bursts out, "What a bitch!"

"Cold doesn't quite capture it, does it?" Margaret says as she turns the key. The truck sputters and stalls. She turns it again and coaxes the engine to life. "If I don't get this old girl over to Philby soon, he's going to refuse to resuscitate her once and for all." She pats the dashboard as the engine settles into a quiet rumble. "That detached demeanor comes too often with a professional life that's steeped in dealing with human suffering up close and personal. Sad." She shakes her head. "That girl's going to need a girlfriend."

"I can do that."

"You have a lot on your plate, but I think it may be part of your journey right now. Two best friends are in need. *But*—and this is a big *but*—you'll have to put yourself first. Radical self-care. It's essential."

She says no more until she has pulled into a circular driveway outside a lovely cottage with natural weathered shakes, a muted purple door, and overflowing flower boxes under a multipaned window. "And here's where it begins." She puts the truck in park. "*Be* in this moment. This is about self-nurturing. Breathe that in."

Emily pauses before climbing down. She looks back at Margaret. "If I put myself first, I won't get a 'big butt' out of it, will I?"

"Very funny. Now off with you, and *be* in every moment. It doesn't get any better than Beth."

Chapter 40

Margaret turns left onto Old Creek Road, a shortcut through a section of woods belonging to the Land Trust. The bright strains of Vivaldi's "Spring" mingle with the brisk wind whipping in the window. Feeling buoyant, she pulls the clip from her hair, letting it fly around her face. She laughs and pats the truck's dashboard. "I promise. I'm calling Philby as soon as I get ho—"

The truck lurches, sending her body forward and back with a snap. Shocked, she looks in the rearview mirror to see a dusty blue pickup about to ram her from behind again. Several young males hang out the windows, whooping and hollering. The driver blasts the horn—quick, short jabs, then in a sustained blare. She steps on the gas, but the old truck has no punch and responds by rattling and shimmying. Fear rises from her gut into her throat, and sense memory takes over as her heart hammers her ribcage. Flashbacks dance in and out as she struggles to keep the truck under control. Taunting voices. Hateful snarls. Jeering laughter. Prelude to the torment. Prelude to the punches and kicks. Prelude to the grasping and grabbing.

The truck bounces over thick tufts of meadow grass. Low-hanging branches scrape along the windshield. She jerks the wheel

OTHER WISE   275

and slams sideways into the thick trunk of an oak. A moment later, she's thrown forward as the blue truck rams into the driver's side, just behind the cab.

"Witch your way out of this one, bitch," a curly-haired teen screams from the passenger window of the four-door pickup.

The driver backs the truck away a few feet, revving the engine, while three of the others leap out. They pull at Margaret's door, but it won't open. One meaty hand reaches in and grabs a fistful of her hair, yanking her head out of the window.

"You think a little fire is all we have for you? Better keep a close eye on those precious dogs of yours and better sleep with one eye open." He loosens his grip but then snaps her head toward him again. "Or better yet, why don't you do us all a favor and move as far from here as you can get?"

Her head twisted around, she is looking up into a face flushed scarlet under tawny hair. The dark eyes glisten with anger. She knows there is no reaching him. Nothing she can say.

"Torch the truck. Torch the truck," two of the younger ones begin to chant.

A third boy hollers, "Burn the witch. By the time they find her, she'll be burned to a crisp. A crispy old titter! It'll look like an accident." He laughs and the others join in.

At the click of a lighter, her heart freezes.

"Our tracks are all over the place, asshole." The one holding her hair yanks her head up and then drops it against the window frame. "Lucked out this time, bi—"

A blast rips the air, shattering a tree limb. The young man dives to the ground, covering his head with his hands. The others jump back into the truck.

"You'd best get your asses out of here. Cops are on their way."

Margaret stares open-mouthed. On a nearby slope, a man stands holding a shotgun in practiced hands. A large dog, lean and muscular, stands at his side, taut with attention. The man motions with the weapon for the one on the ground to get into the truck.

Her assailant crawls toward it and scrambles up into the truck bed as the driver gasses it and backs all the way to the road, sending dirt and grass flying. Once on the pavement, he squeals off, blackening the road with sharply etched tracks.

The man lays his gun on the ground and walks over to the truck, the dog loping along beside him. "'Fraid I've just managed to stir them up more."

He tugs at her door until it finally gives with a metallic shriek and offers his hand to help her down. The truck is tilted higher than she'd realized, and she stumbles. He catches her in both arms and leads her over to a grassy spot well away from the truck. "Let's take a look at you." He urges her to sit down.

"I'm a bit dizzy is all."

He reaches out to steady her. For a confused moment, she shrinks away from his helping hand but then looks into his eyes. They're hazel and not as dark as they'd seemed when he startled her in her backyard. "Have I just leaped from the frying pan into the fire?"

He grins. "What's a man got to do to get a little thanks around here?" He plunks down beside her, his dog coming around to his other side. "Just saved your bacon from a gang of thugs, all testosterone and reptilian brain, and you think I'm some sort of threat?"

She stares at him for a while. He doesn't look away.

She sighs. "Sorry. You're right. God. I thought they were going to light the truck on fire and—" She shivers at the memory. The click of a lighter. The soft whoosh of a flame.

"You got a sweater or something?" He goes back to her truck and returns with her backpack, dropping it on the ground beside her. "You got a phone in there? 'Cause we better call the police and a tow truck."

"But you said the police were on their way."

"Bluffing. I don't have a phone on me. I just wanted them gone and not coming back anytime soon."

She pulls her phone out of her bag and calls the police and Philby Burdock's garage. She reaches Annie at home and asks her to pick up Emily from her massage. To Annie's long-winded questions, she simply says her truck broke down and then hangs up.

"Got the impression those boys didn't choose you at random," the man says. "Sounded more personal."

"Grudges get passed down the generations, I'm afraid. I was hoping it wouldn't get this far."

"Care to talk about it? I've got nothing but time."

"And you would be?"

The briefest hesitation, then he says, "Sam. Sam King. I would have properly introduced myself at your house yesterday if you hadn't invited me to leave."

Again, Margaret holds him with a stare, her blue eyes searching for a way in. "Well, Sam, what do you say we make a fresh start of it? I'm Margaret, but I think you already know that."

He looks away. "Guess I got us off to a bad start just appearing that way. Didn't mean to scare you. And I didn't mean any harm in calling your dogs bitches. That's just the way we always referred to female dogs when I was coming up. Sorry about that."

Margaret is certain he's withholding something. Tiny winged secrets swirl in the air around them, dipping and darting like dragonflies. Playful, tantalizing, innocuous—but present, nonetheless.

"You're clearly from away. What brings you here?"

"You mean to Maine?"

"And to my backyard, specifically."

"Well, I'm on a kind of sabbatical. Going where the road takes me. Figuring some things out. Never been to Maine."

"And once here, why *my* backyard?"

"I'm interested in psychic phenomena, and your name kept coming up. It's true what I said about my grandmother. She had 'the sight.' Also called 'second sight.'" He stares off across the road to the woods beyond. "She left a deep impression on me. Started a lifelong interest in all things extrasensory."

Beside him, the dog yawns and lies down. As Sam pats his head, Margaret takes in the sleek red-brown coat and the distinctive ridge of hair running down its back in the opposite direction from the rest of its hair. "And this is?" she asks.

"C. J. He's a Rhodesian ridgeback."

"I've heard of them but never met one."

"Not likely to get to know him anytime soon. Breed's aloof by nature. But he's comfortable with you. Otherwise, he'd keep his distance even with me around."

"The C doesn't stand for Charley by any chance?"

"No. Just C. J."

"I understand you named your truck Rocinante, so ..."

"No. He may be my traveling companion, but I don't fancy myself a Steinbeck. I am always interested in those who get the allusion, though."

"So, you're not a famous writer traveling incognito with your dog as conversation starter? To rediscover America?"

Sam answers with a belly laugh that has the dog lifting and cocking his head. "If I were—a famous writer, that is—I'd certainly consider remaining anonymous. Meet people on honest ground that way. Which sounds like a paradox, I know." He squints toward the sky as if trying to remember something. "What was it Steinbeck said about fame getting in the way? Something like, '... if people know who you are, they become someone they are not.'"

Both nod, smiling.

"What was her name? Your grandmother?" As soon as it's out of her mouth, Margaret knows the answer. She sees a plump dark-eyed woman. She is smiling, yet there is a deep sadness at her core. Her eyes become mirrors reflecting a double image of Margaret back at her.

"Clementine," he says softly as Margaret nods, mouthing the name along with him.

"Tell me about her."

"My folks died when I was a kid. She took me in. She saw things. Knew things. Made people uncomfortable. But there was a steady stream coming around our farm for her 'readings.' Some people got upset at her for telling them the very things they asked for. Took its toll after a while."

Margaret is quiet, knowing all too well how Clementine must have felt. She slips into Clementine's kitchen and into her anguish. A young woman sits before her, her unborn child dead inside her womb, the birthing imminent. The kettle hisses on the black cookstove. Dust motes swirl in the streak of pale sunlight streaming through the window. The air hangs heavy with waiting.

Fists pound on the door. Someone must be blamed. Clementine bends forward and rocks, arms around her abdomen.

Sam looks at Margaret without speaking. Then goes back to staring across the road.

"A good heart," Margaret say softly. "I wish I could have known her."

"Too good. Heart attack took her in the end."

"I'm sorry."

Sam turns to look at her, his gaze intense. "Better take care of yours."

The sound of a siren cuts the air. C. J. leaps to a wary stance.

"And you'd better make a full report to the police," he adds. "Those guys aren't through with you. Dangerous bunch."

He gets up and turns to help her to her feet. He remains there as she walks to meet the young female officer who has stepped out of the cruiser. Philby's tow truck rumbles to a stop behind the cruiser, and the fire and rescue van pulls in beside him.

As she and the policewoman walk together to the truck, Margaret turns to see Sam and his dog head back up over the ridge.

∞≈

Two hours later, Margaret opens her back door and the girls burst out to greet her. They start down the back hill, stop, and turn back to wait for her to join them.

"You go on ahead." Margaret signals with a wave of her hand. "I'm too tired for a romp just now."

As she lights a fire under the kettle, she catches a whisper of movement behind her, down and to the left. She turns to find stillness. Silence. She drops into the Morris chair and rests her head against its firm cushion. As she closes her eyes, she senses a presence.

"Maggie. It's me. Mattie."

"I know," she says in a drowsy voice.

"You okay?"

"I am, Mattie. I'm fine. Really. Things are just coming to a head right now. But I trust that all shall be well."

"And all manner of thing shall be well." Her brother's voice, sounding strong and grown-up, echoes the thoughts in her head.

Margaret smiles without opening her eyes. As she drifts to the ticking of the clock on the wall, three cracks like distant shots pierce the quiet. Tremors ripple along her legs and arms until her entire body is shivering uncontrollably.

She sits forward with a start as a panic seizes her. Her breath comes in strangled gasps, and her heart thumps erratically. She slides out of the chair, onto her hands and knees on the floor, and surrenders into sobbing.

This is how they find her.

Annie Foss and John Longfeather, having reached her house at the same time, step into the kitchen. Before the door can close behind them, the dogs tumble into the room, nearly knocking them down in their rush to get to Margaret's side.

All four stop before they reach her, instinctively giving her space and air.

Finally, her sobs quiet, and Sophia and Grace pad closer and sit protectively on either side, their eyes never leaving her tousled head and buried face. Annie and John wait without speaking. The kettle begins to burble.

Margaret sits back up on her heels, brushing her hair away from her flushed face. "Well, this is embarrassing."

"Embarrassing nothing!" Annie picks up the kettle just as it begins to whistle. "I just found out you were nearly killed today."

John helps Margaret to her feet and maneuvers her into a chair at the kitchen table. He sits opposite her as Annie pours steaming water into the teapot. He looks directly at Margaret. "You know what the Women would say."

"Get it out before it becomes poison. Yes. I remember. Thank you."

"What happened out there exactly?"

Before she can answer, her phone rings. Margaret starts to

rise, but Annie puts both hands on her shoulders and eases her back into her chair. "I'll take care of whoever's on the phone and anything else that arises. You stay put."

Margaret, feeling thoroughly exhausted, doesn't resist. Then she has a sudden thought. "What about Emily? Did y—"

"Off to Portland to see her young man. When I picked her up at Beth's, she was as relaxed as a person can be. Now, let's get you over to Dr. Alice for a once-over. You could have injuries hiding somewhere, waiting to surface in the middle of the night."

"Maybe you're right," Margaret answers quietly.

John and Annie exchange concerned glances at Margaret's acquiescence.

"A cup of sweet tea first," Annie says, "and we'll take you on over. I'll call her."

While Annie makes the call, John places his hand on top of Margaret's.

"She says to bring you over after you've had your tea." Annie gathers up the girls' water bowls and goes to the sink to refill them.

Margaret wraps both hands around her mug and holds it to her chest. "They were all caught up in a frenzy. A pack feeding on each other's energy. I was reduced to a thing—a target again. I have to admit, I was damned scared." She looks at John and then at Annie, who has joined them at the table. "I was really scared. And that pisses me off!"

Her companions nod but do not speak.

"If he hadn't come along …" She stops, shivering at the thought left unspoken.

"Who? Who came along?" Annie asks.

"The stranger from the other day. Sam King. He scared them off with a shotgun."

John shakes his head. "Guess I had him pegged all wrong. I could have sworn he was up to no good."

"Oh, there's more there than he's willing to share yet. But I think he comes by his wariness honestly. Keeps his defenses high, which translates as a gruff sort of belligerence, as we saw in my backyard."

"Well, I guess I have to trust your assessment since he saved you and all.

"Things have gone way too far. It's past time I met the Kennedy women head-on. There has to be a way to put it behind us. For all our sakes."

"Well, I won't argue the merits of that right now. We have to get you to Dr. Alice. But, you talk to us first before you go doing anything."

"I will." She gives them a weak smile.

"I want to hear a promise on that," John says, his dark eyes holding hers.

"I promise. Any thoughts of going it alone were knocked out of me when my truck hit that tree. This is going to take a village, as they say."

"Good. That we can work with."

As Margaret gets up from her chair, Grace backs away and yelps as her hindquarters rub against the table leg. Bending to pet her, Margaret sees a bloody patch on her fur. Shaking again, she drops to her knees and looks to John for help.

After examining the dog carefully, he says, "Looks like something grazed her. More blood than wound. Not serious. Your yellow balm will fix it right up. Where's your medicine bag?"

"Oh, my God! I think I heard gunshots earlier." She stands, looking from one to the other. "They threatened the girls. If I had been able to get at them, I could have killed them right then and there. A primal rage surged up in me and that's what scared me most. The fact that I could have killed them." She looks down at her wounded dog. "And now I feel it again."

"When those we love are threatened, of course, we're capable of killing!" Annie is flushed with outrage.

Margaret nods. "Intellectually, I've always known that I could kill, but I've never experienced the raw lust of it before. That's more frightening than being driven off the road. Even more frightening than the flick of the lighter by the gas tank."

John, usually a reserved and stoic presence, puts his arms around the two women. Sophia and Grace watch them in perfect stillness.

Chapter 41

The beam from a flashlight bobs along the path through the trees as Emily pulls into her yard. When she realizes it's her mother, she's surprised that she is glad.

"How is he?" Janet calls out as she approaches.

"Good. Really good. The doctors are amazed at his progress."

As Emily opens the door, Janet gives her an almost hug as she enters ahead of her.

"I didn't tell him about Jacquie," Emily says. "No point in worrying him when there's nothing he can do."

Her mother frowns, confused. "Wait. What about Jacquie?"

"Oh, I didn't tell you, did I? Jacquie's boyfriend beat her up. She's in the hospital."

"Oh, my God, Emily. Is she all right?"

"He really messed her up. That sick son of a bitch! She's beautiful and talented. Fun and funny and accomplished."

"That's the problem for some men. They can't handle that kind of power in a woman. Too intimidating. Makes a weak man feel impotent and that makes him strike out."

Emily fills the kettle and lights the stove. She pulls the fixings for an omelet from the fridge. "So how does someone like Jacquie, who grew up with someone like Ned as her best friend, end up falling for someone who's violent? I just don't get it."

"Well, men like that don't walk around with a sign on their forehead saying, *I'm a batterer.* Most are pretty good at hiding the violent streak during the 'honeymoon' stage of a relationship. But sooner or later, it creeps out as hot-headedness or erupts suddenly as rage."

Emily shakes her head, deep in thought. "I'm making a broccoli omelet. Join me?" She glances at her mother. "How do you know all this?"

"Yes, to the omelet. As to your other question … Let's just say I've known my share of too-charming-to-be-real types. I was in group therapy once, and there were a couple of abused women there. You'd think it would have saved me from a more experiential education, but alas …"

Emily turns around to see that her mother is smiling. "I never knew."

"You were off at school by the time they came along. Anthony was the first, and then, since I'm nothing if not a slow learner, I met Ralph. I was lucky in both instances to get out. After Ralph, I actually worked at a women's shelter and had my eyes opened even further. My radar is so finely tuned now, I can spot an angry dick from a mile away."

Emily turns from the stove, laughing with feigned shock. "Mother!"

Janet joins her briefly in laughter, then both turn back to the seriousness of it. "Your friend may not be out of danger from him, you know."

"I was afraid of that."

"She'd better press charges. Even if nothing comes of it, she'll have established a record."

Emily pours the tea and slides half an omelet and a slice of sourdough toast onto two plates. The two women sit at the counter and eat in silence for a while.

"In spite of everything, you look particularly relaxed tonight," Janet says. "Radiant even. It's nice to see."

"That would be thanks to a woman named Beth who gives an incredible massage. I pretty much came apart after we found Jacquie, and then her mother shut us out at the hospital. Beth neutralized the effects of both those things. It's a good thing Margaret's friend picked me up afterwards because I don't think I could have driven." As she places their dinner plates in the sink, she adds, "You should go."

"I beg your pardon? You want me to leave?"

"No! You should go to Beth for a massage."

"Oh, I don't have time for such indulgences."

Emily flinches but chooses to ignore the dismissal. "On my way home from visiting Ned, a story came to me. A character just started talking to me right there in the car, and an opening scene presented itself."

"Sounds like I'd *better* go, let you get to your writing."

Emily impulsively hugs her mother. Janet stiffens and pulls away. She looks around for her flashlight, grabs it up, and turns toward the door. But then she turns back.

"Don't let that story slip away. Get it down. Writing has always been your saving grace. That and Lily May, of course."

Emily opens her mouth to respond, but her mother is out the door.

◈

Three hours later, Emily is still at her keyboard, the story flowing as if she is but a channel—a conduit through which the character can spill her tale. As she writes, she realizes this is no short story. This is a multifaceted tale that needs lots of space and time to expand, to unfold. This is a novel.

She smiles as a third voice enters a conversation already in progress between established characters. Her fingers can barely keep up as the scene explodes in a wildly funny argument. She knows this portion will require no rewrite in later drafts. It's good. Damn good.

Finally, she leans back and stretches. "A good stopping point."

As she crawls into bed, she is still smiling.

ॐॐ

As the early morning sun shimmers through the trees, her characters are already talking in her head. They continue, each vying for attention, as she steps off the back porch and heads toward the pond. She stops at the bench and removes her right shoe. She brushes the bottom of her sock and then feels inside the shoe, trying to discover the rock or wrinkle that's bothering her.

"'Morning," Otis calls as he approaches from the direction of the house. "How's that young man of yours doing?"

"It'll be a long haul, but he's going to be all right." A pebble falls out of the shoe, and she puts it back on.

"Can't keep a good man down, that's for sure." He sits, nodding his head. "Or woman. Have you seen Margaret since her accident?"

"Accident? What—"

"I hear she's okay," he quickly adds. "Sorry. I thought you'd have heard."

"What happened?"

"Accident's not exactly the right word. She was run off the road and into a tree. Truck's a goner, but Mert says she's just a bit banged up."

"When? Where?"

"Late yesterday afternoon sometime. Over on Old Creek Road. It's a shortcut from Hall's Village over to her place."

"My God, Hall's Village is where she dropped me off for a massage. It must have happened after she left me. What's going on, Otis? First her shed is burned down and then this?"

"She attracted some nasty-ass—pardon my language— enemies in her young years. There's a whole extended family of them. They've been making crazy claims that she did some sort of harm to some of their tribe way back when. All a lot of hogwash, of course, but it's become a part of the family story they tell themselves. Now it's infected the young ones. A bunch of damn hoodlums."

She gets up. "I have to call her. I have to go get my phone and call her."

"It's pretty early, Em. Maybe you should take your morning run first. Give your body a good workout and spend some time in nature before you launch into a day full of other people's troubles."

She hesitates and then shrugs. "I think you may have something there, Old Man." She smiles at him as she begins stretching.

"Haven't lived all these years for nothing, you know." Otis rises from the bench and heads for the toolshed tucked behind a living wall of flowering vines in purples and blues at the edge of the garden. "Time for me to get to work before Mother Nature sees fit to take over the place altogether. She and I have an agreement. I honor her work, and she lets me have a little space in which to do mine. But if I start dawdling, it's all fair game to her." He gives Emily a backhanded wave.

As she returns from her run, Emily slows as the path narrows in its approach to the back side of the pond. A blue jay screams as it bursts into the air. She looks to the low quivering branch it's left behind and stops. Through the branches, she sees the heron standing poised, patient. Its coloring is subtle, muted tones of blues and grays, but for the thin black line etched along its wing tips. A lovely ruff of delicate feathers curls out along its breast. She shivers as the cool air in this shaded spot seeps into her glistening skin and under her sweat-soaked clothing, but she doesn't move. Doesn't want to move away from the serenity emanating from this beautiful water bird.

It turns, looks at her, then walks away, leaving silent trails gliding out behind it along the water's surface. Emily's breath catches. Such grace. Such stillness within movement. She watches as it stalks away, its eyes ever scanning the depths, its long legs and S-curved neck lending the hunter a regal elegance. Shivering again, Emily resumes the path toward home and the call she must make.

"Are you all right?" she says to Margaret's quiet hello.

"I'm fine."

"I should have called you. Asked if everything was all right. Thanked you for Beth."

"Stop it, now." Margaret's tone is sharp, surprising Emily. Then her voice softens as she asks how Emily felt after the session.

"More relaxed and … positive than I've felt in a long while."

"Savor that. Let Beth's good work settle in."

"Are you up for a visit? I'd really like to see you. Or do you need to rest?"

"That would be lovely. I've a pot of chili simmering. Come around eleven for an early lunch. I'll make a batch of corn bread."

"See you then."

After ringing off, she tries to call Jacquie at the hospital but is told there is no such patient listed. She wonders if the hospital isn't taking precautions because Jacquie is an assault victim and calls Ned's mother.

After telling Natalie she will be visiting Ned around two that day, she asks if Natalie can help her get in touch with Jacquie.

"Of course, dear. I'll call Marie and get you on the list down there. She may be going home today, but I'll check. Poor dear. She's a long way from recovery—in a different sense from our Ned. She's suffered a betrayal of the worst kind."

"I know. She deserves so much more in a man. Someone like Ned, not some coward who … Sorry."

"I know. We had hopes once that she and Ned would become a couple, instead of just friends. We thought it would be the ideal marriage. Oh! What an idiotic thing to say. Sometimes I just natter on without thinking. 'Nattering Natalie,' my husband calls me. With great affection, of course."

"They would have made a beautiful couple."

"Maybe. But it turns out his heart was meant for someone else. A lovely girl who's come along at just the right moment." Natalie laughs. "Now, let me call Marie. What Jacquie needs right now is a good friend."

As she puts down her phone, Emily's chin trembles. Natalie's words stung unexpectedly, and she'd had to pretend they hadn't. Now she imagines Ned's parents watching their dream of a golden couple dissolve. In its place, a not-so-golden picture of their beloved son and a wild-haired redhead who has yet to prove herself in the world in any way.

"*Stop it!*" she orders, and heads for the bathroom.

The cold blast of the shower raises goose bumps and sends shivers along her spine.

"There!" she says out loud. "Nothing like a little shock to bring you back to yourself." She throws her head back, wet hair flying, sending a spray of water up the walls of the shower stall. "Ned loves me. That's all that matters. That's all there is. So, snap the fuck out of this wallowing."

As the water grows warmer, she imagines herself under a waterfall. Ned is with her. They're laughing, wet skin to wet skin. She feels the heat of his body, the urgency of—

The faint ringing of her phone pulls her to attention, and she hops out of the shower and grabs it. One voice mail message.

"This is Jacquie. I only have a minute before my mom comes back. She's taking me home to her place. She's treating me like—" The message ends.

Emily hits the call-back button, but Jacquie's phone goes straight to voice mail. "It's Emily," she says. "Call me when you can. I'm here for you."

Feeling momentarily impotent, she resists the urge to pace and fret. She's done all she can, and now it's time to write. Time to slip back into the stream of the story waiting for her in a file labeled: Stillness Speaks.

Chapter 42

Margaret sits in the backyard looking out over the fields. Her untouched tea resting on the arm of the Adirondack chair has cooled. Her mind is strangely blank. No thoughts. No images. No visions. Nothing but the landscape before her.

The dogs splash through the stream and gallop up the hill toward her. She smiles as they each grab a stick from the pile beneath the oak tree. "You're going to make me get up, aren't you?" She leans forward, pressing her palms into the wide wooden arms of the chair, but an odd weakness spreads like water through her suddenly slack muscles. She slumps back down. "'Fraid you're going to have to hang on a minute, girls. Too pooped to pop at the moment." She tries not to let her panic seep into her voice.

The girls sit in front of her, a perfect symmetry between them, their heads cocked to each side, looking like bookends. She reads concern in the wrinkled brows above twin sets of brown eyes.

"I know. I know. Not like me at all, is it? I'm feeling more like eighty-two than sixty-two. Just need a little more rest, that's all. A little more time to work some things out."

The headache she suffered following the accident has finally eased off. After her visit to Dr. Alice with strict instructions to

rest, she let Annie fuss over her for as long as she could stand it
and then sent her on her way. She smiled at John Longfeather's
succinct advice— "Be quiet and be still."—and nodded agreement
at his parting words: "For as long as it takes." And she slept soundly
through the night.

When she woke in the morning, she felt strong and refreshed,
and puttered in the kitchen making chili and baking pies. Then she
came out to sit here in the garden before making the corn bread,
and time got away from her.

The girls lower themselves to lie on the ground, crawling
closer to her chair in the process. They rest their heads on their
outstretched paws, facing each other, again in perfect symmetry.

Margaret leans her head against the slanted chairback and
closes her eyes. Silence inside. The stillness is unnerving. It's not
the expansive dancing silence she finds in meditation, but a dark
and desolate nothingness. No voices. No images. Nothing but an
unsettling void. A yawning chasm of emptiness.

She sits forward, opening her eyes. Where are they? she wonders.
Where are the usual simmerings, the barely perceptible buzzings,
like faint static on an old-time radio? Where are the flashes of color,
the flickering images? Where are the glimpses of happenings, the
snapshots of faces, the bits and pieces of fleeting conversations?
Where are the words that sometimes hang in the air, the puzzle
pieces that swirl, arranging and rearranging themselves?

If gone, are they gone for good?

She leans over and retches violently. Sophia and Grace are
instantly on their feet, pacing nervously in front of her chair, eyes
fixed on her. Finally, she stops and lifts her head. "I'll be okay in a
minute."

Again, she slumps back in the chair. Her pulse throbs at her
temples and in her neck. She is cold despite the warmth of the day.
But mostly, she is scared.

This is not the fear she felt when the boys ran her off the road
and threatened her—the in-the-moment-of-danger kind of fear.
This is a deeper fear rising from a dark place in her mind. This is
the fear of losing herself, the self she's always known, has always

been. And beneath it sits the fear of sinking into infirmity, of slowly losing energy and strength. The fear of becoming an invalid, unable to care for herself, incapable of living alone. Fear of sinking slowly into oblivion with the full knowledge of her steady decline.

Invalid. *Invalid.* Invalidated.

"Stop it. Now!" Her voice cuts through the air as she sits upright. "Be still. Stay grounded. It's only fear and the spiraling thoughts that spring from it. Sit with it. Be with it. All of it."

She folds her legs up into the chair in a tight figure eight. Tucking her chin slightly, she straightens, sitting tall. Partially closing her eyes, she rests her gaze on a patch of brown earth in front of the chair—a patch worn smooth over time by her own feet. She slows and deepens her breathing, and then rests in the simplicity of watching it.

Her awareness settles on the gelatinous mass in her chest. Her breathing falters as panic flutters beneath her breastbone. From somewhere, she hears her own voice easing her back inside her breath. Telling her to feel the fear. Feel the panic fully from the inside out. Look at it with curiosity. Look at it with empathy. Look at it with love.

The mass expands inside her, thick and moist and sticky, closing around her lungs and heart.

Be in it. Sit with it. Feel the fear. Feel it fully. With curiosity. With empathy. With love.

Little by little, the mass recedes, dissolving into itself. Then there is emptiness again. And silence. And an odd sense of ease. Carefully, she unfolds her legs and sits back in the chair. A line from a Frost poem comes to mind: *Little—less—nothing!—and that ended it.* Does the empty silence signify an end? The end?

"Fear is a part of life. I will listen when it arises to protect me, but I won't let it stop me from doing what I must."

With that, she again presses her hands to the arms of the chair, plants her feet squarely in the dirt, and stands.

ೋೕ

"Hello? Margaret?" Emily calls as she rounds the house into the backyard. She feels a moment's disappointment that the outdoor table is not set for lunch, but then looks to the darkening clouds building along the western horizon.

"Door's open," Margaret calls from the kitchen.

As she approaches the screen door, the smell of Margaret's kitchen drifts out to greet her, and she realizes how hungry she is. She's had nothing but an apple and a handful of nuts since her run.

"Smells incredible in here," she says as she steps inside. The spicy kick of chili. The clean, sharp bite of freshly chopped scallions. The crusty scent of corn bread beginning to crisp in the oven. Underneath it all, the lingering fragrance of something tart yet sweet. "Can I move in? Can I come live with you?"

Margaret turns from the stove, smiling. "Well, I certainly wouldn't object, but I think you'd quickly tire of having a bossy old lady in your hair. Have a seat." She indicates the chair she usually takes for herself.

Emily rounds the table. "I don't want to take your favorite chair."

"I'm changing things up. Too much routine is the death of the aging brain. And of spontaneity. I'm stepping out of my rut. So, help an old lady out. Sit."

Margaret says this with a laugh, but Emily senses something serious in her manner. "Okay. If you're going to feed me like this, the least I can do is help you out."

"I'd hoped we could eat in the garden, but rain's coming in."

"Fine with me. Every time we plan a nice visit, some emergency jumps in and sends us spinning. So, let it rain, and ask those visions of yours to take a rest for a while too."

She smiles at Margaret, who is setting two bowls of steaming chili on the table. Margaret's eyes meet hers, but there is no laughing response in them.

"Don't think we have to worry about that. Things have gone pretty quiet of late." She sets down a tray of condiments. "Help yourself."

Turning, she grabs two oven mitts and bends to lift a cast iron skillet out of the oven. The burst of fragrant heat bathes the kitchen just as a gust of cold wind sweeps through the screen door, carrying a roll of distant thunder. Emily's stomach grumbles loudly.

"Better dig in," Margaret says. "Sounds like it's ready just in time." She plunks the skillet of golden-crusted corn bread on the trivet in the center of the table and places the oven mitts protectively around its edges. She slices two thick wedges and slides them onto small plates with a pie server. "There's butter or olive oil and maple syrup in the little carafe." She pours them each a glass of iced tea and sits.

Emily sprinkles cheese on her chili and watches it melt before adding a spoonful of chopped green onion. Then she follows Margaret's lead and drizzles olive oil over the top of the corn bread. "I am ravenous. This will keep me going for the rest of the day and then some." She digs her spoon into her bowl.

"But first," she continues, "I want you to know how incredible that massage was. And then, and even more important, I need you to tell me how you are and what in the world happened after you dropped me off."

Margaret takes her time stirring her chili, her gaze intent on her bowl. "Well, my truck and I were forced off the road and into a tree by a group of angry young men." Emily gapes at her, and Margaret waves her hand as if to settle her. "More of the old stuff coming back around from the family I told you about before. Always a smoldering bunch, their low opinion of me flares up from time to time. I'm their go-to target."

"But this isn't some simple case of—"

"Lately, it's come to a head. I won't ignore it, but I'm taking some time to work out the best approach to bring it to an end, or at least a ceasefire. On a positive note, I had an unlikely rescuer. And that's what I'm choosing to focus on right now."

"Oh?" Emily says, spoon halfway to her mouth.

"Sam King is the stranger who recently appeared in our midst. He's camped down by Old Creek. He heard the commotion and scared them off with a shotgun blast."

"I'd have fainted dead away. Seriously."

"When he helped me down from my poor truck, I thought I might."

"Margaret! I can't imagine what that must have been like." Emily rests her spoon on her bowl and sits back in her chair.

"Well, that part's over now and I'm fine, so let's enjoy our lunch."

"What do you know about this man, Sam King?"

"More than I did when we first met. He's still a bit of a mystery, but my initial fear of him was unwarranted. He's traveling around with this gorgeous Rhodesian ridgeback named C. J. Says he's doing some research and sorting out some personal things."

"So why here?"

"Said he's never been to Maine. And he has a personal interest in what he calls 'the sight.' There's more to it than that, but I'm not sure just what." Margaret shrugs.

"Sam King, you say?" Margaret nods. "Camping out and traveling with a dog?" Emily wrinkles her brow in studied concentration. "There's something …"

"Nothing to do with *Travels with Charley*. I actually asked." Margaret laughs before taking up a spoonful of chili.

"Hmm."

As they slip into silence, Emily savors the taste of sunshine, summer garden, and deep rich soil in the food Margaret has made. The corn bread is the perfect complement to the chili with its hint of maple syrup in the batter.

"How is Otis and your mom?" Margaret asks.

"Otis is looking healthier than he has in a long time. He's all enthusiastic about some new plantings he has in mind, but he won't share the plan." Emily laughs. "I'm sure it will have some whimsical or ironic elements."

"And your mom? How's she doing?"

Emily is struck by Margaret's use of the word *mom* and not the more formal *mother*. She hesitates before saying, "She's doing—*we're* doing well. I'm almost afraid to say that out loud."

"Don't be. Shout it out loud. You're coming to know and understand each other. It's a good thing. Honor it by believing in it."

"Can you see it?" Emily searches Margaret's eyes, asking for reassurance so she can relax into this. So she can trust it won't suddenly dissolve.

Margaret looks away, busying herself with blotting up a puddle of tea on the table next to the pitcher. "I feel it."

"But you don't see it."

"Truth is … I don't see anything about anything." Margaret's voice quavers. "They're gone. The visions. The images. The voices. Everything. Gone."

Emily looks up into sadness in the blue eyes across from her. She leans forward. "Surely, they'll be back," she says with a brightness she knows fools neither of them.

"We'll see." Margaret laughs at the unintended pun. "Or not," she adds with a smile.

"How does it feel?" Emily asks earnestly. "Without them, I mean."

Margaret leans back and closes her eyes. "Strangely empty. Quiet." She opens her eyes, looking surprised, "Lonely."

Emily is silent. Listening. Waiting.

"My life has always been underscored by a barely audible …" She struggles for the word, her forehead furrowed, pale scar crinkling. Then the word explodes on the exhale. "… *vibration*. It's the closest I can come. A sort of a humming that's pregnant with meaning, with content … with context.

"My constant companion, it simmers until something triggers a release. Afterwards, I have to tease meaning from whatever shows up. It's like piecing together a cosmic puzzle that's been dropped into ordinary time." She stops, shaking her head. "It's hard to articulate. Perhaps you, the writer, can find better words than I."

"No. I couldn't. And I'm sure it will return. It has to." She hesitates before continuing. "*If*, of course, you *want* it to."

Margaret stares at her.

"Do you? *Want* it to?"

"Ah." Margaret sits back. "The heart of the matter. You'd think I might have a ready answer, but I will have to sit with this." She gets up and begins clearing the table, effectively ending the conversation.

As they share the washing up, rain beats on the roof and rattles against the windows. Thunder rumbles by to the west, and distant lightning flashes in the now dim kitchen. Over tea and slices of pie, Emily tells Margaret of her attempts to reach Jacquie and her plan to visit Ned that afternoon.

As they finish up and Margaret hangs the dish towels on a wooden rack beside the sink, Emily tells her about her novel. "These characters, or this one in particular, just started talking. I'm simply following along, trying to get it all down. It's ..." She looks up at the ceiling as lightning flickers across it and smiles broadly. "It's incredible!"

"Perfect timing," Margaret says. "Just what you needed with all that's going on."

"My mother called my writing my saving grace."

"How very blessed you are."

"I am, aren't I?"

"All the more so because you realize it. Awareness and gratitude magnify our blessings. And multiply them. Don't you think?"

Emily ponders this a moment. "They do." Her smile fades. "I feel kind of guilty, though. Here I am doing the happiness dance, while Ned is on a long and painful road. Jacquie too."

"But for both of them, it's the road out. And while they're on it, they will need the strength and compassion you can offer. Losing yourself in the story that's come to you is like stepping into grace every day. It will sustain and energize you so you can be your best self for them. Or at least that's how I think it all works."

"I like the way you think."

❧

Margaret watches as Emily runs to her car in the slackening rain. Emily starts the engine but then thrusts the car door open and runs back.

"Samuel J. Kingston," she calls to Margaret as she approaches. "Sam King." She steps into the doorway. "I think he's Samuel J. Kingston, the science fiction writer. He doesn't have the fame of Steinbeck yet, but he has a loyal and growing following."

"Well, what do you know?" Margaret is smiling. "Think I'll give him a Google."

"It's been nagging at me since you told me about him. Then it hit me. I think there may even be psychic elements in his novels."

An hour later, Margaret sits back in her desk chair, mulling what she's just read. She closes her laptop and heads for the kitchen. Grabbing her bag, she feels around inside it for her keys as she heads for the back door. She stops short. She has no truck. She's going nowhere.

She calls the girls and heads off through the side yard and down the hill toward Annie's.

≈≈

Margaret stands on the crest of the hill leading down to the river and watches him climb toward her, head down. "Well, if it isn't Mr. Kingston of *Skylark 99* fame," she calls out.

Startled out of his reverie he looks up. "Lucky for you C. J.'s off in the woods somewhere. He doesn't take kindly to unexpected visitors."

"And I don't take kindly to untruthful acquaintances, Samuel J. Kingston." He opens his mouth to respond, but Margaret hurries on. "But since you saved my hide earlier, I'll overlook some harmless deceit. It was harmless, wasn't it?"

"I certainly hope there was no harm done. I was just hoping to keep my dubious reputation from getting in the way of a deeper conversation with you. Please, call me Sam."

He stands level with her now as a light rain begins again. "Care to join me?" He indicates two webbed lawn chairs sitting under a tarp suspended from his camper truck. A small fire bowl squats in front of the chairs, a mound of dying embers glowing orange.

"New car already?" he asks as they sit.

"No, it's my neighbor's. Though I guess I'm going to have to break down and get a new truck soon."

"Maybe something with a little more pep than the one you wrecked? With a nice little handgun in the glove box?" He smiles.

"I'll put *pep* on the top of the list. As to the gun, no thanks. I walked away from those a long time ago."

"I'd think those hoodlums would have taught you a lesson about self-protection."

"The energy of a gun is not energy I wish to carry around with me. I don't begrudge anyone else theirs, but they're not for me."

"You sound like my grandmother. The energy talk, I mean."

"Well, some of us are more sensitive to the energy signature of things than others. Once you've felt a gun's, you can never take it lightly. Believe me."

"I do. But I still think you should reconsider. For your safety."

"I appreciate your concern."

They sit silently as Sam stirs the embers in the bowl and then adds some kindling and a few sticks of wood from a nearby basket. Soon a bright blaze is crackling before them.

"Ready to tell me more about your reasons for seeking me out and for keeping your identity a secret, Mr. Science Fiction Writer?" Margaret says with a smile.

"I'm always looking for the real thing. Someone with my grandmother's gift of second sight. From what I can tell, you're it. More so than anyone else I've come across. Pretenders and quacks abound, along with people with a modified version of the sight. From what I've heard, you're extremely prolific and extraordinarily accurate."

Margaret looks off into the distance.

"I have a writer's curiosity and a grandson's need to understand and honor the most important person in my life. I'm planning a book about her and I didn't want my identity to get in the way, to make you wary."

"You don't look at me and the details of my life as material?"

Sam doesn't answer.

"Because I would have to ask you not to. I would have to ask you to respect my life as mine. Clementine would understand."

"That's a hard one. It's hard to disentangle my writer self from the rest of me. But my grandmother would be sorely disappointed in me if I didn't honor your wishes. I will write my tribute to Clementine using the details I know of her life. I promise not to use the specifics of yours, but I hope you can give me a look at your gift from the inside out."

Margaret stares into the fire. "It often doesn't feel like a gift."

"What then?"

"That's a good question. It's … an ability. A faculty that allows me to perceive things in ways that are outside the norm. It's no different from other abilities that sit just outside the bounds of what the world calls normal. Genius level intelligence, for example. Extraordinary mathematical skill. Natural musical talent."

"But the world at large has very strong opinions about your particular faculty."

"You're right. People have to have their labels for things they don't understand."

"I heard you found a lost boy in the woods. Surely it must have felt like a gift then."

Margaret smiles as the image of Joey Allen laughing and running around at the August Supper comes back to her. "Yes. It did, indeed."

"Tell me how you felt that night. Tell me how you found him. Walk me through your process."

As Margaret describes the night of the rescue, she is acutely aware of the silence inside her. The memory of that night is just that, a memory. There is no accompanying crackle of energy waiting to be activated, to be called upon to offer some guidance. This inner quiet is so unsettling, she steeps herself in the memory of the night on the mountain to offset it.

Sam listens intently, his head cocked to one side, a hint of a knowing smile on his face. "So, when you looked at the map, did you see where he was or hear a prompting in your mind, or what?"

"It's hard to separate it all out. Things happen simultaneously. I looked at the map and saw the landscape around him as if on a movie screen. I heard his whimpering at the same time. I saw the boulders and the flash of red. And I heard the water. That was enough to send John Longfeather to the clearing behind the Grandmothers and to the exposed root ball of the fallen pine."

"Anything else?"

"I saw other images, had other impressions. But they seemed unrelated to Joey. Looking back, I realize I always experience a myriad of things. Then I sort through them, prioritizing and selecting the ones that seem to go together. The ones pertinent to the task at hand. It all happens instantaneously."

"That night, did you travel there yourself? Energetically, I mean."

She looks across the fire at him. "Yes." She sits very still, remembering. "One minute, I was at the search headquarters. The next, I was leaning over the little guy, reassuring him and singing an old lullaby." She stops.

"What is it? What?" Sam prompts her.

"The lullaby. My grandmother. My father's mother, Lucinda. She sang it to me." She looks at Sam and sighs. "I always thought she'd died before Mattie and I were born. But no. She was a presence very early on. Always singing or humming." Tears come as she breathes in the memory. "I remember her voice. I remember the smell of her. Rosemary, sage, and lemon verbena. How could I have forgotten until now?"

"Maybe Clementine has something to do with it. You've agreed to help me with her story, and she's a conduit for this memory. A grandmother for a grandmother."

Margaret is still shaking her head in wonder. "Lucinda had it too. She passed it to my father, and he passed it along to Mattie and me."

"Mattie?"

"My twin brother."

"He has it too? Can I meet him? Talk to him?"

"He died. When we were little." Her voice trails off as she closes her eyes.

"I'm sorry."

"I really thought she died before we were born, but I remember her rocking us on her lap. And I remember the emptiness when she died. We were about two. She fell and ... Oh, God, it was so ... How could I have forgotten?"

"Clementine used to say to me that if we remembered every

sorrow, we'd crumble beneath the weight of them. She said our hearts hold what we think we cannot bear until we're ready. Ready to look and have a good long cry. Only then can we see the sweet on the other side of sorrow. And she believed there is always a sweet side."

Margaret nods, gazing into the fire.

"So, now that you've opened up this memory, are you ready to explore it further?" Sam asks. "What memories do you have of her abilities? How do you know it came from her? Did she offer you any instruction for handling it?"

Margaret raises her hand, imploring him to stop talking. Closing her eyes again, she strains to recall the glimpse of memory she's just seen, but to no avail. Her head aches dully as her mind remains a frustrating blank. Shaking her head, she looks over to him. "Nothing. I can't. I guess I'm trying too hard. Best to let it go for now."

Sam nods in agreement, but she can see the disappointment in his eyes. He pokes at the dying fire.

"I have to get Annie's car back to her and take the girls off her hands." On a sudden impulse, she adds, "Perhaps you could come to dinner tomorrow evening and we could talk some more?"

"I'd like that. In the meantime, maybe you'll have a helpful vision or two. Or maybe a memory will surface. Or maybe nothing will happen, and we'll just have a pleasant dinner together." He laughs, and they both stand up.

"Sounds like a plan." She smiles and offers her hand. "Thanks. To you and to Clementine. Between her and my grandmother, I feel less alone than I did when I sat down here."

"Perhaps someday you'll share your story with the world. You could provide others with insights and advice—the very things you needed when you were growing up."

"I guess that would be the upside to notoriety. Food for thought, Sam. Food for thought."

As she pulls out onto the road, a blue pickup truck approaches from the opposite direction. Her heart races as the truck passes by, an elderly man in the driver's seat. Shaking, she pulls onto the shoulder. Again, she notes the silence inside, the disquieting emptiness, and the dull ache in her head. She leans her forehead on the steering wheel.

"Yes, Emily," she says aloud, lifting her head to look out the windshield. "In answer to your question, I *do* want it back."

At Annie's, she remembers to turn her phone ringer back on and finds two messages waiting. One is from John telling her about a vehicle he's just seen at his cousin's dealership; the other is from Dr. Alice checking in on her.

Within an hour, she is signing the papers on a new car—a hybrid, sage green and basic. John's cousin promises delivery the next morning, and she gives the small vehicle an affectionate pat.

"Time for a change, I guess," she says. "Thought I wanted another truck, but this'll suit my needs just fine. And if it gets the gas mileage you say it will, all the better for the planet. Thanks, Henry."

Back at Annie's, Margaret gratefully accepts a bowl of chowder before heading home. As she eats, she tells her friend about Sam's identity and reluctantly confides that she may have lost the very "sight" he's come to ask about. Annie offers a flurry of cheerful assurances, but Margaret sees the doubt in her eyes as they wave goodbye.

As she and the dogs approach her house, she smiles to see a tall figure in the backyard loading his truck with the last of the blackened debris from her workshop.

Waving, she quickens her pace to greet him as Grace and Sophia run ahead. "Hello, Kenneth. I can't believe you've managed to clean up so fast. I figured it would be several more trips yet."

"Had some help. John and a friend just left with a couple of loads, and this is the last of it."

She stands back, admiring the cleared area and the freshly raked ground. "It's so much easier to imagine it now. It's actually going to happen." She turns to Kenneth, leaning on his rake. "Thank you."

"Piedmont Lumber will be delivering materials tomorrow morning, and my crew and I will get started on Monday."

"Your timing couldn't be better. The thought of watching the new rising up out of the old is just what I need." As she speaks, she steps into the empty space and slowly turns full circle. She imagines the building rising up around her, smelling of raw wood warmed by a late-summer sun.

A memory surfaces with the smells. An elderly man bends over a table saw, easing a piece of wood through the whirring blade. Its high-pitched whine slices the air along with the board. He wears a multipocketed leather apron, and the stub of a yellow pencil sticks out from behind his ear. Behind him stands the studded outline of a shed.

Margaret stops turning, giving herself a moment to regain her equilibrium and absorb what she's just remembered. "Kenneth. The boy who set this fire. His grandfather was a carpenter, very particular about what jobs he would accept. He wasn't interested in making money, just the work. He was a true artist."

"And?" Kenneth furrows his brow as he waits for her to go on.

"I just had a memory of him, and it made me wonder if the boy might have some of that talent. Or an interest in carpentry."

Kenneth is smiling again. "Are you by any chance wondering if we might let him apprentice on this job? Community service in lieu of juvenile detention?"

"I guess I am. I hadn't worked it out in so many words, but, yes, I wonder if that might be possible."

"You'd have to go into it with eyes wide open. I mean, the kid may be beyond help.

"Don't get me wrong," he rushes to add. "I would love nothing better than to turn this kid around by showing him the satisfaction of creating something with his hands. But I also know that sometimes our best intentions are not enough to bring about our desired outcomes."

"But you don't object to my exploring this? I mean, you'd be the one tasked with teaching him."

"If you decide this is viable, I'm all for it."

Spontaneously, Margaret steps back into the space where her studio will stand. She reaches out her hand for him to join her. "At sunrise on Monday, I'll ask John Longfeather to offer a blessing of the studio. I'd like it if you could be there. Unless that feels uncomfortable. The blessing will still hold."

"I'll be here."

Chapter 43

The words are flowing again, the story has taken a surprising twist, and Emily is trying to ignore the buzzing of her phone. She reaches over and hits decline. Within seconds, her phone signals a voice mail is waiting. Still, she ignores it. But worries creep in, derailing her train of thought. *What if it's about Ned? What if Otis has—* Sighing, she retrieves the message.

"Emily? It's Jacquie. Call me when you can."

Jacquie sounds as if she's trying for light and nonchalant, but Emily senses an undercurrent of anxiety. She calls her friend.

"Jacquie, how are you?"

There is the briefest pause before Jacquie says, "Doing pretty well, actually. I wanted to thank you and Margaret for ... well, for all you did. And I wanted to apologize for my mother. She can be a bit of an ice queen."

"We knew she was in protector mode, and you don't have to explain about mothers to me!" Emily laughs.

"Well, thank you for being kind about it."

Sensing she may be about to hang up, Emily asks, "How are you, really, Jacquie?"

"Well, my eye looks like something out of a horror movie, but they don't think there's any fracture and my sight will be fine when the swelling goes down. My wrist *is* fractured, though. Luckily, I have a great staff and a sous chef who could have his name on his own place."

"Okay. That's the physical you. How about the emotional you?"

Emily hears the sharp intake of breath on the other end, and when Jacquie resumes, there is a slight quavering to her voice. "I honestly don't know how to answer that one. I still can't believe he …"

Emily resists the urge to jump in with reassurances and soothing platitudes. Instead, she sits with her friend in the silence that hangs between them.

"I can't believe I was so taken in," Jacquie finally says.

"Are you up to lunch at the Spotted Zebra and a little face-to-face conversation?"

Jacquie doesn't respond.

Emily waits.

"Yes." Her voice is almost a whisper. "Yes. I think I would like that." Her voice grows stronger with each word. "Yes."

"I'll pick you up in half an hour."

Emily calls her mother as soon as she hangs up with Jacquie, asking if her mother will you be around that afternoon. "I'd like to bring my friend Jacquie over after lunch if she's willing. I'd like her to meet you. To meet with you."

After a brief pause, Janet says yes.

৯৩

Seated at a corner table in the Spotted Zebra Cafe, Jacquie orders a large bowl of white bean and kale soup and a demi-salad and eats it all. "Suddenly, I'm ravenous," she says with surprise. She smiles, wincing.

"I figure hunger is always a good sign," Emily says. "Especially for a chef."

"I'm going back to work tomorrow. It'll be good to get back to it."

"Your staff and customers will be happy."

"Well, I won't be showing my face outside the kitchen anytime soon, and no amount of makeup is going to mask this shiner. But my staff will take it in stride." She laughs for the first time since Emily picked her up, and again winces. "Of course, I'm not looking forward to the looks of pity and the awkward silences I expect I'll get when I first get there. But once that's out of the way, it'll be good to plunge in and not come up for air until we close."

"What about being back there? Are you prepared to walk into the room where it happened? Maybe you could do a test run when no one's there? I'd come with you."

Jacquie sits back in her chair. "I love and appreciate your directness, Emily. Everyone else beats around the bush and avoids talking about what happened. Sure, I'm feeling fragile, but I want to talk about it." She looks around at the noisy lunch crowd in the small café. "Just maybe not here."

"Well, I was hoping you'd come with me to my uncle's house and meet my mother. She's got some experience with what you've gone through. If it feels comfortable to you, we could talk with her about it. But only if it feels right."

Jacquie pushes her dishes away. "I'd like that."

෨෴

When the younger women arrive, Otis retreats to the garden. Emily isn't sure what to expect when her mother asks Jacquie if she can talk about what happened, but Jacquie doesn't hesitate.

"Brian came in through the back door of the restaurant while I was pulling ingredients from the storeroom and said he wanted to talk. I was hefting a sack of flour to replenish the bin for the house rolls and I told him I was a bit behind in my prep and asked if it couldn't wait."

Jacquie's hands tremble as she wraps them around her warm mug of coffee. She looks back and forth between Emily and Janet before continuing.

"He'd been moody lately. Distant. Prone to long silences. On edge. I'd asked him a few times what was wrong, and he'd snapped at me. Told me to leave him alone. Stop nagging him. I was uneasy about that, but not to the point of feeling frightened or anything. I was irritated with him, and I promised myself we'd have a talk and I'd get to the bottom of it once things settled a bit with the restaurant.

"But when I asked if it couldn't wait, he flew off the handle. He grabbed me and spun me around and started yelling. He said things that made no sense. Accused me of treating him like he didn't matter, like he was dirt under my feet. Shouted that my precious restaurant meant more to me than he did. Then he accused me of screwing my sous chef! Said he was going to get some of what Eddy was getting right there in the storage room. He pinned me against the shelving, and I pushed him away. He came back swinging with both fists. I don't remember anything else until the hospital."

Tears running down her cheeks, Jacquie shakes her head. "I don't know what I did to make him think those things. I don't know what I could have done differently. I was in the process of starting up the restaurant when we started dating. I laid everything out very clearly every step of the way about what the restaurant would involve. About the time and focus it would take. About my total dedication to making it a success. And he was on board. I don't know what shifted. What I—"

Janet cuts her off. "This wasn't about what you did or didn't do. This was about *him*. His behavior was indefensible. And *he* is responsible for it."

Janet's voice softens. "Jacquie, abusers are adept at hiding their violent tendencies right up until the first punch. And make no mistake: he's an abuser. This wasn't a one-time thing. And I say *first punch,* because there will always be more. If you hear only one thing I'm saying to you today, hear this. With the first punch, you both step over a threshold." Janet straightens, her voice taking on a chillingly serious tone. "After that first one, there will always be more."

Emily sits mesmerized, listening to her mother counsel her friend. Her manner is gentle but firm. She assures Jacquie that the beating was not her fault while insisting that she must have no further contact with Brian. Repeatedly, she reminds Jacquie that abusers have to do their own work if they want to change their ways. Repeatedly, using different words each time, she explains that Jacquie cannot help Brian. Repeatedly, she suggests counseling with a trained therapist so that Jacquie can find her way back to wholeness. She gives her a number to call to get the process started.

In spite of her mother's careful patience and obvious expertise, Jacquie says, "How could I be so stupid? How did I not see—"

"Stop it."

Janet's sharp tone snaps Jacquie's head up. She stares at Janet, mouth open.

"You are not a stupid woman, and you know it." She holds Jacquie's gaze with her own, a fierce intensity shining in her eyes. "He is a master manipulator. You did nothing wrong. There is nothing wrong with you. I repeat, you … did … nothing … wrong. There is nothing wrong with you."

In the silence that follows, Janet reaches across the table and takes Jacquie's hands in both of her own.

"This is where the healing begins. Right now. In this moment. Jacquie, you are not alone in this and you are not in any way at fault in this. Do you hear me?"

Jacquie looks into Janet's clear gray eyes. "Yes. I hear you. But, I have to be honest. It's going to take time for me to really believe it."

"That's right. It's going to take time and lots of self-care and a damned good therapist. But you will get there. I promise. And I'll be here for a while yet, so I can help if you'd like."

Emily loses the next few words her mother speaks, lost in the echo of the words *for a while yet*. In her mind, she sees taillights disappearing down the drive. Then she forces her attention back to her mother's voice.

"… the legal system will deal with him regardless of what you may or may not want. He has broken a number of laws, and they don't need you to press charges. So. All you have to do is focus on your healing. Physically and emotionally."

Janet looks at her daughter and then back at Jacquie. "Emily said you might want to go over to the restaurant today to prepare yourself for reentry before going back to work tomorrow. Would you like for the three of us to go together? Now?"

Without hesitation, Jacquie nods.

Forty minutes later, they walk through the back door of Jacquie's restaurant, Jacqueline's. Jacquie pauses and takes a breath. Emily and Janet stand behind her on either side of the dimly lit entryway. All three are silent.

Emily notices the large round clock over the swinging doors that lead into the dining area. Its second hand clicks softly as it circles the face, briefly touching each black numeral before ticking on to the next.

Finally, Jacquie leads the way into the kitchen area and flicks on the overhead lights. The stainless-steel work surfaces and appliances shine. The hanging pots and pans, some battered and tempered by good use, gleam.

Jacquie releases a satisfied sigh, rolling her shoulders back, and then straightens and walks briskly toward the storage area in the rear. After a beat, Emily and Janet follow. As they stand back, giving Jacquie space, Emily is suddenly thrown back to the day of the assault. She sees Jacquie on the floor powdered with flour, her head bleeding, the area in disarray. Nausea rises hotly in her throat, and she bends forward, hugging her stomach with one hand and covering her mouth with the other. Turning, she staggers into the kitchen, trying to catch her breath. She pulls out a tall stool from the corner and sits, lowering her head and focusing on her breathing.

Jacquie is unaware of her friend's distress as, her hands on her hips, she surveys the area, now clean and orderly and free of all evidence of her ordeal. Finally, she reaches up and takes down a small sack. She lifts it to her nose and squeezes it with both hands. The fragrance of lavender and mint wafts through the air.

"I'm ready now," she says as she replaces the sack on the shelf. "Thank you."

Janet nods, a smile of approval on her face. Then she turns to Emily, and her smile disappears. She and Jacquie hurry to Emily's side.

"Oh, my God, Emily! Are you all right?" Jacquie asks.

"Sorry. I didn't expect it. I was concentrating on you and it blindsided me." Rising from the stool, she hugs Jacquie. "I'm so glad you're all right."

"Yes, I am. And now you've helped me to reclaim this place and my sense of balance. No one will ever take that away from me again. No one. Ever." She turns to Janet. "Thanks to both of you."

Janet reacts with a cautionary gesture. "And—"

"And the help of a damned good therapist!" Jacquie finishes for her.

Chapter 44

Margaret puts down her phone. John's voice and his promise to come on Monday at sunrise has helped to ground her. She walks to the small table in the back corner of the kitchen and looks down at the nearly finished puzzle. A lake is spread out under a starlit sky. A sliver of the moon rises over silhouetted treetops along the far side. Her heart and breath slow as she stands there. Peace settles over her as she imagines stepping into this serene landscape, walking right into the water as its silken warmth swirls around her ankles, calves, knees....

Without thought, she slips the last few pieces into place and smiles at the sense of satisfaction that fills her. She walks into the living room and on into the library, stopping at puzzles in various stages of completion as she goes. Eight puzzles in all. The number surprises her.

"Maybe this is getting out of hand," she says. "No wonder two-thirds of the town think I'm a crazy lady." As she circles back toward the kitchen, a brightly wrapped package on the table by her reading chair stops her.

She reads the tag dangling from a cluster of ribbon curls. *It spoke to me. I think you'll see why! Love, Annie*

Margaret shakes the package and laughs. "Might as well make it nine!"

She carries the package to the kitchen and sets it on the table at her usual place, ignoring her earlier intention to change up her routine. Deciding to enjoy the festive wrapping a bit longer, she measures loose tea into the strainer basket in a single-serving teapot. Then, very slowly, she pours hot water into the pot, covers it, and places it on the table. She reaches for her favorite Hilda Hanson mug and then changes her mind, her intention surfacing anew.

From the back of the dish cupboard, she pulls out an oddly misshapen mug with spatterings of bright paint fired into the glaze. A gift from Anita Parker. A thank you for suggesting she let her inner wild woman loose on the potter's wheel. Anita Parker with the shy ways and buttoned-up style. Anita Parker who would shrink into the furniture in a group setting. Anita Parker with the sparks of dancing colored lights emanating from her body that only Margaret could see. Anita Parker, now famous for her distinctive quirkiness, her flair for surprising elements of color and design, her panache.

Margaret pours tea into the mug and reaches for the package. "What is it this time, Annie?" she asks softly as she unwraps it.

Delicately carved into the top of a square wooden box is a simple stand of birch trees. As she runs her hand along it, marveling at the beauty of the piece, a mild warmth radiates outward from the center of her palm. She places her other hand on top. With both hands pulsating with heat, she cocks her head in a listening posture and waits.

Seconds pass. Then minutes. Nothing comes. No images. No whisperings. No snatches of conversation. Only silence and the emptiness that has become her companion of late. She sighs, placing her still warm hands over her heart.

Suddenly, she is sobbing, her chest convulsing beneath her palms. An overwhelming sadness rises, and she surrenders into it.

Feeling oddly removed from the woman sobbing in the kitchen chair, Margaret listens to what comes from within. Guttural, primal sounds erupt with each spasm in her chest—soundings that plumb the depths and carry wounded fragments of a fractured self to the surface. One after the other, they tumble into the room. With a sense of curious detachment, she watches as this deep-seated grief wells and spills forth.

The wooden box is in her lap, and her body is folded over it as her crying quiets into occasional shudders. She places the box on the table. Her hands explore it, noting the recessed hinges in one side and the tiny latch hook on the front. She flicks the hook with her thumb and lifts the lid.

"Oh, Annie," she breathes. She plunges her hand in and scoops up wooden puzzle pieces. She lets them run through her fingers back into the box, enjoying the clatter and the mild woody fragrance as they tumble. The weight of her grief gives way to the lightness of child's play as she handles the thick chunks of brightly painted wood.

Aware that the girls are sitting on either side, attention fixed on her every move, she pats their heads and rises to let them out.

"Time to be off doing doggy things in the natural world, my empathetic friends." As they scramble out the door, she starts to turn away, but then thinks better of it and steps into the yard.

A hint of autumn flavors the air as she stands on the crest of the hill. She shivers, random thoughts floating through her mind. Thoughts of time passing and seasons turning. Thoughts of change being the only constant. Thoughts of life going on no matter what.

"Okay, Margaret," she says aloud. "Time to explore this new way of being in the world. Everyone you know lives without the added dimension you've always taken for granted. This is just another in a series of losses that make up any lifetime. Every lifetime." She smiles up at the lavender cast of the sky. "Something beneficial always comes in to fill the void. You know that!"

She bends to greet the girls as they clamber back up the hill, each carrying a stick. She tosses the sticks into the shadowed side yard, and they race to retrieve them. Laughing, she wishes she could bottle their exuberance or soak it in by osmosis.

Back inside, she walks to the two puzzles on the harvest table.

She fits the last few pieces into the unfinished one: the riot of bright paint splotches against a stark white backdrop. It looks less like joy and more like chaos today. She gazes at the finished one Emily called *refuge*. "Interesting pairing," she says as she dismantles both puzzles and sweeps them into separate brown paper bags.

She returns to Annie's gift. Tilting the box up, she sprinkles the pieces out onto the table. She takes her time sorting them, swirling each piece between fingertips and thumb before placing them in clusters of like colors.

She immerses herself in the process and slips into what feels like sacred time. Without thought, she turns on a nearby lamp as the kitchen darkens. Otherwise, she maintains an easy but focused attention on the work at hand.

The images begin to take shape—a face here, an outstretched hand there, the curling smoke of an open fire, the thick trunk of a tree shimmering with reflected firelight. Suddenly, Margaret sits back.

She knows the painting photographed for this puzzle. She remembers it propped against the wall of her father's studio, taller than she was at the time. She remembers squatting before it, mesmerized by the figures rendered in thick broad strokes. A circle of cloaked women bend over a fire, some seated and one standing, her arms raised, hands spread wide. Only three faces were visible. Two in profile, mostly hidden by loose hoods and escaping strands of hair. The third, although facing forward from across the central fire, was partially blocked by the raised hand of the standing figure. But Margaret knows whose face it is. It is her mother's.

In his early works, her father always incorporated her mother's face. It would be in shadow, or partially hidden, or just visible on the periphery, without enough detail to be recognizable to any but those who knew his little secret.

That's what he had called it the first time Margaret pointed out the face. "My little secret," he'd said. And then he winked and placed his finger to his lips. She remembers now how she giggled and winked back and felt so very special—coconspirator with this god of a man.

She recalls as well that he had not signed this particular painting in his usual red, and she searches through the scattered pieces for any with the merest hint of white. Fitting them together with care, she at last looks down on the familiar sweeping script, white against a dark background. *Maxwell Meader.* And though she has seen the flamboyant signature hundreds of times, her breath catches and the tears come.

"Oh, Annie," she whispers. She resumes fitting pieces into place with ease, her eyes ever scanning the table for color and shape and specific arrangements of slots and tabs. Finally, she comes to a section that stumps her momentarily. She gets up and stretches and circles the kitchen. As she passes the sleeping dogs, Sophia stirs, raises her head, and then lays back down, assured that all is well.

When Margaret sits again, her fingers gravitate to three of the pieces in a cluster of muted blues and greens. She slowly moves them around one another until they snug together, forming most of a stylized four-leaf clover. Smiling, she acknowledges the puzzle maker with a nod.

"Patrick Kelly, I presume," she says to the empty air. "And since I now know it's you, I suspect you've incorporated dropouts to highlight your logo, and then you've placed it in the lower-left corner of your puzzle."

She quickly arranges more pieces from the pile of blues and greens until the clover is outlined by artistically shaped empty spaces—curved openings, mere slashes—serving to highlight it. She then slides the completed logo down to the lower left-hand section of the nearly completed puzzle, where it clearly fits.

"Yes." She nods, satisfied, and then runs her hands over the surface of the puzzle, stopping at her father's signature. Tracing it with her fingertips.

Reaching for her phone to call Annie, she gasps. Three a.m.!

She turns back to the puzzle, remembering the words scrawled in black paint across the back of the actual canvas. *The Elders Speak.*

Her father painted it when her parents lived in New Mexico, long before she and Mattie were born. She wonders now if that wasn't the happiest time of their lives together, and wishes she could sit with him and ask him all her questions about the paintings that came out of that happy time. They'd always included her mother. Some, like the print above Emily's mantel, depicted her alone against a backdrop of early-morning or late-afternoon sun. Face turned away or in profile, thick dark hair hanging below her waist. But most incorporated her into the midst of gatherings, circles of people, all at one with the landscape and closely connected to one another.

Sadness wells in her chest, pressing up under her breastbone. That's what they had known in the Southwest. Connection. Inclusion. Community. So, what had brought them back to the family land in Maine? Why hadn't they sold it and moved her father's mother back to New Mexico with them? How might life have been different for them if they'd stayed? Would he have suffered less from his visions? Would he have—

"No time for such unanswerable questions, Margaret!" But the image of circles stays with her. The thought of being connected. Of staying connected. Of opening more and more fully to connection.

Tired now, Margaret stares at the puzzle, mentally filling in the missing sections of the painting from memory. Finally, she turns out the lights and heads up to her bedroom. The girls fall in behind her as soon as her foot touches the bottom step.

She slips into bed and turns on her side. The night is as still as her mind. Drawing her knees up to her chest, she turns her face into the mattress, trying to quiet the part of her mind that has begun scanning, searching for the sizzle of sensation, seeking a hint of an undercurrent. She rolls onto her back and sighs before drifting into sleep.

The dream is vivid, the colors bright, the sounds sharp, the sensations keen. She is wandering a long corridor. She has to give a presentation and has forgotten her notes. She can't find the room. Her stomach cramping, she runs into a bathroom with overflowing toilets. Gushing water spreads across the floor, rising. She lifts her arm to swim. It is covered in tattoos. She lifts the other. It too is brightly inked. She flails as the room morphs into an amphitheater.

She is standing center stage, naked. Crouching, she covers her breasts. The jeering crowd throws lumps of coal, but they turn into birds and flap toward the rafters.

She is sitting cross-legged on a woven blanket at twilight. A purple mountain range rims the distant horizon. A black bird with iridescent wing and tail feathers alights on a solitary tree. It calls out a triplet of raucous notes, and a second bird joins it on the slender branch. Together they call out, and a third lands above them. The collective calling continues until there are nine birds sitting in the tree. Their song softens into a mournful chant. A dead bird lies on the blanket in front of her. Lifting her voice, she joins the dirge.

She awakens to bright sunshine warming the bedcovers. Throwing them off, she crosses to the antique rolltop desk in the corner. She pulls open a deep lower drawer and runs her fingers along the spines of three fat sketchbooks standing on end. Pulling out the middle one, she climbs onto the bed and opens it.

The familiar smell of charcoal and old paper nearly stops her as she flips through the pages. But she keeps searching until she finds the first sketch of the series she's looking for. Feathers. Her father's deft hand capturing the delicacy, the softness, the underlying strength of each shaft, transmuting it to essence. More slowly now, she turns the pages until she reaches it, the single feather rendered in color, its iridescence otherworldly. Black nearest the shaft, it broadens to a fat splotch of white, then tapers into a shimmering mix of blue, green, and teal. The word *magpie* is written in black ink in barely visible letters along the rounded end of its tip. The word, at first glance, looks like a part of the feather itself.

On the next page is a silhouette of a spreading leafless tree, its branches filled with birds—stark black figures against the off-white page. Crawling up from the base of the tree are the words *mourning song* in the same tiny script as on the feather.

Margaret closes her eyes, remembering. Her father's voice, a deep baritone the color of mahogany, is telling her a story of his time in New Mexico, the story of the magpies. Of how they gathered in the back garden and sang over the body of one of their own. It lay beneath the sycamore tree, frozen in death, its song forever lost, its mate plumped beside it in the red dirt.

"A funeral," he said. "They actually held a funeral, Maggie Mine." His eyes glistened as he spoke. "I'll never forget that sound. The sound of a whole tribe lost for a moment in their common grief, giving themselves over to it completely before suddenly rising up and flapping away on the wind."

Smiling, Margaret opens her eyes. "I heard it in my dream last night, Daddy, and now I'll never forget." The words, *community* and *connection* slip back into her mind.

Downstairs, her phone rings. Startled that anyone would be calling so early on a Saturday morning, she looks to the clock and laughs. Nine-thirty! The ringing stops before she can get off the bed, and her answering machine clicks on. After the beep, she hears a voice she can't identify leaving a garbled message.

The spell of the moment broken, she closes the sketchbook and carries it down the stairs. The girls practically fall over each other to greet her at the bottom. She opens the door to let them out and smells the rain before she sees the gray clouds rolling in from the north. She lights the stove beneath the kettle and rummages in the fridge.

Suddenly, the girls scrabble at the door as a hard rain pelts the windows. Words filter into her mind as she goes to the door, and she grabs a pen to catch them before they disappear.

> *belly heavy clouds*
> *float then hover overhead,*
> *letting loose at last*

The blinking light reminds her of the forgotten answering machine, and as she towels the girls off, she debates letting the message wait until after she's eaten. But curiosity gets the better of her, and she hits the button and then returns to the stove to catch the kettle as it begins to whistle. She is pouring the water into the teapot as a male voice fills the room. She stops with the kettle in midair.

"Ms. Meader? Miss Margaret Meader? This is Reverend Charlie

Weston of the Savior's Light Church. I'm hoping to come by and have a word with you later today. Please call me back at this number. Thank you."

She scowls as she continues filling the pot and scoops oatmeal into a bowl. She doesn't know the reverend. A wariness fills her. Nevertheless, she decides to call him after she calls Annie.

Her cell phone rings just as she sits. It's Annie.

"I was just thinking of you."

"Sounds like your intuition is getting back on track."

"I can always hope. I wanted to say thank you. The box is exquisite. And the puzzle? A Patrick Kelly of my father's painting! You shouldn't have. It took my breath away. A simple thank you isn't big enough to express how that made me feel."

"Margaret, what you did for Jake and me ..." Her voice trails off, and Margaret knows she is crying.

"Friendship. It's reciprocal. So, I will no longer say 'you shouldn't have.' I'm glad you did."

As she talks, Margaret walks to the table and runs her free hand over the surface of the puzzle, then snugs three more pieces into place. "This particular painting was the perfect choice. It brought back special memories. You are an instrument of grace in my life, Annie Foss. And I'd like to invite you for dinner tonight if you're free."

"Oh, you don't have to do that."

"I know I don't *have* to. I want to. And before you answer, it won't be just us. I've invited Sam Kingston, and I'm going to call a few others as well. Short notice, I know, but it will mean those who are meant to be here will be here. So, what do you say to a little impromptu supper of soup and bread?"

"Your soup and bread? I wouldn't miss that. And I must say, I'm curious about the mystery man, Mr. Kingston."

"Five-thirty?"

"Let me bring dessert."

"I'd never refuse that!"

With the phone still in her hand, Margaret retrieves the reverend's number and, with a deep breath, clears her mind of pessimistic assumptions.

When he answers, the reverend launches into a roundabout explanation for his earlier call, the gist of which is a mission to intercede for the "boys" who forced her off the road. Her stomach tightens, and her throat constricts around her ready reply.

"Reverend," she cuts into his dissertation. "I'm not sure I understand. What would be the purpose of your visit exactly?" Her voice is sharper than she intended.

"Well, as I was saying, I'd like to help you. I'd like to offer my help in resolving the issues you have with the families of the boys involved in your recent accident. If we could meet face to face, I can explain what I have in mind."

"I will be at home this afternoon until two, but I have obligations beyond that time. And you should know, Reverend, that this was no accident and these were not boys. Just so we're clear before we begin."

There is a pause before the reverend responds. "I did not mean to trivialize what happened to you with my ill-chosen words, Miss Meader. I do understand that you were the target of an act of violence. I look forward to seeing you this afternoon then."

"I'll be here."

࿇

Margaret has three pots of soup simmering on the stovetop and has just placed a linen towel over three loaves set to rise when the front doorbell chimes.

The rain blows into the hallway on a gust of wind as she ushers Reverend Charlie Weston into her house. Stomping his feet on the bristled mat, he sheds his coat and hat after snapping his umbrella closed, spattering them both in the process.

Smiling, she leads him through the house to the kitchen and indicates a chair at the table. She places the teapot and a platter of sliced blueberry cake between them as she takes her own seat. For a moment, they chat about the rain and the slight nip, that hint of autumn, in the air. As she pours them each a cup of tea, he begins.

"I'll get right to my point, Miss Meader. Some of my congregants have come to me recently with grave concerns about the series of unfortunate incidents that have befallen you. They and I want to help resolve the problems you have with the Kennedy family. So, first, we want you to know we care about you. Some have told me that these issues go back many years."

Margaret remains silent, looking out the back window at the rain while holding her teacup in front of her. Finally, she looks at him over the cup. "I would love nothing more than to be done with it all. I'm open to any ideas you might have, Reverend."

He puts down his fork. "Well, I hear they mistrust you because of your ... your ..." He looks to her as if seeking help in finding the words, but she simply stares at him, wanting to see what he'll come up with. "Your strange ways," he finishes feebly.

When she continues to stare at him, he plunges on. "Perhaps if you were to assure them you mean them no harm. That your powers are not ... that you've never intentionally ..." He stops for a moment. "Perhaps if you ... If you kept a bit of a lower profile? Perhaps people wouldn't—"

"Oh. I see." She rises and takes his empty plate and cup to the sink. "Well, I thank you for your suggestions as to what *I* need to do to rectify the situation. Your intentions, Reverend Weston, are, I'm sure, well-meant, and I appreciate your concern for me. Please tell your congregants that you have done your part and that the next time I'm assaulted, I'll have myself to thank for not fitting into the box you have constructed for me." She stands at the doorway, extending her hand toward the front hallway.

Slowly he rises, his mouth opening and closing without forming any words. He puts his hands out toward her in a beseeching posture, but then drops them to his side and, head down, walks to the front door. She stands aside as he grapples with his coat and steps out into the rain without opening his umbrella, hat still in hand.

She is trembling as she heads back to the kitchen. "Well," she says aloud. "I can certainly do the low-profile part since my strange ways have diminished considerably. But I don't think that's going to make any difference."

The ringing of her phone startles her.

"Margaret? Kenneth here. Everything all right?"

At the sound of his voice, the tension eases out of her body, warmth flooding in to replace it. "Kenneth! Fine. Everything's fine."

"You sounded upset."

"Oh, sorry about that, just the aftermath of an unpleasant visit. But all's well now."

"I'm calling to tell you the building materials won't be delivered until tomorrow instead of today. Since they messed up in their scheduling, they're going to do a Sunday run. I hope that's all right for you?"

"Not a problem. In fact, it's actually better. I'm having some friends over for dinner and hope to eat outside since this weather is supposed to clear by early afternoon. I was about to call you to see if you'd join us. It's just a soup and bread affair. And I know it's short notice."

"I'd love to come. Beats an evening of my own company and leftovers. What can I bring?"

"Just yourself. And Maxie and Gulliver, of course. Five-thirty?"

She hangs up, smiling, and hits another number. "Hello, John, this is Margaret. I'm hoping you and Sesalie might be free to join me for an impromptu supper tonight?"

"Let me check." She can hear his muffled voice talking with his wife, then he's back. "We'd like that. What should we bring?"

"Just yourselves. It'll be simple fare and dessert à la Annie. Oh, and you should know, Sam Kingston, the stranger camping by the river, will be here too. Hope that's all right?"

There is a pause. Then, "Sounds like an interesting evening."

With two more calls, she confirms with her childhood friend Catherine and her neighbors Hilda and Bryce. Humming, she gives the soups a stir and a taste and preheats the oven.

Chapter 45

As she rushes into the hospital lobby, Emily admits to herself that she's glad Jacquie chose not to come. She never knows how much time they'll give her to visit Ned, and she is looking forward to diving into her laptop and her story while she waits. The thought of Jacquie poring over her cookbooks and resting at home before returning to the restaurant for tomorrow morning's Sunday brunch crowd eases her guilt.

As she enters the small private waiting room outside the ICU, she's surprised to find it empty. Walking to the glass partition with its view of the hallway that runs along the individual care units, she stops short, nearly dropping her bag. The curtains in Ned's unit are open, the bed tightly made and empty. Her heartbeat quickens. Has he had an emergency and been sent off to the surgical suite? Or has—

"Did no one call you?"

The familiar voice that she can't place spins her around. It takes a moment for her mind to register the broad smile on the intensive-care nurse's face.

"He's graduated to a private room, hon. They're just getting him settled in now."

"Oh my God, Belinda! I didn't know what to think for a minute there."

"His mom and dad didn't make it in today. Both sick. Not at all surprising with what they've been going through. I was just about to call them with the update.

"He's in room 310. It's a big, bright room with a lovely view of trees and sky. And there are three visitor chairs. Just go to the nurse's station around the corner. They'll tell you when you can go in. You're limited only by visiting hours and how he's feeling, hon. Do him a world of good to have you around, and you'll have a comfy corner for working on that book of yours. Best scoot now."

When the nurses tell her she can go in, Emily is suddenly apprehensive. As she enters the room and approaches his bed, where he appears to be sleeping, she feels oddly shy. Her ICU visits had been brief, and the beeping, whirring machinery surrounding him had felt like another presence in the small unit. She looks down at him, not wanting to disturb the peace she sees on his face. There are fewer machines now, a sense of spaciousness around him, and a deep almost disquieting stillness about him.

He opens his eyes. And smiles.

She bends to kiss his forehead, but her lips land on his mouth instead—easily, gently, sweetly. "Don't speak," she whispers, placing her finger to his lips. "Just rest. You've just made a big move. Exhausting, I'm sure."

His smile broadens, and she can see signs of strain from that simple act as his facial muscles twitch and then slacken.

"Close your eyes and rest. I'm not going anywhere."

She pulls one of the leather wingback chairs over beside the bed and sits. For a while, she talks softly to him, watching as he sinks back into sleep. Then she silences the ringer on her phone and pulls out her laptop.

Chapter 46

Sam Kingston arrives first and Margaret warns him that the dinner has morphed into a small gathering. The others arrive minutes later. Exchanging introductions and mild pleasantries, all admire the setting as they step into the backyard. On the table under the chandelier three Crock-Pots with ladles and two stacks of Hilda Hanson's earthen bowls sit. Along the crest of the hill overlooking the fields, two long tables are set end to end, covered with a white tablecloth. At each place setting, a plated salad of mixed greens, sliced pears, goat cheese, and walnuts waits. Two glasses and a colorful Anita Parker bread plate sit to the right of each salad. Up the center of the tables, cloth-covered bread baskets alternate with fat water pitchers and stoneware pitchers of beer. Condiment bowls are scattered along this central line, and potted herbs serve as fragrant centerpieces.

Margaret seats herself nearest the serving table, indicating the chair beside her to Kenneth and the one at the other end of the table to Sam Kingston.

Sophia and Grace, having greeted Max and Gulliver with shivering doggy exuberance, have led them down the hill to splash in the stream and cavort in the nearby field.

Easy small talk punctuated by bursts of laughter carries them through the salad course as the group settles into a comfortable rapport. As Margaret clears the salad plates, she invites her guests to serve themselves soup. Once they are settled back at the table with steaming bowls and hunks of grainy bread, the conversation segues into a pointed curiosity about Sam.

"Sam and I got off to a rocky start," Margaret admits. "But he came to my rescue when I was run off the road into a tree."

"What!" Kenneth drops his spoon, the handle hitting the edge of his bowl with a loud clink. All heads turn to him. "Margaret! My God, you could have been killed." He reaches over and covers her hand with his.

"Some old business coming back around, I'm afraid," she says. "But Sam sent them packing with a shotgun blast."

Catherine reaches for her water glass, her hand visibly shaking. "This goes back to our childhood. It should have ended in our teens after the—the assault and the mess that followed."

Everyone at the table is quiet. No one is eating.

John speaks softly into the silence. "We need to put our heads together. End it once and for all." He takes his wife's small hand in his as she nods vigorously.

"It's hard to reason with fear," Annie says.

"Margaret has helped some of the very people behind this," says Catherine. "Yet they remain steeped in ignorance."

Sam leans forward. "Can you tell me—us—about this old business that's coming back around?"

Margaret looks around the table. "Everyone all set with soup? Bread? There's—"

"Ever the gracious host and adept changer of subjects." Hilda shakes her head, smiling.

"These are Hilda's signature bowls, Sam," Margaret lifts her bowl in salute. "She and Bryce are the very heart of our art collaborative. And their gardens are like something straight out of Findhorn."

Hilda laughs, her freckled nose crinkling. "As I said, adept changer of the subject."

"Okay, okay." Margaret smiles. As she drizzles olive oil on her bread, she formally introduces Sam as Samuel J. Kingston. "I think it's only fair for you to know there's a writer in our midst before you spill any personal secrets or fantasies." She laughs. "Sam is interested in me because his grandmother also had what he calls 'the sight.' He plans to write a book about her and promises he won't use any of my personal information as material, only background."

She looks into his eyes across the table. "I now ask him to assure everyone here of the same before we go on."

Sam looks at everyone, one by one. "I don't intend to invade anyone's privacy. I just want to better understand what life was like for my grandmother. The novel will be *her* story, not Margaret's or yours. And, truth be told, I like Margaret." He raises his glass of beer to her. "I hope this is the beginning of a long friendship."

"Why the false name?" John's expression is unreadable.

"Sorry about that. I wasn't trying to be dishonest. I'm not famous by any stretch, but my books are popular. Shortening my name lets me move around under the radar." He looks at John. "I got off to a bad start with you. I can imagine what a jerk I must have seemed. I'd like to prove myself otherwise and start fresh, if that's possible."

"Well, since you have Margaret's stamp of approval ..." With a curt nod and hint of a smile, he raises his beer to Sam.

The four dogs come galloping up the hill and collapse in panting heaps beside the table as everyone goes back to eating.

Catherine is the first to reopen the conversation. "When we were kids, Margaret's pronouncements were just a part of our daily play."

"Can you describe what you mean by 'pronouncements'?" Sam asks.

Catherine laughs, her dimples appearing and disappearing. "We'd be playing and she'd say, 'Your mom's missing glasses are in the clothespin bag,' or 'Your grandmother's coming to live with you. But don't worry. It's the happy one.' One time, she began to cry and said, 'Mr. Jenkins drowned another bag of kittens in the pond and I can't get their crying out of my head.'"

"What a thing for a child to have to bear," Hilda says softly.

Margaret nods. "I quickly learned not to blurt things out when others were around, like I did when Cat and I were alone."

"No one's called me that in years." Catherine laughs. "Cat and Maggie. What a pair we were!" Her smile fades. "Until I abandoned you."

Margaret opens her mouth, but Catherine rushes on with her hand raised. "I know we were just kids, Margaret, but I need to say this. I think Sam should hear everything – the whole story."

She looks around the table. "My parents finally forbade me to have anything to do with Margaret. She was blamed for anything that went wrong and they didn't want me, or rather themselves, to be caught in the crosshairs.

"When kids attacked her, the grown-ups did nothing. Nothing. They said she brought it on herself." She stops, letting that hang in the air. "Her father was dead and her mother was ... fragile. So, she had no one. And when I look at my granddaughter today, my heart breaks for little Maggie."

"As I told Catherine before," Margaret says, "she *did* do something. Though I didn't have the word for it at the time, I knew she stood in empathy with me. There were others too. Annie's husband Jake was my protector when he was around." She grins at her friend. "And there was our teacher, Miss Welks."

"Ah, Miss Miranda Welks." Catherine sighs, smiling.

Margaret looks at Sam. "There need to be characters in your book who represent the Catherines and Jakes and Miss Mirandas, those lights in our lives who make things bearable. Those characters show us how we can be lights too." She holds Sam's gaze with hers for a moment before standing. "And speaking of lights, I think it's time to light the candles and fire bowl. The shadows are deepening, and there's more food."

"And more food for thought, I hope," Sam says as he rises.

Everyone pitches in to clear the table. They remove the white cloth to reveal a pale yellow one underneath, and then put out bottles of wine and platters of fruits and cheeses. Margaret lights the chandelier, Annie lights tea lights along the table, and John squats to light the fire bowl sitting a few yards from the table on a circular platform of stones.

"So," Sam begins once they're reseated, "I hope you'll share some more Margaret stories. It gives me the flavor of life lived in her orbit."

Annie clears her throat and sits up taller, the warrior queen taking her place at the table. Then her eyes fill and she apologizes. "Jake and I met while he was in the service. I first met Margaret when we moved back here to his family home. Her mother had broken her leg, and she and her husband Joe were down from Camden taking care of her. As I was looking through our unpacked boxes for the wineglasses we'd bought in Italy, Margaret told me that the moving van had departed with them! She said the company would claim they had no such box and the police would eventually find it in the driver's warehouse in Methuen. Along with other 'mistakenly kept' boxes."

Annie laughs, then stops suddenly. "She was there for us when Jake got sick. And with us when he died."

All sit in silence as the evening settles around them and the pulsating song of the night swells.

"She helped him to leave … and me to let him go. Later, she brought me a message from him. A little private thing only Jake and I would know."

Everyone waits for her to decide to go on.

"Margaret is the first to say she's not what they call a medium. But she's received other messages like that. For strangers too."

Margaret nods. "Once, some song lyrics got stuck in my head. One day, walking the beach at Long Sands, I sang them out loud. A woman walking up ahead of me turned around, her face ashen.

"Her mother had died suddenly the week before. She said her mother's singing had underscored her childhood. It was an integral part of who her mother was. The song I couldn't get out of my head had been one of her favorites." Margaret smiles. "She took my singing as a sign that her mother was okay. She thanked me and danced off along the water's edge like a child, splashing through the wavelets that slid up the beach on the incoming tide."

"Do you remember the song?" Hilda asks.

Margaret's rich alto lifts into the evening air. "'Daisies and buttercups and sweet summer roses, gathered in a ribbon and laid at my feet. Summer is waning, the gardens are blooming, soon to be fading, as two seasons meet.'"

For a while no one speaks as the breeze sharpens, carrying a trace of autumn into the August night.

"Margaret knew what was wrong with my mother before the doctors did." Sesalie's voice is soft. Her smooth brown face, cheek bones finely etched, shimmers in the candle light. "The specialist called us ignorant Indians and tried to send us away. But we pushed for the tests. Like Margaret advised us to. … They found a rare heart defect."

"And," John adds with a laugh, "she knew who our boys would be before they were born. Called Gregory 'Curious George' in the womb. We thought she meant he'd be an active little monkey, but he came in as quiet and easygoing as can be. A deep thinker, a seeker … Curiosity dances in him."

Margaret smiles. "After … um … When I was in need, the women of John's family took care of me. Treated me like one of their own."

She looks up into the flickering field of stars. For a moment, she leaves her companions at the table and steps into a memory, lush and full with sensory detail. Another night sky, another crackling fire, another circle. A circle of women.

Bryce clears his throat. "She told us once that we would have a grandson. But we were unable to have kids, so we shrugged it off. We figured she must make mistakes just like the rest of us."

He smiles, lightening the weight of his words. "Then three years ago, Jeremy came into our lives. A student at U Maine, he showed up at a farmer's market and asked if he could study our farming techniques. Next thing you know, he's living in our stable every summer, immersing himself in organics and digging in.

"One day—" Bryce swallows, visibly wrestling with emotion. "One day, he told me he grew up in foster care, and we were the grandparents he never had.

He brushes his sun-bronzed hand through his thinning hair.

"About a month ago, Margaret told me not to drive my truck until I had it checked. Well, ... me being my thick-headed self, I told her I'd just had the darn thing inspected and I had to take a load of pottery to Boston. I said I'd check it out when I got back. You can imagine the look she gave me!"

Everyone joins him in a good laugh.

"She was adamant. Said I should have it towed to Philby's for a good going-over." He takes a long drink of his beer as they wait for him to go on. "Worn ball joint." He shakes his head. "That wheel was ready to go. Once on the pike, it's highway driving all the way to the city. The accident wouldn't have affected just me and my truck."

"And that's just one of the many times Margaret has saved our butts," Hilda says. "She knew Leona Stark was embezzling from the art cooperative and Norman Langston was running a scam at the senior center. His fundraising for a gallery for artists over sixty? Pure pie in the sky. Pure Norman Langston pocket money. Without Margaret, we'd still be in the mess of it."

Margaret nods to Sam. "Of course, a lot of people promptly forget any butt saving. Doesn't fit the narrative. One good *bad* story and they're off." The fire snaps, sending off sparks, the apple wood burning blue. Her voice softens. "But to be perfectly honest, I did bring some of the troubles on myself. My mother begged me to make myself small. But my temper kept getting the better of me." She pauses, wincing at an unwelcome memory.

"Once, I lost control completely and I did the unthinkable. After that, Ruth Larson had every reason to hate me. Eventually, it ..." She sucks in a shuddering breath and looks down at her folded arms. "Eventually, it led to ..." Her voice cracks. She stops, head bent.

John leans in. "It's okay, Margaret. You don't have to talk about it."

She looks into his gentle eyes. "Maybe it's *time* I talked about it. About him."

"Margaret, you—"

She puts up her hand and clears her throat. "Just let me do

this." She leans her elbows on the table and rests her head on her fingertips, absently rubbing the faint scar above her left temple.

"His name was Ches. Chester Bramwell. He was from away. Moved here junior year." She stops, remembering the day she first noticed the tall, lean newcomer with black hair and thick brows, the slightly crooked nose and infrequent smile, leaning against his locker and looking at her, his dark eyes unreadable.

"Senior year, he and Ruth Larson started going out. It seemed an odd pairing, but then I didn't really know him. Their breakup a few weeks later was big news. The gossip storm engulfed the school. But I was busy keeping my head down.

"Then Ches began sidling up to me as I walked between classes. He'd walk with me for a while, then peel off and disappear. No words spoken, just an accompanying presence followed by a … tangible absence." She is staring at a spot midway down the table, her voice trancelike.

"One day, he asked for my help with his calculus homework." She looks around at her friends. "My defenses went up. I'd been played before. An innocent seeming question, a setup for a nasty joke. A promise of belonging, a prelude to mockery. I wasn't about to fall for that again. But he persisted.

"We met in the library. One session in, we talked a bit. Two sessions in, he made me laugh." She swallows, tamping down the rising emotion. "Three sessions in, he aced a test. Then he asked me out, and I said no … the first three times."

As she slips inside the memory, she leaves the cool August night and steps into a warm April afternoon. "We hiked Mount Pennatticus to the overlook. Sitting on the ledge, feet dangling, I felt free with him. We talked, and I took out my sketchpad and began to draw. The rocks and boulders below gave way to greening fields and grazing horses in the distance. I said something he found funny, and I turned to see him lost in laughter—his head thrown back, mouth open. I began to sketch him, wanting to capture his essence. He pretended to protest, wrestling for the charcoal. Then he kissed me." She stops, her eyes welling.

"My first kiss." Her smile is small. Shy.

She clears her throat and sits up straight. "Then at school, things got bad for me. Ruth accused me of stealing money from her locker. Other accusations followed, and Mr. Jones made me retake a physics exam, even though I always made As. So, I was labeled a thief and a cheater as well as a witch. And they nicknamed me Maggot." She puts her hand over her mouth and breathes audibly.

"The following week, Ches and I went out to the mountain again to get away. He held my hand going up. And at the overlook, he kissed me again."

She crosses her arms over her abdomen and leans forward, her gaze on a potted rosemary plant.

"That's when we heard voices approaching. We separated just as they appeared." Closing her eyes, she sees them again, stepping from the bushes. "Nancy and Kevin Pill. Red Kennedy and Jimmy Barker. Ruth Larson and her brothers Bert and Dave."

"Margaret, you don't have to—"

"They moved in slowly, surrounding us. I felt Ches tense. He stepped away from me and slipped his hands in his pockets, attempting an air of nonchalance he couldn't quite pull off. He said, 'Hey, guys. What's up?'"

Her jaw tightens. "Bert Larson answered. 'What's up is the stench of witch in the air.'" She begins to rock in tight, tiny movements.

"They crowded in on me. Grabbing me. Shoving me toward the ledge. Ches lunged at them, and someone pushed me, and I fell and hit my head." She rubs her forehead, accentuating the white crescent over her brow. "I struggled to get up, blood in my eyes. I wiped at it until I could see Ches in front of me. He was reaching out to me. His eyes wide. His mouth open. ... And then he was gone. Over the edge." She lifts her face to the sky, eyes squeezed shut.

"I think I screamed. I felt a sharp pain ..." Her voice lowers to a whisper. "... then nothing." Tears slip down her face. She sits in trembling silence, the scene playing out again in her mind.

Her friends take up the narrative.

"They left them there." John's voice is rigid with anger. "Ran away. Hikers found them. Her unconscious. Ches dead."

"Then they started vicious rumors." Catherine's voice is

strained. "They said she'd pushed Ches. That he'd been stringing her along and roughed her up. His parents pressed charges. Margaret's mother hired a Boston lawyer and the truth—some of it, anyway—eventually came out."

"They claimed self-defense." Sesalie's voice quavers, her blue-black hair falling around her face. "Said Margaret had provoked them. That Ches got caught up in the scuffle."

"His death was ruled accidental." Disgust hangs in Catherine's every word.

Annie reaches out to Margaret. "Oh, Margaret! I can't imagine reliving it just now."

Margaret stirs, exhaling loudly. "I had to say it out loud. That sweet innocent boy died because of me. I've never been able to talk about it. Except with Joe. And I didn't tell him everything. I didn't tell him how …" She struggles for composure. "How it all goes back to what I did to Ruth when we were kids."

"Oh, Margaret, surely you can't—"

"On the way to school that day, she added a new verse to her usual taunt."

Margaret continues in a shrill singsong rhythm. "'Poor mad Margaret, her Old Mad Dad is dead. Her daddy …'" She falters. "'Her daddy blew his brains out with one bullet through the head. Crazy brother Mattie saw what he had done and tried to fly into the sky. He took off on the run.'"

There is a collective gasp around the table.

Margaret continues in a softer voice. "The other kids picked it up and danced around me until I wanted to scream—" She looks off over the darkening fields. "Until I *did* scream."

"Well, of course you di—"

"*Vile* words." Shaking her head, Margaret continues, her tone harsh. "A sickening image had flashed into my mind. A dark secret, a very private family secret. And even as I screamed the words, I knew I shouldn't." She looks around the table, blinking to hold back the tears.

"When I saw the look on Ruth's face, I felt her humiliation. Her shock. Her shame. I *felt* what she was feeling, and I didn't care. A giddy something slithered through me." She looks down. "Then it was gone, and I watched Ruth crumple. I *saw* her fragile spirit flutter and go still.

"I knew then that speaking what I saw could be dangerous. That *I* could be dangerous." She stares across the length of the table at Sam.

"You were just a child, Margaret," Annie says, and others murmur in agreement.

She nods. "And so were they."

Silence sits, a palpable presence at the table. Kenneth places his hand on hers.

Then John speaks into the quiet. "But we're all grown-ups now. They learned nothing from what they did to you and Ches. Instead, they infected their children, and on it goes.

"We have to do something. And whatever that looks like, we have to stand in it together. You're not alone, Margaret. You never should have been alone." His usually quiet voice has risen, and all four dogs lift their heads to look at him. "And don't even think about going near them by yourself!" His dark eyes are fixed on her, his expression stern.

She nods as she wipes her eyes. "I won't do anything foolish, I promise. They've sufficiently scared me."

"Good," Hilda and Bryce say together.

"On a hopeful note," she goes on, "I had a vision. I saw Agnes Kennedy sitting down with me in my soon-to-be-built studio." She smiles and nods at Kenneth and John.

"I went to see her and the family recently." She raises her hand to allay any protests. "And was promptly invited to leave. But I felt something shift in Agnes while I was there. Ruth did her best to keep her in line, her own hatred crackling in the air, but I did feel the shift. Her grandson is the one who set the fire. She loves that boy with a grandmother's love and she doesn't want him going to jail. Agnes is the key to making inroads."

"So, your visions have returned?" Annie asks, her voice rising with excitement.

"No. This was before—"

"What do you mean?" Catherine who has been absently twisting her hair, sits forward. "What's happened to your visions?"

"Truth?" She looks across at Sam. "They're gone. Seems I've lost 'the sight.'" In an attempt to make light of it, she taps her head. "All's quiet in here these days. And when I say it's quiet in here, I mean *unnervingly* quiet!" She laughs.

Annie rises. "I think it's temporary. And if it's not, we'll raise a heavenly racket to fill that empty space!" Everyone laughs, dispelling the tension. "And speaking of heavenly, I'm going to get the dessert."

Everyone rises and stretches, putting on jackets and sweaters while John builds up the fire. The only conversation is light and immediate to the tasks at hand or to the chill in the air.

Margaret puts out covered teapots and carafes of coffee as Sesalie distributes mugs. With a flourish, Annie presents a three-tiered blueberry and whipped cream confection and places it in the center of the table. As she passes out generous servings, everyone helps themselves to coffee and tea.

"Kenneth begins work on the studio on Monday," Margaret announces as they eat. "And John will offer a brief blessing at sunrise. Anyone who cares to join is welcome. Also, I've had a word with the county attorney about an idea I'd like to share." She waits until all are looking at her. "The boy who set the fire is the great-grandson of Clarence Kennedy. He was a master carpenter of some reputation. As an alternative sentence, I'd like to arrange for the boy to help rebuild what he destroyed."

For a moment no one responds. Then John nods. "Old Clarence was a master, all right. Finer work you'd never find."

"A real artist." Bryce takes a drink of his coffee. "I've come across his work many times." He raises his mug. "I like the way you think, Margaret."

Catherine, though, looks wary. "Just so long as he doesn't see it as a way to get off easy or to do more harm."

"I'm hopeful but not naive. Besides, it may be moot. The idea will have to be evaluated and approved, and it may be way too late for that."

"Regardless of the outcome," Sesalie says, "it's that kind of thinking that opens up dialogue. Good for you." She raises her cup to Margaret.

Sam is leaning on his elbows, steam rising from the coffee mug in his hands and making his face shimmer in the candlelight. "This studio? Was it your father's?"

"No. Sadly, my mother had his torn down after he died. A long time ago."

"What kind of work did you do in it? Surely, from what you've told me, you didn't do psychic readings?"

Margaret laughs. "No. No readings."

"Then what? Why a studio?"

"I'm a bit of a poet and—"

"A bit of a poet!?" Hilda laughs.

Margaret continues. "Haiku mainly. Paired with simple watercolor sketches. Very simple and very sketchy. Which I realize is a redundancy."

Hilda turns to Sam. "Galleries are falling over themselves to sign her, the mysterious artist known only as M—." She slaps a hand over her mouth and looks from Sam to Margaret. "I hope it was all right to say that."

"Don't worry," Sam said. "Maxwell Meader's daughter deserves to stand on her own reputation. And her psychic abilities would just become fodder for the art world's publicity machine. Far be it from me to bring that down on your head." He bows toward Margaret.

Catherine laughs, and all eyes turn to her. "I'm sorry. But speaking of heads, I just remembered … It's not nice, but …" Again, she is laughing.

"But what? You can't stop there, Cat."

"I can still see Nancy Pill and Agnes standing in the schoolyard in the rain." She waves her wiggling fingers around her head. "Frizzy purple strands sticking out from under plastic rain bonnets. Stinking to high heaven of burnt hair and permanent wave solution."

Margaret tries to suppress a smile. "They weren't the first to get a bad batch of that home permanent, but somehow it had to be my fault. It didn't help that I had predicted it."

To their questioning looks, she adds, "Earlier, when they said I had ring worm and head lice, I struck back. I said I wasn't the one whose hair would turn purple and fall out. In another moment of fury, I sank to their level." She shakes her head. "But, you're right, Cat. That purple rain was something to behold."

"Jake told me everyone conveniently forgot about the time you saved one of their older relatives," Annie says.

"Yes. Gertrude. The summer I was ten. She was out in deep water at Nelson's Pond when a cramp seized her and she went under. I'd had a feeling something was going to happen, so I got to her first. She came up flailing, her face sprouting huge red splotches, and so I side-stroked her to shore."

"And?" Annie is gazing intently at her.

"And, she survived. Her friends rushed her to the hospital. I assume it was anaphylaxis."

"No one ever thanked you?" Annie's voice rises with indignation.

"No. But I rode my bike home feeling incredibly light. It's a familiar feeling after a vision comes to fruition." She wraps her sweater more tightly around her. "It's as if the pull of gravity has diminished somehow. It's very satisfying, like when I fit that final piece of a difficult puzzle into place. Only more so." She throws her head back and raises her hands skyward. "And what I wouldn't give to have it back again!"

"What would you give?" Sam asks.

She looks at him. "Thanks. I'd give thanks."

"Ah." John nods and smiles.

"I think you will get it back," Annie says. "I think the trauma caused it. I can't believe you were given this gift only to have it snatched away." She stands and offers seconds on dessert around the table.

"Saw Bobby Dolloff yesterday," John says. "Asked after you. Kind of worships you since his accident."

"What happened?" Sam asks, looking from John to Margaret.

"His tractor flipped over on a steep section of his back field.

Pinned him underneath. Would have bled out if not for Margaret."

"Specifics, Margaret?"

She sighs, thinking back. "A jumble of images had presented themselves the week before. You have to understand, for every image that proves useful, there's often a half dozen that don't— that never make sense. But in the midst of this particular batch, one stood out. The colors were brighter, the sounds sharper, the sensations stronger. A grinding noise made me cringe. Then I felt dizzy. Then I saw the overturned tractor, its engine grumbling and rasping. One of its tires loomed above me, slowly turning against a stark blue sky. Then it was gone."

"What did you do?"

"There was nothing I could do. It was a premonition, but I had no clue as to when or where it would happen."

Kenneth again covers her hand with his.

Prompted by this comforting gesture, she continues. "Then on the day of the accident, it all came back in Technicolor. I was standing by the back door rinsing off my boots. I was looking down at the muddy puddle beneath the spigot and I saw Bobby's face, bright-red blood mixing with the mud beneath him. Luckily I got Carol when I called 911—she never questions how or what I know—and she dispatched the rescue squad." She slumps back in her chair as if the very memory has drained her.

"So, do you think seeing the mud helped to trigger it?" Sam asks.

"Hmm." She shakes her head. "I rarely see a connection between what I'm doing in a given moment and what comes to me. It truly is a mystery. As Iris Dement so aptly puts it in her song, 'I think I'll just let the mystery be.'"

"Yes," Sesalie says. "The Great Mystery is surely a central element to your grandmother's story. That and love."

"Here's to the mystery!" Bryce lifts his coffee mug, and all follow suit.

"And to love," his wife adds.

"Speaking of which, tell us about your grandmother, Sam," Kenneth says, his hand still covering Margaret's.

Sam leans back, smiling. "She was a paradox. A down-to-earth, no-nonsense, plain-spoken woman with a faraway look in her eyes. Present, yet attentive to something just out of reach of the rest of us. Here, yet there. Bustling around the kitchen listening to an inner symphony, while making me feel totally seen and heard and loved.

"It never occurred to her to turn people away when they showed up at the door. An hour or so later they'd be gone, leaving her with honey or eggs or potatoes. One time …" He laughs. "A woman offered to give her the 'pick of the litter.' Meaning one of her ten children!"

Everyone laughs heartily.

"She never took cash. That changed the dynamic for her somehow. The exchange of gifts was one thing. Cash money was something else again."

Margaret nods.

"What kinds of things did she tell them in the readings?" Catherine asks.

"Wish I had paid more attention. There were bits of advice about everyday living. Warnings like, Fanny should not marry Henry under any circumstances." He smiles. "And predictions. When important ones came through, I could feel her intensity, like electricity in the air. Those were the times when she was the most quiet and exhausted afterwards."

Sam visibly withdraws, lost to them for a while. Then, just as two of the tea lights on the table go out in puffs of white smoke, he says, "Then there were the people who blamed her for what she foretold, angry people who confused her with the message."

Margaret speaks quietly. "Your book will be the perfect tribute. I'll help in every way I can."

Sam nods his thanks. "That's why I've come."

৯৶৽

Margaret sits alone in the backyard after her guests have departed. The candles have all gone out and the fire has died to glowing embers. The air is crisp and still. The quiet inside and around her body, though not comfortable, is at least becoming familiar.

She scans the sky as she remembers a fragment of a recent dream. She'd been floating in a sensory-deprivation tank as part of a scientific experiment. No stars. No images at all. No crickets. No sound at all. No breeze. No sensations at all. No up. No down. No frame of reference. No way to orient herself in space. No way to say she wanted out.

Chapter 47

Four a.m. The floor is cold underfoot as Margaret searches with her feet for her slippers and gathers up her robe. The room is dark except for the faint glow from her beside clock.

Showered and dressed, she is in the kitchen when she sees the bouncing reflection of headlights on the trees in the side yard and hears John's truck rumbling up the drive. When John cuts the engine, she can hear the softer whir of Kenneth's truck, and then the *thunk, thunk* of two doors closing. She welcomes them in, letting the girls run off with Max and Gulliver.

"There's coffee, tea, cinnamon rolls, and—"

The sound of cars coming up the drive and more bouncing lights stop her midsentence.

Annie is the first through the door, followed by Sesalie. Just beyond the back step in the predawn light, Margaret sees Catherine and her granddaughter stop to greet the Allens and little Joey. She turns to Annie with a questioning look.

Annie shrugs. "Word got out and people wanted to come. Despite the ungodly hour!" She laughs. "And judging by the look of the sky, we'd best get out there before we miss the moment altogether." She heads back out the door. "Oh, and we brought food."

Margaret watches as Annie hefts a small box sitting just outside the door and heads across the yard. John and Sesalie brush past Margaret and out the door as Kenneth comes to stand just behind her, his nearness mildly unsettling.

"I didn't expect this," she says. "I hope it doesn't disrupt your plan to get started."

"I'm not at all surprised, and you know what they say about the best-laid plans."

"I guess we'd better get out there."

As they step outside, more people appear from around the house. Margaret and Kenneth join John and Sesalie in the staked-off area of the building site, and a crowd of friends and neighbors encircles them. Margaret spots Sam hanging at the back and nods to him, smiling.

Annie is passing out candles, and the gatherers light them off one another as she whispers instructions. All fall silent, even little Carly and Joey, who stand holding hands in the early morning light.

As the silence settles, more and more people filter into the backyard, surrounding them in an ever-deepening circle.

Finally, John picks up a gardening shovel and digs a deep hole in the center of the space. All the while, he chants softly in his native tongue as Sesalie beats a hand-held drum with a soft mallet. The rhythm—a steady thum-thump, thum-thump, thum-thump—gradually slows, and Margaret feels her heart beat entraining to the sound until she is deeply relaxed.

When the hole is finished, John takes an earthen bowl from his bag and fills it with a handful of dirt from the hole. He lights a bundle of cedar and sage. When the flame catches and flares brightly, he blows it out. Thick, sweet smoke plumes from the tip, and he passes the smoldering stick over and around himself, Sesalie, Kenneth, and Margaret. Raising his voice, he recites a blessing in words no one but Sesalie understands, and yet everyone understands. Then he rests the still smoldering bundle in the dirt-filled bowl.

The drumming stops as the first sliver of the sun crests the horizon, and everyone blows out their candles.

John lifts his head. "We ask Great Spirit to bless this space. We ask Great Spirit to bless Margaret as she does her work in this space. We ask Great Spirit to bless all who enter here. We ask the ancestors to hold this space and Margaret under their wise protection. We ask the sun and the moon to shine brightly upon it. We ask the rains to smile gently upon it. We ask the wind to breathe sweetly upon it. We call this ever after, sacred space."

He holds the smoldering bowl aloft, asking everyone to think of the smoke as visual prayer and to send good wishes up with it.

A child's laughing voice breaks the silence. "Look! A baby dragon! Look, Nana Maggie!" Joey is pointing at the sky.

All heads look up to see a great blue heron high overhead, its long neck hunched back into its shoulders, its long legs stretched out behind. Gracefully it sails away, its broad wings pumping in slow, measured beats.

"Means good luck," someone murmurs.

"It *does* look like a baby dragon."

Margaret turns to see Otis standing beside Sam Kingston, grinning up at the heron. Scanning the circle further, she spots Emily and her mother and smiles.

She scoops Joey up into her arms. "Do you suppose he has a name, that baby dragon?"

"Wing-a-dee!"

"Good-bye, Wing-a-dee!" she calls, waving at the now faint silhouette. "Thanks for coming by." Turning back to Joey, she says, "And thank *you* for spying him with your little eye."

Joey laughs as she places him in his father's outstretched arms. Then he scowls as his tone becomes child serious. "Mommy says I have sharp eyes, but they're really round and soft and wet."

"Well, I'm glad your round and soft wet eyes spotted Wing-a-dee. Thank you. Thank you. Thank you." She plants a kiss on his soft cheek with each thank you.

Turning in a slow circle, Margaret acknowledges those gathered in her backyard, now lit by the first rays of this day's sun. "Thank you for getting up in the dark and coming here to shine the light of friendship and community on this project, this new beginning.

Though Kenneth and his crew will be doing the actual work, you have brought the spirit of an old-fashioned barn raising with you today.

"The great blue heron"—she looks up at the now empty sky and then at Joey, slurping from a juice box— "is known to be a solitary being, standing alone in perfect stillness, at one with its surroundings. But it is also a part of a nesting community. I too am a solitary being at times. But I would not be able to do the work I do without the nourishment of this vibrant community."

She holds up a handful of puzzle pieces and sprinkles them into the hole.

Annie steps forward with a small bouquet tied with a strip of burlap. "A little tussy-mussy from my garden. All Jake's favorite flowers," she says as she tosses it in the hole.

Sesalie removes a strand of beads from around her neck. "From the grandmothers." She squats, chanting quietly, then slides the beads from their string into the hole.

John sprinkles the top layer of ashes and sand from the smudging bowl on top of the offerings. With eyes closed, he circles the smoldering stick over the hole as he recites a quiet prayer. Then, lifting his voice, he asks those gathered to repeat after him each line of a final blessing chant.

A hesitant chorus of voices responds to the initial call of his clear tenor voice. Then, as he builds in volume, the response grows stronger until an easy, rhythmic rapport is reached. Margaret closes her eyes and stands inside the communal heartbeat.

When the voices fall into silence at last, she opens her eyes to the sweet sound of a bell. Three times Sesalie rings the ting-sha, waiting for each delicate tone to disappear before sounding the next. Margaret's body stretches forward, following each note into resolution and beyond.

"The blessings be. It is done."

With these simple words, John hands the shovel to Margaret.

She bends to the task of filling in the hole, the smell of fresh earth rising into the clear morning air. As she works, the others move away, talking quietly at first, then more and more loudly as a celebratory tone takes over.

Margaret squats and packs down the loose dirt with both hands. As she rises, Kenneth holds out a closed hand. "To mark the spot." He places a flat heart-shaped rock into her cupped palm. Her eyes well as she smiles up at him.

"Come and get it!" Annie calls, and Margaret turns to see her harvest table set out on the crest of the hill and spread with food. "Let's eat and be on our way before the real work begins."

Noticing Emily and her family gathered in a small circle of their own, she heads for them, inviting Kenneth along.

Janet extends her hand as Margaret approaches. "A beautiful beginning. Out of the old, the new is born."

Beside her, Emily smiles.

Margaret takes Janet's hand and holds on for a moment. "Thank you. Sometimes we're forced to make changes we didn't know we needed to make." She pats Janet's hand as she releases it. "That old shed had out-served its usefulness long ago. But, being the frugal Scot that I am, I never would have let it go. Now, I'm freed to move in the new direction my work has long been wanting to go."

She introduces Kenneth around, and when she comes to Otis, he nods to her. "When the new building's up, come by and get some plantings. I'm thinning out my perennial beds, and I can't think of a better place to send them."

"I can't think of a better garden to steal from. Thanks." She exchanges a quick hand shake with Uncle Mert and turns to Emily.

"And how is our Ned doing? You've both been on my mind."

Emily's green eyes glisten. "He's doing wonderfully well. He's in a private room and off the machines. I can sit with him for as long as I want. His folks have been sick, so it's just been the two of us for the past few days. Him sleeping. Me writing."

Margaret pulls her in for a warm hug. "There's someone I'd like you all to meet." She scans the yard and calls to Sam. "This is Sam Kingston." She introduces him around the circle. "Emily is a writer too."

"An as yet unpublished writer," Emily says as she shakes his hand. "It's a pleasure to meet you. I've read and reread *Silenced*. It's like taking a master class in writing the short story. You should see my dog-eared copy!"

"I'm glad to hear you say 'as yet' unpublished. A positive attitude and faith in yourself is crucial in the writing game. Also, talent, diligence, a thick skin, a daily habit of butt to the chair, and a generous dose of luck," he says in one long breath. "Once you write the best book or story you've got in you, then you're ready for luck to drop by." He laughs. "If you're interested, I'd be happy to sit down with you and discuss your work. I'll be here for a few weeks at least."

"Really? That would be ... Oh, my God, that would be ... Thank you." Emily flushes a deep red.

Mert grins. "Our little wordsmith at a loss? Pretty impressive, Mr. Kingston."

"Call me Sam, please."

"What brings you to our neck of the woods, Sam?" Otis asks.

"Research," he says with a mischievous glance at Margaret.

"Sam had a grandmother who was ... rather like me. He's writing a book about her."

"That so?" Otis scowls at Sam, his sharp eyes studying the man. "Hmm."

"I take it you aren't so sure about me, sir."

"Don't know you, do I?"

"Well, all I can do is assure you I mean no harm and then prove myself a man of my word."

Otis looks over at Margaret, giving her the briefest nod accompanied by another noncommittal grunt.

"Sam came to my rescue recently," Margaret says, "and it gave us a chance to talk."

"I've investigated a number of people with the sight," Sam says, "but found none as remarkable as Margaret. And none so much like my grandmother Clementine." His voice thickens with emotion. He clears his throat and looks down at the ground.

"Remarkable is the right word." Otis smiles at Margaret. "I didn't know your dad well, but I remember old Lucinda. Same blue eyes as you, and the same canny ways."

Margaret stares at him. "You remember my grandmother?"

"Oh, sure. Delivered groceries to her. A lot of folks were afraid of her, but she was sweet as could be to me. Used to make me sit down for cookies and milk and get me to talking. As I was leaving, she'd say something about the very thing I *hadn't* told her! The thing that was bothering me. I always left feeling better." Smiling, he stops and looks up at the sky. "One time as I was getting on my bike, she told me to take Burgess Lane home instead of my usual route across the bridge. When I got home, my mother was frantic. The bridge had collapsed."

"You never told us that story," Janet says.

"Three people injured. One dead."

"Margaret?" Catherine calls from across the yard.

Margaret asks if the group can stay for a bit and excuses herself to thank those who are ready to leave.

Someone touches her elbow, and she turns to find Betsy Frank and her husband Carl standing behind her.

"Margaret, we're heading off now, but we wanted you to know that we stand with you. Everyone here"—she sweeps her hand toward the yard full of people—"stands with you. I mentioned to a couple of people that you were dedicating this spot today, and look what happened!"

"Thanks, Betsy." Margaret turns to Carl. "You're looking terrific."

"Well, as you knew before we did, the cancer's in remission." He clears his throat, awkward for a moment, then bends down and embraces her tightly. "Thank you. You sent Betsy home with the first hope we've had in a long time."

"I'm just the messenger, but you can hug the messenger anytime."

"We're leaving in a few weeks for a trip across the country," Betsy says. "No more wasting this precious life." With a quick hug, Betsy collects her empty baking dish and they leave.

Margaret turns back toward Emily's family group but is intercepted at every step by well-wishers as they depart.

Bobby Dolloff and his wife Clara are the last. They hang back shyly and then step forward just as Betsy rushes back.

"I nearly forgot, Margaret." Betsy is beaming. "My sister Liz is pregnant! Shortly after she signed the papers on her new home—yellow, with a secret passageway between two of the upstairs rooms—she got the news. She's over the moon. She's going to have her little Rose Marie after all." And Betsy rushes off again.

Margaret turns to Bobby and Clara, laughing. "There goes Hurricane Betsy."

Bobby joins her laughter while Clara, eyes briefly meeting Margaret's, offers a sweet smile.

"Pissed me off—" Bobby begins, but notices his wife's cautioning look. "Don't worry, Clara, Margaret's not the type to get all bent out of shape over a cuss word or two coming from the likes of me." Turning back to Margaret, he continues, "Made me some angry to hear what those guys did to you on the road. They come near you again and they're gonna have to answer to me and my brothers and most of the rest of the county."

"Thank you, Bobby. Really."

Fingering the tiny gold cross at her neck, Clara says, "I don't know how you knew what you knew and I don't care. The important thing is that Bobby is here today because of *you*." Clara's voice rises. "My folks are ashamed of bad-mouthing you all those years ago. They'd do anything for you now. Us too." She gives Margaret a fierce hug, surprising her with its strength. "We'll be back with any help you need as this building goes up. Bobby already told that to your builder."

As the two disappear around the corner of the house, two uniformed men and a sandy-haired kid approach. Both men wear sheriff department insignia on their shirts. The taller of the two says, "Ms. Margaret Meader?"

At her nod, he gestures to the teenage boy. "This is Raymond Kennedy. Raymond is responsible for burning down the outbuilding and is to serve community service by working with …" He pulls out a folded paper from his back pocket. "With a Mr. Kenneth Chisholm on building a replacement. Is Mr. Chisholm here?"

Kenneth steps over and introduces himself.

"Before we leave him in your charge for the day, this young man has something to say to you both." The deputy looks at Raymond, who's standing with his head down.

The youth steps forward and looks up for the first time. His eyes pass from Margaret to Kenneth and back again. Then he looks back down and says, "I'm the one burned your shed. I'm sorry. Thank you for letting me work it off."

His head comes up again, and he meets Margaret's eyes. His are dark brown with amber highlights that glint in the morning light. "I really want to learn carpentry." He throws his shoulders back, straightening, and his voice takes on a reverent tone. "My great-grandfather was a carpenter. I never knew him, but my grandmother says I'm just like him." He looks down at the grass. "I'd like that, to be just like him," he whispers just loud enough for Margaret to hear.

"What do you think he'd say about you burning down the workshop, Raymond?" she asks.

Raymond remains silent for a long time, head still down. Margaret senses a war going on inside him.

"Even though it was yours," he finally says, "he'd probably say it was pretty stupid and all kinds of wrong."

"And when you say, 'even though it was yours,' what do you mean?"

He looks up again, his brow furrowed. "Because of all your spells and shit that you make in there. He'd be against all that witchy stuff, for sure." Suddenly, the boy looks frightened. "Are you going to keep on making that stuff in the new one?" He steps back. "Will I be helping to make a witch hut or something?" He looks up at the deputies flanking him and then at Kenneth.

Kenneth steps forward. "I assure you, Raymond, Ms. Meader is no witch. That was a workshop filled with beautiful artworks that you burned down, and arson is a very serious crime. You need to turn yourself around so that you are never tempted to light a match to anything again. Building something new is a way to do that. Get it?"

Margaret touches Kenneth's arm and smiles up at him, then addresses the boy again. "What if we take it one day at a time, Raymond? You come each day and pay attention and listen to Kenneth. You learn from him and his crew and work hard. When the workshop is finished, we can talk about all the things you've heard about me. But let's make that a separate thing from you learning to be a craftsman like Clarence Kennedy, the finest carpenter this area ever saw. What do you say?"

She waits until he raises his head and looks at her with only a hint of caution. "All right."

"There will, of course, be rules. Set by me," Kenneth says. "Break the rules and all deals are off. And no friend or family member comes on the worksite without my approval. Got it?"

"Got it," Raymond says, head back down.

"Okay." Margaret ushers him over to the table where the remains of the breakfast buffet have been consolidated into a tidy spread for the work crew. "Help yourself to breakfast. You have a full day's work ahead of you."

He looks at her hand, resting lightly on his left shoulder. "Thanks," he says just under his breath.

As she turns back to the deputies, she notes a flash of color by the corner of her house. She looks in time to see Agnes Kennedy in a red sweater walking away.

"I'm not sure this is the best idea, Ms. Meader," the younger of the two deputies says as he hands her a packet of papers.

"Be that as it may," the older deputy says, "he will be delivered here daily by his grandmother, Ms. Agnes Kennedy, and only by her. And one or the other of us will stop by intermittently to check on how things are going. This is all mandated by the judge, as you'll find in these papers. Good luck." He shrugs. "Hope it works out."

The other deputy snorts, shaking his head as they walk away.

Margaret returns to the small group remaining. At their hushed questions, she explains the arrangement with the attorney general's office for Raymond's community service. To their concerns, she simply replies, "Baby steps. We have to start somewhere."

Margaret puts her arm around Emily's shoulders and walks

her over to the site of the blessing ceremony. She stops at the spot where the heart-shaped stone sits atop the freshly filled hole.

"Today I am reminded of the vision I had when we first met. I saw you as a child digging a hole and burying something. Since that day, I've watched you rediscover talents and reawaken dreams. I've seen you uncover inner resources and slip into a new way of being in the world.

"Your life is opening up. You've stepped onto the path that's been waiting for you. Your partner—the one you can safely let inside—has appeared. Friends and guides and mentors are showing up, some for a brief space, others for a lifetime. And it's all because you were willing to do the work of unearthing and reclaiming precious parts of yourself. Of stepping into your power, your wholeness. And taking leaps of faith." Tears come, wetting her eyes. "It has been my privilege to witness all this. And though changed in some ways, I want you to remember that I am here for you and Ned always."

Before Emily can respond, her mother calls to her, telling her it's time to go.

"Coming," Emily calls back. She rolls her eyes. "Some of the work is ongoing," she whispers to Margaret.

After promising to call later, Emily hugs her, letting go reluctantly when Janet calls again. "You are the wisest person I know, and that has nothing to do with your visions. You have been a lifeline, and I don't intend to let go of you anytime soon." Blushing lightly, Emily runs to catch up with her family.

When Margaret turns to collect the dogs, all four have gravitated to young Raymond. He is bent to one knee, petting and talking to them with gentle affection. As she calls out to Kenneth that they're off to see Annie home, Grace hangs back. She nudges her nose up under the boy's hand for a final caress and then runs to join the others.

Chapter 48

Annie is unusually quiet as the two women walk along the streambed and then up the hill. As they enter the woods and begin the gentle descent toward Annie's house, she suddenly stops and turns to Margaret.

"Are you really all right with it? Living without it, I mean?"

Margaret notes the tears forming at the corners of her friend's dark eyes. "To be honest, Annie, I really don't know. Let's just say I'm adjusting and I trust you'll be here if I start feeling not so all right."

"I don't know what good I'll do, but I'm definitely here. Jake is too."

"I know. I'm counting on it."

They continue in silence, then Annie says, "I'd dissolve into one big puddle."

"Pardon?"

"If I were to lose my sight or my hearing or something. You've lost one of your senses. It was just as important to you as the other five are to the rest of us. That helps me better appreciate the magnitude of your loss. I really don't know if I could handle it."

"Of course, you could. You've been through one of the worst

things that can happen to person. You are one of the strongest people I know."

"Losses. I know they're a necessary part of life. Wishing it were otherwise won't make it so."

"Otherwise." Margaret laughs at a sudden memory followed by a new insight. "But we all have gut feelings and flashes of intuition. Right? Maybe not as detailed or vivid as what I had, but on the same continuum. I still have access to that. I'll just have to hone my awareness to recognize it in this more subtle, fleeting form."

৵৶

Annie waves them off as Margaret and the dogs turn up the path toward the deeper woods. After a mile and a half of gradual incline, the trail steepens. As the dogs race ahead, Margaret chooses a sturdy walking stick from some deadfall and slows her pace. There is no need to rush. This is her time.

Letting go of all thought, she simply climbs, totally aware of the placement of each foot on the earth. Totally aware of each breath in and out. Totally aware of the warmth radiating from her body and the feel of the walking stick in her hand.

She hears the rush and splatter of water as she approaches the falls. A quick flashback of her last visit here with Betsy, Liz, and Donna has her thinking about Donna's family and the lost brother who died in a very different landscape, but one he loved intensely.

Her next thought is of her own sweet brother and his death in these very woods. But now the memory flows in on a gentle wave of sadness, no longer sweeping over her like a tsunami, devastating in its intensity.

"Hey, Mattie," she says out loud. She kneels beside the catch basin at the base of the falls and dips her cupped hands in. She draws them out dripping with overflow and splashes her face and neck with the startlingly cold water. With a shake of her head, she yelps.

Sophia and Grace, followed by Gulliver and Max, scamper out of the woods. They dance around her, barking playfully. Laughing, she scoops up more handfuls of water and splashes all four. They jump back in surprise and then come back in for more. One after the other, they race up the terraced embankment beside the cascading water, kicking up dirt and debris as they go. When they disappear from sight, she can hear them splashing in the pool above. They reappear at the top of the falls and then disappear again, crashing through the woods before circling back and racing down to prance and bark around her again.

Suddenly, all four dogs stop. Alert, heads pointed toward the curve in the path, tails up, they stand still. Margaret stands among them listening, her head cocked, heart thumping. Then just as suddenly, her companions relax. Turning to her, they seem to ask permission to resume their play.

"Stay," she commands, her heart still racing. All four sit, but as soon as their rear ends hit the ground, they're up again, their instincts sending them back into a wary stance.

The raucous call of a crow breaks the silence as it lands on a nearby branch. Bird chatter resumes, underscoring the black bird's solitary cry. Then the intermittent skittering of squirrels and chipmunks softens Margaret's vigilance.

"Okay. Time to find our way home."

But the four dogs don't move.

At the snap of a branch, Margaret looks up to see a young man coming around the curve in the trail. Swinging a long walking stick much like hers, he steps into a broad shaft of sunlight and stops. He is tall, his skin a mixture of burnished copper and gold. His head is shaved but for one long clump of straight dark hair falling from a top knot at his crown. He is wearing a faded black T-shirt with a Burning Man logo on the chest, cargo shorts, and black hiking sandals. His brown eyes scan her and each of the dogs before he steps forward.

"'Morning," Margaret offers.

He nods in reply.

The dogs remain at her side but relax into a sit.

"Lost?" he asks. His voice is surprisingly deep, like that of a much older man.

"Oh, no. I know these woods well. We're just out for a good romp." She smiles down at the dogs, ruffling the top of Sophia's golden head. "You?"

"No. Just passing through. Lovely spot," he says, looking up at the falls.

"Yes. One of my favorites."

He approaches slowly and then stops an arm's length away, looking down into her eyes, searching them. "You've lost something, though. Yes?"

She pulls back, uncomfortable under his gaze.

He takes a step back as well, lowering his eyes to the ground. "Sorry. Forgive my intensity. Been in my own company too long, I'm afraid. Sometimes I forget myself and just blurt things out. It's just that ... I just ... I'm the one who got lost for a moment there."

"You said you weren't lost."

"May I be frank?"

She considers this. "Please."

"There is an aura of emptiness surrounding you. It's dark and silent and in sharp contrast to the light and vibrancy within you. I stepped into it and got lost for a moment. You've recently suffered a great loss. Something's missing now."

Margaret stares into his eyes. They are deep brown, nearly black. Unguarded. Vulnerable. She feels as though she could reach in through them and touch his deepest self.

"Yes. I have lost something. But I've found something too." Her words surprise her as she speaks this truth out loud. "I've found that it didn't define me. Neither the gift I had, nor the loss of it, defines me."

He nods. "Ah. Yes. You've landed on the other side of ordinary wisdom." Putting his hands in prayer position in front of his heart, his walking stick leaning in the crook of his elbow, he bends forward. "I bow to you, Sister Grandmother. Namaste. I am honored to have crossed paths with one who is Other Wise. I carry your lesson with me as I go forward."

As he walks around and past her, Margaret mulls the synchronicity of his words, noting a sweet sensation flowing through her body. She turns to ask the question that has suddenly arisen.

But he is gone.

The dogs have returned to their play around the catch basin. A crow calls out. Another answers. A flapping of wings draws her eyes to the patch of visible sky overhead. Three sets of iridescent black wings bank to the left and disappear beyond the trees. High above, a lone heron glides across the blue brightness.

ༀ–ༀ

When she reaches home, the work crew is breaking for lunch. The four dogs, after greeting each man wetly, collapse in the shade beneath the oak. Kenneth begs off her offer of food, saying he's taking Raymond to town for lunch and a chance to talk with the boy.

She watches the two walk away. Master and apprentice. Filled with hope for this arrangement brimming with potential, she smiles.

As she's preparing her own lunch, there is a knock at the front door. Detective Jay Horner stands on the doorstep, his face anxious, his manner hurried. "Sorry to disturb. I've come to ask your help with something."

She ushers him on through to the kitchen and heads for the stove. "Coffee?"

"Afraid I don't have time. A teenage girl has gone missing. Alissa Cates. Thirteen. We think she's been abducted. I'd like to give you a description and the basics and see what you—"

"I'm sorry, Jay." She turns to face him. "I wish I could help but I can't." She stops, blindsided for a moment by a feeling of impotence.

He looks across the kitchen at her, his expression more hurt than upset. "Maybe you could just—"

"It's gone." Unable to face him, she looks down at her hands. "My ability to see things is gone. Believe me, I'd help you if I could."

"Oh, Margaret." He crosses to her. "I'm so sorry. Are you all right?" His own cause forgotten for the moment, he focuses completely on her, his empathy bathing her in momentary peace.

She looks up at him. "Thank you, Jay. You are such a good man."

"What happened?"

"I was in an accident and shortly afterwards everything was gone. So much of what I used to think was *me* disappeared. It doesn't bother me for my own sake. It wasn't that helpful in my everyday life. But not being able to help …"

"I'm sorry I brought this to your door."

"Don't be. Please. You couldn't know."

He takes one of her hands in both of his. "I wish I—"

"Look, I know you have an investigation to run and you're needed elsewhere. You don't have to stay. I understand. Go."

He sighs heavily. "I do have to be off. Time is precious in such cases, as you know. But I'll keep you posted and I'll come back by when we can talk more."

"Where was she last seen?" she asks as they walk to the door.

"Leaving the Big Barn Thrift Store in Halliston. She was walking that strip of highway that goes over to the Willow Well Plaza to meet a friend."

"Do you have a photograph?"

He takes out his phone and brings up a school photo of a girl with a round face and straight blond hair. Her cheeks are sprinkled with freckles and her eyes are on the green side of hazel.

"Sweet. All innocence. A child still." Margaret shakes her head sadly. "Her parents must be frantic."

"Just a father. The mother died of breast cancer last year. He's nearly catatonic."

"Poor man." She shakes her head again. "I trust you'll find her. Not because I 'see' it, but because I know you. I'm sorry I can't offer more than my prayers. "

"Your prayers are enough. Take care now." His shoulders slumped, he heads for his car.

Margaret remains in the doorway, watching him drive away. Then, her appetite gone, she goes into the sitting room. Three puzzles in various stages of completion are spread out on tables around the room. Taking up a large ceramic bowl, she sweeps the puzzles off into it one by one.

The only puzzle remaining is in the kitchen—the gift from Annie, the photograph of her father's painting. She gazes at it as the clock over the stove ticks off the minutes in the otherwise silent kitchen. She studies the intricate symbols woven into the cloaks of the Elders gathered around the luminous fire rendered with a fine brush by her father's meticulous hand.

Slowly she disassembles it, placing clusters of jig-sawed pieces into the beautiful wooden box Annie so carefully chose. The tears come then as she lifts the box to her chest, the puzzle pieces rattling inside. She carries it up the stairs and places it on top of her father's sketchbook on the desk.

At the sound of a backhoe grumbling to life, she looks out the back window. A well-muscled man in his late fifties, clearly the stone mason, is directing the backhoe operator as he swings a massive rectangular block of fieldstone around and into place, laying the beginnings of a foundation along the perimeter of the site.

√∞√

Several hours later, a quiet knock at the back door gives her a happy reprieve from the work of unpacking the afternoon delivery of art supplies.

"Margaret?" Kenneth calls before she can get past the boxes and out of her temporary workroom off the living room. She sees him through the screen door, just turning away from the back step, as she comes into the kitchen.

"Here," she calls. "Sorry. I was trapped in the back room." She laughs and then looks at the clock as a chorus of truck engines starts up in the dooryard. "Oh, my. I didn't realize the time." She steps out the door.

"Just checking in with you before I leave for the day." Grinning, he sweeps his arm toward the completed foundation. "What do you think?"

She walks over to it. "Oh!" She looks up into his face. "It's really happening, isn't it?" She bends down, placing her hand on the sun-warmed stone. "That man is an artist. I watched him work for a while. I was stunned by his strength and mastery with the stone. And now just look at what he's done." She straightens up.

"Yes. Edgar is a marvel. The guys call him the Stone Whisperer." He laughs. "We were lucky to get him."

"And Raymond?" she asks, nodding toward the boy sitting in the grass by the fire bowl. Grace has nestled beside him while the other dogs are still at play on the hill. "How did he do today?"

"Off to a good start, I'd say. He's a quick study and a natural. A good worker. By midafternoon, the crew was treating him like a worthy apprentice—guiding him and teasing him good-naturedly. I think this is a good fit for him. You should feel very good about it."

As they talk, the boy turns toward the side of the house and gets up. Grace starts to follow as he heads toward the side yard. He bends to pet her and then points for her to go over to Margaret and Kenneth. As he does so, Margaret catches movement at the corner of the house and turns to see Agnes Kennedy waiting for her grandson, her body rigid and still.

Kenneth excuses himself and strides across the lawn toward her. Margaret starts to follow but thinks better of it, watching as he extends his hand to the tall, thin woman who has hated her since childhood. They shake, and Agnes quickly refolds her arms across her chest as if protecting herself against unwelcome news. But as Kenneth speaks, she drops them to her sides, her body visibly relaxing. Though Margaret can't hear his words, his enthusiasm is easily translated via broad gestures and a smiling voice.

As he turns to head back toward her, he gives a brief wave to the two Kennedys and calls out the time for tomorrow's workday. Agnes, her hand on the boy's shoulder, looks over at Margaret. Without smiling, she nods and is gone.

Grace sits looking after them, and Margaret goes over and kneels beside her. "My sweet goodwill ambassador. Good for you." And she ruffles the golden head.

This brings Sophia, Max, and Gulliver on the run, and they

nearly knock Margaret over in their exuberance to be in on the affection. Laughing, she tumbles on the grass as they dance around her, licking her face and nudging her with their noses.

Kenneth slips his laptop into his briefcase and slides rolled-up plans into a blueprint tube. "Hate to break up the fun, boys, but it's time we headed out." He leans down and extends his hand to pull Margaret to her feet. "We'll be back in the morning, just not quite as early as today."

She smiles. "Thanks for participating. It was such a beautiful way to begin. You helped to lay both a metaphorical and a literal foundation today. Thank you."

Without thinking, she reaches up and brushes a clump of curling hair away from his sea-green eyes. Tiny lines around them crinkle and deepen as he smiles.

Neither moves until the dogs run barking to the top of the hill as a flock of Canada geese swoop down to land by the stream. Margaret steps back first, but his eyes don't leave hers as he calls after his dogs, telling them there's no time for wild goose chasing. He grins at her and says more quietly, "If I didn't have a dinner date, I'd let them have a last romp and we could watch them try to take off into flight."

Margaret's head is buzzing. *If I didn't have a dinner date* has sent her spinning. She hasn't heard any of his words beyond that. "Well, you'd best get on your way," she manages.

"My daughter's taking a cooking class," he goes on, "and I'm the guinea pig. Tonight's offering is the latest in a series of vegan delights." He grins again. "And though I tease her, everything's been great so far. She wouldn't appreciate me inviting anyone to her experimental dinners, but I'd like for you to meet her."

As he heads for his truck, he turns back and says, "Let's plan on it soon. What do you say?"

"I'd love it. Enjoy your dinner."

Once Kenneth and his dogs have left, all seems especially quiet in the backyard. Margaret corrals the girls into the house and sets out their dinner bowls. As they eat noisily, she heats the kettle and sets up a tea tray. From the shelf, she takes down a delicate saucer with scalloped edges tapered to wafer thinness. It is one of the few remaining pieces from her mother's cherished set of "good china." On it, she places a plump cinnamon roll that Annie squirreled away for her before laying out the morning's feast.

She fills her favorite teapot and carries the tray out to the backyard table between the Adirondack chairs. She sits in silence as the late-afternoon shadows lengthen around her. Leaning back, she spreads a napkin on her lap. Holding the saucer level against her chest, she savors each bite of the sweet doughy roll between sips of soothing tea.

At last, she folds her hands in her lap and closes her eyes, listening to her surroundings—the light chatter of birds, the pleasant rustle of a warm wind teasing the leaves, the satisfied groans of Sophia and Grace as they settle beside her chair.

When she awakens, it is dark and still.

Too still.

No night sounds. No brook babble. No wind.

No Sophia. No Grace.

Sitting forward with a start, she looks up. The stars twinkle in the blackness, distant and cold. The empty silence closes in around her. She rises and starts down the hill. Propelled forward by an inexplicable urge, she stumbles and pitches forward.

Tumbling through the darkness, she loses all sense of direction. Her head throbs. Her stomach lurches. Her mind shuts down.

A harsh clanging. The sudden intrusion of sound after its total absence sends shrieking pain through her head. She rolls herself into a fetal ball, covering her ears, but the sound is coming from deep inside her, rising up and clambering to get out.

"Relax into it, Maggie. You know what to do. Relax into it."

The voice is a whisper seeping in under the noise. Mattie's voice. Mattie's grown-up voice. Calm. Compelling.

In spite of the pain, she unwinds her body until she is floating, loose and relaxed. The clanging is still there, and she breathes deeply, letting it fade to the background of her awareness.

"That's right, Maggie. Floating. Drifting. Breathing."

As his gentle voice repeats the words, different sounds separate out from the painful noise. A railroad crossing signal. As soon as she identifies it, it softens in tone and insistence, giving way to a far-off whistle. Then the clacking of passing train cars sends out a rhythmic vibration into the now solid ground under her.

She sits up. Jigsaw pieces in subtle tones and muted colors dance in midair around her. Lit from within, they whirl and swoop, fitting themselves together a few at a time until a picture emerges—an old barn, its wide boards winter-warped, its roof caving in at one corner. A railroad track snakes away over rolling hills, bypassing a crumbling warehouse in the middle distance. Deserted, most of its windows are broken. Hanging shards of glass reflect the stars.

The smell of moldy hay and ripe manure drifts to her on the night air, along with the sound of soft sobbing. A church bell tolls in the distance.

A wet nose nudges her hand, and her eyes snap open. Four glistening brown eyes gaze up at her. Sophia and Grace whimper, their entreaties accompanied by the swelling chorus of crickets and tree frogs and night birds. She is seated, the slats of the chair hard beneath her. She looks around, wondering how long she has been asleep.

"It wasn't a dream, Maggie." Barely a whisper now, his voice fades to silence.

A new silence. An old silence. A full silence. Crackling. Buzzing. Humming.

"I'm all right, girls," she soothes, as she hurries into the house, fumbling through her bag for her cell phone.

When he picks up, Detective Horner's voice is strained, heavy with weariness.

"I know where she is, Jay. Alissa Cates. I know where she is."

Made in the USA
Columbia, SC
29 May 2024

36313438R00224